EILEEN STEPHENSON

IMPERIAL PASSIONS

THE PORTA AUREA

BLACHERNAE BOOKS

Blachernae Books
Rockville, MD

www.eileenstephenson.com

Publisher's Note: Imperial Passions—The Porta Aurea is a work of historical fiction. Apart from the well-known actual people, events, and locales figuring in the narrative, all names, characters, places, and incidents are a product of the author's imagination or are used fictitiously. Any resemblance to actual people, living or dead, or to businesses, companies, events, institutions, or locales is completely coincidental.

Constantinople image by Byzantium 1200, cover design by Jennifer Quinlan

Imperial Passions—The Porta Aurea / Eileen Stephenson, 1st Edition

Print:
ISBN: 978-0-9996907-0-3
ISBN-10: 0-9996907-0-1

E-book:
ISBN: 978-0-9996907-1-0
ISBN-10: 0-9996907-1-X

To Melissa, Suzanne, and Kathleen

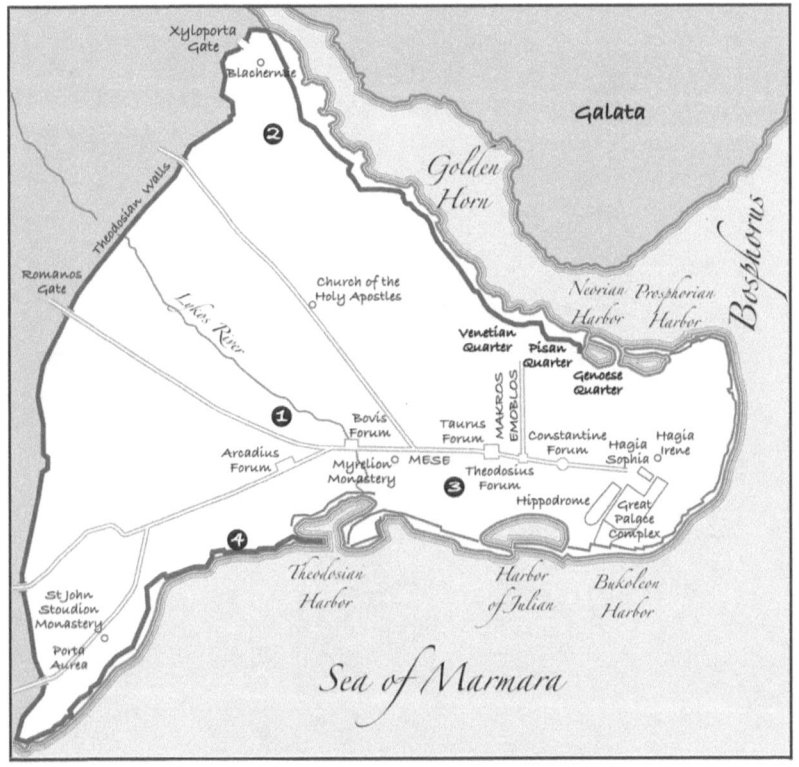

Map of Constantinople – circa 1050

❶ Residence of Adrian and Theodora Dalassenus
❷ Residence of John Comnenus and Anna Dalassena
❸ Residence of Constantine Ducas and Xene Dalassena
❹ Residence of Isaac and Catherine Comnenus

Note

The capital city of the Eastern Roman Empire, commonly called the Byzantine Empire, was Constantinople. However, the people of that city seem to have rarely called it that. Writers from this period called it Byzantion, Byzantium, the City of Byzas, the Queen of Cities, or just "the city", as if there was not other place worthy of that title. This novel uses all of these names for that great city.

Main Characters

---

1 Asterisked* names indicate that no record of the individual's actual name has **survived.**
2 At the time this story takes place, the use of surnames is inconsistent. Not everyone had a surname, and of those who did, not all of them took their father's name. For example, Anna Dalassena's father, Alexios, only had the nickname of "Charon" and no recorded surname, while Anna took her grandfather's **surname.**
3 *Italicized* names indicate a character created for this **story.**

Ducas Family

Constantine Ducas—husband of Xene Dalassena
John Ducas—Constantine's younger brother
Irene Pegonitissa—John wife

Comnenus Family

Manuel Comnenus—general under Basil II; deceased when story opens
Isaac Comnenus—eldest surviving son of Manuel
Catherine of Bulgaria—Isaac's wife and the daughter of Tsar Ivan Vladislav of Bulgaria Manuel Comnenus—son of Isaac and Catherine
Marie Comnena—daughter of Isaac and Catherine
John Comnenus—youngest child of Manuel
Eudokia "Donya"* Comnena—sister to Isaac and John
Michael Dokeianos—general and husband to Donya Comnena
Theodore, **George***, *Helena and Anastasia* **Dokeianos**—*children of Donya and Michael*

Rulers of the Eastern Roman ("Byzantine") Empire

Basil II—emperor for almost 50 years until his death in December 1025
Constantine VIII—Basil's dissolute younger brother; deceased in 1028
Zoe—Eldest surviving daughter of Constantine VIII; empress upon his death
Romanus III Argyros—Zoe's first husband; deceased/murdered before story opens
Michael IV—Zoe's second husband
John the Orphanotrophos—a eunuch and eldest brother of Michael IV; power behind the throne
Michael V—Michael IV's nephew and adopted son of Zoe and Michael IV
Constantine IX Monomachos—Zoe's third husband

"La Skleraina"—Monomachos' mistress

Theodora—Zoe's younger sister and ruling empress following the death of Constantine IX Monomachos

Michael VI Bringas—bureaucrat named emperor by Empress Theodora on her deathbed

OTHER CHARACTERS

Eudokia Makrembolitissa—friend of Anna Dalassena

Michael Keroularios—Eudokia Makrembolitissa's uncle; eventually named patriarch

Michael Psellus—court functionary and historian

Katakalon Kekaumenos—renowned general

George Maniakes—renowned general

Gagik—abdicated king of Armenia, later in service to empire

Nicephoros Bryennios—renowned general

Nicephoros Botaneiates—renowned general

Leo Tornikios—general and nephew of Constantine IX Monomachos

Alusian and Aron—brothers of Catherine of Bulgaria, wife of Isaac Comnenus

Anna* Alusiana—daughter of Alusian

Michael Maurex—a young sailor, later to become droungarios/admiral in Byzantine navy

Maria Kourtikios—a physician

Imperial Passions

"Imperial is the mind that rules over passions."

—Theodosios of Dyrrachion (ca. 1000)

Sailors have told me of the two currents that run through the Bosphorus. One is the surface current of murky blue water; the other is the deeper, hidden river that can drag a ship in the opposite direction, sometimes into the deep. My life has been like that of a ship sailing that treacherous way— living the quiet life of a Roman woman, and yet with invisible streams pulling me into an altogether different place. There were sharp changes in direction when I could not see what lay ahead and was too anxious to remember what was behind. But those years are past now, and I will soon approach the safe harbor, where those I have loved will be waiting, and so I put down my story that it might be preserved and recalled.

CHAPTER ONE

Byzantium

Summer 1039

He slapped her cheek like a whip hitting the back of a stubborn donkey that stifling summer day.

"Don't interrupt me," Constantine Ducas said, his lip curled and turned back to his brother, John, as though slapping his own wife was of no consequence.

Xene had been standing beside her husband, asking him what he'd like her to bring on her next visit, when his arm rose to strike her with no warning. A red handprint marked my cousin's cheek as she slumped to the floor, her brown hair flying loose.

I slipped from behind my grandmother to help Xene struggle up, as my Uncle Costas leapt to defend his daughter.

"What in the name of heaven are you doing?" he barked at Ducas. "She did nothing to deserve that." Xene's thin body trembled in my arms. She reached out a shaking hand for a stool as tears ran down her flushed cheeks.

"That stupid, barren cow you saddled me with?" said Ducas, his handsome face contorted, "She's annoyed me once too often. She knows well enough what I need."

My uncle's fists rose to defend his daughter, his face ruddy with anger. "What—"

Ducas stood up then, his beard jutting out.

"Back off, old man. She's my wife, and I can do what I want with her."

The two men stood only a foot apart, animosity rising like volcanic steam between them, neither willing to yield.

"If you don't stand down, I will take her, here and now, before you all. She's my wife, and I have every right to do so," Ducas said in a low growl.

Xene made a mewling sound, half fear and half shame, before choking it back.

John Ducas had been watching the scene with amusement. He no longer made a pretense of affection for his brother's wife. But even he now caught his breath in a gasp. This was too much.

"Constantine . . ." he stammered, pulling his brother back. John was not as tall as his blond, blue-eyed older brother, but his stocky build might be enough to hold Constantine.

My chest felt tight from holding my breath, with Xene frozen in my arms. The sounds of the guards playing dice outside the door felt like the only normal part of that moment. My grandmother moved in front of us, her face as pale as a marble queen's.

Uncle Costas lowered his fists. He had survived many battles and ten years of captivity in Egypt, but he was almost forty years older than his robust son-in-law. And he had to live in this tower prison with the man.

After five years of imprisonment together in this lonely tower, these two men—my great-uncle, Constantine Dalassenus, and his son-in-law, Constantine Ducas—had lost whatever bonds of affection or friendship that may have once bound them. The tension had festered like an ugly boil in recent months. Ducas blamed only my uncle for their confinement, not the political winds that put them there, as he blamed Xene for not having children.

Grandmother and I pulled Xene, trembling and stumbling back from her husband. John Ducas drew his brother to a table on the other side of the room, next to the narrow slit window looking out of the city to fields beyond its walls. He poured them both cups of wine from the wineskin we had brought. Grandfather kept a grip on his older brother's shoulder, neither speaking but with their eyes flashing.

"It was my fault, all my fault. He gets angry when I forget what he's told me to bring," Xene whimpered after our visit, as the tower guards escorted us down the steep stone steps to the ground level to let us out. It took an hour to walk home from that remote tower, the path through a field half-overgrown with weeds. Xene pulled her maphorion closer to her face to hide the tears and purple bruise forming, but we encountered few passersby that Sunday afternoon. I stayed quiet rather than lash out at Ducas and upset her more.

"Constantine just lost patience with my stupidity—you can't blame him. And the heat is so oppressive; that can make anyone lose their temper." She always had excuses for him; he never had one for her.

Grandmother's eyes kept me silent. My tongue almost bled from biting back my hatred for the monster Xene's husband was. We walked close on either side of her, Grandfather moving ahead of us through the narrow, winding streets, his face like a dark cloud. Grandmother and I said our good-byes to Xene at the gate to our house. Grandfather escorted her the rest of the way home.

Inside our walls, Grandmother and I rested on a bench beside the old elm tree that shaded the house. She shook her head in disbelief. "Oh, Anna, I tried to tell Xene about that man before they married, but she would hear nothing of it. She was besotted with his looks, told me he looked like a statue of Apollo. Well, he did, but I told Costas I thought he was no good. Did he listen to me? Of course not. Ducas never cared for anyone but himself, and maybe that weaselly brother of his. All that mattered to your uncle was that Xene wanted Ducas, so Costas got him for her."

She raised an eyebrow, recalling that time. "Men don't think about what misery it can be, married to a man like that."

"I thought he wanted Xene, too," I said. "I was little then, but I remember their wedding. He acted happy that day." I stood up and paced, wishing I could think of something, anything to hurt Ducas as much as he had hurt my cousin.

Grandmother removed her maphorion and raised her plait up to let the breeze cool her head. Over fifty now, her face held a few lines around her eyes and her hair was more gray than dark brown. I removed my maphorion as well and laid it on the bench beside her. Grandmother gave me a level look, as though she thought I was ready for the truth.

"After they were betrothed, I overheard him boasting of the prestige of being married to a Dalassena, to your cousin. He was excited about her rich dowry. That made him happy. But I never, not ever, thought he wanted or loved her for herself."

She gave a frustrated snort and shook her head. "Ducas was fortunate Xene was so taken with him, or your uncle would never have considered him. Of course, no one expected they would be imprisoned like this. Who would? But as bad as prison is, striking his wife and threatening to rape her in front of her family is worse than anything even I expected of that man."

I swallowed, a bitter taste in my mouth.

She turned to me then, her brown eyes locking with mine, her chin jutting out. "You're a Dalassena, too. But, Anna Dalassena, I promise I will never see you married to someone like that. Never."

The air felt sticky and sultry the morning after that terrible scene. Cool breezes usually blew across between the Golden Horn and the Marmara, but that day the air barely stirred. I moved sluggishly through the morning's chores while looking forward to a refreshing visit to our bathhouse after the midday meal. In my morose preoccupation with Xene, it hardly registered that my grandparents had closeted themselves for some urgent discussion. I presumed they were discussing Xene, trying to find some solution for her predicament.

My grandparents, General Adrian Dalassenus and his wife, Theodora, had raised me after my parents' deaths nine years earlier. Xene lived with us at the time while her father was on campaign. She had lost her own mother at a young age and cared for me when my parents died. She stayed with me for many of those sad nights, holding my hand as I wept. We visited their graves and left flowers for them. The doll she found in the market brought the first hesitant smile back to my face weeks after their burials. She became part sister and part mother to me then—something I could never forget.

The Dalassenus family fortunes had tumbled down over the past ten years, since Empress Zoe's husbands—first one, then the other—envied the esteem the army and people had for my Uncle Costas. The first one, Romanus, tried to blame the Aleppo defeat on him, but Uncle's soldiers were still billeted in the city, so the emperor backed off. This new emperor, Michael, had a powerful ally in his brother, the eunuch John the Orphanotrophos—the Orphan Master. This cunning man with a minor title had slowly gathered the empire's reins of power into his own hands. He learned from Romanus's mistake, and Uncle's army had been disbanded long before they arrested him and Ducas.

These jealous emperors imagined my uncle harbored a secret desire for the throne. They did not realize that Uncle Costas knew the difference between politics and soldiering and had no interest in the former. Besides, he was an old man—nearing seventy on that hot summer day—with no interest in taking on the responsibility for an empire.

The Dalassenus men were soldiers with no pretensions to the *dynatoi*. Those privileged families lived in seaside villas and palaces overlooking the Sea of Marmara, filled with elegant gardens sloping down to the sea, marble statues, and mosaic floors. Our house in an undistinguished neighborhood, though spacious and comfortable, had no marble or mosaics, and the garden grew more food than flowers.

Grandmother kept me busy in the morning—in her gardens behind the house, my disinterested efforts at the loom and with a needle, and the endless sweeping and cleaning a house needs. Grandfather, who would never be called to lead another army with his brother in prison, took charge of my education. Grandmother had urged him to teach me whatever he knew, even though most of it would have been what a son, such as my Uncle Simeon, would have been taught. He filled my afternoons with grammar, rhetoric, mathematics, philosophy, and history—mostly military history.

Grandfather could take the driest story of a battle in a history book and transform it into the saga of drama, death, and victory it was. We often created stick figures, tied together with vines or leftover threads, with which we acted out the fighting while Grandfather described the soldiers' campaigns. Grandfather's stories of the great events in Roman history taught me better than any book of history. He wove tales of military maneuvers and political intrigue into my lessons that kept me more eager to learn than a colorless tutor who had never carried a sword into battle would have. These lessons spilled into our evening chess games, where he taught me the strategic thinking of generals and kings.

After a refreshing bath that afternoon, I sat on the terrace behind our house in the shade of a vine-covered trellis, shelling a bowl of peas. My black and white cat, Athena, stretched languorously under the bench I sat on. Grandfather recounted Emperor Basil's defeat by the Bulgarians over fifty years earlier. Grandfather's appearance reminded me of the great white egrets that flew in the marshy ground down near the Lykos River—long-legged, thin, and with a steel gray beard in contrast to his soldier's tan. His mind was still sharp, even as age and old wounds had sapped his physical agility. His hands, firm and covered with freckles and age spots, stacked pebbles on the table to recreate the mountain pass named Trajan's Gate, arranging and rearranging the soldier stick figures to show me how the battle had progressed.

My head snapped toward the house when I thought I heard strange voices coming from that direction, but it was only angry squirrels. I sighed with impatience and kicked at the sweaty sandals I had removed, wishing for a breeze to blow Trajan's Gate away and cool us off.

"Grandfather," I said, squinting against the sun as I looked up at him, "why are you telling me about such a terrible defeat? I think I prefer the stories of victories."

"Do you?" He raised a snowy eyebrow at me. "Won't learn much if all you know about are victories." He removed the straw hat he wore and wiped the sweat from his glistening face with the sleeve of his juppe before moving into a shadier spot under the trellis.

"Best soldiers learn most from defeats—best lessons from their own," he said in his laconic fashion. "My father fought there, and other soldiers I knew later. Told me how the Bulgarians surprised our men, storming down the mountains, slaughtering thousands of our soldiers. None forgot that rout. But Basil survived. The loss made our eventual victory sweeter."

I swatted away a pair of bees that buzzed around my face and continued shelling the peas. I wondered if it would be cooler under the willow tree by the river at the back of our property. Trajan's Gate held little interest for me just then, but the discussion did distract me from thinking about Xene.

"But wasn't the old emperor a great general who had many victories? How could he have lost?"

Grandfather leaned forward, an unexpected intensity in his narrowed gaze. This startled me so that the bowl almost slipped from my lap. Why would he think a battle fought so long ago was important for me to understand?

"Basil was young then, not much experience. Good soldier, yes, but he didn't know the enemy's tricks. Learned them at Trajan's Gate. Never made those mistakes again."

He gestured at the pebbles and sticks used to demonstrate the battle. "Survived defeat, learned from it; that led to success. Basil discovered that." He stood up, stretched, and paced around the terrace before he gave a quick glance at the house. He pulled his light silk juppe away from his body to let the air through.

I peered down at a few peas that had slipped from my fingers onto the ground and kicked them into the dirt in irritation.

I followed his eyes. Grandmother was gesturing to him to come in.

"Good lesson to learn," Grandfather said, referring to the day's subject. He swept the pebbles and stick figures from the table onto the slate tiles beneath our feet. "Anna, finish with the peas and then come inside," Without waiting for my response, he strode toward the house.

We had few visitors since no one wanted to risk offending the emperor or the Orphanotrophos. However, I could see the back of a tall stranger just leaving when I reached the house.

The house felt dark and cool after the midday sun and should have been quiet at that time. Instead, servants rushed around as though preparing for a feast. Grandmother's usually cheerful face looked creased with worry as she glanced from me to Grandfather. She had pulled an apron over her loose light brown silk tunica. If Grandfather reminded me of an egret, Grandmother was more like a mother hen—always busy with her chick. She moved with the energy of someone years younger as she gave instructions to the servants scurrying past me.

"Anna," she called to get my attention. I stepped into the hallway, bemused by the unusual burst of activity in the house. Grandfather stood beside her, concern on both their faces. "Something has happened . . ." She stopped and looked at Grandfather's set face, unable to finish.

"Emperor's not satisfied with what he's done to my brother. I've received word his soldiers will come here tonight. We're to be exiled,"

Grandfather spoke with a gruff finality. "It's bad, but better than prison. We'll be sent on a ship leaving for Amaseia on the Black Sea and go to Costas's estate there."

My sweaty hands felt unsteady as I put the bowl of peas on a table.

"But why? We've done nothing wrong. And why so far away? Couldn't we just go to our farm in Thrace?" I could not control the plaintive note in my voice. Grandmother moved to put an arm around me. I felt we were like the helpless mice I sometimes saw in Athena's clenched jaws, about to be consumed.

"Doesn't matter," came Grandfather's brusque response, his face reddening. "We've no choice. Thrace's too close; the greater the distance, the better. The emperor just wants us gone from the city. Pack a bag with what you'll need on the journey. Not too much—they might realize we were warned. And wear traveling clothes to bed. They'll give us little time to prepare." As an afterthought, he added, "Alethea and Maria have agreed to come with us."

Alethea was our cook, who kept me cowed with her impressive size and bossy manner. Maria, a serving girl of about my age, might be good company.

"What about Athena?" I asked, grasping for some reason that might change our plans, and reached down to gather the cat in my arms.

Grandmother peered regretfully at the cat and stroked Athena's soft fur, but she shook her head. "I don't think we can take her. She can stay here with Nicholas and Leo. They'll look after her."

Our steward, Nicholas, came back into the room. "Lady Theodora, would you have a minute? Samuel's arrived."

The warehouse down near the Neorion harbor had been Grandmother's dowry when she married my grandfather. She had always handled its affairs since Grandfather had been so often absent on campaign and had little interest in commerce. Samuel, a Jew, had managed its daily operations under her direction for years, holding goods coming into the city or being readied for shipment out.

Grandfather walked me to the stairs and put a hand on my shoulder.

I turned to him with tears in my eyes and asked, "What about my cousins? What about Xene and Romanus?" Romanus was the grandson of my grandfather's oldest sister. His father had died a few years earlier in suspicious circumstances in the emperor's custody. A young boy, he still lived in the city with his mother, my cousin Eugenia.

"Emperor's not interested in fatherless boys. Xene's husband is already imprisoned, so he won't bother her. No, the Orphanotrophus just wanted me this time," a regretful tone crept into his voice. "Can't think why—we've done nothing. But as I said, it could be worse—we could be imprisoned. Or blinded. Or dead."

I wiped the tears from my face with my sleeve as Athena leapt back to the floor.

"Tears are no help. We'll be back someday, little chick," Grandfather said with a wry smile. "Now, upstairs to pack your bag. And don't forget Trajan's Gate—the key to victory is to survive and learn from defeat."

Dinner started as a quiet affair, each of us anxious about the imminent arrival of soldiers and the journey into exile. Grandfather tired of the gloominess, though.

"Thea, when we went on campaign, we always marched to songs on the way," he said to brush away the evening's somber tone. "What do you say I teach you ladies some of them?"

Grandmother looked relieved at the proposal. "All right, Adrian."

After a quick trip to his room, he returned carrying a small drum and a tambourine, which he handed to me.

Grandmother broke into an unexpected laugh; the tensions built up in her over the past two days dissolved at this diversion. Grandfather took the drum and began to tap on it, at first with a light touch and then with more energy. Alethea and Maria joined us, and for the next hour the four of us learned the soldiers' marching songs, to laughter and jokes, with Amaseia the destinations in the songs. Two or three times Grandfather let slip some of the raunchier lyrics, garnering a look of reproof on Grandmother's face and hilarity from the rest of us. Even grumpy Nicholas was there with a reluctant smile of enjoyment.

We women went to our rooms when darkness fell for what sleep we could manage, Athena curled up next to me. Grandfather kept watch for the soldiers he expected downstairs in Grandmother's workroom overlooking the courtyard.

Thunderous knocking jolted me awake and frightened Athena, who scampered off the bed with a startled hiss. I crept to the window to see the courtyard.

"Dalassenus! Open up, we come from the emperor!" came shouts from the street as someone pummeled our gate. It had to be after midnight.

The clamor from the other side of the wall confused old Leo, our gatekeeper, who scrambled first to the house and then back to the gate as the bellowing became more insistent. Grandfather emerged from the house and gestured to him to open the gate.

As soon as Leo slid the last bolt back, the soldiers pushed the gate wide open, and a dozen of them with torches rushed through. Old Leo got knocked down in their haste to enter and dropped his lantern when he fell, looking stunned at the impact. The flame ignited some straw on the ground before he could pick it up, but it soon burned itself out. A pair of soldiers, each of them twice Leo's size, picked him up while they yelled in their foreign accents, demanding to know where his master was, not seeing my grandfather in the dim light. These tall, blond men with their barbarian accents had to be in the emperor's Varangian Guards. One of the big soldiers roughly shoved the stable boy, who had emerged half-asleep from his loft above the horses. The poor boy's face scraped against the wall's rough stones as he fell.

The curved blades of the soldiers' *rhomphaia* glinted in the torchlight, mirroring the sickle moon in the sky. A tall, blond man, broad shouldered and with a double-headed axe hanging from his belt, appeared to be the leader and pushed his way to the front. Grandfather stepped into the torchlight to greet the soldiers.

"I am Adrian Dalassenus. Do I speak with Harold of the Varangians?" Grandfather said in a loud but calm voice.

The leader of the soldiers, the man Grandfather called Harold, responded to the welcome with a loud announcement in barbarian-accented Greek as his soldiers surrounded the house: "Dalassenus, the emperor has decreed that you are suspected of conspiracy against him. You and your household leave tonight for exile."

"Yes, yes, I understand. Can I give you and your men some refreshment while my family readies itself?" Grandfather asked, his hands spread out in a gesture of conciliation. Nicholas must have been alerted for this since he appeared with a wineskin and cups.

"Anna." Grandmother startled me with a grip on my shoulder. She had entered my room without a sound, and I peered around at her anxious face. "Are you ready? Gather your things. We'll need to leave now."

I nodded, unable to get words out. I watched the belligerent soldiers in our courtyard tease old Leo and jab at him with their weapons while Nicholas poured them wine. I turned away, alarmed by the scene below, and knocked a small alabaster box that had been my mother's to the floor, where it shattered. The carved stone of a soft ivory tint and amber-colored swirls was broken into pieces that could never be repaired, like the life I had lived to that day. I was about to pick them up when I heard my grandmother's insistent calling.

I gathered up my traveling bag in shaky hands, ready to leave when I remembered Athena. She was hiding under the bed, shaking and her ears back. I coaxed her out and calmed her with a few strokes before kissing her farewell. I placed her on the bed, where she sat with a questioning turn of her head before I raced downstairs.

Final instructions were given to Nicholas and in minutes we departed into the midnight dark streets of Byzantium. I walked between my grandparents, trying not to trip on the uneven paving stones. Alethea and Maria followed close behind.

The soldiers carried torches to light our way through the Forum Bovis and east on the Mese before turning toward the sea. The salty smell of the Marmara's waters grew as we neared the Theodosian harbor, the one closest to our home, where an imperial dromon lay anchored. The Varangians handed us over to the captain at the dock and watched us board the ship, which swarmed with dozens of oarsmen and sailors. Harold and his men did not turn away until the dromon had sailed some distance from the pier.

The ship's captain, with his bulk, long black hair streaked with white and dark protruding eyes resembled a sea monster. He paced the deck shouting orders to scurrying crew. His creased face dripped perspiration, I suspected as much from fear of the Orphanotrophus as the heat, still oppressive at that late hour. The dromon creaked as it headed out of the harbor, slipping between the beacons on the two mole towers at the harbor's entrance. The ship sailed alongside the silent city's seawalls. Two cabin boys leaned out over the ship's prow with torches to keep us from running aground.

Few lamps still lit the city at that hour, but we had to be sailing east to approach the cape of the peninsula and reach the Bosphorus. The Boukoleon, one of the Great Palace's residences, stood above the seawall near that point. Light from torches in each arch of its long portico caught my eye even before we reached it. On the landing where the emperor's own ships docked, a hooded monk stood between the two marble lions guarding it, his face half-hidden in his cowl.

Grandmother was questioning one of the sailors but turned to see where the light came from. She gasped at the sight of the monk and jerked me back into the shadows to shield me from the man's view as we approached. I stood so close to her that the scents from the herb garden that always lingered in her clothes overcame the salty air. I came close to weeping, wondering when we would see that garden again. Distracted by these thoughts, I almost missed her words.

"He does not care about us since we are just women. But there is no need for him to see us," she whispered, her arm encircling me while she watched the man. I realized then that the monk on the landing was the vile Orphanotrophos, and I peered at him from our shadowy corner.

This man's plots and schemes had ruined so many lives. Yet from a distance, he looked ordinary—not tall, with a slightly rounded belly, and the robes of an innocuous monk. His habit covered all but his beardless cheeks and sandaled feet, the breeze lifting the robe about his ankles. He looked like the kind of man you would pass on the street and not recall.

My grandfather stood in clear view, unbowed and unafraid, speaking to the sailors and laughing by the deck's railing as he would in his own home. A eunuch who pretended at piety with monk's robes without monk's vows did not intimidate that battle-scarred old man. That eunuch may have sent us into exile, but Adrian Dalassenus refused to tremble and hide. The fear of that eunuch seemed to drop like a suffocating blanket on everyone else on the ship except him.

That was my last sight of Byzantium, aside from the dark contour of the dome of the Great Church of Holy Wisdom, Hagia Sophia, in the distance as we sailed north past the Golden Horn to the Bosphorus.

Once we were out of sight of the city, the captain anchored near a small island to wait for the dawn. I heard him mutter something about only a fool or a madman attempting to sail the Bosphorus at night, no matter what some monk in the palace said. The strait made for a dangerous passage even in daylight, and a shipwreck for certain when sailing in the dark. The four of us women huddled in cramped quarters, dozed fitfully.

I awakened in the morning and emerged onto the deck to find we were under way, the two sails open to catch the wind that would carry us to our destination. The summer sun sparkled on the water, where an occasional fish leapt high into the air. The menace of the night before had faded into a day somehow alight with unexpected promise, as buoyant as the ship.

I walked to the railing to stand next to my grandfather. He glanced over at me, his face damp with sea spray, and then put an arm around me.

"A fine day for sailing, don't you think?" he asked me.

"Yes, Grandfather, I do," I answered, the wind twisting my hair. I rested my head on his shoulder. "How long will it take to reach Amaseia?"

"Maybe a week to get through the Bosphorus and the Black Sea, and then overland to Amaseia. If the weather holds."

"How long to get through the Bosphorus?" I asked. I could see the oars had been pulled in since the sails pulled us in the right direction for this stretch.

"By this afternoon. It's not far, but the passage is slow this time of year with many merchant ships to watch for. The wind may not hold. We'll need to stop, too, for fresh water in this heat."

We watched together as a forest and a small fishing village perched on the coast came into view and disappeared after we passed it.

"Sorry we had to leave. It's a mystery why the emperor decided we were a threat now, after all these years," he said in a conciliatory tone as he looked at me. "I suspect the Orphanotrophus is using us as an example to others who might try. I'm an old man—I've no energy or interest in causing him problems. I have my opinions, but you're the only one who listens to them." He winked at me.

I snorted, amused. Then, suddenly, I realized I had forgotten about Xene in all the turmoil since the previous day. She would have only our cousin Eugenia for company with us gone. And Eugenia—busy raising her son, widowed and living on her brother's charity—could offer little help or comfort.

"Grandfather, does Xene even know we are gone?"

"Yes. Sent notes for her and Eugenia with Nicholas. He'll deliver them today." His face took on a grim expression at the thought of his niece. "I suggested Xene go to Simeon if she needs help."

My Uncle Simeon was a monk at the city's most renowned monastery, St. John Stoudion. But his vows limited what he could do.

"Sunday was awful," I said, shaking at the memory.

"I know. Never dreamed Ducas would do that. The bastard." He frowned out onto the blue-green waves flecked with white foam. "But Costas will still be there. He'll do what he can."

That thought helped little. My uncle was an old man, and Ducas no more than thirty.

"Those soldiers frightened me last night," I said, changing the subject.

"Did they?" he asked wryly, rubbing his beard.

"Weren't you worried?" I asked.

"No. Remember the big blond fellow, the one I called Harold? Saved his life a few years back in Bulgaria." Then in a quieter voice, he said, "He sent to warn us yesterday, but we had to look intimidated, or Harold would be on the next ship out."

"I wish I'd known," I said, squinting at him with a crooked smile.

"Then you wouldn't have looked frightened enough. Someone might suspect Harold."

Grandmother and Alethea joined us then on deck to report that Maria suffered with seasickness. Grandfather took my grandmother aside to cheer her as best he could. She was a strong woman, but she had left her home and her only surviving child, my Uncle Simeon, behind in his monastery.

I stayed with Maria for much of the sea voyage to help with her seasickness. Even after we had passed through the curves of the Bosphorus and reached the more placid waters of the Black Sea, her condition did not improve until we had docked at the port of Amisos and our journey continued on land.

After a night at an inn in Amisos, Grandfather hired a cart and some horses, so a few days later, after over a week of travel, we arrived at Uncle Costas's estate on the outskirts of the theme's capital of Amaseia. My cousin Damien, Uncle Costas's only son, lived on the farm with his young family. Our precipitous departure gave no time to warn of our arrival, but the Dalassenus family stood by each other.

The cart racketed along the dirt road toward the farm, dust rising in the air. The bustling, noisy streets of the great city of Constantine seemed like another world as the only sound now came from a few sheep bleating listlessly in a field. In most of the city, the walls and buildings stood so close by each other that the sky was only just visible. Even the farm in hilly Thrace did not have vistas like this valley's. Here, the wide sky spread like a golden bowl above our heads, sunlight stretching across to mountains in the south.

We turned from the road onto a long path that approached their house. A dark-haired boy unhitching a donkey from a cart saw us and ran into the house to alert someone. A woman emerged with a baby on her hip, the boy at her side, and cautiously regarded our bedraggled party. She had last visited Byzantium seven or eight years earlier, but Grandmother recognized Damien's wife, Irene, at once.

"Irene—it's me, your Aunt Theodora," she cried out, waving her arms above her head.

Irene approached us, confused as people are when they see someone they completely do not expect, almost as though seeing a ghost.

"Aunt Theodora?" she began haltingly, then looked at the rest of us. "Uncle Adrian? What's happened? How did you come to be here?"

The quiet summer day was soon filled with greetings and the story of our exile and voyage. Maria, Alethea, and I scrambled out of the cart with our meager possessions.

Just before entering the house with my grandparents, Irene turned to the dark-haired boy we had seen first. "Demetrius, fetch your master. Go quickly; I think he's in the olive grove."

While everyone else disappeared into the house in a wave of conversation, I lingered in the tidy courtyard, an oak tree shading its center. Grandfather's chestnut horse and the donkeys that had pulled our cart drank thirstily from the trough, their slurping reminding me of my own parched throat.

The preposterous charges that brought us here made no more sense to me than Ducas's cruelty to Xene did. Then, as I stroked the side of his horse, I recalled Grandfather's admonition that last afternoon in Byzantium: "Don't forget Trajan's Gate." One defeat, no matter how terrible, is not the end if you have survived. With that slim thread of a promise, I entered my cousin's house.

CHAPTER TWO

Amaseia

Summer 1041

Uncle Costas' estate lay far from the crowded streets, noise, and markets of Byzantium. Our family farm in Thrace, at less than two days' journey from the city, was almost next door compared to this distant outpost. Old Emperor Basil had settled many of his soldiers on estates like this, seeding the borderlands with men ready to be its defenders.

Damien was Uncle Costas's only son, named for his grandfather, who died in the battle at Apamea. Like all the Dalassenus men, Damien had been raised to be a soldier, but he returned home after almost dying in the Aleppo debacle eleven years ago. His slight limp testified to those wounds.

The constant scrape of tension we had lived with in the political maelstrom in Byzantium disappeared in the country, and my grandparents' faces lost their worried frowns. Up before dawn, I helped milk the cows and goats in the warm barn before returning to the house for breakfast with Damien's boisterous three young sons. The boys and I then fed the chickens—a lengthy affair that usually involved the boys chasing the chickens around their yard. There was always laundry to do and what mending Grandmother would trust me with. She had long since decided that my tangled efforts at weaving were hopeless, so she excused me from that particular task altogether.

Later in the day, with competent tutors rare in this remote district, Grandfather and I spent a few hours teaching Damien's two older boys,

Constantine and Alexander, their letters, grammar, and arithmetic. In the evenings after dinner, someone would read from one of Uncle Costas' books or play a game of chess, while Grandmother sewed.

Most girls were either already married or at least betrothed at my age of sixteen. At home, the family had been out of favor with the emperor and living under the constant suspicion of rebellion for so long that no one even had inquired for me before we were exiled. I imagined now all the mothers of the young men in Byzantium saying, "Marry a Dalassena and end up exiled, in prison, or dead."

In recent months, a few young men in the district presented themselves to my grandparents—the rough sons of retired soldiers or a wealthy merchant's conceited offspring. Some of them were handsome enough, but none of them either knew of, or had an interest beyond the town's borders. Grandmother saw my stifled yawns and would give a quick shake of her head to Grandfather. I had no regrets when these few marital prospects dissipated like the morning mist.

On that particular day in late July, I had little expectation that matters might change.

"Mistress, your grandmother wants you to come downstairs now," Maria was breathless with the exertion of bringing ewers of fresh water upstairs in the late afternoon heat. "We have a guest tonight, someone with a letter."

"Really?" I had been sewing a small nightshirt for Damien's new daughter. "Do you know who it is?" I asked.

"No, but he looks like a soldier," she said, setting the pitcher on my table. "A fine-looking, young one, at that," she added with a toothy grin before moving on to the next room with her ewers.

I loved hearing the latest news from the city. However, even good-looking soldiers might not be overly congenial—respectful of my grandfather and cousin while ignoring me. It was not easy to tell if soldiers frugal in their use of words spoke little from fear of making an offhand remark that the emperor or the Orphanotrophus might hear of and take offense to, or from a natural disinclination to speech. So I washed, ran the tortoise-shell comb through my thick brown hair, and went downstairs for supper with just a bit more anticipation than normal.

"Anna, you're finally here," Grandmother spoke in a rush, just finishing her instructions to one of the servants. Her eyes glowed as she continued. "We've received a letter from your Uncle Simeon. John Comnenus, the younger brother of the new strategos, Isaac Comnenus, brought it for us."

She paused to speak to another servant, giving instructions for Alethea's dinner preparations before continuing. "He's in the study with your grandfather and will join us for supper. I've invited him to stay here tonight, so he won't need to rush back."

General Isaac Comnenus, the new military governor of our theme, headquartered nearby in Amaseia had not yet visited us. Grandfather said Isaac Comnenus had once served under his command, acquitting himself well before leaving to join his own uncle's troops. He had never mentioned a brother.

The servants soon appeared with platters of food, their rich aromas luring the men from the study. Damien and Grandfather emerged in animated conversation with a solidly built redheaded young man with a neat beard. The man's deep, friendly laugh at something Damien said made me smile. He looked like some exotic bird with his bright hair and green silk tunic, a gold scroll design embroidered on the hem. Feeling dull in comparison, I looked down and smoothed the blue tunica I wore as Grandfather escorted him over to us.

"John, let me introduce you to my wife, the Lady Theodora, and to my granddaughter, Anna. My dear, Anna, this is John Comnenus, General Comnenus's younger brother. He has been kind enough to bring us a letter from Simeon."

Uncle Simeon, although Master of the Scriptorium at St. John's, knew he was watched by the emperor's spies. In theory, he was above such worldly matters, and his valued work on the Menologion, the book of saints' days for the emperor, was only partially completed. None could equal his drawings, and the scriptorium, the largest in the city, benefited from the organizational ability Uncle Simeon had inherited from Grandmother. Although valued for his work, and permitted occasional visits to Uncle Costas, he knew to be cautious when sending letters.

John Comnenus gave us an uncertain smile. We sometimes got odd looks since many dynatoi families did not permit their women to meet with male guests at home. Uncle Costas had decreed that a foolish custom many years earlier and the rest of the family followed his lead. John recovered quickly, though, greeting us as we waited for the servants to bring the platters into the dining room.

"Ladies, I'm happy to finally meet the mother and niece of Father Simeon," John said, glancing first at Grandmother and then at me. "He told me how much he misses you and hopes you'll return soon to the city."

"We're grateful you took the risk to bring us my son's letter, given our family's standing with the palace." Grandmother's eyes glowed.

John Comnenus smiled. "Oh, he took great care. We only spoke twice before making all other arrangements through someone we both trusted, away from any spies. He hid the letter in the false back of an icon he sent you and your husband as a gift."

Grandmother's mouth arched humorously. "Hmm, and probably said a few prayers over it for good measure." Turning to Grandfather, she asked, "Have you read the letter yet?"

"No, we thought we would wait until after supper when you and Anna could hear it, too." Irene had given birth a few days earlier and was still recovering.

Damien's eyebrows rose in scrutiny of the dinner platters the servants carried in. He was not a man to let a meal get long delayed, with or without a guest. I caught Grandmother's eye and glanced briefly at my hungry cousin. With a gracious smile, she walked the young soldier to our dining room. A breeze cooled the warm evening air, blowing through the windows open to the garden.

Grandfather sat down, said grace, and passed the platters—small fresh loaves of bread, still warm and fragrant from the oven, lamb, olives, asparagus, and soft cheese. A servant poured the light, sweet wine from Bithynia mixed with a little water—refreshing in the summer.

I glanced curiously across the table at the stranger. A head taller than I was, John Comnenus stood as tall as Grandfather with a broad, muscular build. His face had the look of someone who smiled often, with lively blue eyes and freckles sprinkled over his cheeks. I suddenly realized those blue eyes were gazing back at me. Blinking, I looked down at my plate, embarrassed at my boldness, hoping he didn't think I had forgotten good manners after so long in the country.

Damien dismissed the servants after they had brought out the food and drink.

"John, we saw Isaac briefly in town a few weeks ago, but he didn't say why he's here. Wasn't he assigned to Bulgaria in the past? Never so far east before," Grandfather said.

John leaned forward, quickly swallowing the bite he had in his mouth. "I expect you know Isaac's wife, Catherine, is the daughter of the old deposed Bulgarian king, Ivan. But did you hear the news about her brother, Alousian?" he asked.

Grandfather's eyebrows rose, and he shook his head, "No, nothing. We get little news here."

"Alousian rebelled a few months ago and joined a cousin who had raised an army trying to regain the Bulgarian throne. The emperor sent Isaac here rather than forcing him to fight his own brother-in-law or, more likely, keep him from being tempted to join the rebels. A few weeks later, the emperor remembered me and sent me to follow him. Of course, Catherine and their children stayed behind in the city," he said, drily, "for their own safety, obviously."

"Why would Alousian do that? I've met him a few times; he was quite Romanized and didn't seem interested in returning to Bulgaria," asked Grandfather.

"It was one of the emperor's brothers," said John, speaking of the emperor's four avaricious brothers, all eunuchs. "Constantine, one of those useless eunuchs, was appointed domestic of the Scholai, and with the backing of the Scholai troops, he demanded that Alousian vacate his villa overlooking the Marmara. I was once in it—it's almost as splendid as the Boukoleon at the Great Palace."

He shrugged. "I guess Constantine wanted to live as well as the emperor. Anyway, Alousian had few alternatives but to vacate the villa with little more than the clothes he and his family wore. He escaped the city hiding in the back of a wagon hauling shit out of the city, worried his life would be forfeit next." The disgusting, if amusing ruse caused us all to laugh. "He must have thought his only choice was to join his cousin Peter's rebellion.

I thought the emperor must have had need of Isaac Comnenus, only to send him to the Armeniakon theme rather than to prison, with his brother-in-law in rebellion. Of course, we were about as far from Bulgaria as you could get within the empire's borders, and keeping Isaac's wife and children within sight of the Palace must give the emperor and Orphanotrophus some comfort about their general's loyalty.

"John, we've heard rumors about the emperor's health. Any truth there?" Grandfather asked.

"He commanded the army in Bulgaria for a while, but when he's in the city, he stays in the Palace. He leaves the court's business to the Orphanotrophus, so that might be the reason for the rumors."

My grandparents and cousin exchanged looks at this news before John continued.

"Even so, gossip escapes. The empress is almost never seen, like she's a prisoner in the Palace. She only leaves it to attend services at the Hagia Sophia. A story circulated a few months ago that she tried to poison the Orphanotrophus which may be why. Zoe's only companions are eunuchs and ladies loyal to the Orphanotrophus and the emperor. They say she rarely sees the emperor and never shares his bed."

"Zoe may be Basil's niece, but she certainly lacks his intelligence," Grandfather said as he stood and moved around the table, refilling our wine cups. "Can she truly think Michael would want to bed a wife if she tried to poison his brother?"

"Maybe fear is driving Michael from Zoe's bed," Grandmother said with a shudder, her scowl betraying her cynicism. "Or a guilty conscience. Could be both. I don't want to think what could have happened to Costas."

Everyone knew the story that Zoe killed her first husband, Emperor Romanus, drowning him in his bath with Michael's help. Even worse, Zoe and Michael married the same day old Romanus died. The old emperor had been no friend to our family, jealous since Zoe's father had first wanted Uncle Costas to marry her, and he was only the second choice. Still, he didn't deserve to be murdered so she could marry another.

"The emperor fills the coffers of priests and monks with gold coins, trying to expiate the sin of murder," Grandmother said in disgust.

Grandfather patted her hand, knowing how much this angered her, her mouth turning down in a rueful frown.

The crickets' insistent hum grew louder with the setting sun, the sky turning deep purple hues around the mountains to the south. A servant knocked and entered with a couple of oil lamps. The light shone brightly on the young soldier's face. I realized I'd been staring again at John Comnenus when another servant entered with a bowl of peaches. The conversation veered to the mundane topics of crops and weather until she left.

At the meal's end, we retired to the study to read Uncle Simeon's letter, eager to hear its news. I sat at the chess table by the window while the rest clustered close to the table upon which two brass lamps sat.

John handed the icon of the Theotokos and Christ child to Damien, who pried the back off with a small knife to find the letter. The icon's golden halos shimmered in the lamplight as he set it aside on a table. Unfolding the stiff parchment, he began to read:

"My beloved family:

Greetings from St. John Stoudion Monastery. I am well, surviving the recent earthquake, thanks be to God and the intercession of the Theotokos. We had minor damage to the monastery's stables, easily repaired, though several nearby tenements were destroyed, so the families are staying in the guesthouse until they find other lodgings.

I visit Uncle Costas almost weekly. His health is good, but the tedious confinement drains him. Relations with Ducas continue strained, as he blames Uncle for their confinement. Ducas lately forbade Xene to visit them. To keep the peace in their tiny quarters, Uncle won't speak harshly of his son-in-law.

My fist tightened around the marble pawn I held, the memory of our last visit still sharp as a knife after two years. Grandmother's face reddened as her hands lay unmoving atop the sewing in her lap.

"Bad news from Sicily. Father, your good friend George Maniakes easily defeated the Saracens in Sicily with the Varangian Guard, but had difficulty with the emperor's brother-in-law, Stephen, who accompanied

him. Stephen managed to allow the Muslim general to escape by ship after the battle, and George—you recall his temper—became enraged with Stephen to the point of cursing and striking him. This rough treatment from a man of George's impressive size angered Stephen, who sent word to the Palace that George planned an uprising against the emperor. George was arrested on his return. The emperor then put the luckless Stephen in charge of Sicily, where the Muslims routed him within a few weeks. We lost many soldiers and much gold, left behind in Stephen's abandoned camp."

Grandfather covered his face with his hands. He looked up finally and shook his head. "George didn't deserve that, but I wish I'd been there to see him pounce on that stumpy weasel Stephen. Must have been quite a sight."

"Better news from Bulgaria. The Orphanotrophus decided the treasury needed refilling after the cost of the Sicilian disaster and generous gifts to his brothers had depleted it. He decreed that Bulgarian subjects should begin paying their taxes in coin instead of from each farm's production, as Emperor Basil permitted. The peasants struggled to make their payments, with coins being rare in those remote farms. When some could not, the tax collectors forced them off their farms, leaving many homeless and prey to wild animals and starvation. Traveling monks told us that often the tax collectors benefited more from the sale of these farms than the emperor did. Rebels rose up, led by Peter Delyen, the son of a Bulgarian ruler, and his cousin, Alousian. Their army looked to break Bulgaria apart from the empire. Emperor Michael led an army to Thessalonica, which the Bulgarians attempting to take, but some of his soldiers were Bulgarians and took the opportunity to desert to the rebels.

"This is better news?" Damien asked. "The taxes were sufficient until the Orphanotrophus and his greedy brothers took over."

"Despite this, the emperor's army, with a large contingent of Varangians, put up a notable defense of Thessalonica when the rebels attacked,

defeating them and killing many. We hope that will soon be the end of it, but I doubt the new taxes in Bulgaria raised as many coins as were spent to defeat the rebels the tax precipitated.

Before the emperor left for Thessalonica, he and the Orphanotrophus convinced the empress that they should adopt his nephew, the son of his sister and the luckless Stephen. The empress gave this boy, who is also called Michael, the title of caesar. So if the emperor dies in battle or succumbs to an illness, this boy will inherit the crown. Only his family connection could justify the elevation of such an unremarkable young man so close to the throne.

I hope this letter has found you all in good health and spirits. I pray for the day when Uncle Costas is free and you can return to the city. Please give a cordial welcome to my messenger. We know him well at Stoudion, raised here with his brother as charges of the old emperor. You have my prayers for God's blessings on you all."

No one spoke at first. None of the news sounded promising, but Xene's news troubled me most.

Uncle Simeon was too discreet to mention in a letter if Ducas had hit her. But forbidding Xene to visit her husband and father left her isolated in the city since our cousin Eugenia had departed a year earlier with her son to live with relatives in the country.

I recalled that even before the slapping incident, I tried to speak to John Ducas, asking him to urge his brother to be kinder to Xene. Naively, I thought it might help Xene, and John did not seem as harsh as his brother. I should have known better from the way he almost worshipped Constantine with an extreme devotion. His face glowed when Constantine spoke, lapsing into passivity and indifference when conversing with others. Oddest of all, though, were his tears at parting from his brother. My grandfather and uncle, soldiers like the Ducas brothers, never wept at parting as John did, no matter their grief at his imprisonment.

I gritted my teeth at that acid memory.

My grandparents had been taking leave of my uncle and Ducas that day while I stood outside, waiting for them when John Ducas approached. In his early twenties, his appearance differed greatly from his strikingly handsome brother's—not much taller than I was and dark haired. Seizing the chance to speak, I reached out a hand to stop him as he passed.

"John," I began in a soft voice so as not to be overheard, "can I speak with you for a moment?"

John looked pointedly down at my hand, which I quickly removed. He replied with formal courtesy, "If you wish," then glanced impatiently at the chamber's door.

"I wanted to ask if you would speak to your brother about how he treats Xene. You must see she tries to please him, but he always seems angry at her, berating her. You know she's trying to do what he wants," I trailed off at his look.

His lips curled up in an ugly sneer as he rolled his eyes.

"Well, shouldn't she be trying to please him, do what he wants? Isn't that every wife's duty? If she can't manage to give him children, she should at least try to please him."

"Yes, but—" I started.

"How my brother treats his wife is his affair, not mine. Nor yours. Don't bother me about this again." With that, he turned and entered their rooms. My cheeks had burned at his rebuff. I felt stupid not to have guessed that John would not be troubled by his brother's behavior toward Xene.

I shook myself back to the present. Grandmother looked up from her sewing and bit off a thread, before breaking the silence. "I hadn't thought the empire's affairs could have gotten worse than they were when we left, but I was wrong."

"Hmmmph. Obvious, but I feel bad for George. He doesn't deserve prison," said Grandfather.

"If this keeps up, there won't be many generals left to defend the empire. At least, not many good generals left. It sounds like we'll still have Stephen," Damien added. "John, I imagine Isaac worries about spies among his men?"

"Of course," John said with a wry grin. "He's tough but he lacks George's temper. Besides, Stephen has no interest in visiting here in Armeniakon, not so pleasing a destination as Sicily." He stopped to take a sip of wine before continuing. "We *do* need a few competent generals who aren't in prison. Still, he's careful about what he says—anything could be twisted."

"You and Isaac would know," observed Grandfather. "I recall your cousin Nikephoros, one of the Orphanotrophus's first victims after Basil died. Easy to convince the old Emperor Constantine your cousin was a traitor. He was always drunk while the Palace eunuchs sent him a constant stream of whores."

"I didn't know my cousin Nikephoros well, only met him a few times. I was still a student at Stoudion then. He went home to Thrace after the blinding and died not long after. Isaac knew him well and swore the charges were lies." John sounded defensive about his cousin.

"None with sense believed them. Just the first of many," Grandfather said as he patted John on the back. "Can't hold my own tongue, so lucky I've not been arrested. But I've no reputation like Costas or Nikephoros, nor any fancy villa. That clan only picks the fattest targets."

I had been sitting by the window at the table with the chessboard, absentmindedly rolling the cool marble game pieces in my hand and enjoying the breeze that warm evening. Uncle Costas had brought this set back from Egypt after he was released from ten years as a hostage in Cairo.

John sat nearby, and I noticed him glance at me and the table, looking intrigued. Chessboards and game pieces were rare but becoming better known, and I wondered if he knew how to play. Feeling self-conscious from a stranger's attention, I put down the pawn that I had been holding and went to sit next to Grandmother.

"John, played chess before?" Grandfather's eyebrow twitched with interest.

"So that is chess? No, I've never played it. Is it difficult?" He peered at the chess table.

"Not difficult to learn or even play. But difficult to win, difficult to master. Want a try at it?"

"If it's not too much trouble, I would. I'm sure you recall the times on campaign when there isn't much to do. Chess could be a welcome distraction."

Grandfather's eyes twinkled. John had walked right into his trap.

"Anna, I think it's time for us to retire for the evening." Grandmother sighed, folding her sewing away. She was not as fond of chess as the rest of us, and since Grandfather's infamous chess lessons could go on for hours, she would rather excuse us. "John, thank you again for bringing my son's letter. I hope we'll be seeing you again soon, as well as your brother. We enjoy the company."

And so I left for the evening, never having spoken to our guest, or him speaking to me.

Awakened early the next morning as usual by the clacketing family of storks nesting on the roof above me, I went out to help with the milking and my rambunctious young cousins. I had to admit that, aside from the storks, the country held a deep peaceful quietude, with sweeter air than in the city. Even so, I missed the sea scents that blew off the Marmara and Bosphorus, pungent with seaweed and fish.

"Were you up late last night learning chess again?" I asked Damien as he limped in to breakfast, his sons not quite up yet.

He laughed. "Not too late. I had the excuse of needing to check on Irene and the baby. Our guest, however, was snared like a fly in your grandfather's chess spiderweb. He must have been there for hours." He picked up a small loaf of bread and began chewing on it, grinning at me.

"I hope Grandfather hasn't scared him off," I laughed. Recalling the news of the night before, I changed the subject. "Damien, is there anything we can do for Xene? She must be miserable."

He frowned. "I don't think so. As her husband, Constantine can forbid her visits. And it isn't all bad—if she's not visiting our father, she doesn't have to see her husband either."

I had to concede that point.

Xene was his much younger sister, born after Uncle Costas had returned from his hostage years in Cairo. Damien had been born a few years before that exile. He and the rest of the family had loved this late, surprise baby with a sunny disposition. Her parents and brother had indulged her, and until her marriage, she had seen few disappointments in life.

Quick, solid footsteps in the hall announced another early riser. John Comnenus entered the room, his corselet already pulled over his tunic, not looking too exhausted by the previous late evening.

"Good morning, Damien, Lady Anna," he said. I was surprised at the pleasure I felt that he recalled my name. "I'm not interrupting anything, am I?"

"No, we were just discussing the news in the letter you brought us. Uncle Adrian didn't keep you up too late last night teaching you chess, did he?" asked Damien. "He can be intense about it."

"He did keep me up, but I managed to keep his wine cup filled a bit more often than my own, so it wasn't too bad. I'm used to getting up early, no matter how late I'm up the night before."

"Refilling his wine cup—that's one way to get him to finish his lesson at a reasonable hour," Damien laughed.

John said, "Waiting for a battle can get dull, but a game like that would help pass the time. I'll have to see about getting a game board and pieces that I can take with me."

I spoke up then. "I think Grandfather knows someone in Amaseia who could carve the pieces for you."

Damien gave me a questioning look, before saying, "I'll find out the artisan's name and bring it to you next market day."

Grandmother bustled into the room to join us. Damien took the opportunity to bid his farewells to our visitor and departed for the fields and tenants.

"Good morning everyone. John, you don't look too exhausted from your chess lesson last night," Grandmother said. "We do get worried when visitors get trapped in Adrian's drills. He can be a bit too focused on the game sometimes."

"No, not at all. I enjoyed it immensely," John said while glancing over at me, almost laughing. It looked like he had picked up the family dynamic. I gave a small smile back. "I hope to continue the lesson on a future visit, if it wouldn't inconvenience you."

"We would love for you to return anytime. I imagine you and your brother Isaac would enjoy having something other than army food, and the opportunity to relax in something more comfortable than soldiers' quarters."

John rose to leave. "Thank you, I know we would. But I do need to get back to town, so thank you again for your hospitality." He gave Grandmother a respectful bow, walked out to the stable yard and his waiting horse, and was gone.

Grandmother sat down to breakfast and began eating a little bread and cheese, looking after him with a speculative eye. "He's a pleasant young man, don't you think?"

I shrugged, attempting to be casual. "Well, I didn't speak much with him. Still, he seemed agreeable and brought us the letter, even with all the spies in the pay of the Palace. I just wish we'd gotten better news in it."

Grandmother's smile faded at that reminder.

After that first visit, John Comnenus stopped by every few weeks and seemed eager to learn chess from my grandfather and cousin. Although we spoke infrequently, his warm personality showed through. My difficulty with his visits was that I did not have an opportunity to play chess myself on those evenings, being relegated to sewing or to reading aloud. The family had a respectable library of about twenty books—histories, Homer, plays, poetry, the Bible, and a book of the lives of the saints. My grandparents found the writing in the books difficult to see, so those of us with younger eyes, Damien or Irene or myself, took on that duty.

One particular evening during one of John's visits Irene was reading one of her favorites, the epic poem of *Digenes Akrites*. Its excitement and romance thrilled Irene, but Digenes's improbable feats had bored me after a few readings. So there I sat, making a half-hearted attempt at sewing, listening to my least favorite book, and not enjoying myself.

"John," Grandfather said, moving his rook, "when will you be bringing your brother out for a visit?"

John's attention had been on the game, but he looked up to give a polite response.

"I've been trying to pull him away, but you know how focused he can be. From what we can see, the previous strategos assigned here was indifferent about defense, lax in his reports, overly zealous with tax collecting, but not quite as much in sending the tax revenues to the emperor. Quite a mess to clean up." John shook his head in disgust, lost his concentration, and then made the absolute worst move he could have, from what I could see. "And he's had to visit the theme's fortified towns to make sure they are adequately manned and supplied, what with all the Turkish attacks on the frontier. Not a simple matter when the emperor does not send the all the soldiers and supplies he's promised."

Grandfather gave John a self-satisfied glance, made his move, and said, "Checkmate."

"What?" He leaned back in his chair, surveying first the board and then the rest of us. He looked discouraged at the defeat, never yet having won a game.

"There must be someone else I could play and have a chance to win against?" He looked around, glancing at Damien, who chuckled at John's frustration. John glanced at me and then looked at Grandfather. "What about Lady Anna? Can she play?" He appeared to think I would be a weak opponent.

Grandfather, setting up the game again, raised an eyebrow and looked at me. "Umm, yes, Anna can play. Anna, would you like to play a game with John?"

Out of my seat in an instant, I flung the sewing aside and left the ridiculous Digenes off killing bears and dragons and bandits. "Yes, Grandfather, I would be happy to play chess with John," I said, trying not to appear too eager.

Grandfather eyed me with interest as I passed him on my way to the chess table. Damien looked entertained at the thought of me playing chess with John, who appeared eager at the prospect of an opponent he might overcome.

I settled opposite our visitor at the table. John glanced up and gave me a friendly smile. He was playing white and so made the first move— king's pawn, one square forward. I smiled back at him but then turned my attention to the game.

Growing up, my uncles and Grandfather taught me to play chess, I think before I learned to read, but I can't remember. Once, before the emperor had him arrested, Uncle Costas and I were playing, but Uncle was not playing the game well. I realized he was doing it so I could win. I became angry with him and childishly scattered the game pieces. "I can't learn if you make it easy. I want to do it on my own," I cried at him. My determination at such a young age surprised both of us. He gave me a pensive look and apologized. After that, it was a long time before I won a game with him, but in time I did.

So while John may have been a soldier, he had not been playing chess long and did not realize that in chess, as in war, the first rule for winning is to know your opponent's strengths and weaknesses. Equally important: do not make assumptions based on appearances.

I moved my king's elephant pawn forward one space, and looked up at John, catching his light blue eyes and holding them. We looked at each other for a long moment before he glanced back down at the chessboard. Then he looked back up at me, curious to see if I was still looking at him. I was. I had tried to put him off his game, but looking in his eyes, my heart thumped oddly. I looked back at the board, not taking my eyes from it for many moves, striving for control of the center.

After we had been playing for over an hour, Grandfather wandered over to get a better look at the game's progress; I think it surprised him that it was still going on. However, I hadn't wanted to embarrass our guest by winning too quickly. Finally, I sacrificed a horse to put my rook into position and made my move.

"Checkmate," I said.

John looked a little stunned but then gave me an amused look, sitting back in his seat. He'd not seen the checkmate coming.

Grandfather looked down at the game, trying to gauge my strategy. "So, John, never seen Anna play chess before?"

Damien was barely suppressing his laughter. Grandmother was shooting looks at him to be polite while trying hard not to laugh herself. Irene finally put Digenes down, realizing that no one was paying attention to her brave hero's exploits.

"Well, no," John said, giving me a direct look. "Lady Anna, you appear skilled at the game."

That got a laugh out of everyone.

"Anna can sometimes outwit Costas, and on occasion I can defeat her, but she's the best in the family besides Costas," said Grandfather, smiling. "She learned from Costas when she was maybe five and has years of experience, playing every day, plus the energy of youth. You had no chance."

"Grandfather, you shouldn't flatter me," I said, looking down to avoid John's eyes that peered into me. "My uncle and Grandfather have been kind enough to teach me the game, and here in the country there are so few diversions that I've had many opportunities to practice."

"Well, you seem to have taken advantage of them. I only hope to attain your level of mastery someday," John said. "I trust you'll give me an opportunity to play another game with you?"

I looked up at him. He was smiling good-naturedly at me, not at all irritated by my win, as many men would be. Even though I had won the game, I felt embarrassed by my success and somehow confused about what the outcome had been.

"I would be happy to," I said, pushing a stray strand of hair behind my ear and feeling uncomfortably warm.

Grandfather spoke up, "And if you get Isaac to take time for a visit, then we can teach him, and you'll have a worthy opponent. Knowing Isaac, he'll learn it quickly and challenge us all."

"Sir, I will redouble my efforts in that regard," John said, finally looking away from me. "I believe the carver in town will have the set I ordered finished in a few days. Once I show it to him, with the promise of a real challenge here, that should convince him to put aside his work and visit."

"John, that would be lovely. Now, Anna, we have an early day tomorrow, so I think we must excuse ourselves," Grandmother said. I didn't think it was so late, but Grandmother seemed tired, and I couldn't object. Damien and Irene also bid John good night, and the four of us left our guest, about to start another game with Grandfather. Trailing behind the rest, I looked back at John, his face lit by the lamplight, as he glanced up, smiling at me as we left the room. I could not recall any other soldier who had visited us looking at me quite that way.

CHAPTER THREE

John Comnenus

Autumn 1041

R ed and gold leaves spun around that breezy late October afternoon, a month since John's last visit, when we'd played chess—a
month I'd spent daydreaming about him, imagining the clever
conversations we might have when he returned. I was helping to finish storing the last of the hay, carrying the bundles from a cart into the
barn, where Demetrius hefted them up to the loft, and Damien stacked
them to be stored until winter. Everyone else had finished their chores,
drifting back to the house for shade on that warm day. We were almost
done ourselves.

I glanced around at the golden fields, shorn of their abundance
and surrounded at their distant edges by a forest full of dark trees. For a
moment I thought I heard thunder, but the billowy clouds held no hint
of rain and I turned back to the cart.

I'd emptied about half of the sweet-smelling sheaves from the cart
when a rough hand pulled me away, twisting my arm around my back.
The sharp edge of a cold blade scraped against my throat. I struggled
against my captor before another man darted in front of me—dark
skinned, but not like the Africans who worked on the wharves in the city.
Arabs or Turks maybe.

"Who are you? Let me go! You're hurting me. Damien, help me!"
My voice rose shrilly.

The one holding me muttered something in a foreign tongue to the
other and then hissed at me with foul breath, raising his blade to my

mouth. I couldn't understand his words, but their meaning was clear—be quiet. He pulled me closer to his body while I tried to squirm away. He smelled of a disgusting mix of horsehair, sweat, blood, and greasy food. His companion looked no better, and smelled worse, the stench of black teeth rotting in his mouth overpowering from even an arm's length away.

Demetrius rushed from the barn, waving a scythe and shouting at the two men to release me. My captor must have made a joke about Demetrius to his partner, both laughing at the lad.

"No, Demetrius, no, go back," I called out, desperate to keep the boy from these brigands. Why didn't I think he would be first to reach me?

The black-toothed one pulled a curved blade from its sheath and dodged Demetrius's flailing swipes. He danced around the boy, playing with his prey before striking. He stabbed into the belly, twisting the blade before pulling it out. Demetrius fell to the ground, blood gushing from the wound, groaning in agony. The scythe lay in the dust beside him, blood splattering its blade.

"What have you done?" I screamed at them, horrified at the sight of the boy lying in a puddle of his own blood, eyelids quivering, whimpering.

The one with rotten teeth stepped closer to me, his eyes gleaming. He grinned and slapped me so hard my head snapped back. I felt dizzy when he began groping my breasts with one hand while the other fumbled with my skirts. His partner was rubbing himself against me from the back.

Black-teeth grinned at me, appearing to enjoy my struggles to get loose. Over the man's shoulder I could see Damien standing in the barn's doorway, an arm raised. The wind whistled and Black-teeth's face took on a shocked expression before he shuddered, his eyes rolling back. He crumpled, the shaft of a hatchet protruding from his back, blood arcing in the air. His companion stopped rubbing himself against me. He looked at Damien in stunned surprise. My cousin's fist now gripped a large knife, his arm raised and ready to let it fly. My captor still clutched me as a shield, cursing as he backed away to the side of the barn, where two horses waited.

"Anna, don't let him get you on a horse," Damien called. I didn't think I would have a choice, though.

The man held the knife too close to my face to risk speaking more than an involuntary grunt of pain as we stumbled away. When we reached the horses he grabbed a lasso from his saddle and quickly bound my wrists and ankles. I was not to be just a shield; he planned to take me with him.

Just as he was about to throw me across the back of one of the geldings, we both turned at the sound of hoofbeats.

Two soldiers, dusty and trail-worn and still some distance away, galloped toward the house. My heart leapt when I recognized John Comnenus.

"Aye, yah," my captor said in frustration. He shoved me away, throwing me to the ground. My shoulder was bruised in the fall, but relief surged through me—he would leave me behind. Snatching the reins of his companion's now-riderless horse, he raced away, streaking through the fields.

I lay dazed on the ground a moment before struggling to sit up. My face throbbed from the slap, swelling into a bruise, and my shoulder ached. In seconds, Damien had rushed over.

"Damien, I'll be fine, please just go see to Demetrius," I said between chattering teeth. Being soiled by the touch of those filthy men overwhelmed me. The disgusting stink of their bodies lingered in my nostrils. Worse was the thought of what had happened to Demetrius.

John and his companion raced toward us.

John slid off his horse and began cutting the ropes. "What happened?" he asked.

I looked weakly up at him, still too dazed to explain.

"Turks," said Damien. He had come back around, looking grim and glancing over his shoulder after the cloud of dust trailing our attacker. "I've never seen them raiding in so far from the border. I killed one of them but the one that got away would have taken Anna with him if you hadn't arrived."

"John, let's see if we can get the bastard," said the other rider.

John looked at me and, realizing I was not badly hurt, gently squeezed my arm and mounted his horse. "We'll be back as soon as we can."

"What of Demetrius?" I managed to croak out to my cousin after they left.

Damien just shook his head as he finished untying me. "At least the bastard paid for killing him."

Finally free of the ropes, I stood on shaky legs. I couldn't seem to stop trembling, and realized I was sobbing.

"I'm sorry, Damien. I didn't think when I called out that Demetrius would try to fight them." I felt overcome with remorse.

"It's not your fault, Anna. Those two. . ." he stopped, shaking his head. "Let's get you back to the house; Irene and your grandmother will help you get cleaned up."

Damien shook his head as we limped away from the barn with its puddles of blood. "Demetrius was a good lad. Dear God help me, I've got to speak to his mother now."

I looked into the sky and realized everything had happened in less than half an hour. The sun had barely moved, and the boy who had greeted us on our arrival here two years earlier was with the angels now. The lad had dreamed of being a soldier, like his patron saint, St. Demetrius, and now he was gone after his first battle.

John and his companion returned as the last rays of sun disappeared from our valley.

I had calmed down by that time and felt a little giddy after drinking unwatered wine for the first time, on Grandmother's instructions. She and Irene bathed me, cleaning the scrapes, soothing me with assurances that John would take care of the man who'd escaped. They left then, to offer condolences to Demetrius's family.

"Isaac, I didn't realize it was you with John," said Grandfather in surprise as the two men entered the house.

"Adrian, good to see you again. I never expected those two brigands we were tracking would lead me to your gate. It was good fortune for your granddaughter we were here. I don't want to think about what they might have done with her."

I stood on shaky legs to greet John and the man who I realized was his brother, Isaac, the Strategos. Up close now, and without the terror of the attack at the barn, I saw their family resemblance. Their coloring and the shape of their faces—both redheads with wide-set blue eyes and square jaws—held the greatest similarity. Isaac had the greater height, though, and walked with the gruff confidence of a man used to giving orders and seeing them obeyed. John, on the other hand, while a stocky, physically strong man, had a gentler demeanor.

"Young lady," Isaac said to me, "you won't have to worry about the other one. We chased him for miles; he lost his companion's horse before his own horse took lame and threw him. We made quick work of him then."

Marie entered the room with a tray loaded with food and goblets of watered wine.

"John and I left a few days ago with a dozen soldiers to inspect a fort in the east and resupply it. Damned good thing we got there when we did." Isaac stopped to take a sip.

"What happened?" asked Grandfather, an eyebrow raised.

"More Turks," said John. He leaned against the window ledge, arms crossed on his chest. "A raiding party, maybe fifteen of them, bold as lions, laying siege to it."

"Only ten or eleven of our men at the fort, low on arrows and food. I wouldn't have bet much on their chances of surviving if we hadn't shown up when we did," said Isaac.

The blood drained from Damien's face, realizing how close they had been. "They had to be, what, over a hundred miles from the border?"

Isaac raised an eyebrow, considering. "At least. But no need to worry about them now. We finished off most of them. Been tracking these last two for a couple of days"

Isaac turned to Damien. "Where did you learn to throw a hatchet like that? That was neat work, the way you took care of him."

Damien flushed but smiled at the compliment. "Learned from the Varangians. Took some practice, but it's not something I'll ever forget."

John turned and gave me a quick wink. If I had not just been through such a frightening experience, I might have giggled.

"Isaac, you and John look as though you could use a bath after all that," I heard Grandfather say. "Anna, ask Maria to ready a room for them, and bring water for them to wash before dinner."

I nodded and left the men to see about dinner and their accommodations.

I sent Maria to ready a room and water for bathing for our guests and then dashed to the cellar to pour wine from an amphora into a jug for dinner, spilling only a little on my way to the dining room.

In the kitchen, Alethea had already revised the evening's menu to include lemon-spiced chicken, olives, cheeses, and the small loaves of bread that were her specialty, followed by an apple, walnut, and honey confection that we all loved so much at this time of the year.

I returned to my room and sat on the edge of my bed until my hands stopped trembling. Calmer, I stripped off the plain homespun overdress I wore for outdoor work. The lid of the cedar chest holding my clothes creaked open, and I considered my choices. Nestled among the fennel and lavender—keeping away the hungry moths—was the red silk tunica Grandmother had just finished embroidering for me, with its blue-and-gold diamond shapes bordering the cuffs and hem and a braid pattern in the same colors for the neckband. My hand lifted it out and, almost without thinking, I slipped it over my head and tied its sash around my waist. A few comb pulls through my hair and I emerged into the hall, where Grandmother waited for me.

Grandmother looked me over, a wry smile on her face, and her forehead crinkled.

"What's wrong? Don't I look presentable?" I refrained from twirling around to show her how well the dress fit me.

"No," she said slowly, a look of amusement on her face. "You look fine."

We gathered Irene from the nursery, and as we descended the stairs the men emerged from the study. Isaac had draped his arm over John's shoulders as they walked, and they grinned at each other in plain affection. Isaac's booming voice and broad gestures displayed the confidence that whatever he wanted to accomplish was doable. John looked happy to let his brother gather all the attention.

The servants brought platters into the dining room. Grandfather steered the conversation to news from the outside world.

"So, Isaac, what word on the Bulgarian campaign? The letter John brought gave some idea about it, but nothing since," Grandfather said.

"Why, yes." Isaac looked surprised and glanced around the table. "You must not have heard—my wife, Catherine, only sent word two weeks ago. The Bulgarian revolt is over. Her brother, Alousian, realized they had no chance after their defeat at Thessalonica. His idea of the best solution was to capture and blind his cousin, Peter, who had a hand in starting it, and then take him as a peace offering to the emperor. Worked out well for him, not for Peter."

Isaac stopped for a moment at Irene's shocked gasp.

"Who could do that to their own cousin?" she said.

I felt as queasy as Irene. Grandfather had explained how most thought blinding a humane way to cripple an enemy, more merciful than execution, but I thought it was gruesome. Isaac, John, and my grandfather, battle hardened and less squeamish, seemed to consider it just another casualty.

"Too many," Damien said, his face grim as he looked into the cup where his wine swirled.

Isaac continued, "The emperor was relieved to end the fighting and sent Alousian to the Orphanotrophus back in the city with instructions to be generous with a reward. I expect Alousian is already sipping wine on his old veranda again. After that, the emperor had a triumphal return to the city through the Porta Aurea." Isaac sat back for a moment, relishing the neat resolution to his brother-in-law's rebellion.

He cleared his throat and continued with a more sardonic comment. "Unfortunately for Alousian, he has to deal with Catherine now. She was fond of Peter and I'm sure angry with her brother. I can't say the situation makes me want to rush back home soon to mediate that quarrel."

"You're fortunate the emperor sent you here rather than to a cell like my father's," Damien said.

Isaac gave him a sharp look. "He's keeping my wife and children under imperial 'protection'. It was better to be here than anywhere else— no allegations of illicit conspiracy with Alousian likely, plenty of opportunities to impress the emperor by cleaning up my predecessor's mess, and scaring off a few Turks. On the whole, I would almost ask Catherine if she has any other relatives interested in rebelling. I might get promoted to dux."

"So then the army and emperor are back in the city?" asked Damien.

"They are, or were," Isaac said slowly. "But the strangest thing she wrote about was the emperor's victory parade. He rode through the Porta

Aurea and all the way up the Mese to the Palace looking terrible. His face and hands were hugely swollen, his fingers as big as sausages. No question, the emperor looked sick."

My grandparents and Damien gaped at this. Old men sometimes had an ailment that caused their bodies to swell, but the emperor was not old, only about thirty summers.

Isaac continued, enjoying the attention. "He looked pale and often stopped to wipe the sweat from his face. Catherine wrote that the crowds cheered as he approached on horseback until he neared and they saw how he looked. Then they grew silent, everyone just staring. The rumors about his health must've been true. A few days later, he left for the Monastery of St. Demetrius. When the empress realized he'd gone, she followed after him. I'm not sure what she expected, but Catherine said he wouldn't see her."

"If he's as sick as it sounds, then maybe he's hoping for absolution from the monks before he dies. He has much to atone for," said Grandmother before breaking off a piece from a warm loaf of bread.

Although noteworthy, this news seemed of little importance for us. Even if the emperor died, the Orphanotrophus's positioning of his nephew in the succession left us little hope. I glanced across the table and saw John looking at me. He gave me a quick smile before turning back to Isaac.

Grandfather cleared his throat and smoothed his gray beard before asking, "Any word on Costas or the others he's locked up?"

Isaac raised an eyebrow trying to recall, then shrugged. "No. Could be a good thing. Maniakes and the rest have influential families still in the city who keep an eye on them, as well as a little gold to put in their guards' pockets, so I expect their quarters are no worse than Costas'. Doesn't your Simeon have some influence with the emperor? Where they're kept is not the Great Palace, but it's not a dungeon. They have enough to eat and they've still got their eyes."

Finally, Grandmother stood up. "Enough depressing talk. I think it's time for us to move into the study. Perhaps Irene could read this evening."

"I hope that doesn't mean you won't teach me a little of your chess, Adrian," said a grinning Isaac as he rose from the table. "John's tried to, and I've played with him a few times, but I haven't it figured out yet."

Grandmother's eyes widened in polite dismay at this. I knew we wouldn't stay long if I did not think of an alternative as we walked to the study.

"Grandmother, the air is pleasant this evening. Would you like to walk in the garden?" I asked. I wanted its peace after the terrible events of that day.

"Oh, may I join you?" inquired John. He had been looking over the chess table with Isaac and Grandfather. "It might be better to let Isaac learn at the feet of a master without my interference." My spirits lifted at his words.

"Why, yes, of course, John. I don't think you've had a chance to see our garden before," said Grandmother pleasantly.

It was late in the year for such warm weather. Many of the flower and herb beds had been turned over, and the winter plantings were just in, so there wasn't much to see. But the air was fresh, and we had late roses, a few red blooms climbing up the side of the house. The three of us wandered through the garden as the evening's shadows lengthened, Grandmother pointing out where the herbs grew, the vegetables in the kitchen garden, and the fruit and nut trees. John nodded and commented politely.

"Does that rosebush always bloom this time of the year?" he asked as we approached the terrace near the house. "Seems late for flowers."

"Oh yes," replied Grandmother as she sat down on one of the garden benches, glad to be off her feet. I sat next to her while John sat on the bench across from us, the mosaic of Odysseus and Penelope that Uncle Costas had had laid down so many years ago under the arbor between us. "Costas planted it when Xene was born years ago, and most years it does have these late blooms. It was a gift for Sophia, his wife. He was so happy to have another child after the ten years he spent as a hostage in Egypt."

A servant brought out a pair of lanterns that threw a soft, flickering light. A few moths danced close to them while the heavy, fecund scent of earth surrounded us.

"Wasn't it Uncle Costas who said that he and Aunt Sophia had been apart enough, and so he had her join him whenever visitors arrived, no matter who they were? And once she started, all of the women in the family followed suit?" I asked, already knowing the answer. John would not know why the women in our family were not like most other dynatoi families—the ones who kept their women always in the gynecaeum and away from guests other than family.

Grandmother eyed me, surprised at my feigned ignorance. "Yes, he did. And the women in the family have enjoyed the chance for company and conversation. I think the men in the family are grateful too, if we don't contradict them too much."

"You can count me grateful too. Otherwise, I would have missed the opportunity to get to know you both," John said, his blue eyes focused on me.

"John," I began, "how is it that you were raised at the Stoudion, if you don't mind my asking? Was Isaac raised there, too?"

He leaned forward, resting his elbows on his knees, hands clasped, giving me a direct look. "It happened my father was in his sixties when I was born and died when I was five. My mother had died a year earlier. My father, Manuel, had served Emperor Basil for many years, so he made sure Isaac, our sister Eudokia, who we call Donya, and I were taken care of."

So here was another instance of the old saying—an old cat with a young mouse. An old husband with a young wife. My parents had been like that; I think my father had been almost fifty when he married my mother, who was seventeen at the time. The many years of rebellions and invasions Basil had faced when he came to the throne kept some of his soldiers from marrying until they were older. That left more than a few orphans when these men did not live to see their children reach adulthood. I was fortunate my mother's parents could care for me.

John continued, "The old emperor sent Isaac and me to Stoudion and Donya to the Myrelion convent. Isaac, being ten years older than I am, stayed for only few years before joining the army himself. I lived there more than a dozen years. Old Father Michael, you remember he helped with your uncle's letter? He had responsibility for raising the orphaned boys the emperor sent there, usually about a dozen at a time. Being the sons of soldiers, I doubt you would find a rowdier group in any monastery." He paused, smiling in recollection of fond memories.

"Our older brothers or uncles would visit and take us hunting in the forest outside the city gates. I loved hunting the most—the freedom to ride and be outside the confines of the city. But Father Michael was patient, almost like a real father to us. He saw us all reach our first beard, and most joined the army. I visit him when I can."

"He must be glad of your visits," Grandmother said. I could tell she regarded John's devotion to the old monk with favor.

"Yes. I was visiting him before leaving to join Isaac when I saw Father Simeon." He stopped and gave an embarrassed smile. "I wasn't one of the more attentive students in his scriptorium— more interested in horses and hunting. But he'd heard I would be sent here and thought I might get a private letter to you."

"Ah, a fortunate coincidence, then."

"Yes. He does seem to know more than most monks about what's going on in the city. Maybe more than a coincidence?"

"Uncle Simeon is friendly like that with everyone," I said. "He'll speak with the poor traveling monks begging alms and a place to stay even though many people ignore them. He says he learns much about the world outside the monastery's walls from them."

The sun had long since set behind the distant western mountains, and the air was rapidly cooling. Grandmother pulled her mantle closer, shivering. "It's getting chilly now. Perhaps we should join the others and see how Isaac is doing with Adrian's game."

In the study, the men were laughing. Isaac's face held a look of humorous outrage. Irene sat with the story of Digenes Akrites forgotten in her lap, laughing at the men's banter. It had been a long time since I'd heard as much laughter in an evening, with Isaac the bright pebble thrown into our quiet pond, merry ripples emanating from it.

Isaac looked up at us when we came in, pointing at John for emphasis. "John, when we get back to Amaseia, we are going to play this game every night until I can beat this old scoundrel." He winked broadly at his brother. "I need to learn to cheat at this as well as Adrian does."

"Isaac, I didn't know you were such a sore loser. Can't stand to lose. Explains why you almost always win in battle," Grandfather said with a grin.

"You can't expect to win against Adrian your first time playing him. The only ones who can win against him are my father and Anna," Damien said as he sat down, starting to wheeze with laughter.

"What? A woman can defeat Adrian, but not me? The great Generals Dalasseni, I can tolerate that, but a woman, and such a young one?" He peered around the room, lit with a few oil lamps and candles, until he saw me. "Young lady, can you really best your grandfather at chess?"

I was still laughing, but a blush of embarrassment covered my cheeks with the attention from someone I hardly knew. "Yes, sir. I have been playing chess since I was a child. Uncle Costas and Grandfather taught me."

John stood beside me. "Isaac, I can vouch for her abilities." There was a hint of amusement in his voice as he glanced over to me. "She let me play for at least an hour before checkmating me."

Even more laughter erupted.

"Isaac, did you know our Anna is the daughter of Alexios Charon? She may not have his way with a sword, but she is just as intent on winning as he was," Damien said, winking at me. "Maybe as much as you are."

I hardly remembered my father, who had been dead over ten years. Even so, it gladdened me to hear such praise.

Isaac replied, looking dubiously at the game board, "Really? The blood of Alexios Charon? In that case, I will need a lot more practice at this before I take you on, young lady. I saw your father in battle once, when I was just starting with the Exkoubitores. All I can say is that I was glad we fought on the same side."

Grandmother smiled at them with a raised eyebrow, looking wistful.

"Anna, we have much to do tomorrow, so I think it's time we said good evening to our guests. Gentlemen, we will leave you to your chessboard. Don't let Adrian keep you up too late." And we were gone, Irene joining us.

We made our way upstairs to our rooms, chatting about the day's events, our visitors and their news. "Isaac makes me laugh," said Irene, smiling at the memory of the scene in the study. "I haven't heard Damien and the others laugh that hard in a long time. I just wish he had some good news about Costas and Xene."

"After almost seven years of Costas's imprisonment, I've learned not to expect much good news," Grandmother said soberly. "I'm just grateful when the news isn't too bad. All we can do is pray for a miracle."

"That is, in truth, all that we can do now," Irene said with resignation. "Good night, then." She disappeared into the nursery to check on her three boys and baby Sophia.

Alone in my room, I looked out the window over the quiet courtyard and to the fields beyond it, where the barn stood. I realized I might have been dead, or worse, by now if John and Isaac had not arrived when they did. I wiped my eyes and said a prayer for Demetrius, who had tried to save me at the cost of his own life. Those two men had thrown away their own lives and his for nothing. What a waste.

The harvest moon hung overhead, tinged orange and as bright and round as one of the orchard's peaches. The only noise now was the sound of the men's voices downstairs. I felt a little safer, less afraid, hearing them. I strained to make out John's voice among them, the youngest of those four but with the deepest tones. A bolt of pleasure shot through me when I recognized it.

I thought suddenly that I might never have met John if we had not been exiled or if Isaac's brother-in-law had not rebelled. Strange the twisting paths the fates lead us on.

The men's voices diminished. I pulled the shutters closed and climbed into bed.

Restless thoughts kept me up that night—replaying the attack, the terrible moment when Demetrius was killed, Damien's axe thudding into the Turk's spine, blood spilling from their wounds, the relief I felt when I saw John galloping toward me.

John had been there when I needed him, but would he, or anyone else, be there whenever I needed help? My world had changed when that cold blade had slid against my throat and I witnessed the death of an innocent boy. I shivered and pulled the blanket up. In my heart, though, I knew the world had not changed, just my experience of it. Surrounded in the cocoon of my grandparents' love and care, even in exile, it had been so easy to pretend I was safe.

CHAPTER FOUR

Sailing Home

Winter 1041 to 1042

Afew days after Christmas, word arrived that Emperor Michael had died on December 10th. He'd taken monk's vows and been shriven of his sins at the end. As expected, Empress Zoe then named her adopted son, her late husband's nephew, also named Michael, to succeed him as emperor. After that, nothing else happened as anyone expected.

John Comnenus rode out on a frosty day shortly after Epiphany with news and a letter from Uncle Simeon.

"The new Emperor Michael has recalled Isaac," he said as Grandmother handed him a warm cup of wine. "We'll be leaving within the month, once the new strategos arrives."

Grandfather handed me Uncle Simeon's letter to read, his old eyes no longer able to discern the small letters. I unfolded the parchment, blinked, and read the words aloud.

"Father—the emperor has freed Uncle Costas and Ducas. He has ended your sentence of exile. You can return home now. Simeon."

Grandmother, whose persistent cough had worried us all, looked ecstatic, murmuring, "God be praised," over and over again as Grandfather embraced her. I glanced at John and caught him reflecting my own smile.

There had been no more signs of Turkish raiding parties since the attack in October. Isaac said he thought the brigands he and John had pursued looked more like criminals trying to escape their sultan, and not a sign of imminent invasion. With that reassurance, Damien decided he would return with us to Byzantium to see his father and sister. John and Isaac invited us to accompany them on the journey since we would be traveling at the same time.

Even so, we worried. Uncle Simeon's letter did not explain why Uncle Costas had been freed, but neither did it hold a warning. My grandparents' quiet apprehension about returning so soon after Uncle's release shadowed us.

The journey could take several weeks, depending on the weather, but we hoped to be back in the city before the first of March and the start of Lent. Grandmother's ill health that cold winter kept her bundled in blankets close to a brazier most days and left me to do much of the packing. One of Damien's trusted tenants would stay in the house with his family, do the spring plantings, and keep watch over Irene and their children. Autumn's bountiful harvest meant provisions would not be lacking during his absence.

Every night I was early to bed, exhausted from the regular chores as well as the packing, and slept through to the cock's crow with the sun barely up.

Finally, it was mid-February, and all was ready. My grandparents, Damien and I, along with Alethea and Maria, would leave in the morning, meeting with Isaac and John and their soldiers. I would miss Irene and her brood, but the excitement of returning home overwhelmed me. After almost three years, I would see Xene and Uncle Costas again, our house in the city, my cousins and friends there. It almost seemed that our problems were gone.

We made heartfelt farewells the next morning. Irene with her three little boys and the new baby, Sophia, had become so dear to me that I almost didn't want to leave. My only regret was leaving them behind.

A servant drove the carriage Grandmother, Alethea, Maria, and I rode in, with Grandfather and Damien and two menservants on horseback. Frost covered the ground and the four of us shivered under our blankets. The canvas roof provided at least shelter for us—much better than being on horseback as the icy drizzle fell. Our party met Isaac, John, and the half dozen soldiers returning with them to the city at a crossroads not far from our estate.

John and Isaac rode over to us, their horses steaming the air with hot breath. They were bundled in gloves and winter traveling cloaks over their metal-linked corsets.

"General, this dreadful weather should keep most bandits off the roads, but I'm glad not to have to take a chance that it won't."

"Lady Theodora, I don't think we'll have that worry," Isaac said, giving a rueful glance at the dismal sky. Gesturing to one of the soldiers following behind, he said, "Phillip is in charge of the men. He'll help when your wagon gets stuck in mud." He gave smart salute before riding ahead to join Grandfather and Damien.

John looked after his brother but lingered a few moments. "If there's anything you need, you have only to tell Phillip or one of the other soldiers to ride ahead and bring me back."

"Thank you, John. I appreciate your consideration," answered Grandmother.

John saluted, directed a warm smile in my direction, and rode off to join the others.

Grandmother looked after him, an eyebrow raised. "John is such a thoughtful young man. Wouldn't you say so, Anna?"

I glanced at her. "Ah, yes, Grandmother, I suppose he is."

Behind me, I heard laughter. Maria and Alethea were chuckling in the seats behind us.

"Lady Theodora, I think she finds the young soldier quite agreeable, wouldn't you say so, Maria?" said Alethea.

Maria laughed. "Oh yes, I think she does too."

I flushed with embarrassment. Grandmother said nothing but smiled wryly.

"I don't know what you two are talking about," I shot back. It infuriated me that Alethea could see right through me and have the nerve to jest about it. That Maria did too made me wonder just how obvious my interest was.

The carriage got stuck four or five times in the muck of the road the first day. That evening, the women had a room to ourselves at the inn where we stopped. Alethea, suspect of the quality of the food we might encounter on the road, had packed enough for us for a few days. Isaac and John ate with their soldiers in the dining room, Grandfather and Damien joining them for the soldierly camaraderie. Alethea contributed some of her sausages and bread to augment the innkeeper's fare.

The men's raucous laughter rose from below, lively even after the day's journey. The four of us women were just happy to be hearthside, exhaustion especially on Grandmother's face. Alethea passed around the bread with slices of cheese and sausage while Maria poured watered wine into cups for us.

"I wonder how the house will be after we've been gone for so long?" I mused.

"I expect Nicholas kept the house in good repair. He's reliable, and Simeon visited on occasion. He'd have been diligent," said Grandmother, and yawned. She looked pale, her eyes tired as she nibbled at her meal. "Your grandfather sent word ahead of our return."

I didn't say anything about Nicholas. He had worked for Grandmother's parents as a boy before coming to our house. He was devoted to her. But he ignored instructions and often found a way to avoid doing anything Grandfather asked of him, much less me. With Grandmother, he was different. I changed the subject.

"Grandmother, who do you think we will see first?" Questions bubbled up as I tried to arouse her enthusiasm about our return, gripping her chilly hand in excitement.

She smiled at that thought. "I expect we will see Simeon first, or perhaps your Uncle Costas. I so want to see my son again. I'm not sure where Costas would have gone after being released. He could be at the house, or he may not have wanted to return to it until we were back and could be staying at Stoudion's guesthouse with Simeon. That might have been safer for him."

"And what of Xene? I want so much to see her again," I said.

"Child, I don't have the answers to all of your questions and won't until we are back." Grandmother yawned again. "I'm getting into bed. We'll have another long day tomorrow."

Grandmother slipped into the bed as Alethea, Maria, and I continued our excited talk in subdued tones about what we had planned for when we were back. Alethea yearned to see her own son, who owned a bakery near our house, and having fish from the sea to cook again. Maria missed her parents. We were up for another hour discussing all our plans in excited, hushed voices. We put out the candle, and I joined Grandmother in the bed while Maria and Alethea slept on pallets on the floor. I lay on my back for a time, looking up at the ceiling beams in the fading red glow from the hearth.

I had not mentioned what I hoped for—a betrothal. Most girls my age were already betrothed, if not married. My prospects were better with Uncle Costas out of prison and a new emperor on the throne. Still, Byzantium's mothers and grandmothers might need more time before deeming me a safe choice for their sons and grandsons. Of course, John Comnenus didn't have a mother or grandmother. That might make it easier if he were interested.

I did not imagine the way his eyes met mine—I felt like they pierced into my soul. My grandparents liked him—a man from a family of soldiers, like ours. They knew him well enough to realize he was no Constantine Ducas.

Curled up next to Grandmother, without knowing how it happened, I realized how much I wanted it to be John. John Comnenus. It was a relief to admit it, rather than hold back any longer. I rolled onto my back and closed my eyes, praying that John Comnenus really did want me as much as his eyes said he did.

The next morning, the sky had cleared, and while it was cold, at least we did not have to contend with as much mud on the road as the previous day. Well, not so much, but muddy spots still got us stuck a couple of times, once when John was there. He helped Grandmother and the rest of us down, then he and the driver and a few soldiers heaved the vehicle out of the muck. John's warm hands lingered around my waist as he lifted me out of and back into the cart. I loved the look of his hands as they reached for me, and their solid warm feel.

Our next two nights were spent in monastery guesthouses, first on the road, and then in the seaport of Amisos. The men made arrangements with the brave captain of a ship to sail to Byzantium. Damien said the captain's sizable fee reflected the dangers of sailing in winter. What cargo he could carry would augment his fat profit.

The ship provided only cramped accommodations. Grandmother and I shared one small bunk of rough wood in the small curtained-off area of the hold that the women received. For Alethea and Maria, there were hammocks that would be hung from the ceiling to sleep in. The confining space smelled stale from decaying straw spilling from a corner; I would try to avoid being there any more than necessary. I scrambled on deck to watch as we left port after stowing my belongings.

For February, the weather was fine, with the sun shining and the wind billowing the sails. We stood against the railing watching the fishing villages pass by when Maria suddenly turned pale. Alethea grabbed her.

"Come with me. Let's find a spot so you can vomit away from the rest."

Grandmother glanced toward the ship's bow and saw John and Grandfather talking.

"Anna, let's go over and join them. Perhaps John can tell us what to expect for the next few days."

The men were discussing our expected arrival in the city, which looked to be within the next week if the weather held.

I looked at John, trying to think of some sparkling topic I could ask him about, instead settled on a boring subject.

"John, have you traveled this way often?"

"Not often, Lady Anna," he said, squinting down at me. "Mostly north of here, to Bulgaria, on the Black Sea. Isaac's mother and his wife were both Bulgarian, and he speaks their tongue well, so most of the time that's where we get sent."

"Oh, I didn't realize that you had different mothers," I said, feeling thoughtless.

He laughed, not bothered at all. "Our red hair comes from our father. Isaac's mother was the granddaughter of one Bulgarian king, and his wife is the daughter of another one. His mother had Isaac and an older son, who died young. My mother, Maria, was Greek and had Donya and me. Isaac's mother and his brother died of the pox when Isaac was about five. Father married my mother two years later."

"Oh. Does your sister live in the city?" I asked.

"Last we heard, she does." He looked uncomfortable. "Her husband, Michael Dokeianos, was catepan of Italy in Bari. It's a troublesome place, so he sent her and the children back to the city."

Grandmother's eyebrows rose in surprise. "Anna's father, Alexios, was sent there many years ago. Long before Anna was born, though. He said Bari was lovely."

John shrugged. "That may be, but Michael's had the worst luck there. Frankish mercenaries attacked and defeated his army last year."

"What happened?" she asked.

"Have you ever met a Frank?" he began, looking over at us.

Grandmother nodded, but I shook my head.

"These Franks are big men, much taller than most Romans," he said, raising his hand a good six inches above his head to demonstrate.

"They are like the Varangians—blond and fierce, maybe not quite so tall. They sometimes call themselves Normans. Any army aiming to defeat them must be well armed and well paid in gold. Michael's difficulty was that the emperor had not sent the men's pay in months. Some deserted. Worse, Michael's army had men from different parts of the empire, speaking different tongues. They often couldn't understand each other. It was a disaster before the first arrow flew."

"The emperor knew that the soldiers were due their pay but didn't send it?" I asked, my teeth starting to chatter in the cold. Soldiers won't fight if they aren't paid but I did not understand why the coins weren't sent.

"I don't know what the emperor or the Orphanotrophos thought," John said with a frown. "But the Bulgarian rebellion cost gold. Perhaps the money went there. Of course," he looked around to make sure we were not overheard before continuing, "if the emperor's brothers had not caused Alousian to incite rebellion among people already upset about taxes, then perhaps he would have had the gold to send to Italy."

He had a point. "That's awful, John," I said. "Your brother-in-law must have felt humiliated."

John shrugged. "Plenty of coins go into the treasury. But even aside from the cost of Bulgaria, the emperor sends gold purses to monks to pray him out of hell. And then the Orphanotrophos made another brother, Constantine, the domestic of the Scholai. That fool couldn't find money for his soldiers, but he's decked out in jewels and fine silks. And, of course, their brother-in-law, Stephen, lost a fortune in Sicily. Not much left for the soldiers."

Grandmother had seen this before when Uncle Costas was sent to Aleppo. She shook her head before answering with a world-weary note, "No, there isn't."

John looked disgusted.

For the next few minutes, we stood in silence, gazing at a passing village as the ship slipped over the waves to the north before Grandmother said, "Anna, I think Alethea and Maria may need us. Perhaps I have something to help Maria's stomach."

Nursing occupied my next couple of days. Maria's tendency to seasickness was unabated. She had almost become accustomed to the ship's movements when a late winter storm forced us into the harbor at Sinope for a day. Eager to be on our way, we stayed on board the rocking vessel to be ready when the weather cleared. The four women kept inside our shelter, avoiding the icy deck and waves threatening to fling careless travelers overboard. Finally, though, I'd had enough and ventured on deck to escape the smelly cabin atmosphere.

The clouds blew carelessly about a gray sky, and the crisp, fresh air smelled sweet after our stuffy confines. I wondered if this was how Uncle Costas felt after finally being freed from his tower cell in Byzantium. The deck swayed at alarming angles, but milder air had melted the ice, and I had a firm grip on the railing.

"Good day, Lady Anna," a voice called from behind me.

Looking around, Isaac waved to me from the captain's deck, chatting with a couple of the sailors there.

"Good morning, General," I replied, waving back. After a few minutes, he joined me at the railing, his usual boisterous self.

"I've been wondering how you ladies fared. Can be dreary, cooped up in this weather."

I smiled up at him. He really was a much bigger man than John, although with the same flaming red hair and beard. "General, for four women who are not sailors, we've done well enough. Looking forward to standing on dry land, though. Thank you for asking." I did not want my manners to be found lacking. "And how do your men fare?" I inquired.

He laughed. "In good spirits—we've sailed together many times. They've too much time on their hands, playing at dice more than they should. But better dice than fighting. The ship has been pitching too much to play chess during the storm, but John and I tried a few games before the storm began." He gave a wry look. "I think I'm still better at dice than chess."

I smiled at that, "So John's been getting the better of you?"

"I'm not used to my younger brother winning," he admitted in a humorously sarcastic voice. He clearly hated losing to anyone. "Being the best at chess in your family, do you have any suggestions I could use to trip up John?"

"Uncle Costas is better than I am. However, General," I began, warming to my topic and turning toward him, "know that chess is a battle. For the king to win, he needs the backing of ministers, the church, the military, castles, and the people, just as the emperor does. The king might still win if he loses one element, but not more. Watch your opponent to learn his strengths and weaknesses. No one set of moves will work in every game but you'll need to get control of the center, the heart of the board, to win."

He regarded me with more interest than before.

"Young lady, it sounds as though you have spent many hours learning your grandfather's and uncle's lessons."

"Oh yes, many hours," I said. "In the country, we don't have much else to do in the evenings but tell stories and play chess. Often, Grandfather would explain the battles as though they were chess games, and chess as though it was war."

The ship heaved again, and it became harder to keep a solid grip on the railing. The wind blew my hair around, making it difficult to see.

Isaac noticed the worsening waves and my difficulty staying steady. "Young lady, it's time I brought you back to your grandmother. We don't want you blown off the ship." He proffered his arm to me. I slipped my hand into the crook of his arm, keeping a tight hold as we cautiously made our way from the deck to our shelter.

"Thank you, General. It was kind of you to escort me inside."

Isaac gazed down at me, giving me an appraising glance.

"It has been my pleasure. Perhaps sometime, after I have bested John once or twice at chess, I can challenge you to a game."

"I would like that," I said, and returned to the stuffy cabin.

Eventually, the wind and waves calmed, and the weather turned sunny, if chilly and we set sail again. I needed to get out of the cabin for a little fresh air and pulled on a warm cloak to cope with the raw elements. The occasional fish emerged briefly amidst the whitecaps on the slate-colored sea, their tails flapping, and beyond them, the pine tree-covered shore. Sailing as long as we had been, we must be approaching the Bosphorus.

Looking around, I saw Grandfather and Isaac Comnenus deep in conversation near the ship's bow while his brother John and some other soldiers were in the stern, apparently playing at dice. Delighted, I breathed in air untainted by too many unbathed people confined together for too long, hoping there would be no need to return to the cabin soon. I stood for several minutes, exhilarating in the feel of the ship bringing me home, when I heard someone approaching. Looking up to make sure I wasn't in the way of a sailor going about his duties, I saw John Comnenus slow his pace, looking hesitantly at me.

"Lady Anna, I see you've come out to enjoy this fine weather. Your grandmother and servants have not joined you?"

"No, they still felt the chill in the air and declined. I see that you and your soldiers thought it would be good to get outside."

He glanced back at the men, still at their dice, but did not seem particularly interested in them. "Yes, we are used to all sorts of weather. It's boring being closed in for so long."

We stood, awkwardly regarding each other, neither of us seeming sure about what to do or say next. Finally, I broke the silence.

"It looks like they are playing at dice. You haven't taught them chess?"

He laughed, the awkwardness between us relieved a bit. "A few of them, yes, but it's difficult to keep the pieces steady with the ship constantly moving and swaying. Easier playing at dice."

"You're probably right," I agreed as I gripped the railing more firmly against the swelling waves.

John joined me, leaning against the ship's rail and gazing out on the sea, his red hair whipped about by the breeze. "I do need to work on my game, though," he commented, ironically amused. "I wouldn't want you to think you can always beat me at it."

"Well, you won't get any better without practice. Once we no longer have to worry about the ship, back in the city, perhaps you can visit and play a game now and again with me. And Uncle Costas, too, since he is out of prison," I added.

"I'd like that." After a moment, he added, "It sounds like your Uncle Costas' reputation is not just on the battlefield."

John was right. Aside from ten years as a hostage in Cairo, my uncle had loyally served the emperor and was respected more than any other general, which was why the old Emperor Constantine had considered him first to be married to his daughter, Zoe, who became empress. But Uncle had been living far from the city, on the Amaseia estate then. The old emperor was dying, and he needed a husband for Zoe quickly, so instead she was married to Romanus Argyros, who lived in the city. According to Grandmother, it was just as well. Aunt Sophia had died only a short time before that message, and he was not eager to marry again.

The wind picked up, pulling my hair loose from my cloak. "Yes, it is," I said before changing the subject. "You must be looking forward to seeing your sister again, and Isaac's family when we are home. Do you expect to be sent on campaign this year?"

"No idea. Alousian complicated Isaac's situation, so I'm not sure how that will work out. But Isaac knows politics, and I expect he'll find a way." John looked out at the sea, a bit amused at his brother's quandary. "We're likely to be home for a while before being sent out again."

"Do you live with your brother?" I asked.

"Yes, when we're in the city, with my sister, too, sometimes—I enjoy spending time with their children. Without a wife and children of my own, it didn't seem sensible to acquire a house that would be empty most of the time," he finished with a small shrug.

"I think you're right—not a sensible expense," I commented. So he was not married, and it did not sound like there were any plans afoot. "My grandparents' home is in the Ta Kyrou suburb, near the river. I wonder if Isaac's and your sister's houses are far from us?" Extracting information from soldiers meant a persistent but indirect approach.

"Ta Kyrou? Isaac's house would not be far. His wife's dowry included their house on the Sea of Marmara, not far from Stoudion. It isn't so nice as her brother's house, so less of a temptation to greedy imperial relatives."

"You and Isaac and his family must visit us when we are home."

"I would like that, Lady Anna, but I think I would be more interested in playing a game of chess with you. It has been a long time since that first game."

I glanced up at this to see his blue eyes looking intently down at me, a bit of a question in the smile on his face. Warmth spread through me; was I blushing?

"Yes, I'd be pleased to play with you," I stammered.

At that moment, Grandfather and Isaac wandered over, in good spirits. John and I turned to greet them and I tried to bring up a topic less likely to make me blush than a discussion of playing games.

"Grandfather, are we getting close to the Bosphorus? We've been sailing so long that we must be." Suddenly, I felt impatient for the journey to be done.

"Yes, the ship should reach it by sunset, so we could be back in the city tomorrow. Right now the captain and crew are readying the ship for the passage. You remember all the twists and turns?"

"Yes, I remember being on deck for part of it."

"We won't be so rushed this time of the year since fewer ships are out. Isaac, have you sailed this way often?"

"A few times. Every journey's different. The powerful currents running just below the surface can push a ship places it didn't plan to go. I've seen even experienced sailors caught unawares."

The ship's cabin boy was nearby and must have overheard our conversation. He looked to be a few years younger than myself—thin, wiry, and still beardless, with thick inky-black hair. I seemed to recall that his name was Michael. His attentiveness helped when Maria's seasickness required additional buckets.

"General, sir," the boy spoke up, "we'll be stopping today to pick up a pilot and fresh water to take us through. The captain wouldn't venture the straits without one—they are the most treacherous waters I've ever sailed through."

"That they are," Isaac replied, looking down at the boy. "Have you been sailing long, boy, to know the dangers?"

"Oh yes, sir, for five years. I have been through the Bosphorus many times, and the Dardanelles and Marmara, the Black Sea and Aegean on many voyages on merchant ships."

"So how long do you think it will take to reach Byzantium?"

"Sir, the distance to the city from here is not far, so no more than half a day." He spoke energetically, warming to his topic. "We sail only during daylight and in winter the southerly winds push against the current and slow us. Still, we will not need to watch for as many other ships as in summer."

Grandfather must have been considering the boy's comments and asked, "If the captain has sailed this way so often, why must he hire a pilot to take him through where he has gone before?"

The boy grinned and shook the hair from his face. "The villages here earn much from their pilots. If a ship does not hire their pilots, there can be fires lit on shore that confuse sailors, causing ships to run aground. They're wrecked, and their cargo disappears. So it's better to hire the pilot."

That got a cynical laugh from the men, acknowledging how many would sacrifice their integrity for a few trinkets.

"I think you may be correct in that, boy," remarked Isaac with a shake of his head. Looking over at the cabin boy, he asked, "What's your name, boy? How long have you been on this ship?"

"Michael Maurex, sir. I've sailed on this ship for a year. The captain is better than most and fair to the men, or I'd not have stayed this long," he replied diffidently. He looked over his shoulder briefly, checking to see if the captain or mate had need of him, then relaxed after seeing them otherwise occupied.

John gave the boy a friendly look before asking, "You must miss your home, though. Don't you plan to return to your family?"

"I've no family left and sailing's a good life. Every day different and many places to see." He added, more quietly, "I tried to join the Imperial fleet, but you need a connection even to be a cabin boy, and I've none, so I'll likely continue with the merchant ships."

Isaac and John exchanged glances before the older brother spoke up. "Michael, when we get to the city, I think we could find you a place with the navy. You would have to prove yourself to the Droungarios of the fleet, but I think my brother and I could be a connection for you."

Michael flushed, a wide smile crossing his face. "General, I'd be most grateful for that. You'll not regret it. Thank you." Then, hearing the captain's call, he was off with a quick wave and another thank you.

Isaac remarked, "He seems a promising lad; perhaps he'll do well in the navy. And it would not be amiss to have another friend there, don't you think, John?"

"Isaac, you have friends and contacts everywhere—from cabin boys to Strategos and Dux. I suppose that one more could prove useful. Perhaps we could send him over to Isaac Kontostephanos. Isaac's a good man but tough. If the boy does well with him, they'll both be grateful to you."

I left the men to their conversation, returning to the hold to let my companions know that we would begin sailing the straits in the morning and be back to the city by the afternoon.

The next morning was gray—gray sky, gray water, gray misty fog swirling over the water and coastlands. I came up early to watch the pilot start the ship through the passage, Alethea and grandmother soon joined me, all of us bundled in thick woolen cloaks, while Maria stayed in her hammock.

John came up behind us, surprising us as we stood watching the pilot and captain readying the ship before weighing anchor.

"I thought I might find you here, Lady Theodora. You've all come to watch, then?" he said, glancing over at Alethea and me.

"Yes, for as long as we can stand the rolling of the ship." There was suddenly shouting and calling back and forth between the captain, the pilot, and the crew, raising the anchors.

The triangular sail unfurled above us, billowing out with the cold wind. We could hear the rowers below begin pulling on their oars and the creaking of the ship as it turned into the waterway.

"I'm told the current keeps the ship to the port side through the passage until we get to the city. Then it pushes us to the Golden Horn. The rule is ships must stay to the left, the port side, otherwise they could collide. Even this time of the year, when few are sailing," John said.

Grandfather, Isaac, Damien, and some of the soldiers had joined us on deck to watch. After a few minutes, the soldiers went to play at dice, and my grandparents strolled together around the deck, heads bent in conversation.

John was standing on one side of me, Alethea on the other. Damien and Isaac had wandered to the opposite side of the ship.

I felt tongue-tied, trying to think of something to say to John.

It was difficult to have a conversation about anything other than the blandest of topics with Alethea standing next to me, and she appeared determined to stay with us.

"You mentioned Isaac lives not far from my grandparents. Where does your sister live?" I asked, feeling insipid. .

"She and her family live closer to the Great Palace, near the Church of St. Mary Kyriotissa. Her sons attend the school near the Hagia Sophia, so it's convenient for them." The conversation continued, each of us sharing some bits of information about our families, watching the cliffs pass by, the mist dissipating in the weak sunlight.

The ship moved sharply to starboard as the sea lane narrowed and twisted, and I lost my balance. John caught me, his arm around my waist, his solid bulk not at all disturbed by the ship's motions. His hand held mine briefly as I steadied myself—warm and substantial. My hand felt like a perfect fit in his. Just at that moment, I happened to glance over at Alethea, who was giving me an ironic look of amusement. I noticed that she had not lost her balance. Perhaps I needed to keep a better grip on the railing. Finally losing interest in our tedious conversation, she walked over to speak with my grandparents.

John glanced around and then began speaking in a low, urgent voice, "Lady Anna, you know I am the son of a soldier and a soldier myself, and that it is all I want to do. You, too, are the child and grandchild of soldiers, so you know the life we lead." He swallowed, looking distinctly uncomfortable but determined.

Distracted, I pushed aside the hair that had blown into my face and turned to look at him.

He continued in a rush, eager to speak in privacy. "I think that we would be well matched, and I've asked Isaac to speak to your grandparents about a betrothal between us." He stopped but began again, as though he felt he must speak now or never speak to me again. "But I thought to speak with you about it. If you're opposed, it's early and I can tell Isaac that I've decided against it, and you'll not be dishonored. I hope you will favor it, though."

The world seemed to shrink to this tiny spot where we stood talking. I shut my mouth, which had gaped open at his speech. I had always expected to be told of my betrothal, not asked. This extraordinary question left me so startled that I looked around to see if anyone else had heard. No one was close by, and I looked back at John, whose expression managed to convey both apprehension and military resolve.

With an effort, I mustered my thoughts. The border between propriety and impropriety was clear, but a joyful laugh bubbled up.

"John, yes. Yes. Oh yes, I do favor it." I tried to take a deep breath, but my chest felt both constricted and freed, and then the words just tumbled out in a rush. "I'd so hoped for it myself."

Relief registered across his face.

"I don't like the idea of a marriage where both are not willing. I wanted to be sure you favored it," he finished, smiling at me.

"I do, and thank you. Not all men would think that my desires mattered." John's respect for my feelings was no small matter. Most men would count a woman's opinion as unimportant.

My grandparents would have to be agreeable, but I thought that likely. And there would be negotiating about my dowry and his bridal gifts and a house; and his sister, Donya, and Isaac's wife, Catherine, would need to meet me and find me acceptable. Those small concerns shrank to almost nothing in that magical moment, looking on the bright, elated face of the man I would marry.

CHAPTER FIVE

Uncle Costas

Spring 1042

Ships and fishing boats glided through the waterway as we neared Byzantium and home. The sun, high in the sky, had not warmed the air much, and I pulled my heavy cloak closer as the wind whipped my hair about.

My grandparents stood beside me, Grandmother's face with a rare glow to it and Grandfather's arm around her. Alethea and Maria were nearby, pointing at the shining dome of the Hagia Sophia, laughing at the miracle of our return. John and Isaac had climbed to the captain's deck, I presumed so John could tell Isaac of our conversation without being overheard.

The captain stepped down to our deck to greet the harbormaster's boat and pay the required fees. My eyes kept returning to John and Isaac, who finished talking and descended the steps to join us.

"It won't be long now," Isaac boomed. "Tonight we'll be sleeping under our own roofs." He adjusted his tunic before calling out instructions to a few of his soldiers.

"I need to find out what's been happening, not just dispatches. They tell me nothing," he said in a low voice.

John glanced at his brother and said, "I expect Catherine will know. Just wait till you get home."

Isaac gave a noncommittal grunt. "Yes, I expect she will."

Isaac looked relieved when one of his soldiers came over with a question about their accommodations in the city. The two of them wandered off, going over details. My grandparents also left to gather together our belongings.

John and I stood close, leaning on the railing. Hidden in the folds of our cloaks, our hands found each other, his so warm in the February air.

"Isaac spoke with your grandfather," John said. "Your grandparents think we would make a good match but want to wait until we're back in the city to make the final decision. Your grandmother wants to meet Catherine and Donya, too."

I gripped the rail with my free hand, letting his words sink in. They favored it. My heart seemed to spin at the news that I was almost betrothed.

We sailed into the Golden Horn and docked in the busy Neorion Harbor. Even in the cold February lull, the Neorion's docks swarmed with local fishermen hauling in their catch, weavers delivering silks and brocades to warehouses for export, and dockworkers lugging goods to merchants' shops. Isaac and most of his men bid us farewell and quickly departed, leaving John to see to their baggage. Grandmother sent the young cabin boy, Michael Maurex, to find Samuel, the warehouse manager the family employed, while Grandfather, Damien, and I assembled the family's possessions for transport home with the help of Maria and Alethea.

Samuel appeared just as we finished unloading onto the dock, followed by a hired cart and two sedan chairs. He welcomed my grandparents as though they were his own family. The three of them chattered away as dockworkers loaded the cart, and I stood a little to one side, not wanting to intrude. Suddenly, John stood next to me.

"Anna, I need to leave now. Isaac expects me." John spoke softly, but he was all I heard as the other dockyard noises faded into the background. "I will call on you soon." He smiled down at me.

I stood for a moment, gazing at him, pushing a stray strand of hair back. "Don't let it be too long."

"It will be soon," he said, his voice husky.

John glanced quickly in my grandparents' direction and reached to give my hand a hurried, hidden squeeze before bidding them farewell.

I watched as the carters and dockworkers hefted the soldiers' heavy chests into wagons. It wasn't long before John left for the barracks near the Great Palace. I kept him in sight until he disappeared up a street heading in that direction.

Turning back to my family, I realized one sedan chair was waiting for me, and another for my grandmother. Many ladies used curtained sedan chairs, but I had been too young for my own before. Now I felt self-conscious stepping into it, like a pretend lady. I almost would have preferred sitting with Grandfather, Damien, Alethea, and Maria in the cart.

Our burly carriers lifted the chairs and followed close behind the cart, whose driver called out repeatedly, "Make way, make way." We followed the main road through the quiet Genoese Quarter, which lay closest to the Neorion, before turning into the Pisan Quarter. Most Latin merchants returned home for the winter and would not return for a few more weeks.

Our chairmen then carried us south onto the Street of Porticos, where many of the city's shops were. Now I regretted the honor of a sedan chair whose curtains did not permit easy viewing of the sights I had almost forgotten.

I peeked out from behind the curtains in wonder at the abundant displays. Colorful awnings rippled in front of the shops lining either side of the busy street like the banners of so many armies. Shopkeepers hovered in front of their establishments, calling out to attract the attention of passersby. My head spun at the colors and variety, so different from the paltry selection available at Amaseia's occasional market day. We passed shops for fabrics, pottery, spices, wine, cheeses, olives, metal goods, candles, woodwork, and leather goods. The odors of briny fish and pungent spices, almost forgotten in exile, permeated the air. I had forgotten the exuberant cacophony of the people, horses, donkeys, and carts in the city. I wanted to jump from the chair and run my hands over the fine silks, taste the olives, and wander the stalls just to know that I had returned to the Queen of Cities.

Too soon we had passed the busy shops and reached the Mese. Further east lay the road to the great church of the Hagia Sophia, the perfume purveyors, gold merchants, and the Great Palace, but our house lay in the west, toward the Forum of Theodosius. The crowds thinned out after the Street of Porticos, and we picked up speed. We passed taverns, brothels, food stalls, and tenements lining the Mese before reaching the forum, where an ancient central column honored the long-ago Emperor Theodosius. I was ecstatic to see that old and shabby monument, unchanged in our time away, again. The buildings circling this forum housed many government offices, with a few taverns and food stalls and a church, about which lurked a few beggars. This late in the day government officials, proudly displaying their badges of office, had begun departing for home. Our caravan moved on.

The cart and our carriers picked up speed now, pushing through to the oval Forum Bovis, after which the Mese split into the northern road to the Romanos Gate and the southern road to the Golden Gate, the Porta Aurea. We took the northern road to our house on a quiet street off the main thoroughfare.

Shaking with impatience, I completely pushed aside the curtains to peer ahead for the gate to our house. Samuel had sent a boy to let the household know of our imminent arrival. Old Leo and Nicholas stood watching outside for us when Grandfather called out, and they came running. Grandmother and I stopped our carriers and stumbled from our sedan chairs to join the rest in happy greetings.

The house, vacant for almost three years except for Nicholas and Leo, sprang back to life with our voices and footsteps filling it.

Damien looked around for his absent father as we began unpacking the cart and brought our boxes into the house. He cornered Nicholas and questioned the steward while running a hand through his hair. He walked over to where Grandfather was helping me move a large box.

"Adrian, Nicholas says that my father is in the guest house at Stoudion. If you can do without me for a time, I'll go to the monastery and bring him back."

"Of course, you must go." Grandfather put down the case and gripped Damien's arm. "Go at once."

Suddenly, my cat, Athena, appeared, surprising me with a jump into my barely raised arms. My cat had not changed during my long absence, but her irritable glare said, "Where have you been?" I carried her outside to the patio, where we sat for a time in the setting sun, cooing to each other. Sitting on the worn bench as the sun faded, I noticed among the fallen leaves the remains of the stick figures and pebbles Grandfather had used to explain the battle at Trajan's Gate the day before we had left. He had been right—surviving to fight another day was the important thing.

The unpacking continued, and we became familiar again with the house and grounds—things we had forgotten, things that had changed, and things just as we remembered them. Alethea seemed to be experiencing the most change of us all in her kitchen. While Nicholas had made sure it was well stocked for our return, it had been just him and Leo using it for the past three years. They had not kept it to her standards.

"This kitchen is a disgrace; it is filthy. It was a good thing we left Anna's cat behind, otherwise the mice feasting on your crumbs would have taken over the house." Alethea's voice was strident with outrage.

The two men retreated from her onslaught, eager to help with our boxes and out of her range.

Later, after helping Grandmother with her boxes, I had some time for my own unpacking. I brought a lamp and brazier back to my room for light and warmth. The air in the room smelled musty and unused, but appeared much as I remembered it. Someone had put it back in order following our hasty departure—my bed was tidy and the broken pieces of my mother's alabaster box swept away. I opened the shutters to let in fresh air and glanced out the window. Two figures entered through the gate, one carrying a lantern. For a moment, with the shadows, I did not recognize them before realizing the man limping was Damien, accompanied by Uncle Costas, moving slower than I recalled.

Alethea assembled a delicious meal on short notice from provisions Nicholas and Leo had on hand. It was cheese fare week, so at least there was no meat to prepare. Dinner included olives, warm bread, pungent cheese, of course, and carrots. The meal's wine, a fine vintage from Grandfather's estate in Thrace, celebrated our homecoming.

Grandfather and Damien sat on either side of Uncle Costas. He still had the same broad chest and strong hands I remembered, but his face held more lines, and his hair was closer to white than the steel gray he'd had three years earlier. Grandmother and I sat across the table from them. My uncle, a man of more than seventy, looked tired.

"Costas," Grandfather said after savoring a few bites, "how did you find life at Stoudion? I mean, you aren't the monkish type. You know you would have been welcome to stay here."

"Stoudion's guesthouse was none so bad. Thought it would be better for you if I was there in case the emperor changed his mind."

He looked at Damien and continued, voice catching, "Son, I'm glad you made the voyage. I just wish Irene and all the grandchildren could be here. And our Xene."

Damien covered his father's hand with his own, overwhelmed. "I, too, Father."

Grandmother reached across the table to squeeze my uncle's hand. "We're all glad."

I recalled then a question we had all been curious about.

"Uncle Simeon surprised us when he wrote, but his note didn't tell us how you came to be released. What happened?"

Uncle Costas sat forward in his chair, resting his elbows on the table, raised an eyebrow at me, and looked around at our curious faces. He shrugged before responding.

"Child, or perhaps I should say young lady, you've grown so much," he said with a corner of his mouth turned up. "The guards did not explain when they unlocked the door. They just told us to go. But John Ducas was there to greet his brother, as was Michael Psellus, the tutor Xene had hired for him. Psellus is a court official, so maybe he had the new young emperor's ear."

"But what about the Orphanotrophus? He permitted that?" Damien asked incredulously.

Uncle Costas blinked at his son in some surprise before speaking. "You didn't hear? The Orphanotrophus is gone. Exiled. The new Emperor Michael lacks the same affection for that bastard as the old Emperor Michael did. It didn't take long before the new one sent the uncle who had put him on the throne into exile himself."

"Dear God, Really?" asked Grandfather, startled as we all were. "I thought he was invincible. That's the last thing I would have expected."

"Put not your trust in princes, even if the prince is your nephew." Grandmother shook her head as she poured more wine into our cups.

Uncle Costas raised an eyebrow as he took a sip of wine. "Very true, Theodora. Rumor at Stoudion says the emperor instead is spending a great deal of his time with his new favorite uncle, also a eunuch, Constantine."

"Wasn't it Constantine who tried to take General Comnenus's brother-in-law's house?" I could not recall with certainty. "If he's the same one, he's no improvement over the Orphanotrophus. We heard terrible things about him."

Grandmother's eyes narrowed in concentration trying to recall.

"Anna, I think you're right about Constantine being the one who did that." Grandmother turned to Uncle Costas. "Do you know Isaac Comnenus? He was appointed Strategos in Amaseia during the Bulgarian uprising and brought his younger brother, John, along. He said his wife's brother, Alousian, joined the Bulgarian revolt after Constantine confiscated his house. John and Isaac visited us often over the past few months, and accompanied us back here."

Uncle Costas considered. "I've met Isaac once or twice, not John. Knew their father well, though. The Roman army never had another soldier half as clever as Manuel Comnenus—he could get out of the tightest spots." He laughed, reminiscing. "I was glad we fought on the same side, out of fear of him embarrassing me with one of his tricks. You know he couldn't stop from winking whenever he was plotting some trick."

My mind wandered to the subject of John, musing on how long it would be before our betrothal. The Lenten season about to commence meant a delay until after Easter for it to be official, but the negotiations could start. I would have to tell Grandmother about my shipboard conversation with John. I decided to speak with her of it in the morning, when the men would be out.

It was easy to decide to speak with Grandmother that night. It was more unsettling to actually speak with her about John the next morning. She had loved and raised me, and I trusted her opinion.

As it turned out, I worried needlessly.

"So you think John Comnenus would make you a good husband?" Grandmother's eyes searched my face as she held my hands. We sat in the room off the main hall she used as a workroom. The south-facing

windows gave her the brightest light all day, as well as a view of the courtyard and easy oversight of the household's activities. "You are our only
grandchild, and we would see you wed to a good man."

"I think so. In all the time we have known him, he's been only kind
and thoughtful. John does not seem like the kind of man Xene married."

"Hmm, Constantine has been awful to Xene, but there are even
worse examples of bad husbands than him." Grandmother sat back in
her chair, pondering me. "I know Xene didn't expect things to end up the
way they have," she said frowning.

I blinked, hoping I was not mistaken in John's character.

She tapped her fingers on the table, a habit she had when planning
something. "And there are plenty of examples of bad wives. Since we
don't want you to be one of those wives, I think you'll have to start taking
on some responsibilities. You have helped a lot over the past year, but you
only learn to run a household by doing it. So what shall we start you on?"

In short order, I found myself with new duties. I had not expected
to find myself taking charge of the kitchen, managing the provisioning
of our household, and the more difficult task of managing Alethea, but
practically speaking, keeping a family fed was a wife's primary duty. So I
plunged in. And was promptly flung back, like a fish flopping about on
the fishmonger's counter. Alethea contradicted, disagreed, and changed
everything I asked her to do or order or serve at table. When I got angry
with her, dinner was burned. This went on for at least a week before I
finally went to Grandmother in tears.

"Anna," she looked up from her sewing with a sigh, "Alethea has been
our cook for many years. She knows what she is doing."

"Yes, but she's not doing what I told her to do," I said, my dignity in
tatters.

"Could that be because she knows what you should be doing? Have
you asked her for suggestions? If you asked her, you might learn something. A good servant is your partner, not a tool; she is not ignorant."

I stopped sniveling. Wasn't I in charge? Perhaps, but I was the ignorant one. If I was going to have my own household, then I needed to
learn how to do it. Grandmother saw the light of understanding dawn
on my face.

"Why don't you go back to the kitchen now and discuss what needs to be done? Ask Alethea what her ideas are, and if she suggests something different from your plans, ask her why. She will have good reasons."

And that was when my real education began. Most days I would go to the nearby shops with Alethea and Leo, who had the task of escorting us and carrying our purchases back. Most of the dynatoi families would never have permitted their daughters to do this. I learned who were the reliable merchants and who might sell old foodstuffs at the price of fresh. And we often purchased bread from the bakery owned by Alethea's son, Matthias, which lay not far from our house.

Grandmother explained her reasoning for sending me out this way one afternoon.

"The other dynatoi ridicule merchants and traders, and this city is full of merchants and traders. Who do they think pays the taxes to fight wars, or for the salaries of bureaucrats who make the laws?" She came from a family of merchants and didn't think much of those attitudes. "A lot of the dynatoi spend their days thinking up ways to get out of paying taxes and helping themselves to the imperial treasury. If they worked half as hard as the merchants and traders do, rather than showy frivolity, maybe they would have enough to pay the taxes they owe and not pick the empire's pockets."

She gave me an ironic frown. "No use complaining, though. Just the way people can be." With that, Grandmother locked her account book in a chest and we left for supper.

While I was receiving an education in the fine arts of kitchen and household management, Grandfather and Uncle Costas attempted to contact Xene. Uncle sent his daughter several letters asking to visit her, but the only response he received came from Ducas, stating that a visit was not convenient. Damien was so upset at this that he would not even approach Ducas, afraid his anger might make things worse. Finally, Grandmother and I thought to ask, and since we were only women, our visit was allowed.

The sun shone brightly for that chilly mid-March day. Nicholas hired sedan chairs for us, which would wait and bring us home. Ducas's house, in a fashionable district close to the Great Palace and the Marmara, resembled many of its neighbors—a tall house with little land and just a small walled courtyard. As we emerged from our chairs, I glanced up at the elegant stone building to its roof four floors above ground. A small attic balcony protruded from the red roof tiles.

The steward greeted us as we entered the house.

"Please follow me. Lady Xene is in the gynecaeum," he said. We had rarely visited after Uncle Costas and Ducas were imprisoned seven years earlier, but I did not recall there being a gynecaeum in the house before.

We saw just a few servants as we passed rooms with thick carpets, marble-topped tables, silk curtains, and cushioned chairs. The house was as silent as tomb, as if none dared make a sound. Our footsteps echoed on the stairs to the top floor under the eaves where the gynecaeum appeared to be. I had not been to this floor on my previous visits.

Grandmother finally spoke to the steward, her gentle voice jarring in the hush, "Is General Ducas at home this morning? I would like to congratulate him on his return home."

Inclining his head, the steward answered, "The general is not at home today, but I will be sure to give him your congratulations when he returns."

Grandmother's curiosity persisted, "Oh, is he just gone for the day?"

The steward fended off the question. "Lady Theodora, the general does not always keep me informed of his activities. I believe he is only gone for the day, but his plans can change."

Grandmother was getting out of breath as we climbed up the last flight of stairs. Even in the dim light, the floors appeared dusty, and the paint on the walls was peeling—there was no marble or carpet here. The steward knocked softly on the door at the top landing.

"Lady Xene, your visitors have arrived," he said, not unkindly.

We could hear the sound of quick steps, and then the door opened to Xene, her face alight at seeing us again. I looked over her shoulder at the room as I embraced her. The gynecaeum was a good size but sparsely furnished with a few chairs, a bench, and a table. Light spilled in from the door to the small rooftop balcony I had seen when we arrived. Xene had the company of a plump servant girl, and they appeared to be engaged in needlework, which was scattered about the room.

"Anna, Aunt Theodora, I am so glad to see you again." Her eyes spilled over with tears. She looked me up and down. "Anna, I don't know that I would have recognized you, you look so grown up now."

"Isn't she?" Grandmother's voice was tremulous as the two of them embraced, a few tears falling on her cheeks. "And how have you been? We've missed you so." Grandmother had cared for Xene after my Aunt Sophia, Xene's mother, died a few months before I was born, and they were almost as close as mother and child.

"I'm doing well." She turned to the lingering steward. "Sebastian, would you please bring refreshments for our guests?"

The steward thus dispatched, we sat down to catch up after almost three years of separation. Grandmother and Xene spoke while I looked around, taking in the details I had missed at first glance.

The plain room's walls had nothing other than a simple icon of the Theotokos in a corner, its paint chipped and faded. A pitcher of water with two cups sat on a corner of the table. The rough-hewn furniture would have been more appropriate in servants' quarters, not those of the mistress of the house. The lone cheerful aspect was the half-opened door to the balcony, letting in sun and the early spring air. Xene's dress of ordinary brown homespun was unlike the fine silks or soft wools she had always worn in the past. I had been in the gynecaeum of other families— busy places with children and servants running in and out—but none so dreary as this. Of course, Xene had no children.

Grandmother found it difficult to speak of Uncle Costas and his efforts to see Xene, but it had to be done.

"Your father has written to Constantine about visiting you here and bringing Damien, but your husband told them that it wasn't convenient," Grandmother spoke gently, looking into her face.

Xene looked down, eyes hidden, before making a stiff, rehearsed response. "Constantine does not wish me to receive any men when he is not at home, and his schedule has been unpredictable, so it has not been convenient."

"Not even your own father or brother?" I asked.

She breathed out a painful sigh. "Constantine does not want me to, so I obey his wishes."

Grandmother shot me a look telling me not to push Xene.

Changing the subject and trying to put on the best face possible, I smiled at Xene while reaching over to squeeze her cold hand, realizing in that moment that over these past three years my hand had grown bigger than hers.

"I have missed you, cousin," I said. "Without you around to help me, Grandmother has discovered how poorly I really sew." I laughed at the memory of how often Xene had redone so much of the sewing that I had been tasked with before we had left for exile.

Xene laughed, too, while Grandmother gave us an amused look.

"And I thought it was the sea voyage that caused Anna to forget all the fine sewing 'she' had done before we left." Then turning to me, Grandmother continued with a rueful chuckle. "Well, I have given up trying to teach you. You'll just have to hire a seamstress once you are married."

"Once she is married? Oh, Anna, are you betrothed?"

"Not just yet, but we got to know General Isaac Comnenus and his brother, John, while we were in Amaseia. We sailed back with them, and young John Comnenus has expressed an interest in Anna." Grandmother finished with a twinkle in her eye, "And Anna seems to have an interest in him."

I blushed at that and nodded, rattling on about John like any besotted young girl. My discourse ended when the steward returned with refreshments: a tray with wine and biscuits.

"But I've been talking too much of myself. Xene, tell me how you've been."

None of us brought up the ugly scene when we had last been together, but its ghost sat with us that day.

Xene had been pouring the wine, but at my question her hand trembled, and she spilled a bit of the wine on the table, which upset her more.

"Oh, what a mess I've made. Constantine will be angry with me," came her anxious comment, so focused on his temper.

I spotted a rag on the floor, picked it up, and began wiping what was a trifling spill while Grandmother sprang to help Xene pour. Our efforts calmed her and she returned to her chair, apologizing for her clumsiness. Grandmother and I exchanged glances as I sat down with my wine cup.

Grandmother tactfully changed the subject to the sewing Xene and her maidservant had been doing, admiring their careful stitching and making humorous comparisons to my poor efforts. My cousin glowed at the compliments, and I was relieved to see some of her old confidence reappearing.

Noticing again the doors to the rooftop porch, I said, "So you can be outdoors, then, on good days, up above the noise and the smells of the streets? That must be pleasant. Can I see the view?"

"Oh yes, you must both see." Xene pulled us over to the door. "If you look straight ahead to the south, you can see the Marmara through the trees, especially in this season, when the leaves are not out yet. And then to the east is the Great Palace, but it's hidden behind the Hippodrome."

Her perch had a spectacular view of the ships' high masts peaking above the rooftops and seagulls gliding in slow circles. Looking east, I could see the distinctive pattern of the hippodrome's striped bricks, columns, and porticos. I had never been in that old racecourse, only passing the outside a few times. Most dynatoi women, and certainly no children, attended with its unruly crowds, although the empress and other women in the imperial family and their guests sometimes would join the emperor in the kathisma, the imperial box.

"Even on cold days, I love standing here, looking out over the city. Do you know, if the wind is blowing toward me, I can hear the crowds shouting at the Hippodrome on race days?" Xene leaned wistfully on the railing, as though contemplating an escape from the boundaries of her life. "They sound so happy and excited that I wish I could be there." Her thin fingers meshed between mine, squeezing my hand.

I laughed, thinking how unlikely our attendance at a race would ever be, but went along with her daydream. Impulsively, I said, "Someday, Xene, we will attend the races together, and we'll stand in the kathisma with the emperor." Putting my arm around her shoulders, we looked toward the Hippodrome. "Promise me you'll bring me with you if the emperor invites you, and I promise to bring you if I am asked. Promise me, won't you?" I encouraged her in my fantasy as I gave her arm a squeeze.

"I promise, but I don't think I'll be the one invited into the kathisma." She shook her head wistfully. "Still, I promise to come with you if you are."

We stood, arms linked, looking out over the city's busy expanse before a cold gust sent us back inside.

We left Xene a short while later with promises to return soon. Grandmother and I followed the steward outside to our chairs without speaking, our footsteps echoing through the polished halls. Despite being in different sedan chairs, I could almost hear my grandmother clucking in distress at Xene's predicament. Neither of us would look forward to describing my cousin's situation to Grandfather, Uncle Costas, and Damien on our return home.

My icy hands lay in a knot in my lap. I sat back in the chair with my eyes closed, feeling a terrible weight on my chest. Ducas had put his innocent wife in a prison almost as painful and humiliating as his own had been. For once, I felt no urge to peek out of the sedan's curtains at the shops and people we passed.

CHAPTER SIX

Catherine and Donya

Lent 1042

John visited us several times in our first weeks back home, meeting Uncle Costas and playing a few games of chess with him. We had no time alone, of course, but just seeing John, I felt more certain of my affection. He stayed with his sister, Donya, rather than with Isaac, helping with her children since her husband still had not returned from Italy. He said the embarrassment over her husband's recent military failures left her overwhelmed. I was impatient to meet her and Isaac's wife Catherine, but Lent was half over before a time could be arranged for their visit to our house. Grandmother said impatience was my greatest fault, that that should be my special effort for Lent. I did try.

Custom dictated that my grandfather and Isaac would sign the betrothal agreement on behalf of John and me, as the eldest men in our families. Often, though, the mothers, grandmothers, aunts, and sisters made the real decisions in these unions, giving their blessing before the men even knew of their plans. I knew Grandmother would not feel comfortable about my situation until we had met John's sister and sister-in-law.

A betrothal should be a simple matter. Yes, there would be negotiations on my dowry and John's wedding gift to me. But John and I wanted to be married, my grandparents approved, and Isaac seemed agreeable. I felt as eager as a racehorse, ready to sprint ahead.

The day of their visit finally arrived. We had cleaned the house until it shone, and Alethea's refreshments sat ready. I wore a pale blue silk tunic with embroidered neck and armbands, my brown hair loose down my back. Grandmother had on her best gown in deep blue.

I watched for their approach, expecting the usual sedan chairs. Instead, a grand party on horseback approached the gate. The two ladies had the company of three escorts—two of Isaac's soldiers and a maid for the ladies. Catherine, the daughter of a king, must have been accustomed to a more elegant style of travel than I was. The escorts quickly dismounted and helped the women down, the men following old Leo to a shady spot with the horses for a rest while the women made their way to the house.

I stopped gawking at this cavalcade and reached Grandmother's side just as they made their entrance into the house. Catherine looked to be only a little taller than I was, but she held herself regally erect, accentuating the impression of height. She removed her maphorion, revealing abundant black hair held in place with an elaborate arrangement of gold netting and hairpins, glinting in the spring light. Catherine's gown of heavy silk brocade in rich red and gold shades had stylish wide sleeves and a gold sash belting her trim waist. Her face was attractive, but a square jaw kept it from prettiness. The scattering of pale freckles across her fair-skinned face softened it into a less intimidating aspect.

Donya, sparrow-like in size and color, wore a plainer dark green gown and an apprehensive expression. A petite brunette, she looked little like her flamboyantly large and colorful redheaded brothers, much less the splendid Catherine.

We exchanged cordial introductions in the entry hall before Grandmother escorted us all to the library, where Catherine's maid sat apart from us at a table near a window overlooking the garden.

Alethea had done well preparing Lenten refreshments for our guests, as evidenced by her excellent bread, a bowl of dried figs, and wine. The serving tray held silver cups, delicate silver forks, and plates.

Catherine glanced casually around the room. It held Grandfather's prized collection of books, the rare chess set, and the family's silver. Our large garden just turning green could be seen from the windows.

"Lady Theodora, you have a lovely home," said Catherine, making the first move. She glimpsed the seascape mural painted on our walls. "I haven't been in this part of the city often, but your home is delightful."

Though unexceptional from the outside, we often received compliments from visitors once they were inside.

Donya glanced around and murmured after her, "Oh yes, it's quite lovely."

"Lady Catherine, Lady Donya, you are both so kind. I know the area is not as fashionable as others, but we are happy with it and are so glad to be back," Grandmother said.

Grandmother passed a tray with our best silver cups to Catherine, whose eyes narrowed for a moment at the sight of them.

"Oh yes, Isaac told us about the dreadful way you and your family were treated by that terrible eunuch," Catherine said. "I'm sure my husband must have told you of our own difficulties with my brother and cousin. It seems there is hardly anyone in the city without a horrible story to tell of what he did to them." She looked genuinely distressed, using a napkin to dab at tears.

Grandmother passed her a plate. "Yes, the Orphanotrophus terrorized many. We can be grateful he is gone now, and we can get on with our lives."

Donya spoke up with unexpected energy. "Lady Theodora, we may be grateful he is gone, but the problems he caused are still with us. My own husband is in Sicily trying to wrest back the territory that man lost the empire. I don't know when the children and I will see him again." She also subsided into a teary silence, dabbing her own eyes with another napkin. This was perhaps not the most auspicious topic to discuss when starting betrothal negotiations.

"Lady Catherine, I understand that you have two children. They must have been happy to see their father again," I said.

Catherine brightened at the mention of her children. "Oh yes, they missed him terribly. Manuel is eleven and, like any boy, needs his father's guidance. He's a good student, but every chance he gets he is out riding and hunting. Boys are like that," she said with a knowing shrug. "I feel better if he hunts with his father or John, which he couldn't for all those months. Maria is eight and truly Isaac's pet. As much as Manuel missed his father, I think Maria missed him more, moping about the house the entire time he was gone." She gave a fond mother's "what can you do?" sigh and took a bite of a fig.

Donya had been nibbling at a slice of bread, nodding in agreement at her sister-in-law's comments, when I turned to her.

"Lady Donya, how are you and your children managing with your husband gone?"

"It's better with John staying with us. He takes the boys, Theodore and George, out hunting with Manuel and Isaac now that they are all back. George is youngest, but they all get along well. All the boys will be disappointed when Isaac and John are sent on campaign again. And my daughters, Helena and Anastasia, fuss over John no end. They are so fond of him."

The mention of John seemed to bring us all back to the purpose of the visit, which was to get to know each other before moving ahead with the betrothal.

"So, Lady Theodora, I understand that you and your husband have raised Anna since the death of her parents," Catherine began.

"Yes, she is the only child of our only daughter, Helena and her husband, Alexius Charon, who Isaac mentioned he met many years ago. Our only son, Simeon, is a monk and master of the scriptorium at the Stoudion monastery." Grandmother smoothed the skirt of her elegant silk gown and nodded to the fine icons in the corner. "Can I pour you some more wine?"

"Thank you, it is most refreshing." Catherine held out her cup.

"I'm glad you like it. It is from our farm in Thrace," she said, making an oblique reference to part of my inheritance. "These cups were a gift from Emperor Basil to Anna's father."

"Really?" Catherine said, glancing at me with interest. An awkward thought struck me—could my father have been in Bulgaria when the emperor had conquered Catherine's father?

Donya made a gentle foray into the conversation. "John said that Anna's father was stationed in Italy many years ago, as my husband was until recently."

"Yes, Alexius was there about thirty-five years ago, when Anna's mother was a baby. Adrian, my husband, met him there when Emperor Basil sent him and his brother, Costas, to Italy," she finished smoothly, adding her famous brother-in-law to the discussion.

Catherine's face was bland, but she clearly understood Grandmother's comments in every way. She might have royal blood, but the Dalasseni were neither poor nor lacking in prestige and accomplishments.

Donya finished off the last crumbs on her plate before giving us a relaxed smile and quaffing the rest of her wine. They left a short while later amid effusive expressions of affection and promises to see each other again soon.

"Grandmother, I'm not sure about Catherine. She was curious about everything, and so formidable. Do you know if my father was with Emperor Basil when he conquered Bulgaria?" I asked as our visitors rode away.

She looked at me, startled at the question.

"Oh my. I hadn't thought of that. It's possible, but I've no idea. We won that war years before your parents married," she said with a frown. "Still, Isaac and John's father could've fought there, too. If she can come to terms about him, she can come to terms about your father."

She shrugged, "Besides, I think she really wanted to be sure you weren't interested in marrying John for his money. Perhaps she worried you might want to leech off of what she and Isaac have. I think she wanted to know what to expect in a dowry. She didn't get an exact number, but she knows you'll come into the marriage with more than the clothes on your back. It was a good first meeting. Next time it will be just Isaac and Catherine and your grandfather and me."

I put the plates, forks, and cups onto the tray. "Donya seemed quiet but sweet," I said.

Grandmother raised an eyebrow at that. "Yes, she did. I expect you'll have an easier time with her than with Catherine. I'll wager Catherine will never forget she was a princess, even if it was just Bulgaria."

The next meeting, with my grandparents, Isaac and Catherine was a week later, but to my unhappy surprise, they reached no final agreement.

"There is no rush. We can't have the betrothal during Lent, and John needs to find a house before the wedding. We need to purchase the linens, cooking utensils, dishes and the like that you need to bring with you into your home." I brightened at the thought of trips to the shops on the

Street of Porticoes that held so many of the fabrics, household tools and even the expensive imported spices my household would need.

Both of my grandparents accompanied me on shopping expeditions, with Grandfather on horseback escorting our sedan chairs. Unlike their usual careful habits, they indulged me outrageously when we shopped for my dowry – purchasing any trinket or household tool that might ever be useful.

One morning early in Holy Week, we were perusing the many fabrics of a cloth merchant. Grandmother and I looked them over inside the shop, deciding which would be suitable for curtains and bed linens, which for dresses. Grandfather chatted outside with the merchants from other shops and the street vendors in the weak mid-April sun. He said goodbye to the men he had been speaking with and joined us as we left the shop, looking subdued.

"What's the matter?" Grandmother asked, sensing his unease.

"Nothing we need to worry about now," he said in a low voice. "But there's talk on the street about the empress."

"What sort of talk?" asked Grandmother, looking perplexed as she tucked a few packages into her chair.

"Talk about how she hasn't been seen for weeks, not even at liturgy at Hagia Sophia. People only see that preening Paphlogonian emperor riding through the city on the finest horse in the imperial stables, wearing an emperor's boots. He'd be nothing without her. The men I was talking to are worried there could be a riot on Sunday if the emperor doesn't go on the usual procession with the empress for Easter. Emptying their shops in case of it."

"Hmm, they never rioted when the Orphanotrophus kept her locked up, but I suppose he was more intimidating than this young pup," Grandmother said, referring to Emperor Michael.

"I think we stay close to home until the talk has blown over," Grandfather said as he put a warning hand on her shoulder. "There'll be time to shop for Anna's dowry before the marriage takes place if we allow a week or so for matters to settle down."

I peered around the street. The shopkeepers and their patrons still thronged the road, but now I noticed clumps of people with sour faces talking while looking over their shoulders for the eparch's men. We might not be the targets of their anger, but that would not matter in a riot.

We only left the house to visit Stoudion for Holy Week services. I spent my time reading and working in our garden. On Wednesday, John joined us for dinner, arriving while I was still outside digging up weeds.

"Hello, Anna," he said.

I had been so focused on my task that I had not heard his approach and spun around in surprise. "John," I exclaimed, feeling a blush rise on my cheeks.

"I didn't mean to startle you," he began. He stood near me, his red hair gleaming in the sun, his hand half raised, reaching out for me. "I thought it was such a fine day for April that I should come out to enjoy the air. Why don't we sit?"

I took off the broad-brimmed straw hat I wore when working in the garden and shook out my hair. We walked over to the grape arbor, where there was a table and chairs. For propriety's sake, there was a clear view of us from the house in that spot. It would be too cool tonight to eat outside, but the afternoon sun combined with the musky scents of freshly turned earth made it pleasant for the moment. The willow tree down by the river, with its leaves still pale this early in the season, was behind John, framing him.

I relished these few moments just for us. Some couples did not meet until their betrothal, so we were fortunate with even this. John brushed a few specks of dirt from his dark blue braccae as we sat in awkward silence for a minute. He cleared his throat and leaned toward me.

"I think my sister and Catherine both liked you. They returned from their meeting full of compliments," he said, sounding pleased.

"I'm glad. I think it will be wonderful to have sisters. Xene was the closest I ever had to a sister." No need to discuss the regal Catherine then.

"I think the rest of my family worried that I would be as old as my father when I married." He gave a rueful laugh. "But I didn't want to wait until I was in my forties, as he was when he married Isaac's mother, or even older when he married my mother. I don't want to leave behind orphans to be raised by others. I wanted to marry at an age where I might see my

85

children grown." John shook his head, reminding me for a moment of a small, lost boy.

"I know. Even grandparents, or the good monks of Stoudion, can't stop you from wanting your parents back," I said.

John shook his head, as though trying to shake off the sad memory. He looked speculatively at the house and then laughed.

"I wonder how long we will be here together before one of your elders comes out to make sure we are behaving?"

I grinned and, feeling a little mischievous, said, "It won't be long. What sort of misbehavior do you think they expect? Should we give them something to reprimand us about?"

John's eyes widened in amusement. "I don't think that would be wise before we are betrothed. Otherwise, they might decide that we are so depraved that the only way to save our immortal souls is to tonsure us and pack us off to the monastery. I don't think I was meant for one."

My teeth chattered a little as a chilly breeze blew. The sun had dropped low in the sky.

He continued, "It's good we've gotten to know each other beforehand. I didn't want to find myself married to someone I hardly knew. I've not had many chances to get to know young women. I certainly hadn't expected to find one when I arrived in Amaseia. That was a happy surprise," he said, smiling at me.

"I hadn't expected to find a young man there, either."

John noticed my shivering and asked, "Are you cold? Do you want to go inside?"

"No, I'm fine." I was loathe to see this time alone with him end.

He stretched out his hands to me. "Give me your hands, then; I'll warm them."

"Oh no, I've been working in the garden; they are too dirty," I said as I hid them under my hat.

He laughed outright at that. "You're talking to a soldier, and you think a little dirt from a garden will bother me? Come, give me your hands." The last was part question, part insistent demand, and after a glance down at my grubby hands, I reached over to him.

His large hands were warm, and mine felt as though surrounded by mittens that had been set on a brazier.

"Are your hands always this warm?" I asked.

"You hands are like ice," he said, surprised. "Yes, always warm. It's a great advantage this time of the year, not as much in the summer." We sat quietly with hands clasped for a few minutes, the heat spreading throughout my body. Suddenly, John spoke again, earnestly.

"So, Anna, tell me what you are hoping for in our marriage."

His request startled me. I had not thought what I might want in a marriage beyond the obvious.

"Umm, I think the usual things a girl wishes for—a good husband and children. A home. I don't think anything out of the ordinary." Perhaps John had different expectations. "Why do you ask? What are you hoping for in our marriage?"

He searched my face. "The same, I think. But I wanted to make sure now. Some people desire positions at court, prestige. I didn't want to disappoint you." He gave a small shrug of indifference to worldly honors. "I'm just a soldier. I'm happy leaving it that way."

"John, I've no interest in court life, either. Especially after seeing what happened to Uncle Costas."

Just then we heard the footsteps. I thought John might let go of my hands, but he didn't, only gripped them more tightly and grinned playfully at me. Uncle Costas approached with a quizzical look on his face.

"Anna, your grandmother sent me out to let you and your young man know that dinner is almost ready. Perhaps you should clean up before we eat?"

John spoke up quickly but had not relinquished my hands yet. "General, I was just holding Anna's hands to warm them. She was shivering, and I didn't want her to take ill."

By now, I was feeling quite warm and finally extricated myself from his grasp. "Yes, Uncle, I'll go in now to get ready." I hurried into the house. At the door, I turned back to glimpse John, standing strong and solid beside my uncle. My heart beat faster at the thought that we would be betrothed in a few weeks and wed soon after, perhaps by summer.

CHAPTER SEVEN

Emperor Michael

Easter 1042

We rose in the dark on Easter morning, to be ready for the Divine Liturgy. Our family attended the services at Stoudion because of Uncle Simeon, as well as its proximity to our house. Many in the city went to Hagia Sophia to see the great procession of the empress and emperor. This year, with the rumblings grandfather had heard, we kept far from the palace and the great church. John and Isaac, however, being active in the empire's service, felt obliged to attend there.

There were a few torches giving light to Stoudion's worshippers that morning, but most carried candles. The priest chanted the reading from St. Luke outside the church, telling the familiar story of the disciples not finding Jesus in the tomb, and their surprise at the angel's news. We filed into the church to the sound of the monks' joyous hymns, the women climbing steep stairs to the gallery, the men below in the nave. I preferred the gallery with its better view. The icons and the iconostasis glittered in the candlelight—exquisite renderings of Christ, the Theotokos, the angels Michael and Gabriel, Saints Peter and Paul, St. John the Baptist, dressed in sapphire blues and ruby reds all with golden halos, symbols of the incorruptibility of heaven. The panels reached far above a man's height, but the prayers rang out clear in the church.

By the time the service finished, it was full light. We returned home for the Paschal feast—lamb Alethea had begun roasting the night before, delicate young asparagus from our garden, early strawberries and wine from Grandfather's estate. Grandmother had sent several baskets of produce to the monastery for the monks' celebration. She had also dispatched old Leo to gather in any stray traveling monks who might need a bed and a place to share the Paschal celebration. We often had one or two staying with us, and Eastertide was no exception, with monks called Father Timothy and a Father Phillip comfortably housed above the stable.

After the Lenten weeks with no meat or cheese or fish, the meal was wonderful. I never appreciated Alethea's cooking as much as I did at the Easter feast and she outdid herself that year, celebrating both the resurrection and our return from exile.

As the meal drew to a close, it was still not much past noon. Grandfather, trying to be casual, announced, "Costas and Damien and I will be walking down to the city, to see how the procession from the palace went this morning. We could use a bit of exercise after this wonderful meal."

Grandmother was not fooled. She looked at him with a narrow eye. "Didn't you say it wasn't safe to be about on the streets?"

"That's true," Grandfather began diffidently with a wave of his hand, "but I think we can manage without any difficulty."

"Two old graybeards and a man who has walked with a limp for more than ten years? I'm sure you will do a good job frightening off the beggars."

The men looked a bit annoyed at her. Grandfather scowled and tried to coax her, "Now, Theodora. . ."

"I'll admit it's probably a good idea to find out how things stand, but bring one of the stable lads with you—and make sure he carries a stick or club along. If there's rioting, you will need some sort of protection."

Grandfather agreed to this small accommodation. The four of them soon set off to see what had happened that morning. They returned by late afternoon.

"So, what did you see?" asked Grandmother as she poured water for them.

"We went all the way down the Mese to the Milion and Hagia Sophia and saw nothing out of the ordinary," said Grandfather. "We spoke to an old monk who helped visitors at the church. Apparently, the procession went perfectly this morning. The emperor and empress emerged together from the palace through the imperial gate into the church and the crowd roared at the sight of them. Perfectly ordinary. Too ordinary maybe?"

"Afterwards, the empress returned to the palace while the emperor joined the crowd outside where he distributed gold coins to the people to much praise," said Uncle Costas.

"Anyone will get smiles scattering gold coins, even the Orphanotrophos, " Damien added. "But Zoe's popular and the crowds have cheered all the emperors who shared her throne."

"I'm grateful to the emperor for releasing me but he's still the son of that idiot, Stephen," said Uncle Costas, his fingers drumming on the table. "After what Stephen did in Sicily, can his son can be any better?"

Grandfather walked to the window, looking out on the garden turning lush with green leaves. He ran a hand through his hair and turned back to us, the lines on his face deeply etched. "Something didn't feel right. It was too quiet when we were out."

We stayed close to home the next day. A chilly rain fell on Monday, unpleasant after sunny Easter. Uncle Costas and I spent the afternoon battling across the chessboard. There is nothing like playing chess with a great general to learn about strategy. Conversation had been sparse as we focused on the game, until he cleared his throat and began speaking.

"So, Anna, about your young man, John," he stopped to consider the board and cleared his throat.

"Yes," I said suspiciously. I wondered if he was trying to distract me from the game, a familiar trick of his.

"You know, it won't be easy being a soldier's wife. He'll be gone for much of each year and you'll have to manage without him then. Have you thought what that would be like?" His focus returned to his carved black pawns.

"I have. Grandmother has told me."

Uncle Costas nodded before he surprised me by moving his bishop. I kept my face impassive despite frustration at not having anticipated that move.

"You know John's brother Isaac is one of our best generals, and married to the daughter of a Bulgarian king. John could find himself in an influential position. You would be expected to do what you can to further his career. Have you thought about that?"

"Oh, John's not interested in politics or anything like that. He just wants to be a soldier, nothing more," I assured him blithely.

"That may be, but sometimes people with ability or connections can get thrust into situations they never expected, the way your king is. Best to be prepared," and he moved his castle straight down the board.

I wanted to dismiss his worries, but then I looked up at his face weathered by love and grief, fear, victories and humiliation. So much of his life had been thrust on him – ten years in captivity in Egypt, Aleppo, seven years a prisoner of the emperor, and other events I knew little of. I swallowed, finally feeling unnerved, my concentration on the game gone.

He glanced up, giving me a direct look, his steel gray eyes still strong, but tempered with hard won wisdom. "Child, all I'm saying is that you should be ready for anything. You will need to pay some attention to politics. You and John come from important families. Unless you are prepared to move out of the city, it will happen."

He met my eyes, moved his knight, and grinned. "Oh, and checkmate."

Tuesday was overcast but dry. We had planned an afternoon outing to Stoudion to visit uncle Simeon since we had not seen him on Easter. During breakfast Nicholas rushed in from the errand he had been on, out of breath and calling, "General Dalassenus, General."

Grandfather, on edge for the past week, rose to meet him. "Nicholas, what's wrong? What's happened?"

Nicholas panted, trying to get all the words out at once. "The empress ... gone ... emperor sent her away."

Grandfather blanched and grabbed Nicholas' shoulder to steady him. "What did you say? Slow down and tell us what happened."

Nicholas' breathing slowed but the shocked expression on his ruddy face did not diminish.

"Eustace, the fishmonger down the road, went to the wharves this morning to buy the day's fish when he heard the emperor sent the empress to Prinkipo during the night."

Grandmother gasped. Over the centuries, troublesome nobles and imperial family members had been bundled off to one or another of the monasteries on the small island of Prinkipo, in the Sea of Marmara. No empress ever went there willingly.

"Sent her to Prinkipo? Why?" Grandfather asked, trying to gauge the situation.

"He said the palace servants were told the empress tried to poison the emperor." Nicholas began to catch his breath, still panting.

Uncle Costas and Damien had also risen from the table by now and were exchanging looks with Grandfather.

"Anything else?" Uncle Costas asked, his face flushed .

"That was all he said, General. But when I was out you could tell people were upset – I could see groups of them becoming angry as they heard the news. Not many people out yet, but the crowds were growing," Nicholas finished.

Grandfather sat down, looked across the table at Uncle Costas before glancing back at the steward. "Thank you, Nicholas. If you hear anything else, be sure to let us know."

"Michael just wants the throne for himself. He threw a few coins at people on Easter and thinks he's bought their loyalty," said Uncle Costas. He looked disgusted at the news.

"It's possible she did actually try to poison him, just to be rid of him," Damien suggested.

"Maybe," said Grandfather. "If she did try to poison him, maybe she had a good reason. And if she didn't, she's got a good reason now."

Damien looked thoughtful and asked, "Won't the Senate need to be informed?"

"They hardly matter, but Michael may want their agreement, to give his decision some legitimacy." Grandfather turned to his older brother, "We should go to the palace to find out what's happening."

"You're right. I don't expect the senate to do anything, though. None of those useless dynatoi cares about anything other than their stipend from the treasury and where they rank in the imperial processions," said Uncle Costas. "Still, I'd rather hear the news myself, than depend on street rumors."

"I'm going with you," Grandmother announced unexpectedly.

The men looked at her, initially speechless, before Grandfather spoke. "Now Theodora, I don't think –"

Grandmother interrupted brusquely. "I want to hear what excuse they give for sending an empress born in the purple room into exile. We'll bring the stable boy with us for protection. I'm sure I'll be fine with you, Costas, and Damien, as well as the boy."

The men began trying to convince her otherwise.

After a moment's hesitation, I decided I would have to accompany them. "I'm going too. Grandmother's right, we won't have any trouble. Everyone will be distracted by whatever the emperor has to say."

I then had the distinct pleasure of seeing all of my elders shocked into silence before Grandmother started to protest. Uncle Costas cut her off.

"Theodora, if you think its safe for you to go, then I think Anna should come too. If she is going to be married to Isaac Comnenus' brother, she might as well get a taste of how the empire works."

I wasn't sure that I needed to know how the empire worked, but an opportunity like this did not happen often and would certainly be more interesting than going over menus with Alethea.

The distance could usually be covered in about an hour, but the growing crowds slowed our passage as we neared the Milion where any announcement would be made. We found a spot under a portico near a sweet smelling perfumer's shop and across from the main gate to the palace, outside of which stood six Varangians. The polished dark oak gate rose well above the tallest man's height and was held in place with iron hinges and bars. Groups of two or three men in senatorial robes were permitted through the gates every few minutes, many of whom my grandparents or uncle recognized.

Suddenly, I heard muttered profanity coming from my uncle and cousin. Looking around I saw Ducas with two other senators. He had recently inherited this position from his father and wore his new official robes. Ducas was the handsome man I remembered, tall and distinguished, his features beautifully proportioned and harmonious. I thought he certainly gave the lie to Plato's conflation of beauty with truth and goodness. Gold borders were embroidered on his red silk robes, his beard oiled and combed, and gem-studded rings glinted on his fingers— all so different from Xene's shabby attire. I didn't think he saw us where we stood in the shadows near the shop, but if he did, he ignored us. He avoided the laborers and tradesmen who milled about waiting for an announcement as he processed through the crowd.

It had been almost three years since I had last seen him that day in the tower. I found myself shrinking back, the way you would from a vicious dog, relaxing only when he disappeared inside the walls.

Surprisingly, the crowd appeared to include almost as many women as men milling about. Most women rarely left their houses, tending their children or grandchildren and all the chores that involved. I realized how much women applauded her for being on the throne in her own right, not just as a wife. For all Zoe's faults, I could not blame them. Too many men treated women as little better than ignorant children.

We waited over an hour before the gate creaked opened again and the senators filed out with solemn expressions. A man in the emperor's attire followed them. His robes were, of course, silk dyed in the imperial purple reserved only for the emperor and empress, and embroidered with the empire's golden eagle, gold around his neck and armbands. A jewel-encrusted crown with pendants of hanging pearls framed his face. Even his sandals were dyed purple with golden buckles.

He was, otherwise, unremarkable. His thin face, scraggly beard with nondescript brown hair, and short stature did not impress me. He looked nothing more than a sparrow dressed in peacock's feathers. Surrounded by a dozen Varangian guards armed with their rhomphaia, the populace at first maintained a respectful demeanor towards him. He climbed onto the stone platform used by the eparch to make announcements with a smug expression, and began to speak.

"My people, I come before you today with sad, grave news," he said. But, I mused, if it was so sad, why was he smirking?

"In the last few days I have learned that Empress Zoe has been plotting to murder me with poison. I know this will be as much of a shock to you as it was to me—that my own adoptive mother whom I have loved and cared for as dearly as I would the mother who gave birth to me, would be so heartless and cruel," he paused, looking for sympathy from the sullen, skeptical crowd. He must not have seen much evidence of sympathy, though, and his smirk faltered. He continued, hurrying through his prepared words.

"Court officials told me of her plot and shown me the evidence for months, but I did not want to believe them until I received incontrovertible proof. I was warned that this might happen by many court officials and even earlier by my illustrious uncles, the dearly beloved late emperor Michael and the ever vigilant Orphanotrophus."

Listening to the speech, the emperor's comments were almost plausible to start, but these last words made no sense. Did he think everyone had forgotten? His uncles were not illustrious, nor were they dearly beloved. Jealous, greedy, incompetent, and cruel were more apt descriptions as far as my family and I, and many others, were concerned.

Continuing to listen to these falsehoods was difficult.

"Last night I presented the damning evidence of her guilt to the empress. She could not deny it, but repented of her sins and begged my forgiveness, weeping at my feet. I condescended to absolve her of her guilt, but she insisted that to fully expiate her sins she must leave the city and enter the convent on Prinkipo immediately. She left during the night by ship and was tonsured there today."

A groan went up from the crowd.

"I am distressed at the loss of her wisdom and counsel, but believe her decision was the right one. Please keep Empress Zoe in your prayers, as I am sure she will do for you."

The thought flickered through my mind—how odd that he would miss Zoe's great wisdom and counsel when she had tried to kill him. Then I heard a loud voice I recognized.

"All hail Emperor Michael," Constantine Ducas called out, followed by hurrahs and shouts of support for him from the other senators and Varangians. At least Ducas had a reason to hail the emperor since the man had freed him after the "illustrious" uncles had locked him up for seven years. Even so, the whole speech sounded like a lie from start to finish.

Most of the crowd seemed to share that opinion and had not joined in the hurrahs. Their brooding faces and muttered comments much like those that filled my mind.

"Filthy little heretic, locking away our empress, our mother," grumbled one sturdy woman, with flour dusting her dress.

"To think that scrawny piece of horse shit is wearing Basil's crown," said an older man more loudly.

Several men called out, "Unworthy." Others said, "Dig up his bones."

"He's nothing without the empress. If she wanted to poison him, they should just let her," came another angry voice, as a stone was lobbed at the emperor.

"Get back to your ship, Caulker, before we dig up your bones," called out another woman, calling him by the emperor's father's old profession. A few more projectiles followed although none did more than graze him.

Michael may not have heard all the words, but he heard the anger in the voices, and felt the pelting detritus. The emperor was fortunate to have the Varangians with him as he retreated behind the palace walls with alacrity. Even the soldiers were too nervous of the crowd to make an effort to apprehend the stone throwers.

After a few more catcalls, the outraged crowd trickled away, with some clustered about the Milion. Other groups walked together, heads shaking in infuriated disbelief. Grandmother and I walked arm in arm back up the marble paved Mese, Damien and the stableboy ahead and my grandfather and uncle behind, heads bent close in discussion.

"Anna, the emperor never did tell us what evidence he had against the empress?" Grandmother said indignantly.

"No, he never did, did he?"

"I didn't hear much in that speech that rang true," said Damien. "There are many words I've heard used to describe Zoe, but I think this is the first time I've heard her described as 'a font of wisdom'. The way he said it, you'd almost think she wanted to be tonsured."

"I'm grateful to the emperor allowed us to return, and freed Costas, but he shouldn't have done this," she said. "That man's family has brought only misery on the empire. He wanted everything for himself. He got rid of the Orphanotrophus, thank God, leaving Zoe as the only impediment to complete control."

"I'll wager he didn't expect to hear people call out 'Unworthy' or 'Dig up his bones'," Damien said.

"Why?" I asked.

Grandmother shook her head, her lips pursed.

Damien answered. "People say that when they want to get rid of the emperor. Hasn't been said in years."

We passed through the Forum of Constantine, with its massive pillar of purple Egyptian marble in its center reaching high above the buildings surrounding it. Atop the pillar stood a bronze statue of the first Constantine, fashioned to appear like Apollo. That monument was already seven centuries old and had seen bad, good and indifferent successors. This trivial upstart sitting on his throne would have disgusted the empire's founder, but there had been worse than Michael. Still, when the people lost patience with an emperor, he never lasted long.

Nicholas reported the next morning that folk in the shops and taverns were agitating to have Zoe returned to the throne, tonsured or not. If not her, then her younger sister, Theodora, confined by Zoe these many years to a convent. The people wanted a ruler with Basil's blood, not this man nicknamed "Caulker." A traveling monk who begged shelter for a few days said he had been staying at a monastery near the palace. He heard the Varangians grumbling noisily about the emperor, and decided that was a sign he should find a place to sleep farther away from the palace.

The Varangians had a reputation of loyalty to the emperor whoever that might be. An emperor who had lost their loyalty was doomed.

After the emperor's speech Grandfather, Uncle Costas, and Damien ventured out to see what was going on every few hours. Our outlying suburb of the city might not be the target of a riot, but if a mob lost all control and began looting, they wanted to be prepared.

I worried about John. We'd had no word from him since the week before. Living with his sister, he would feel responsible for the safety of her and her children. Their house lay in the city's center, near the church of St. Mary Kyriotissa and the Aqueduct of Valens, and the palace.

Not long before sunset, the men returned looking grim.

Grandmother's brown eyes anxiously scanned their faces, before sitting them down in the library around the square table we had there, and pouring them each a cup of wine. I stood by the window, too nervous to sit.

"So how bad is it?" she asked in a clipped voice, taking her seat. Her chin looked as taut as it had the night we had sailed into exile.

The two brothers exchanged glances across the table but it was Damien who spoke up.

"Bad enough," he began, "but not so bad that I think we should start planning an escape." He paused to take another sip of wine before continuing with an unnatural calm. "There seems to be a general understanding that the men of the city will be at the palace in the morning, and they will be armed."

"And most of the women, too," added Uncle Costas. " The women look to be even more upset than the men are."

"They will demand that Zoe be returned," Grandfather concluded.

"What chance of success do they have?" I asked.

"If I hadn't heard what that monk your Grandmother has tucked away above the stables told us about the Varangians, I would say they have no chance. But if the Varangians have turned, then the odds of success improve markedly. Either way, tomorrow will end in bloodshed. I'm sure of that." Grandfather rubbed his hands over his pale face.

"Adrian," Uncle Costas spoke calmly, "I don't think we'll be troubled here. We're far from the palace."

"I hope you're right. Still, we'll barricade the gate, and keep watch tonight. There's a lot of drinking going on in taverns; some of the fighting might start early." His forehead held deep furrows as he glanced at Grandmother.

"Have you thought about what you will do in the morning? Will you go down to see?" Grandmother asked, giving the men a suspicious eye.

The room was quiet. Damien took a sip of his drink, while Uncle Costas sat swirling the wine in his cup, both of them avoiding Grandmother's intent eyes. Grandfather ran a hand through his hair. A man avoiding his wife's question.

Finally Grandfather spoke. "I don't think we'll need to go out early in the day, but maybe by midday, to learn what's happened."

Shaking her head, Grandmother rose and cleared the cups from the table. I could hear the clatter of the dinner dishes in the dining room but no one spoke.

During the night the men took turns watching with old Leo, but Uncle Costas was right, nothing happened beyond a few drunken shouts echoing through our neighborhood. I slept uneasily that night hearing my grandmother pace the hall outside my room.

At dawn, Nicholas and Damien ventured out to the shops near our house, ostensibly to purchase the day's bread and fish. They were gone for over an hour before returning, red-faced from a quick march back.

"Everyone in the streets is armed," Damien began, panting. "The men have swords or axes, or whatever is at hand. The women are carrying stones, gathered in their skirts. We followed the crowd longer than we had planned to, trying to see what was happening."

Grandmother looked incredulous. "There are women out carrying rocks?"

Nicholas nodded as he caught his breath. "Oh yes, lady, at least half of them are women –but not all have rocks. Some have knives. I've never seen such a crowd – we followed them for a while, until they got to the emperor's uncle's house. You recall the uncle, the one called Constantine? The emperor's favorite uncle?"

"Yes, I certainly remember him," said Grandmother.

"Why were they going there?" asked Uncle Costas, taken aback. "Michael isn't there. I'd have wagered they would go to the palace."

"They'll probably end up there, but Constantine's house was closer. We didn't stay long to watch. There must have been a couple of thousand, and they were out of control, looting and tearing the place apart. It looked like they killed Constantine's guards before bursting through his gates," Damien continued in a rush. "I've never seen so many people in such a rage outside of war."

Grandfather stood looking from one to the other, his arms crossed on his chest.

"So was the eunuch there?" he asked.

Nicholas and Damien exchanged puzzled looks, before Damien replied.

"Constantine? I honestly don't know. We did see an ornate sedan chair that was inside his gate. Its carriers ran off before the mob demolished it, hacking it to pieces." Damien shook his head, eyes wide in remembrance at its destruction. "With all its gold and red paint, it did look like it would have belonged to the emperor's uncle. Or it did before they got to it. Now it's kindling. Maybe he was getting ready to leave for the palace. But I never heard any shouts or saw anything that said they'd found him. Maybe he hid, or escaped when he heard the mob coming, or maybe they found him after we left. But we'd seen enough."

Grandfather met his brother's eyes with what appeared to be perfect understanding of each other's intentions.

Turning to Grandmother, he said without preamble, "We need to find out what's happening. Damien, you'll stay here with the women."

Grandmother nodded wanly before replying, "I know. You'll be armed, and you'll take Patricios with you." It was a statement, not a question.

He put his arms around her, and kissed the top of her head. "We will. And we'll be careful."

They left with Patricios, their short swords hidden under their cloaks, while the stable boy carried a sturdy walking stick.

As we learned later, the rioting continued all day as the mob thoroughly destroyed the palaces of Constantine and the rest of the emperor's family. After this warm-up, they advanced on the Great Palace. The emperor's uncle Constantine had indeed escaped from his house through a hidden back gate and made his way to the Great Palace to warn the guards to secure its gates. The guards bolted every possible entrance and stood on its walls shooting arrows and javelins into the approaching mob. They killed hundreds until the people moved beyond the soldiers' range, milling about, alternately shouting to the soldiers to rebel against the faithless emperor, or vowing revenge for their dead fellows.

Inside the palace, the frightened emperor realized the mistake he had made in sending Zoe to Prinkipo. He ordered a ship sent from his dock to fetch her back from the island. She was soon back in the palace, still clad in her black nun's habit. She must have feared Michael would kill her if she disobeyed and gave her pathetic agreement when he demanded that she stand with him on the balcony of the palace's theater near the walls, so the crowds could see her and know her to be safe.

Michael's scheme did not work as he expected. Most in the crowd were so distant they did not recognize the small figure still clad as a nun next to him, and those who did were further outraged that she had not been returned to her crown and imperial purple robes. The shouts and name-calling grew worse until Michael and Zoe withdrew.

Grandfather and Uncle Costas knew many of the men in the mob, old soldiers retired now, but still loyal to Zoe's family. My grandfather and uncle made their way to where it seemed the crowd's ringleaders stood, hovering near the edges of that group as the angry people discussed what to do next. At that point, they found themselves standing next to a soldier they recognized, one Constantine Cabasilas, and greeted him as the men standing nearby argued about what they should do next.

Uncle Costas later told us he'd had a sudden thought, and whispered to Cabasilas, "What about Zoe's sister? Has anyone thought about Theodora?"

Zoe was the middle child of three sisters. The eldest had died years earlier of smallpox, but there was still the youngest, named like my grandmother, Theodora. The two sisters did not like each other. After Zoe became empress, she had sent her sister to live in the convent of Petrion in an isolated corner of the city. Over the years, many people had almost forgotten about Theodora's existence, but my uncle's whispered question inspired his old comrade to suggest retrieving her and setting her on a throne in Hagia Sophia as co-empress with her sister.

In short order, Cabasilas was dispatched to retrieve Theodora who, by reports, was accustomed to her quiet convent and not eager for this return to the purple.

At the same time, Grandfather and Uncle Costas continued to watch the crowd as it seethed about in waves some distance from the palace gates. Some of the mob had spread down neighboring streets, with the most lawless elements setting fires and attacking the unwary. My grandfather and uncle stopped one thuggish attack on a young woman, before threatening another pair who were attempting to break into a perfumer's shop with sword points.

After these incidents, they decided it was time to return home and inched their way through the rioters and up the Mese. Out of breath, disheveled, and red in the face from their quick return walk, they were otherwise unharmed. Clearly, the news was bad.

"We don't think the mob, however out of control it might get, would dare to attack Stoudion or any monastery, but other places, including this house, maybe. With Simeon at Stoudion, I know the monks would find a place in their guesthouse for us," Grandfather said.

Grandmother's sharp brown eyes searched his face before nodding in acquiescence.

"Is it safe to get there now? I'd rather not leave."

"There's some looting nearby, but most of it is closer to the palace. We shouldn't have any trouble now but it could spread. Alethea and Maria need to come with us. We'll leave Leo, Nicholas and the stable boys behind, but if the house is attacked, they'll have to do what they can to protect themselves."

It was then that my hands began to shake and feel clammy.

Late in the afternoon we made our way to the monastery through unnaturally quiet streets. A few drunken men hung about the doors to the taverns, cursing the emperor, but most of the other shops were deserted, their shutters pulled closed. The sound of the rioters roared from the east where the palace lay. It sounded angry and violent, not like the excited noise the spectators at the hippodrome made.

We finally reached the entrance to the monastery where old Father Athanasius, the gatekeeper, greeted us. He was a sweet man, but getting forgetful and no longer moving quickly, depending instead on one of the orphan boys they took in to run errands and announce guests.

"Lady Theodora, General Dalassenus, how wonderful it is that you have come to visit us today. But you have brought so many people with you," Father Athanasius squinted around at us, looking bemused. "Is Father Simeon expecting all of you? I don't think he said anything about it to me."

Grandfather spoke for us with some urgency. "No, Father. We've not had a chance to speak to our son. We are in some need of shelter for the women of our household, if you could call the master of the guesthouse for us, we'll explain the situation to him."

The monk looked around, even more confused. "Oh my, was there a fire at your house? I don't recall any earthquake recently. I'm sure we can find a place for the good ladies, but it seems that we have had many requests for accommodation today. Now where did that boy go? I saw everyone go down to the dock for some reason. No one tells me anything about what is going on. . ."

Father Athanasius wandered off in the general direction of the main monastery building, apparently in search of the guesthouse master, or the boy who would fetch that monk. We waited anxiously. It was no use trying to hurry monks—with their thoughts always on the eternal, nothing seemed urgent with them. I peeked through the grate to the courtyard beyond the gate. It was, like the streets on the way to Stoudion, unnaturally deserted. Why everyone had gone down to the monastery's dock on the Marmara?

After a few minutes I noticed that the sounds of the rioters were growing louder. My grandparents exchanged concerned looks, but the street was still empty.

Eventually we saw my Uncle Simeon approaching with uncommon haste, his face pale.

"Father, what are you all doing here?" he looked frantically over the seven of us, while bending to give his mother and me perfunctory kisses.

"Simeon, what's wrong? I brought the women here so they could stay in your guesthouse. People are rioting. I thought the safest place for them would be here," Grandfather said.

Uncle Simeon's eyes widened in horror, "You thought it would be safer here? You didn't hear then?"

"Hear what?" Grandfather asked. It was beginning to look like this might not have been the best place for us to be.

"The emperor is here, with his uncle Constantine. They are with the hegoumenos. They've begged for sanctuary, and to be tonsured as monks. They sailed from the palace to our dock a little while ago."

Grandfather swore under his breath. Suddenly, the sounds of the angry mob were close and I turned to see an immense number of people swarming up the street that had been empty only moments earlier. Uncle Simeon looked over my shoulder, his usual calm gone.

"Theotokos help us," he prayed, then pulled us in before barring the gate. "Come with me. I'll put you in an alcove in the church. It should be safe there. They won't dare desecrate the sanctity of the church."

Uncle Simeon secured the gates to the monastery before turning us all towards the church. I grabbed hold of Maria and Alethea's hands and we raced through the gardens towards the archway that held the door the monks used. We'd been in the church many times before, but always from the visitors' entrance, never from the monk's. Uncle Simeon rushed us through a back corridor and up steep stairs to a gallery overlooking the nave. He glanced over the railing, then gasped.

"They're here," he whispered, looking towards a few figures we could see through the entrance in the iconostasis.

That time of day, the gallery was in shadows, hiding us while we could see all that transpired below.

The man I had seen proudly attired in imperial purple just a day earlier, was now in the plain robes of a monk, his head still pink where he had just been tonsured. Another man stood near him, also pink with the tonsure, but a beardless eunuch. They were pleading for protection from the Hegoumenos, Matthias, their hands grasping the altar.

The door to the church crashed open below and a voice called out, "They're in here." The rabble rushed in while the two new monks frantically grabbed the altar, crying out "Sanctuary! Sanctuary!" repeatedly. I thought the people would seize the men at that moment, but the hegoumenos raised a hand.

"Stop! Stop! Not one step further, you are in the house of God. I will not have you desecrate it with violence." Matthias, a soft-spoken elderly man, would have had better luck trying to stop the waves from lapping on the shore than to deter this mob.

A couple of the larger men pushed the sputtering hegoumenos to the other side of a door near the altar, shutting it and ending any further monkish interference. Uncle Simeon, up in the balcony with us, was the only monk to witness to the retribution dealt the two miscreants.

One of the men in the crowd, with light brown hair that poked out at odd angles, a beaky nose and receding chin, and wearing the garb of a palace official, pulled away from the mass of people and began berating first Constantine, and then Michael for their sins against the empress. The two men cowered, hands gripping the holy altar.

"Was there anything she ever did that could have justified your cruel treatment?" Looking directly at Michael, his angry rebuke continued, "The empress is your adopted mother and has been only kindness and generosity to you. I saw it with my own eyes. And this is how you repay her? With baseless accusations and imprisonment?"

The crowd surrounding them cried out in assent to these statements, shaking fists and waving swords at the two figures clinging to the altar.

The beardless one began stammering a reply, pointing a finger at Michael. "It was him—I couldn't stop him. I tried to but he would've killed me." He gibbered on, lapsing into incoherent sobbing excuses for what had happened.

The one who had been emperor gaped at his uncle's efforts to absolve himself from any blame. He started to speak, looked around at the crowd and thought better of what he had planned to say, then began again.

"It is true, I sinned against my kind mother, the empress." Michael stopped and gulped hard, looking around to gauge the impact the admission had on his listeners. "But I've repented and taken the holy vows and tonsure, as I deserve for my wickedness. My kind mother has told me she forgives me. Please, please have mercy." With that, he bent his face to the altar and rested his cheek against it, almost daring the mob to pull him off.

The rabble was slowed by this speech of repentance, but not stopped. The anger and outrage throbbed through the air, thirsting for blood. A few men with spears jabbed their weapons at the two, sometimes pricking the skin and rousing the crowd to greater frenzy as bloody cuts appeared. One woman called out to finish them off.

Suddenly, two soldiers entered with about twenty of the Varangian guards. I recognized among the Varangians the tall blonde guard called Harold who three years earlier had escorted my family to our ship and exile. Grandfather whispered that one of the men was Constantine Cabasilas, the one who had gone to bring Zoe's sister, Theodora, back from her convent.

In the fading light I tried to see who the other man with the Varangians was. His shape looked familiar when I realized with a shock that it was John Comnenus.

Cabasilas ordered Michael and his uncle to leave with him, that the new empress Theodora had ordered it, Zoe conveniently forgotten for the moment. All eyes were on the sobbing men gripping the altar, and I moved out into the little remaining light in the church that came through the windows. John had been speaking to some of the Varangians when my movement caught his attention and he saw me, eyes widening in disbelief. Grandmother pulled me back into the shadows.

"Didn't you see him? That's John down there with the soldiers," I whispered urgently to her.

"I don't care who it is, we need to stay hidden until this mob is gone," her voice edgy at my recklessness.

Michael and his uncle were steadfastly refusing to leave the altar, but none were ready yet to physically remove them from it.

Cabasilas tried another way to remove them willingly from the church, but I think he was lying when he spoke.

"I swear by the Holy Relics of the holy St. John of this Church, and by the Theotokos, that you, Michael, and you, Constantine, will come to no harm, by order of the Empress Theodora. But you must leave with me now," he concluded.

It did no good; they still refused to be moved from their sanctuary. At that, Cabasilas lost all patience. He nodded at the leaders of the mob. The two men were pulled from the altar and dragged, screaming desperately, out to the street in their new monk's robes, sick fear in their cries.

I turned to Grandmother, shaking at what I had witnessed. Her pale face was as shocked as mine. The church grew quieter as the crowds surged through the doors back to the open area outside. Almost without realizing it, we were drawn like iron filings to a magnet, turning to look through the windows at the front of the church down at the scene below.

The mob poked and taunted Michael and his uncle, making ribald jokes about the old eunuch, nicking them with their swords, spinning them around until they fell, weak kneed and dizzy, into a heap. Damp spots on their robes showed the fear they felt. Suddenly a beefy man appeared carrying a brazier with several pokers sticking out of it.

"Phillip, welcome, we have been waiting for you so this party can begin," Cabasilas said with sick humor.

It seemed Michael's uncle recognized the man before Michael did, and let out a horrified moan before falling into an unnatural silence, resigned to his fate. Michael took a few more seconds before he, too, realized the inevitable. Yet he, instead of accepting the punishment as his uncle did, he fought frantically, if unsuccessfully, against it. Several men took pleasure in restraining him with the occasional fist.

Phillip came up to the men with his instruments at the ready, the crowd closing in on them. The view from our vantage point was crystal clear.

Suddenly I heard the eunuch speak, "You there," to Cabasilas, "make the people stand back, so all can see how bravely I bear my punishment?"

Cabasilas looked over the crowd before nodding and people spread back in anticipation of the gory show. The old uncle looked in vain for mercy, before lying down on the cold stones, ready for Phillip's hot irons. Phillip started to bind his victim's arms but Constantine stopped him.

"If you see me flinch, then nail me down. Until then, leave me as I am."

With a shrug, Phillip took up the first of his hot pokers, touching close to first one eye of the man, and then the other. Constantine took his punishment bravely, not moving or screaming at all, despite the agony he must have felt. Michael, seeing his uncle's now blind face, began wailing and struggling more. The grinning soldiers forced him to the ground and bound him more tightly. Still he writhed, trying to escape punishment, forcing more men to grab and hold him down. It was not long, though, before he shrieked like a wounded animal from the first wound.

Voices in the crowd muttered, "Got what he deserved," and "Piece of horse shit," and "Dug up your bones." Most approved what happened, but a few of the women fell back in shock.

Still they were not finished. Another anguished scream rose from the man who had been emperor, as the poker pierced his other eye. I stood mesmerized until the mob's cheering broke the spell, and I turned around. Someone put his arms around me as Michael's anguished cries echoed in the square.

The ghastly job completed, the mob dissipated like a morning mist on the Marmara. It had had its fill of blood and laughed in satisfaction at their accomplishments. Monks emerged from the monastery to tend the two blind men in the street, leading them to its infirmary to bind up their wounds.

I finally looked up and realized it was not Grandfather's arms around me as I had thought, but John's. I leaned against him in relief, wiping my tears on his shirt.

CHAPTER EIGHT

Empress Zoe

May 1042

We waited until the crowd dispersed, its violence exhausted, before descending to the nave and departing the church. The empty square held only a shameful silence and the smell of burnt flesh sour in the air. The revolting sight of scattered bits of discarded charcoal hard by the stains of urine and shit where the two men had been held were the last things I remember before leaning against a wall and vomiting. Grandmother and John stood on either side of me, holding me steady as waves of dizziness flooded me.

I trembled with delayed shock, and tears ran down my cheeks. John looked over and gently wiped my face with his sleeve.

"It will be all right, my little Anna. The worst is over," he murmured.

I looked up at John and asked through my chattering teeth, "How did you happen to be here today? I thought you would be with your sister."

He smiled ironically. "I could ask you the same question. I thought you would've been at your house."

I explained to him Grandfather's thoughts about the rioters and our attempt to find a safe haven at the monastery. He gave a short laugh.

"And instead you walked straight into the hornets' nest. The emperor was an idiot. If he'd had any sense he would have sailed far away from here," he said, shaking his head as we walked back to our house. "I'd gone out to see if the rioting was spreading into Donya's neighborhood. A friend of mine saw me and insisted I join him and the other soldiers. I learned of the plan to blind them on the way to Stoudion."

"Was that the only thing they could do? They'd been tonsured. Couldn't they have been exiled the way my family was?" My teeth still chattered but the trembling had diminished.

John regarded me with sympathy before explaining. "It's the only way to be sure that Zoe won't put him back on the throne next to her. People know she's soft hearted, or maybe soft-headed. She might've found a way to bring him back if he was just tonsured or in exile on some island in the Aegean. No emperor can be blind, so he'll never be back."

He continued ruefully, "If I had a choice, I don't know that I'd choose blinding over death, but some say it is preferable."

"Why didn't his uncle make a sound, but Michael howled? I've never heard anything so horrible." The words would almost not come out from between my clenched teeth, the taste of vomit still in my mouth.

John looked down at the paving stones as we walked. "His uncle must've known that the poker only has to be close to the eye to blind it, it doesn't actually have to touch it. When the prisoner struggles, as Michael did, it's more likely to pierce the eye. When the poker pierces the eyes, it's worse. The man can develop a fever. Often he dies."

I grew silent.

We reached home close to sunset. John sat talking to Uncle Costas and my grandparents while I went upstairs to wash and change into a fresh dress. I felt almost myself again after a few sips of wine, when John said he had to leave.

John and I lingered a minute in the shadows outside the door. Leo had lit only one outside lantern that evening.

"I'm sorry you witnessed that scene. It was horrible," John said gently. He leaned against the side of the house, arms crossed on his chest, giving me a pensive look.

"People can be so cruel."

John gave a short laugh then, and shook his head, "Bad as that was, there's worse in the world." He stood up and moved closer to me. "But it's over now. You should try and forget it." He looked down at me, his hand reaching for mine.

We stood gazing intently at each other for a long moment before I found myself in his arms, being kissed for the first time on that April night with the moon coming out. I don't know if it was the danger we had just been through that made me forget how Grandmother expected me to behave, or if I had just waited long enough, but his lips were warm, and his arms were strong around me. I forgot the blindings.

It was a long kiss, and I felt wanton in the pleasure of it. When it ended, we stood locked together, joyfully drinking in the sight of each other. We reluctantly broke apart when we heard Alethea coming to find me.

A quizzical eyebrow raised, she opened the door to the house to see us standing on the steps. Alethea gave me a look, then said, "Don't be long, dinner is almost on the table," before turning back into the house, the door ajar.

John was standing close again, cupping my chin in his hand.

"I think we need to get the betrothal negotiations finished soon," he said in a husky voice, and kissed me again.

"I think so, too," I said, my voice sounding distant to me. He turned and was gone.

Returning inside, I went to the library where my elders were discussing the events of the past few days.

"I cannot believe the mess Zoe has gotten herself into," Grandfather said, shaking his head. His hand trembled as he poured himself a cup of wine. "Even more, I cannot believe we ended up in the worst place in the city to be today."

Uncle Costas' laugh sounded world weary. He finished his cup and refilled it. "Adrian, don't blame yourself. How could we know Michael would be so stupid as to sail to Stoudion? He should have gone to Thessalonica or Athens. As for Zoe, not to excuse her, but she wasn't taught how to rule the empire. Even so, she made a mess of things."

"Maybe it was a mistake to allow a woman to inherit the throne," Damien commented.

"So instead we should have a man on the throne like that young fool now in Stoudion's infirmary?" Grandmother asked acerbically. She looked over at Damien with a narrowed eye. "There have been several woman who have ruled the empire when their husband or son couldn't, and managed better than Zoe or either of her husbands. Not to boast of my one grandchild," she said, gesturing at me, "but Anna could have done a better job."

I blushed and sat down at the chess table, still floating from John's kiss. "Oh, Grandmother," I protested. "Don't say that. All I want is to get married and have children."

"Well, I think you would be superb at it, given the chance. You're much smarter than Zoe," said Uncle Costas, giving me a conspiratorial wink from across the room.

"Hmm," said Damien, "that wouldn't take much."

Nicholas came in and announced dinner. I felt pinned on the twin horns of queasiness from the blinding, and euphoria from John's kiss and could eat little. I excused myself after a few bites and went to bed, pleading exhaustion. Sleep did not come easily.

As much as we wanted to finalize the betrothal contract, events in the following weeks conspired against us. Zoe was back on the throne, joined by her younger sister, Theodora as co-empress. The sisters had an uneasy peace during these weeks, outwardly congenial despite their long sibling rivalry.

The two Emperor Michaels' many relatives had sprouted out like weeds among the empire's offices. The first order of business was to pull them out and send them back to rot in Paphlagonia where they came from. Soldiers and those loyal to Zoe and Theodora received new assignments. John's friend, Cabasilas who he'd joined the day of the riot was sent to Greece; George Maniakes, dispatched to Italy's troubled shores. Gifts of gold coins fell into the laps of those who had stayed loyal to Zoe.

John stopped by when he could. There was some talk of Isaac, and so too John, being sent to the East, perhaps to Antioch, but nothing announced yet. Rumors flew as numerous as the hungry seagulls soaring over the docks.

The most tantalizing speculation was about whom Empress Zoe would marry, since it was clear she could not manage on her own. At first it was said she would marry a court official, a man named Constantine Artoklines. But he died suddenly, some said by his wife's hand who, the gossip said, would rather be a widow than divorced and living out her days in a monastery. Guesses abounded about who would be Zoe's next choice.

One afternoon I was in Grandmother's workroom going over menus and the kitchen's accounts with her. After we finished, I didn't rise to leave, but continued sitting across from her, nervous about broaching the question.

She gave me a quizzical look. "Is there something else?"

"Yes, I wanted to ask if you knew when John and I will be betrothed?" I spoke in a nervous rush. "It's past Easter and it hasn't happened yet." At seventeen I felt certain I was the oldest person ever to be unmarried outside a convent or a brothel.

"My, you are impatient," she said with a knowing smile. "In fact, your grandfather and I are planning to visit the farm in a few days. We haven't been there since we returned, and it's time we checked on how the steward's been managing. We thought we'd bring back wine, cheeses, olives, and other supplies that we could use at the betrothal celebration."

"Oh, that's wonderful," I said in grateful relief. It meant I might have just a few weeks to wait. "I can't wait to see it again." I loved the farm in Thrace, with its hills covered in dusky green olive trees and its orchard full of ripe fruits.

"Well, you won't be going. I thought this would be a good opportunity for you to take sole responsibility for running the household while we are gone. We thought Damien might enjoy seeing it again, but Costas will stay here with you."

Disappointed though I was at staying behind, I thought this a good sign for an imminent betrothal.

A few days later, they departed on the two-day journey, down the Via Egnatia would take them about halfway to Adrianople, near the town of Tzouroulon where the farm lay. With at least a week to see to their affairs, they would be gone for almost two weeks. Plenty of time for me to demonstrate how ready I was to run my own household.

After my initial troubles with Alethea, we had settled into a respectful, if sometimes tense, pattern of interaction. The stable boy, Patricios, had gone with my grandparents to care for the horses and donkeys, leaving Nicholas and old Leo behind.

Nicholas acted sulky after my grandparents left. I often had trouble finding him during the day, getting excuses once I finally did locate him. The explanations were barely plausible, and he clearly did not respect me, often checking with my uncle on my instructions. It irritated me, but I was not sure how to handle the situation.

A couple of days after later, I was in Grandmother's office making notes on her accounts when I looked up and saw a visitor in court attire ride a horse into our courtyard. Surprisingly, Nicholas appeared out of nowhere to greet the man, before coming inside to announce him.

I got up and went to the entry to find out who the man was looking for when Nicholas walked past, ignoring me.

"Nicholas, who is that man outside?" I said, irritated at his rudeness.

He slowed and turned back to me, his face looking as though he had sucked a lemon, "It's a messenger from the palace. He's wants to speak with General Dalassenus," before continuing to the empty library.

He returned after realizing it was unoccupied. "Do you know where he is?" he said rudely.

"Yes, I do," I said, irritated. "Please ask the messenger to come in here."

"Yes, Lady Anna," Nicholas responded, red in the face, realizing he had gone too far.

Uncle Costas was in the garden, sitting in the sun on a bench, reading Thucydides.

"Uncle Costas," I said as I peered at him around the rose trellis, full of tiny green buds, a few bees humming about the bush. "There's a messenger come from the palace who wants to speak with you."

He slowly looked up at me, with an eyebrow raised, an odd sour expression on his face. He carefully shut the book, stood up and started to the house. He looked back at me when I did not follow.

"Anna, you must come with me," he said in a strained voice.

Startled, I hurried to join him.

The man saluted my uncle and began, "General Dalassenus, the Empress Zoe sent me to request that you wait upon her this afternoon. I'm to escort you to the palace."

Uncle Costas stood before the messenger, hands clasped behind his back. He looked pale at the messenger's words, before giving a short nod of assent. "I'll be pleased to accompany you. I'll need to bring my niece as well. My brother and his wife are away and have left her in my care. I don't want to leave her alone."

The man looked startled at that, but clearly could not think of a reason to refuse. I was surprised, too, but my uncle's attitude did not invite questions.

Uncle Costas glanced at Nicholas, hovering in a distant doorway. "Nicholas, please take this man to the kitchen and see that Alethea finds some refreshment for him. Lady Anna and I will need to change into clothing appropriate for the palace."

"Yes, General," came a respectful response and Nicholas escorted the soldier to the kitchen.

I stood gaping at my uncle.

"Anna, would you please ask Leo to saddle a donkey for me and order a sedan chair for you? Then we'll both have to change into clothes fit for a visit with an Empress."

When I did not move, still stunned, he spoke sharply, "Quickly."

Within an hour I returned downstairs in my red silk tunic, hair brushed and arranged carefully under the maphorion I wore to church by Maria, who was almost as excited as I was.

Uncle Costas appeared a few minutes later looking resplendent. His tall, lean frame, slightly bent with age, filled the blue tunic, embroidered with a key pattern in red along the hems, and darker blue bracca underneath the tunic. His dark leather boots and the armor he wore, saved for formal occasions shone as though new. His white hair and beard, carefully combed, may have been an old man's, but his dignified bearing was not.

"Uncle, you look splendid!" I said, wide-eyed with appreciation. "The empress will be impressed."

"As she will with you, too, my dear," he replied with a tight smile. "Shall we depart?" he asked, putting an arm out to escort me.

"Oh, yes uncle, and thank you for bringing me. I've never been there."

"Well, then, it is about time you saw its inner workings."

We left, the messenger leading the way on one of the palace's geldings.

We hadn't been traveling for long before, peeking out from behind the chair's curtains, I noticed the attention we received due to the imperial escort. People stopped what they were doing and stared, then turning to their friends to discuss the sight. Occasionally a soldier would call out, hailing Uncle Costas, and he would nod or wave in reply.

Eventually we reached the same palace gate where Michael had made the speech that led to his blinding. The gate itself was sturdy, made of thick wooden panels and with iron hinges and the double-headed eagle shield gleaming in the sun.

Uncle straightened his clothes, brushing off the road's dust. He glanced at the stately buildings towering over the walls. "Something you'll notice about the palace—most of it is old, very old. Almost none of it's less than a hundred years old."

The Great Palace was not just a single building, but a city within the city. The Boukoleon Palace was the Empress' main residence and the building at the water's edge I remembered sailing past the night we were exiled. There were churches, residences for the imperial family as well as for soldiers, the palace eunuchs, and servants, gardens, stables, a theater, the purple room where empresses gave birth, and the great golden audience hall—the Chrysotriklinos.

The sentries on watch let us pass through the gate and we followed the messenger onto the palace grounds. Uncle Costas was right—the buildings were old. The mortar had softened with age, with some walls sagging slightly outwards like a bent old man. The marbled pathways we walked held unrepaired cracks with small green weeds stark against the white stone.

We passed through gardens where a couple of gardeners were working, before reaching an inner wall where another sentry looked us over before allowing us to pass through its gate into the Gallery of the Forty Holy Martyrs.

This porticoed walkway extended from an inner wall to the Chrysotriklinos. Brilliant mosaics on its curved ceiling told the story of the forty Roman soldiers who became Christian and were martyred not long before the great Constantine became emperor. Each scene in the story was separated by an arch with a hanging oil lamp, unlit at that time of the day. The doomed faces of the holy martyrs, even with their glittering golden halos, seemed designed to heighten the anxiety of anyone meeting with an emperor or empress.

At the end of the gallery lay the entrance to the Chrysotriklinos where the empress would see us. The doorkeeper peered around the polished silver doors as we reached the entrance, as though he had been watching for us.

"General Dalassenus," he said, giving my uncle a warm smile in greeting. "So good to see you again."

"Hector, it's been a long time," Uncle Costas replied, patting the man on the back. "I'm glad to see some things haven't changed." He gave the man a weak smile.

Hector regarded me with curiosity. "General," he began, "umm, I believe it was only you that the empress called for."

"Hector, this is my niece, the granddaughter of my brother Adrian. Her name is Anna. I will have her accompany me to the audience," Uncle Costas insisted.

Hector raised an eyebrow, but then shrugged as though everyone brought their niece to audiences with the empress, and disappeared through another set of silver doors to announce our arrival.

"Uncle, I'd be all right if you'd rather I stay out here," I murmured. I did not want to contradict him in front of the doorkeeper. Just being inside the Great Palace was exciting enough.

"No," he said definitely, looking directly into my eyes. "I want you with me. You are not to leave me in there, even if the empress herself orders it. Make a scene if you need to. Pretend you're still upset from the blinding, or something. Anything. Do you understand?"

"Yes, Uncle," I replied, feeling confused.

Hector was gone for a few minutes, apparently receiving his instructions. Unlike some other parts of the Great Palace, this room glittered like a gem. I gaped in awe of the magnificent mosaics covering the walls and ceiling. Exquisitely rendered roses, anemones, poppies and others I could not recognize encrusted the walls, each panel framed with silver borders and polished to a glittering sheen. Above them on the ceiling were biblical scenes, including the crowning of David, the Annunciation and Transfiguration. The most impressive one was a rendering of Jesus, dressed in Pentecostal red flame-colored robes, surrounded in gold, his arms outstretched.

Finally, Hector returned and escorted us through the double silver doors and into the audience chamber, our footsteps sounding hollow on the vast room's walls. A secretary greeted us with a warm smile, showing us where to make our prostrations. Empress Zoe sat on her throne on a dais raised up four steps from where we stood. The stunning gold chair glistened like a beacon in the night and appeared larger than what a small woman such as the empress needed. I hardly dared look at her and kept my eyes downcast as we approached, a few steps behind my uncle. We reached the dais and prostrated ourselves before her, heads bent low. The empress's rose perfume filled the room.

I glanced up at this woman who inherited the world's greatest empire. The exquisite gown of imperial purple silk embroidered in gold and red, with slippers of the same red color, were of the finest quality. A belt of braided gold cords circled a slender waist, and she wore a maphorion of the sheerest purple silk, over which lay a gold crown studded with jewels and pearl pendants dangling at the sides of her oval face. I had to stop myself from staring at her face, though, which had an unnatural white pallor, with pink shadows painted on her cheeks. Talk in the city was that she busied herself devising cosmetics to stay youthful, but to me her coloring looked more peculiar than youthful.

She glanced over at me with a frown. "General, who is this accompanying you? I asked only for your presence."

"Your majesty, I brought my orphaned niece, Anna, with me. Her grandparents, my brother Adrian and his wife, left her in my care while they are in the country. I could not leave her alone at home," came Uncle Costas's circumspect answer.

The empress sniffed at that, but appeared to decide me not worthy of further attention.

I stood and backed up into the shadows next to the wall. Two ladies from the empress's household stood discreetly in the back, while a young soldier guarded what must have been the doorway to the palace. Light sifting through the high alabaster windows in the dome illuminated the mosaics with their gold tesserae covering the walls. An enormous gold chandelier hung cleverly suspended from the dome's oculus, its oil lamps unlit but unneeded in the sunlight. It was obvious why the building was called the golden reception hall.

I looked again at Zoe's secretary, a man with a beaky nose and receding chin standing at a desk on the other side of the room. I realized I had seen him before. He was the man who had accused Emperor Michael of faithlessness at Stoudion just before the blinding. He whispered some bit of information in Zoe's ear. He then returned to his desk while giving my uncle an ingratiating smile.

The empress began addressing Uncle Costas, an almost girlish smile on her painted face. "General, I want to express my gratitude to you for all of your service to the empire. Your devotion to the empire and my family throughout your life has been honorable and noteworthy."

Uncle Costas turned red, but stood motionless before the throne.

"At this time I would ask that you consider doing us further service. I have recently been reminded that my beloved father thought first that I should wed you when he sensed his time on this earth was coming to an end, so that you might rule by my side. Unfortunately, death approached faster than he expected and as you were some distance away, he chose another for me." She tactfully didn't mention the name of the husband people said she had murdered. "Since I am again in need of a husband to rule at my side, I thought to return to you of whom my dear father thought so well and first proposed." She looked down at him, smiling as though at a fish on her dinner plate, ready for eating.

My mouth gaped at her suggestion and the honor it would mean to our family, even if my uncle did have to be married to this foolish woman. Looking at him, though, Uncle Costas's face had the same flat expression he had when he was about to put me in checkmate.

"Your majesty, you honor me greatly with your memories. I am blessed by your gratitude. Your illustrious uncle, Emperor Basil, was always appreciative, especially for the ten years I spent exiled from my home and family in Egypt." He paused, clearing his throat.

"I did not experience that same degree of gratitude from your previous husbands," he said dryly. His stance relaxed slightly, and he looked down thoughtfully at the mosaics that covered the floor of the dais, a scroll pattern with animals depicted intermittently.

The empress blinked and turned even paler, if that was possible with her cosmetics. The sound of the secretary's scratching across his parchment echoed.

Suddenly Uncle Costas looked up and gave a warm, brilliant smile to the empress. "I recall the first time I saw you when we were both young. You and your sisters were with your father and Emperor Basil, in procession to the Hagia Sophia at Easter. My father and brothers and I were so honored to be in that procession. I must say, I think you are as lovely now as you were then."

Well, that sounded like nothing more than outright flattery to me. The empress might not look like the old fishwife down the road, but she was not a young woman anymore. Anyone could see that.

The empress ventured a cautious smile at the compliment.

"Your majesty, I think you might want to reconsider your proposal." Uncle spoke carefully as he reached up to stroke his white beard. "You know I am a soldier, as your uncle was. I have lived the same hard life as he did and would be inclined to rule with the same stern hand that he did for the many years he reigned. I am an old man who cannot change his ways. Since you came to the throne, you may have become accustomed to more, ah, independence."

He was turning the empress down. I was not sure that was even possible. My uncle would be as strong and good an emperor as Basil had been. It wasn't my place to say it, but I wanted to speak up to him, tell him to say yes. He could not realize what this would mean, for himself and the family.

The empress leaned back, eyes narrowed and mouth pursed. She had spent long years confined to the gynaeceum before her father's death, and until recently the Orphanotrophus and his brothers had locked her in again. No one would wish to return to such restrictions.

"As I said, you do me great honor at your proposal, but I fear that it has been many years since you were ruled by a soldier, with soldier's ways, and I hold you in too great esteem to desire that you be returned to the dominance of one with my simple tastes," Uncle Costas finished.

The empress' mouth hung open at uncle's speech, which almost implied she herself was declining her own proposal. Silently I prayed he would change his mind, but after a few moments of staring down at him, she spoke.

"Undoubtedly you are correct, General Dalassenus. I have grown used to my freedom and comforts. Thank you for making this visit to the palace and I wish you well." Glaring at my uncle she made a motion of dismissal. I hastily dipped into a deep curtsey and moved to leave this room with the cloying scent of roses.

The secretary's pen scratched, and he glanced up at us dismissively, so different from his obsequious welcome. My uncle ignored him and held out his arm for me to take.

We left the audience chamber and passed the bemused Hector, bidding him a polite farewell, on our walk back to the gate where we had left the donkey and sedan chair.

"Uncle, what. . ." I started to say, before he stopped me, finger to my lips.

"All questions will wait until we are home," he whispered.

We didn't attract as much attention on the Mese without our imperial escort. The traffic did not give way as it had on our way to the palace, so the return trip took longer. I tried urging the sedan carriers to go faster through the crowds, to little avail. I needed to know why my uncle had declined to marry the empress.

We finally reached our gates and my uncle returned his donkey to Leo's care after paying for my chair.

Uncle Costas gave me a glance and said, "Let's go inside." I followed him up the steps to the door and through to the library, where he poured a glass of wine from the jug kept there.

"I was afraid I wouldn't get out of there," he said, looking tired and older than when we had left for the palace. He sat down heavily in a chair by the window overlooking the gardens, looking intently into his cup.

"Uncle," I began urgently, eyeing him with frustration. "What happened back there in the palace? Why didn't you accept Zoe's offer of marriage?" anger in my voice. He sat staring at his wine, avoiding me. "Did you know she would ask you?"

Finally shooting me a look, he said, "I thought it likely, yes," then swirled the wine in his cup. "I just wanted to decline the honor without paying for it with my life. Of course, I might have paid for the honor with my life if I had accepted. Amorous empresses can be dangerous creatures."

"Uncle, you know you would have been a wonderful emperor, much better than her other husbands," I protested, my voice rising with frustration. "You should have accepted her proposal. You know, you know it would have helped Xene. How could you not accept?"

"Anna, I'm an old man, much older even than the empress. Do you want me to spend my little remaining time worrying that my wife might poison me or drown me in the bath?" his anger flaring to match mine. "Nor do I want to waste my time trying to rein in that foolish woman's spending on frippery and potions. I would wear myself out to the point of death before even the next new year arrives trying to rule the empire. What would be the point of becoming emperor then, when she'd just have to find another husband a few months later?" he finished grimly.

"You don't know that. You could outlive her," I said, my hands curled into fists. Even so, I had to admit the old man tremors in his hands were more obvious each day.

"Have you thought about what it might mean for my children?" he asked suddenly calmer, in the voice that had explained the logic of a chessboard to me.

"Yes, it would mean Constantine Ducas would have to let Xene see you, that he would have to let her attend court functions and put away the ugly clothes he makes her wear," I said. "He would have to treat her better. You could make him, if you were emperor."

He gave an unpleasant snort of unamused laughter. "Perhaps for a while. You do realize Damien might become Zoe's heir? No, I can see you didn't. You know what that would mean?"

I shook my head.

"It would make Damien and his family the targets for many ambitious men, Ducas first among them. That man has an old family name, alliances with some generals, he's a senator, and he's married to my daughter—he would think himself a more fitting heir than Damien. Do you think he would hesitate to find some way to be rid of my son and his family?" His voice reeked of bitterness at his earlier misjudgment of the man.

"And once he's disposed of Damien and his children, Xene's life would be short. Ducas wants children and it doesn't appear that Xene can give him any."

I stopped short at this assessment, unable to assail his logic, but unwilling to concede.

"But if you were emperor, couldn't you. . ." I began.

"It may look as though an emperor is all powerful, but there are more limits than you might imagine. You know Damien is sick of city politics, has no desire to live here, and certainly no desire to inherit the throne. He wants his children to grow up in peace, not worrying they might be murdered," he stopped, looking so much older than I had seen him before.

I felt sick with frustration at an opportunity that was nothing but a trap. My uncle had strategized this game with the empress much as he did chess with me—looking ahead at how his opponent might move. Only this time he had had the empress sitting across the board from him, with Ducas in the background.

I shook my head with disappointment before I suddenly remembered the other man in the audience chamber.

"Uncle, who was that man in the audience chamber with us? I've seen him before."

"Him? Oh, that's Zoe's secretary, Michael Psellus. Where did you see him before?" he asked, rising stiffly from his chair and reaching for the wine jug.

"At Stoudion, that day . . ." I couldn't quite get the words out.

"Oh, yes, I'd forgotten, that was him there," he raised an eyebrow in grim recollection of that event. "He's always been devoted to Zoe. Well, I'm not sure anyone can be really devoted to that stupid woman. He's more devoted to his position in the palace."

"Do you know him?" I asked. Uncle Costas seemed oddly familiar with the man.

"I do." Uncle had a sour look on his face, mouth twisted. "Xene hired him to tutor Ducas in oratory. They became friendly. I would not be surprised if Ducas had put Psellus up to make this suggestion to the empress. Psellus probably sent word to my son-in-law before we'd left the palace grounds of my decision."

I sat down at the chess table trying to understand what had really happened before thinking to ask, "Why did you insist that I stay with you?"

"The empress believes her womanly charms to be greater than they are. I thought with you in the room, there was less chance of an unwelcome advance on her part," he said wryly.

"Oh," I said, grimacing at the thought of that painted old woman trying to seduce my aged uncle.

I continued sitting, looking out the window to the gardens sloping down to the river. Gaudy spring flowers bloomed that day and the vegetables had begun sprouting, giving the air a promising and fecund scent.

"I keep hoping things might get better for Xene." I felt powerless before the impossible choices presented.

"Anna," he said, raising his hands to rub or wipe his eyes. "I think about that everyday. There is nothing, absolutely nothing, I regret more in my life than offering that man a place in my army all those years ago. If I hadn't, and she hadn't become besotted with him, I would have married her to someone else. I pay for that mistake everyday."

CHAPTER NINE

Eudokia M.

May 1042

The word of my uncle talking the empress out of a marriage proposal quickly spread in the city. Arriving in the women's gallery for the liturgy at Stoudion's church two days later, some of the women gave me sidelong looks and whispered to each other. The men below did the same to Uncle Costas as he strode to the front. He ignored them, focusing his attention on the priests and the icons, the picture of faithful devotion. The priests soon processed in, accompanied by monks' hymns and rising incense, and the whispering subsided.

Irene Pegonitissa, a girl I had known prior to our exile, stopped to speak to me as I left the service. She was a few years older than I was and did not have a hearty constitution, frequently ailing, although she appeared well that day. It surprised me that she would take the trouble to stop me since we had never been close.

"Anna," she said, delicately clearing her throat, "it's good to see you. You must be glad to be back." She rearranged her maphorion, which had slipped from her shoulder.

"Thank you, Irene. I am."

We emerged from the church. My uncle stood circled by a group of men in the square outside the church. He waved briefly at me. Irene saw me wave back at him and peered at him.

"Is that your uncle? The one who's been in prison? I've heard much about him from John."

"Yes, that's my Uncle Costas. John has spoken to you about him?" I asked, curious about why my John would have spoken with her.

"Oh, hadn't you heard? I am betrothed to John Ducas. We're to be married in September." She had the self-satisfied look of a cat after consuming a tasty bit of prey.

I looked sharply at Irene on hearing the Ducas name. I'd heard nothing of John Ducas since our return, and would have been pleased never to hear of him again. Still, Irene must be relieved to be getting married. She had to be at least twenty or twenty-one years old.

"Congratulations, Irene. I'm happy to hear your news," I stammered out.

"Thank you," she replied. Then she came to the real reason for our encounter. "I heard your uncle was considered as a husband for the empress. Is that true?"

Rather than pretend ignorance, I gave her the politic version of the event.

"Yes, she did speak with him about that, but the empress decided he would not be a husband to her taste. I accompanied him to the palace and saw her. She is quite beautiful." A bit of a stretch to say that, but if gossip was to circulate, might as well limit the potential damage.

"I've never seen the empress, but I've heard she is," she looked envious of my visit to the palace. "You don't think she was angry with your uncle, do you?"

"She said nothing that made me think she was angry," I replied. True enough, Zoe had not had angry words for him, but perhaps I was stretching the truth.

"That's good," she said, looking relieved. "Since I'll be marrying John, and his brother is married to your uncle's daughter, any trouble might have delayed the wedding. My father said if John or his brother has problems with the palace, then he'll put it off."

I looked at Irene thinking that at her age she must be more desperate to wed than I was. John Ducas was not as attractive as his brother, nor did he come with great wealth. And my experience of his personality had not been happy, recalling my encounter in the prison with him. Irene's mother gestured to her to leave, and we parted.

I glanced at Uncle Costas who looked to be regaling the men around him with the story of our palace visit. As I waited for him to finish I noticed a young girl, maybe about twelve years old, standing near a group of women. Her clothes were clean but shabby with wear. The child had a sweet, appealing expression on a lovely face surrounded with wavy blond hair. She turned and smiled at me.

I smiled back at her.

"Hello," I said. "I should introduce myself. My name is Anna Dalassena."

She frowned, her forehead wrinkling in concentration. "You're a relation of Constantine Dalassenus?"

"Yes, he's my uncle. You see he is over there," I added, pointing at him. I wondered if anyone had not heard of our visit to the empress.

She looked his way, but I could tell she didn't know which of the men in his group was my uncle.

"My name is Eudokia Makrembolitissa." she stopped, her mouth twisting into a sour knot, unsure how to continue. "We come here to can see my father. He's a monk here."

"Oh, I see." I did understand. In normal times, few men would leave their wife and young child to be tonsured as a monk. Elderly people, widowed men and women, would often be tonsured and take religious vows to live in a peaceful monastery in their last years. Not usually young ones. However, it had happened more often in the years when the Orphanotrophus ruled.

"Some Sundays we go to Hagia Sophia, where my uncle is," she said.

"When were they tonsured?" I asked Eudokia, with some sympathy.

"Maybe two years since they were accused. . ." she trailed off. After a moment, she continued, "Now my mother and I live with my aunt's family."

"I am sorry for your losses," I said. Looking at the bright-eyed child, I asked, "Did you see your father today, with the other monks?"

The girl brightened at the reminder. "Yes, I did. He looked up at us and winked as they left the church."

"I'm sure he misses you very much," I told her.

A young boy came up then. "Eudokia, it's time to go," he told her.

Eudokia joined her mother before turning to wave at me.

Later, on our walk back home, I asked my uncle about the girl.

"The girl's father is John Makrembolites, and her uncle is Michael Keroularios, both of them pretty good soldiers. I heard in prison that they were part of a scheme to overthrow the Orphanotrophus, but the group was caught on the verge of executing it. They both lost everything they owned, were forced to take monk's vows, and be tonsured."

"You and grandfather didn't get forced into that."

"The difference was we didn't actually do anything, just spoke more openly than everyone else did. John Makrembolites and Michael Keroularios were caught in the act of bringing soldiers into the city. They were fortunate the patriarch interceded for them. They would've been blinded otherwise."

"Oh," I said, queasy at the thought of a blinding.

"Now John's daughter is growing up without her father. And he's a young man, used to having a wife, and the freedom to come and go as he desires. It must be as difficult to accustom yourself to the discipline of the monastery as a prison, but better than blinding I suppose," Uncle Costas mused. "The lesson to learn from them is if you decide to rebel, make a foolproof plan. Or be ready for the consequences."

My grandparents and Damien were still in the country. I wondered what they would think about Uncle Costas' news when they returned. And now every time Alethea and I went out to shop for food all that people were speaking about were the latest rumors about who Zoe would marry.

I paid little attention to all of the talk, being focused on my impending betrothal and wedding. I was, that is, until midweek when we received unexpected callers. John's sister and sister-in-law, Donya and Catherine, visited with the intention of speaking with Grandmother, but finding she was away, asked to speak with Uncle Costas and me.

They looked flushed and agitated as they sat down in our library, accepting my offer of wine.

"General," Catherine began, with a furtive glance at me then my uncle, "we've heard some talk about you of late."

My uncle flushed at Catherine's statement, but he said nothing, only giving a slight nod.

"We heard that Empress Zoe proposed marriage to you," her eyes bored into him, intent on his answer. "The word on the street is that you turned her down," she finished in a rush.

"Is what we heard true?" Donya added nervously in her soft voice.

I could see Uncle Costas' jaw clench as he regarded the two women and thought about his response. After a few moments, he spoke with deliberation.

"The empress did summon me to the palace last week, and we did have a short discussion about whether or not I would be a suitable candidate to be her husband. But in the end she came to the conclusion that I would not be. Then we left."

"What do you mean, "we" left? Who was with you?" Catherine asked.

"I was with him," I said. Uncle Costas' look at me said I should have been silent; let him do the talking.

Their eyes widened to the size of plates at that.

My uncle cleared his throat before saying, "With her grandparents visiting their farm, I was loath to leave Anna alone in the house and insisted she accompany me."

The two of them sat in unsettled silence for a few moments before they exchanged glances and rose.

"We won't trouble you any longer, but we will want to see Anna's grandparents when they return. When did you say they would be back?" Catherine asked.

Uncle Costas and I rose to our feet.

"I expect them back in the next day or two," he said in an even voice.

My uncle's face was red and he looked irritable when he came back in the house. He gave me a hard look before returning to the library where he sat down, poured a cup of wine, and began drumming his fingers on the table. I followed him into the room, trying to puzzle out what had happened.

"Uncle, why were Catherine and Donya asking about the empress? It had nothing to do with them." I looked toward the courtyard they had just left.

Finally he put the cup down saying, "Can't say. We'll find out once your grandparents return."

The next day my grandparents and Damien arrived, their cart laden with wine, cheese, nuts and honey from their farm. It was the longest I'd ever been apart from them, and I was glad to see them.

The news of our visit to the palace shocked them. I realized that while Uncle Costas had suspected he might be summoned, he had only shared that premonition with Damien.

"Anna, you went too?" asked Grandmother, her glance moving from Uncle Costas to me. "Were you nervous?"

"A little," I answered. "But there was so much to see, I was only nervous when we were in the Chrysotriklinos with the empress. And even then, I just stood at the back while Uncle Costas spoke to her."

Her brows creased in a worried look, before she said, "You should help Alethea with unloading the cart and putting everything away. We've brought back a lot."

I did not understand then why she looked so anxious.

The next morning, I was in Grandmother's study, going over the household accounts for the time she'd been gone, when I looked up at the sound of horses riding into the courtyard.

"Grandmother, it's John, and Isaac's with him."

She frowned and left to find Grandfather. I went to the door, excited to see my soon to-be-betrothed.

John and Isaac, however, entered without smiling, their faces dark. John only looked me in the eye for a moment before glancing away. I had the strange feeling something unpleasant was about to occur, but tried to push it away. We entered the library where my grandparents and Uncle Costas waited.

Greetings exchanged, Isaac sat on the edge of his chair, looking down uncomfortably at his hands clasped together, pursing his lips as he decided what to say. Finally he looked up at me, then Uncle Costas.

"Costas, you know I have the utmost respect for you and your family. I was pleased at the prospect of John's betrothal to your niece, who's a lovely young woman." He inclined his head towards me.

He then gave my grandparents a direct look. "But recent events have left my wife and sister with serious concerns about whether the betrothal should be announced now, or put off for a time," he said apologetically.

I felt as though I'd been struck. "What, what do you mean, some concerns?" I stammered.

John looked at me and spoke then, gently, "Catherine's concerned because of her brother's rebellion. She worried about her children when that happened. Donya's husband is already out of favor with the palace because of the mess in Italy, so she's worried for her children. If we were betrothed now, with your uncle's refusal to marry the empress, both are fearful she might inflict some further retribution on anyone related to him."

"But he didn't actually refuse her. Uncle Costas tell them. . ." I started to say, turning to him. They needed to understand that.

He just sat there, red faced, rubbing the back of his neck and shaking his head.

"Anna, I'm sorry. I didn't expect this to cause you any problems." His face was flushed with embarrassment.

Grandfather finally spoke, "Anna, they have valid concerns. Zoe could hurt them or their children. You wouldn't want John's family to suffer because of our family—a bad start to a marriage. A short delay to let Zoe forget, and the betrothal can happen. You'll see."

I barely heard what Isaac was saying then, something about Antioch. I flew out of the room refusing to hear any more excuses, any more betrayals. Now I knew why Catherine and Donya had paid that odd visit to us, but they sent John and Isaac to give us the bad news. I pushed open the door to the garden and ran down to the willow tree by the river. The sun shone down on its soft green leaves, oblivious to my distress. I recalled my condescending thoughts a few days earlier towards Irene Pegonitissa, soon to be wed at the ancient age of twenty or twenty-one. A sin of pride that I would have to confess. The way matters were going, I would be lucky to be married by the time I was her age, if ever.

I wiped my eyes with my sleeve. If I ever did marry and had children, I would not let any of my children go through what I was going through. I would not.

I could hear approaching footsteps, but didn't turn to see who it was. I was so upset, I didn't want to talk to anyone. The person stopped a short distance away, not saying anything for a few moments.

"Do you know when I first thought that I would marry you?"

"I don't know that you will be," I replied tersely, refusing to look at John. "Go away."

Undeterred, he continued. "The first time I saw you coming down the steps at your cousin's house. You see, I'd wanted to find a wife. I didn't want to marry and have children as an old man, the way my father did. He never saw us grow up and I want that. And I wanted to marry someone I knew first. Isaac and Catherine were betrothed as children. They never had a choice, and hardly knew each other when they wed, and well... But when I saw you, I knew you were the one."

I turned to him then, angry at his words. "If you knew I was the one, then perhaps you should have stood up for me."

"Anna, it's only a delay, not the end. You'll see, we'll soon be betrothed and married," a soft, pleading look in his blue eyes. He stepped toward me, but I waved him away.

"Maybe it is the end. Maybe someone else won't have your family's qualms. I'm seventeen, I can't wait forever." His inability to stand up for us infuriated me.

"No, it isn't the end. You know it isn't," he took my hands. "To prove it to you, I want to take you and your grandparents to see the land I've purchased for our house."

That stopped the sharp retort I had been about to spew at him. Before my mouth could form a word, he spoke again, trying to calm my fury.

"It's close by. I knew you wouldn't want to be far from your grandparents so it's on a hill overlooking the Golden Horn, in the Blachernae neighborhood. It will take some time to build the house. Isaac and I will be away in Antioch, so I thought to ask your grandfather to keep an eye on the construction."

"You're going to Antioch?" My heart lurched at the thought of him leaving.

"We just heard a couple of days ago. There've been raiding parties in the area. It should only be for a few months," he said. "By the time we return, Zoe will be happily wed to someone else, and forgotten your uncle. Catherine and Donya can relax, and we'll be betrothed and wed. You'll see. It won't be long."

John had grasped my hand and moved closer. He bent his head and kissed me, first gently, then a second time with his arms encircling me. The last of my anger dissipated in that embrace.

The swooshing sounds of skirts alerted us to an impending intrusion and we separated, blushing guiltily.

Grandmother, from a short distance, announced, "John, Isaac said he was ready to leave and wanted to know if you'd be joining him?"

He glanced at me, smiled, and gave a small shrug of resignation, "Yes, Lady Theodora, I will. I just need to make some plans with you and your husband and Anna to see the land I've bought for our house."

The words 'our house' were balm to my spirit and music to my ears.

Uncle Costas could not have been more apologetic.

"I should have expected this, I didn't think it through enough. I'm so sorry, Anna, I was thinking only of how it might affect Damian and Xene," he said later in contrition, an arm around my shoulders. "I hope you'll forgive me."

I sighed, looking away from the gate through which John and Isaac had just left. I wasn't so much angry with Uncle Costas as with the situation. John's words had relieved my worst anxiety, but our marriage was no closer.

"I know, Uncle. It's just frustrating," I said, wiping a few tears away with the back of my hand.

"I know, and I am sorry. But Isaac's right, especially after what Catherine's brother did. It will be best for their family, and his family will be yours. You'll see, Zoe will forget about me when someone else accepts her proposal. You and John won't have to wait too long."

Grandmother often reminded me that I needed more patience and now I'd have months to practice it. The delay was not the end, and the building of our house would have to be my focus as I waited for John's return.

CHAPTER TEN

Rebellion and War

Fall 1042 to Spring 1043

The land was about a half hour's walk from my grandparent's house. Thomas, a burly man with thick mason's fingers and dust in his graying hair, would build our new house and showed us the plans for it and other buildings. John instructed Thomas to make any changes my grandparents and I thought necessary while he was in Antioch.

The land had been farmed for many years, but its aging owner decided the offer of John's gold solidi for part of his holding easy to accept. We strolled through the field as John described where he planned to put the house, the stables, the bath, and the gardens. Towards the back of the lot rose five tall cypresses at the top of a hill, their deep green foliage like spears against the sapphire sky, the air filled with a resinous aroma. The view from that vantage swept over the houses and shops sloping to the boats and fishing ketches swarming below in the slate waters of the Golden Horn, like bees flitting from flower to flower. Barely visible through the trees, where the city walls met the estuary, lay the Blachernae imperial lodge, near the gate leading to a hunting park.

John and I moved into the shade of the cypress, our fingers woven together. The air smelled fresher than the pungent odors nearer to the Mese and the more crowded neighborhoods. We wanted no marble palace overlooking the Marmara as Isaac and Catherine had, instead pleased with a splendid view of the water, and this quieter setting. My grandparents stood speaking with Thomas some distance away.

"So, will this suit you?" John asked, raising a ruddy eyebrow, eyes soft as a spring breeze. "It's not the most fashionable of neighborhoods, but I thought you'd like it."

"I do, John, it's wonderful," I said. gazing at him. "Thank you. It was foolish to doubt you."

John visibly relaxed and squeezed my hand. "Good. You know it's only a matter of time."

We stood close, hands clasped, surveying where our home would be, where we would raise our children, and imagining our future. Smiling into his sunny face, I said, "Still, it's hard to imagine what the house will look like, even seeing your plans. I've never seen a house built before."

John said, "It will keep you and your grandparents so busy that time will fly by. I'm told Thomas is one of the best builders in the city, so between the four of you I know it will be perfect for us."

We turned back to join my grandparents after a final look at the vista. While walking I tripped on what I thought was a rock but looking down I saw it was the broken bit of an old brick.

"That's odd, finding part of a brick in a farmer's field," I said, irritated at myself for stumbling.

John looked down at it, and then pointed to a few others nearby. "See there are a few pieces of them scattered here and there," he said without surprise.

"Where did they come from?"

"There used to be houses here, a long time ago, when the first Justinian was emperor. Plague killed maybe half the people in the city. No one knows for sure how many. Later the houses were torn down and the land sold for farms."

I shivered at the reminder of long ago people who had lived, and died, where my home would be. It seemed as though an otherworldly parade of souls inhabited this piece of earth, and wondered what my place in that procession would be. I shook it off; Justinian had ruled five hundred years earlier, and even the most persistent ghosts would be gone now. It was time for a new house to be built and children born to fill it. God willing, my children would help me find my place in life's pageant.

John made arrangements for payments to Thomas during the construction of our house, bade me a heartfelt farewell, promised to return by the fall, and left a few days later.

A few weeks later, the blinded eunuch, Constantine, formerly Domestic of the Scholai, disclosed where he had hidden the gold from the treasury he had absconded with. The giddy empress used the coins, an enormous sum thought equal to half a year's tax revenues, to reward those who had stopped Michael's attempt to overthrow her. What was left hired jugglers, dancing bears and other entertainments at the hippodrome for the people of the city. Grandfather and Uncle Costas thought such pandering sickening when they heard stories of how soldiers in the borderlands went unpaid and poorly provisioned.

Uncle Costas' estimation that someone would accept Zoe's proposal soon was correct. Constantine Monomachus, a member of the dynatoi and imperial bureaucrat exiled years earlier by the Orphanotrophus for his part in the same rebellion that led to Eudokia's father and uncle to monasteries, accepted Zoe's hand. He married her and was crowned in June. A robustly genial man, the new Emperor Constantine, the ninth with that name, won over his bride to such a degree that Zoe permitted her new husband to move his mistress, nicknamed Skleraina for her Skleros family, into the palace. That scandal soon stifled the talk of my uncle's rebuff of Zoe.

Damien finally coerced Constantine Ducas into allowing him a brief visit with Xene, before taking ship to home and family. Years earlier he had fought beside the father of Irene Pegonitissa, John Ducas' betrothed, who advocated for him with my cousin's husband. Damien had wanted to see Xene again, not knowing when he might have another chance. His visit to her lonely attic gynecaeum, though, gave him no consolation. Uncle Costas, still unwelcome in his son-in-law's home, decided to stay with us rather than return to his estate. Xene needed him close by more than Damien did.

For a man with such a reputation of amiability, the new emperor's first actions were to settle old scores. Few would have argued with his decision to exile the Orphanotrophus to an even more remote and tiny island than he had been on, where the old wretch finally died, unmourned. This new emperor had suffered many years in just such an exile, and all could see the justice of that punishment.

On the other hand, no one expected what happened to the great General George Maniakes, whom Zoe had freed from prison in May and sent to Italy with an army. Maniakes had property in Anatolia bordering land owned by Skleraina's brother, Romanus Skleros. A smoldering feud had burned for years between the two men. Intoxicated with her position as the emperor's mistress, Skleraina incited Monomachus to bring about a final resolution. Soldiers were sent to pillage and destroy the towns on Maniakes' property in July, within a month of the new emperor's crowning.

"He did what?" Grandmother asked incredulously when Grandfather told us of this news one night at dinner. "And the empress let this happen?"

Grandfather gave her a dark look, one eyebrow raised. "Do you think she cares? She spends her days with her pots and potions and gold baubles. She could not wait to leave the empire to her new husband to manage."

"What else?" Grandmother asked, guessing he had not told all.

He glanced over to me.

"Anna's old enough to hear it, whatever it is, if she's old enough to be married," Grandmother said.

"The soldier who told me this said that Skleros raped Maniakes' wife before slitting her throat and setting their house ablaze," he finished in a low voice.

Quite suddenly, I lost my appetite. Grandmother went pale, before saying, "May God have mercy on her soul."

"And on the rest of us," added Uncle Costas, "when Maniakes hears what has happened."

Maniakes reacted as one would expect to the news of both his wife's savage killing and the message he was relieved of his command. He killed the replacement the emperor sent to Italy, and incited his troops to rebellion and proclaimed himself emperor. His progress toward the city was slow as the weather grew colder, but Maniakes was the empire's best general and had defeated Turks and Saracens. Only the emperor and his mistress doubted his ability to achieve the throne.

The emperor sent Romanus Skleros at the head of an army to confront the usurper. To Skleraina's dismay, her brother received justice when he was killed in a skirmish and his body mutilated by Maniakes' men. The rebel army slogged through bitter winter weather in its slow approach to the city. The comet streaking through the sky every night that month left us all with a sense of foreboding. The city was on edge.

A young dark haired sailor arrived at our gate on a brisk day late that fall. Looking out from the window in Grandmother's office, I recognized him as the cabin boy John and Isaac had befriended on our sea voyage home, Michael Maurex. He had grown several inches and his face carried the shadow of his first beard. His tunic, with bands of ochre, were the imperial fleet insignia of a helmsman. I waved to Leo to allow him entrance, and went out to greet him.

"Lady Anna," he greeted me with delight, "I was hoping to see you."

"Michael, I'm so glad to see you again, too," I said. "You must come inside, my grandparents will want to speak with you."

"Yes, thank you. I want to see them, too. John Comnenus entrusted me to carry a letter and package from Antioch to deliver here. I can't stay long, though. I also have to visit General Isaac's family, but I promised I would visit you first."

My heart beat faster at the mention of John.

Grandmother whisked in a small feast for him, sure that the navy's food would never suffice for a growing young man. Before tucking into the roast chicken, Michael opened his pack to remove a sealed parchment letter addressed to Grandfather, and a leather-covered box. Etiquette would not permit him to write me before we were betrothed. Grandfather broke the lead seal, and read.

General Dalassenus-

I hope this letter finds you and your family in good health and spirits. We hear much of the Maniakes rebellion, which is worrisome, but I trust that you will do whatever is necessary to protect your household.

Isaac and I will, unfortunately, need to remain in Antioch at least through the winter. The Saracen raiders have been more difficult to eradicate than we expected.

Please give my best wishes to your wife and family, most particularly your granddaughter, Anna. I have asked my messenger to bring a small token of my affection for her, if you will permit him to give it to her.

John Comnenus

Disappointment washed over me. I had begun to suspect that John's return might be delayed given the lateness of the season and felt despondent at another test of my patience. Michael, though, proceeded to open the leather-covered box and removed a package snugly wrapped with thick red woolen fabric and tied with a cord, laying it before me.

I glanced up at him.

"You should open it," he said, smiling in anticipation. "But you must take care."

I loosened the cord and pulled away the soft scarlet cloth. Inside rested an alabaster box, as pale and soft as a pearl. Its carved lid was covered with poppies, delicate small red stones inlaid for the petals, green stones for the leaves. I had never owned anything as lovely.

Before receiving this gift, my stoic daylight face had often given way to shadows at night. Would my hopes for him be shattered the way my mother's alabaster box had shattered the night we sailed into exile? That night, with the moonlight shining on John's gift, the promise of our new beginning felt sustained. It was a reminder that while one part of life can end, another can be created.

Thomas, the builder John had hired, first finished the stable after he had surrounded our property with a high stone wall to deter intruders. The house was roofed late that year, before the weather became too cold for the men to work on the other out buildings – the bath and cookhouse.

I developed an interest in sewing as I realized all I would need for the house. My skills did not improve appreciably, but I could at least sew the straight seam needed for curtains. Grandmother and I would, on occasion, visit Xene and we would spend the afternoon sewing together, almost like we had before. Ducas was never present during our visits, the rest of the house empty and echoing except for our chatter and laughing.

I'm not sure what we laughed at, or why. Perhaps just being together then. Otherwise, we had little to cheer us. I was anxious to see John, and Xene's hopeless situation worried all of us. Then there was Maniakes and his army, drawing closer each day.

Still, I remember those bits of joy, snatched in that plain room and savored like a ripe peach.

Maniakes' thirst for revenge pushed him closer to the city each day. Grandfather and Uncle Costas never condemned him for rebelling, but wondered at his chance of success.

Monomachus sent an inept palace eunuch to lead an army after Skleros' death. Grandfather said that if he'd sent a competent general who won a victory, that man might be a contender for the throne. A eunuch's mutilation would never allow it. The armies fought their final battle near Thessalonica. The rebel army had, in fact, defeated the emperor's forces led by the bungling eunuch. But as the battle drew to a close chance bestowed its favor on the eunuch when a lance pierced Maniakes's armor and deep into his side. The great man fell from his horse, dead. Some days later, the eunuch processed in triumph down the Mese to the palace parading the fallen general's head. And as we came to learn was his wont, the emperor rewarded him with generous purses of gold.

The rebellion had other implications, as Grandfather learned months later from other soldiers he knew, giving us the news one evening at dinner.

"I saw John Ouranos today. He has been with the army in Dyrrachion," Grandfather began without expression after he sat down.

Uncle Costas looked at his youngest brother as he passed a platter, trying to discern his expression. "And how is our friend John these days?" he inquired.

Grandfather cocked an eyebrow before speaking. "He is well, although his news was not. He says there is no army in Italy now."

My uncle gave Grandfather a sharp look. "What do you mean no army? The empire cannot hold Italy without an army."

"That's true—the empire cannot hold Italy without an army, nor does it any longer. The emperor did not replace Maniakes' army. Nor does it appear that he intends to from what John hears. Bari's catepan has a small garrison in that town, but that's all we hold in Italy now," Grandfather finished.

"We've lost Italy?" came Grandmother's shocked question. "But we've ruled it for five hundred years – how can we lose it and only hear of it inadvertently?"

"Why would the emperor announce such a disaster? The news will seep out in slow drips, and since we still hold Bari, people won't realize how bad a loss it is," Grandfather said, his bushy eyebrows knotted together.

"Perhaps the emperor will launch an attack from Dyrrhachium and regain it," Grandmother suggested.

Grandfather gave her a raised eyebrow. "Not likely. He's not a soldier, just enjoying life in the palace. He might when the treasury doesn't receive the Italian taxes, but it'll be too late then."

Easter passed that year, a year since I had thought John and I to be betrothed, and almost that long since we should have been wed. John's infrequent letters gave no hint of when he might return. Grandmother tried to keep my mind off John, but with little success. Our house was the one solid reminder keeping my days from melancholy.

During Lent, old Patriarch Alexios died and the emperor elevated Michael Keroularios, my friend Eudokia's uncle, as the new patriarch. His reaching this lofty state would have been odd since he had spent most of his life as a soldier and been reluctantly tonsured only a few years earlier, but for the fact he and the emperor had been named in the same conspiracy. Michael Keroularios soon pleased the emperor by turning over a treasure room filled with gold coins that the old patriarch had hidden away.

Eudokia and her mother, Marina, would sometimes visit us, eager to escape the house where they were the not so welcome poor relations. I sympathized with their plight, recalling how it felt to be cast upon family members, unexpected mouths to feed. Now, their situation improved with Marina's brother's new position.

"Mama has had several callers to speak about arranging a betrothal for me," Eudokia said one morning as we walked in the garden. The bright summer sun had us in straw hats, although the heat was not oppressive yet. "Uncle Michael says she should wait until I am older, to make the best marriage for me."

"Twelve is early for that." I felt a pinch of envy for her suitors. Eudokia was just fortunate in her uncle, whereas the Dalasseni were not quite acceptable again. "She should take her time finding you a husband who is handsome, wealthy, and kind. Hmmm, what else could you want in a husband?" I asked her playfully, trying to think of what else she would want. "A soldier, or a farmer, or a poet?"

"Oh, a poet, definitely, and he would have to be handsome. But I don't think a poet's on mama's list. It will probably be a soldier," she said, twisting a strand of her blond hair around a finger.

"Soldiers aren't so bad," I said in mock outrage, squeezing her arm. "Aside from Uncle Simeon at Stoudion, all the men in my family are, and I plan on marrying one myself. If he ever manages to return to the city," I ended, rueful at the thought.

Eudokia looked embarrassed. "I didn't mean to remind you about John," she said.

"Well, its not as though I ever forget him, so don't feel bad," I said. Changing the subject, I asked "Have you seen Irene Pegonitissa lately? The girl who married John Ducas? I saw her at liturgy and I thought she looked as though she might be pregnant."

"Oh yes, she is. She is due to have her baby in November."

I frowned, thinking that Constantine Ducas' rage at his wife's barrenness would be worse than ever, seeing his younger brother with children. I felt sick about what he might say or do to my cousin. How odd to think that Irene, as pale and small as a seagull's down feather would have a child, while my cousin, strong and healthy, would live so long without one. Niggling worries would erupt sometimes, would John and I have the same disappointment, or would God bless us with children? How would Xene feel if we had children?

"She must be pleased."

"I think so, and her husband, too. I saw them at Hagia Sophia when we were there for Easter liturgy. Irene looked weak, still with the morning sickness. Her husband was strutting about as men do, bragging to the other men about the baby," Eudokia said as we sat down on the bench in a little shade.

"Hmm, that doesn't surprise me," I said, recalling my previous experiences with John Ducas. "I wonder what it's like to be pregnant. Do you think you know right away? Just know somehow?"

"I don't think you could. Not until your courses are late. Why do you ask?" she looked at me quizzically.

"Just wondering," I said slyly, and then grinned. "I'll need to know someday."

She laughed. "It won't be too long. John will be back any day. You'll see."

It had been over a year since John had left. The house was built, although there was some minor finishing inside to do. Grandmother decided we should go over and begin the work creating kitchen and flower gardens. We took old Leo, the gatekeeper, and the stable boy along for the heavy work.

One morning a few days after Eudokia's visit, we were in the courtyard loading the tools into packs carried by a donkey to take over to the new house to work on its gardens when Nicholas rushed through the gate, panting.

"Lady Theodora," he started, trying to catch his breath, "ships, in the Marmara. Hundreds. Warships, not ours."

Grandmother stood motionless for a few seconds, blinking as his words sunk in, trying to comprehend. Then she looked at me, asking, "Where's your grandfather?"

"Inside, with Uncle Costas."

"Run. Tell them to come out here," she said before turning back to question Nicholas.

By the time I returned with them, Grandmother had learned more. The ships were Rus, a surprise since the empire had been on good terms with the Rus for many years, and at least three hundred of them.

Grandfather and Uncle Costas exchanged looks.

"Costas and I'll go find out what's happened. Bolt the gate when we leave. Everyone is to stay inside the walls." Glancing at Leo, Grandfather added, "You're not to open them before we return. Do you understand?"

Leo nodded, pale under his tan. The two men quickly departed, the bolts sliding across the gate behind them with reassuring thwacks. As disconcerted as I was, I almost laughed when I saw Leo pull out an old cudgel, resting it on his shoulder. He didn't have the strength to do anyone damage, unless they were already lying prostrate in front of him.

Grandmother and I returned to the house. Her jaw was set and brow furrowed in thought.

"Anna, call Alethea. I need to speak with her. I don't know how bad this will be, but we'll need to be prepared."

When Alethea and I returned to her workroom, Grandmother sat at her desk, and having scraped off an old piece of parchment, begun listing what we had on hand, one column for the supplies in the cellar, another for the garden. She told us what to buy, if possible. The gruesome stories Grandfather and Uncle Costas had told of sieges they had seen loomed large. Starvation and disease always accompanied them.

After Alethea left, I looked at my grandmother as she bent over her list, her hand absently rubbing her forehead back and forth. I sat across from her.

She glanced up at me and stopped rubbing her forehead, her hand reaching across the table to clasp mine.

"I don't want to worry you, but it's been a long time since the city was last under siege. We'll have to be prepared for anything that might happen, including fleeing the city."

"What should I do," I asked, surprised to hear the tremor in my voice.

She gave me a weak smile. "We may need to sew some coins into your clothing—should we get separated, you would have some money. Not yet, but if things get bad."

It was jolting to think what might cause us to be separated.

I asked, "Have you ever been in the city when it has been under siege?"

"It's never happened in my lifetime. Basil ruled for fifty years; no barbarian would have thought to come so close then." She frowned, looking out into the courtyard, and shrugged. "But he's been gone almost twenty years now. Barbarians notice when soldiers aren't patrolling the borders and forts become decrepit."

"I thought our armies were superior. How can they not be?" I asked. That's what I had been taught.

Grandmother glanced at me with a cynical frown. "Yes, they are, or were. Armies need gold solidi for weapons, food and soldiers' pay. After Emperor Michael named that disgusting brother of his as Domestic of the Scholai, I think most of the gold meant for the army made its way into his treasure room."

"But he gave it back to Zoe, didn't he?"

She peered at me with a narrowed eye and laughed. "She only got back what was left after he had lived like Croesus for years. What do you think paid for the free bread the palace handed out, or the races at the hippodrome, or the myriad other entertainments Zoe put on? They may have been free, but they cost the empire. She probably spent most of that gold. Such a waste," she said, shaking her head.

Within a few hours, Grandfather and Uncle Costas returned with word that there was no imminent danger. The Rus prince had sent out a demand for gold as his price for leaving and was waiting a response. In the meantime, the navy's droungarios commandeered any large ships in the city's harbors—merchant ships and large fishing boats—adding them to the few dromons at anchor. They formed a barrier between the seawalls and the Rus ships.

The next day the emperor sent an embassy with a weak response to the Rus. He offered gifts and reparations for the supposed ill treatment some Rus merchant was said to have received from the city's eparch, which was the *casus belli*. The prince, named Vsevolod, rudely abused the embassy and increased his demand to three pounds of gold for each of his thousands of soldiers. The ambassador immediately refused this staggering amount. The Rus either thought the city had springs of gold, or they just wanted to provoke a fight. In any event, it was the fight they got.

The two navies sat in place, glaring across the water at each other for more than a day, neither willing to begin the battle. We had gone to the seawall near the Theodosian Harbor with other crowds to learn our fate that Sunday. The slightest of breezes blew that day and the sun burned both sailors and onlookers. Grandfather and Uncle Costas shaded their eyes while scanning the water.

The Rus had such an impressive number of warships lying so close together it looked as though one could jump easily from one to the other, from one side of the Marmara to the other. On the other hand, the imperial navy looked a bedraggled, ragtag thing, few and widely spaced.

"There they are Costas," Grandfather said, pointing at three vessels outfitted with long ceramic tubes and hoists, strategically located across from thickest cluster of Rus ships and some distance from our own.

Following the direction Grandfather had indicated, Uncle Costas nodded. "Yes, I see them," a note of satisfaction in his voice.

I saw them too. The fire ships, specially equipped to shoot Greek fire, moved close to the Rus. Miraculously, these must have been in port when the Rus attacked. Grandfather peered at the men on the Rus ships. "They have no idea what's about to hit them," he said.

"I see, they're not paying any attention to the fire ships," Uncle Costas remarked dispassionately. "God's mercy be on them," he said with a shake of his head.

Winches pulled the clay tubes into position, aiming for the Rus. Perhaps I imagined it but I thought I could just hear, above the sounds of the sea and the crowd around me, the creaking gears starting to turn. Those gears would propel the deadly liquid across the water onto the enemy. Suddenly a single bright orange light launched across the water to the invaders' ships, followed by flashes from the other two fire ships. The attack had begun, flames arcing onto the enemy ships.

Soon the screams of dying men struggling to escape the unquenchable fire echoed across the water. The men plunged themselves into the sea, hoping for some relief, not knowing water could not quench the flames. The burning concoction consumed dozens of ships in its devastation, the acrid smell of the Greek fire, seared flesh, and inciner-ated wood drifting towards shore. My eyes stung and I pulled a scarf over my mouth and nose.

Stunned at the deadly power of this weapon, the surviving Rus troops soon made the prudent decision to abandon their attack and return home. All of us on the seawalls cheered at the victory.

Prince Vsevolod himself barely escaped, sailing up the Bosphorus towards the Black Sea with his surviving ships. Unfortunately for him, his sailors were unfamiliar with those twisting waters. Some sailed their ships aground, where themata soldiers greeted the Rus army with swords, turning the shore crimson with the invaders' blood.

This foolish Rus prince did more to enrich the empire with booty and equipment scavenged from his dead soldiers and the ships run aground, than he did for himself. Somehow he did get a wife out of it, though. A few months later, the emperor's daughter, Anastasia, child of a forgotten earlier wife, found herself bartered away as part of the peace treaty, soon bound for barbarian lands, a crown in hand to console herself with.

For all of the faults of dead Emperor Michael and his brother the Orphanotrophus, there had not been any attacks on the capital in all his years on the throne. Constantine Monomachus had already seen two in just one year. Like anyone whose family had soldiers, I hoped for peaceful times, but this start to Monomachus' reign was not promising.

CHAPTER ELEVEN

Theodora Dalassena

Fall 1043

Thomas had finished our house in the year since John had left. By the middle of September there was still no sign of his arrival. I had long since exhausted whatever store of patience I had—my biggest fault as Grandmother often reminded me. To distract me, she had delegated many of the household responsibilities to me and had slowed down perceptibly, enjoying this respite. Alethea and I had long since reached an accommodation, and the other servants were little trouble, except for Nicholas. He was the persistent pebble in my shoe, sneaky in making trouble to undermine me. I learned not to trust anything he said outside of Grandmother's presence.

One crisp fall morning Grandmother and I were working in the sunny garden, plucking ripe apples to store in the cellar over the winter. I had climbed on a stool and passed the fruit down to her to deposit in our basket, when she was suddenly not there to take it. The floppy brim of my straw hat made it difficult to see where she had gone, when I saw her lying in the grass.

"Grandmother? What's wrong?" I cried, jumping down.

She gave a soft groan, clutching at her chest. Frantic, I tried calling to the house for Nicholas, but he was playing his stupid game of ignoring me.

"God's wounds, where is that man?" I swore under my breath. I rushed to the house for help and found Maria who went to stay with Grandmother, before finally locating Nicholas and Leo, who carried her to her bed.

"Leo, go to the warehouse and fetch my grandfather back, tell him to hurry," I instructed after we settled her in bed.

Running a hand through my hair, I tried to think of the name of the physician we had seen in the past. It was Basil, like the old emperor, and it came to me. "Nicholas, you recall our physician, Basil Kourtikios? Go tell him we are in need of his help now. Go quickly."

"But..." Nicholas started to say.

I stopped him speaking with a brusque wave of my hand. "Leave now, no excuses," I barked at him.

He turned and left, his eyes narrowed.

Alethea entered the room, eyes wide in shock, and helped loosen Grandmother's clothes, trying to make her comfortable. That accomplished, she left briefly, returning with a pitcher of cool water, and then dipping a soft cloth in it to sponge Grandmother's face and hands.

I sat on a stool beside the bed, stroking her hand, murmuring to her that Grandfather and the physician would soon arrive. Her eyes opened part way, unfocused, while her face grimaced with pain. I leaned over and kissed her sagging hand, pressing it to my cheek, wet with tears. Grandfather arrived. Our desperate prayers for my dear Grandmother's recovery assaulted heaven's gate, for we could do naught else.

Nicholas returned some time later, a woman in tow and a smirk on his face.

"Where is the physician?" I asked when I saw them.

"Lady, I am the physician," said the woman, dark haired and with an olive complexion. "I am Maria Kourtikios, Basil is my father. He is old, infirm with the gout and not seeing patients any longer, but he trained me to follow him." This physician spoke with quiet confidence as she moved towards the bed where Grandmother lay.

Nicholas had a smug look on his face, pleased at my surprise at seeing a woman doctor. He must have known her father was no longer seeing patients. I glared at him, and then returned to Grandmother's room.

Maria Kourtikios spent an hour with Grandmother, examining her and asking questions. Had she been in any pain before that day? Yes, but she hadn't wanted to worry anyone. How long? She thought for some months, but it came and went.

The physician asked for some water, into which she poured a little wine and a pinch of a powder from a leather pouch extracted from her medical bag.

"Lady Theodora, I'll need you to drink this. It should help you feel better," she said.

She lifted Grandmother's head gently and held the cup for her to swallow the mixture. Her eyes soon shut in sleep.

Maria Kourtikios packed up her bag and gestured for us to retreat to the hall.

"Lady Theodora has had a seizure, her heart," she said in an alcove where we could speak quietly. "It may be some time before she feels able to be up and about again. In the meantime, you need to add a pinch of this powder to a little water mixed with wine, no more than twice a day."

I took the small pouch she proffered, grateful for whatever help it might give.

Grandfather's eyes peered at this confident woman in her middle years. His voice held both hope and fear when he spoke, "Thank you, Lady. You think, you think she will recover then?"

The woman gave him a kind smile, and patted him on the shoulder. "That is in God's hands, General. You must pray for her recovery. With rest, the medicine I've given you, and God's help, I hope so."

"I'll escort you home," Uncle Costas said in a quiet voice, walking her downstairs. "Can I first offer you some wine before we depart?"

Grandfather and I did not speak as we watched them descending, still unable to comprehend what had occurred. The afternoon sun slanted into the hall at autumnal angles, seeming to reminisce of the summer just past. I was on the edge of crying again until I looked Grandfather's bereft face.

"I need to sit with Theodora."

"I'll speak with Alethea and Nicholas," I said, not relishing the thought of managing that man without Grandmother.

I walked with him into their bedroom where he sat on a bedside chair. At the doorway, as I was leaving, I looked back to see him reaching out for her hand.

We settled into a routine within a few days. Grandfather pulled out his old army cot, moving it into their room, to be at hand if she needed help during the night. When he had to be out during the day, Alethea, Maria, and I took turns caring for her, between the other daily tasks. Maria Kourtikios stopped by often, and seemed pleased at her patient's progress. I had never encountered a female physician before, although I had known there were some women who chose that profession.

The added responsibilities and worries over Grandmother's illness left me exhausted and short-tempered after little more than a week. Alethea and Maria's moods were little better than mine, they sometimes gave me sharp retorts at my requests. I did not like that, but I could understand, and as a rule they showed me respect.

What trouble I had with servants was with Nicholas. He ignored my instructions, disappeared when I needed him, and often would not respond when I spoke to him. He may have worshipped my grandmother, but he made it difficult for me to do what I could for her.

One afternoon, I sat by my sleeping grandmother, more tired than I could ever remember being, worried about her, frustrated by Nicholas, and irritable with everyone else. Not even realizing it, I started to cry, sniffling and wiping my eyes.

"Anna," came a feeble voice, "why are you crying?"

Startled, I rubbed away the evidence of my distress.

"Grandmother, how are you feeling? Can I get you anything?"

She gave me a direct look that would brook no redirection. "I need nothing but to know why you are crying. Has something happened with John?"

"No, I've heard nothing from John," I had barely thought of him since her seizure. Her brown eyes had regained some of their normal intensity and were fixed on me, compelling me to confess. I swallowed, not wanting to whine, but the fatigue won out.

"Grandmother, it's been hard trying to take care everything." I spoke fast, before I began crying again. "I'm trying to run the house, but it's a battle every day. Nicholas especially causes me problems—he's always disappearing when I need him and isn't respectful."

Her brow furrowed as she listened to my complaints, endeavoring to make sense of them.

"That is the problem?" she asked.

I nodded, feeling like I had failed her.

"We can resolve that. Help me sit up," she said, reaching for me. "Put some pillows behind me to rest against."

Sitting up, her eyes brightened and her face lost some of its pallor.

"Now, go tell all of the servants that I need to see them now, here in my room. If you can't find Nicholas, ask Leo. He'll know where Nicholas is."

Leaving her, I easily found Alethea and Maria, and Peter, the boy who helped in the kitchen. Leo and Patricios were repairing harnesses in the stable. Nicholas, as usual, was nowhere to be found, although Leo, as Grandmother had said, knew where to locate him.

Grandmother's room was not large and the six servants had squeezed into what space there was between the bed and the door. Their faces held varying mixtures of curiosity, concern, and apprehension.

Grandmother began. "As you all know, I am ill and unable to tend to the household. Until I have recovered Anna will be responsible for the house, and you will go to her for all instruction as if she was me."

She paused for a long moment and repeated, "As if she was me."

She stopped, worn out, but looked directly at each of the servants in turn, asking them, "Can I trust you in this?" and receiving each affirmative, even surly Nicholas'. She continued, her voice still firm but softer.

"I have taught my granddaughter all she knows and I trust her completely with this responsibility. Do you all understand?"

Nicholas looked as though he had swallowed an oyster shell. He might not relish taking orders from a young woman he had known since childhood, but I was grown and this was just the way of the world. He would have to accustom himself to it.

Her strength diminishing, Grandmother looked over to where I stood. "I think my grandmother needs some rest now, so you may go. I will be downstairs later to go over assignments."

After the servants had gone, Grandmother drank a cup of water and then lay down again.

Beside her, holding her hand, I said a quiet, "Thank you."

She laughed. "Don't feel bad about it. When I was a girl helping in my father's warehouse, some of the men working there acted as though

I wasn't there, or if they did, it was only to threaten me. I would wager those dockworkers were much worse than Nicholas. My father had to sit those men down and say much the same to them."

"Did it work?"

She frowned, trying to remember, "Yes, mostly. But some never learn."

Yawning then, she closed her eyes and slept.

Grandmother's admonitions improved Nicholas' behavior after that day and he ceased his overt rudeness and unexplained disappearances. Even so, his resentment of me was palpable. I tried to ignore it.

About a month after her seizure, I was reviewing accounts in my grandmother's workroom when I heard the sound of slow steps coming downstairs. Going into the hall, Grandmother stood on the stairs, leaning heavily against the wall.

"I sent Maria on an errand so she wouldn't stop me," she said before I could speak, waving a dismissive hand. "I'm feeling better and can't stay in bed forever."

I stood gaping at her, speechless.

"Well, are you going to just stand there?" her iron-willed brown eyes defying me to escort her back to bed.

The obedient habits of a lifetime took control. She gripped my arm and I guided her to the table in her workroom facing the window that overlooked the courtyard. Leo was there, his rake scratching against the slate tiles as he gathered the fallen red and brown leaves.

"Grandmother, do you think you should be up? What will your physician say?"

"I don't care what Maria Kourtikios says. If I have to stay in that bed for another day I will go mad. So if getting up kills me, better that than becoming a madwoman. Now, show me the account books. Have you kept them up to date?"

She spent the next half hour reviewing her accounts. The return to normal activity brought more color to her cheeks, but it was not long before her energy waned and she relaxed back into her chair. We sat together for a few minutes, speaking of nothing in particular, reluctant to return upstairs. She happened to glance out the window at the gate, and then smiled at me.

"Anna, I believe we have a visitor."

I turned and saw a man in a cloak, probably a soldier from the way he carried himself, had entered the gate and stopped to speak with Leo. I looked harder at the man, and the words came to me almost before my mind knew what I spoke.

"It's John," I said in a hoarse voice, before repeating more loudly. "It's John."

In an instant I was outside and running to him, before checking myself. What if he had come to say he had changed his mind? Then, he turned to me, face alight, and there were no more doubts, his arms holding me close, and his lips on my mouth.

John was determined that we would finalize the terms and sign the betrothal agreement in the next few weeks, before Advent began, with our wedding to occur between Epiphany and the start of Lent.

"We've delayed too long already. The house is ready, I am ready and Anna is ready. No need to wait longer and allow some other impediment to appear."

Isaac and my grandparents agreed and set the dates for an early November betrothal and late January wedding. That left little time to finish acquiring the household items a bride was expected to bring to her marriage, and Grandmother's weakened state would not permit her to venture out to the shops.

Into this breach arrived my widowed cousin, Eugenia, and her only child, Romanus Diogenes. Eugenia was the granddaughter of my grandfather's oldest sibling, his only sister, also called Eugenia. My cousin and her son, apprehensive after our sentence of exile, had left the city not long after we had, staying those years with her brother-in-law's family in Cappadocia. They returned now so Romanus could find a place in the army. He had grown into a handsome young man, just in his first beard, with light brown hair and deep blue eyes, tall, tanned, and muscular. He looked as impatient to make his own way in the world as I was to be married.

Eugenia's eyes darted around the room when she spoke with anyone, as if searching for a spot to hide in should the conversation veer to her late husband. She made sure no conversation touched on that thorny subject, speaking only of the weather, the year's crops, and the misfortunes of others. She faced the gloomy prospect of living as a needy solitary widow in her brother-in-law's house once Romanus had his place.

"I'm so happy we can be here for your betrothal and wedding," she said at dinner the evening she and Romanus arrived. "If there is anything I can do, just ask. I'd be happy to help," she continued, tenaciously cheerful.

Grandfather and I exchanged glances before he answered.

"You know, Eugenia, Theodora and Anna have made some purchases for Anna's dowry, but there are still many more items Theodora wants for Anna. Perhaps you could accompany Anna and me, and help finish that." He shrugged and rolled his eyes at the prospect of shopping. "I'm not good with that sort of thing and Anna needs a woman's hand with it."

She glowed at the prospect, giving my hand a squeeze across the table. "Uncle, I'd love to help with that," she said. "It would be almost as though I had a daughter of my own getting married."

"In the meantime, I'll take Romanus to visit some friends who can find him a spot in the army," Uncle Costas said. "I think I have the time to find him a suitable place to begin his training."

Romanus shot our uncle a grateful glance.

"Thank you, Uncle. I am grateful," Romanus said, his wavy hair falling across his face.

"Happy to do it, son," Uncle Costas replied. "I've got friends still in the taghmata who might be glad of a new recruit."

Grandmother's strength returned slowly, allowing her to spend part of each day in her workroom, a warming brazier close, making lists of all that Eugenia and I had to purchase or accomplish for the betrothal. Uncle Costas found Romanus a place in the Exkoubitores taghmata, delighting his mother, and he soon left for training.

Then, two days before the betrothal, at dinner, Uncle Costas made an announcement.

"I've decided to enter Stoudion and receive the tonsure next week," he said as he passed the breadbasket around the table.

"You what?" I replied, blinking at him.

"I will be taking monk's vows next week at Stoudion. I've given this a lot of thought," he spoke in a firm voice. "I've signed over most of my property to Damien, some money for Xene, and after a few bequests, the remainder will go to the monastery. Perhaps Ducas will allow Xene to visit me at the monastery. If not, I'll spend my remaining time there seeking forgiveness for my many sins."

"Bless you, Costas, for your holy choice," said Eugenia, beaming as she crossed herself reverentially.

A glance at my grandparents, intently studying their cups of wine, told me they already knew of this decision.

"I hadn't known you were planning this," I said plaintively. "When did you decide this?"

"Only recently. I've been speaking with Simeon and the hegoumenos. I never thought myself cut out for the monastic life, after spending so many years in confinement, and Ducas knows that. If I had no worries for Xene, I'd rather end my days on my estate with my grandchildren and Damien and Irene. But at least if I'm nearby, Xene won't feel so alone," he answered.

I looked down at the fish on my plate, appetite gone at this reminder of Ducas.

"He's a vile man," I said, unable to contain the hostility.

"That may be, but he controls the center of my chessboard. I've no other options," Uncle Costas said with a frown.

"I'll miss you," he said gently. "But you'll soon have a new husband and, I pray, God will bless you and John with many children. You won't have time to think of your old uncle then."

"I'll always think of you, Uncle," I responded as I reached to hug him.

The next day Uncle Costas and I played our last game of chess.

"I don't think they let you play chess in the monastery," I teased him. "Are you sure you're making the right decision?"

Uncle Costas gave me a wry look. "I did know that, Anna. Doesn't change anything; I'm finished with games."

We played chess badly that day. Finally, after I checkmated Uncle Costas, we both sat back, pondering the board.

"I'll miss our games," he said, looking across at me.

"I'll miss them, too, Uncle. John is learning, but it will be a long time before he can match you."

He started laughing then and reached across the board to squeeze my hand. "You may play games with John after you are wed, but chess may not be one of them. Later though, when children come, you will have to teach them as I taught you."

"I'll try," I answered with cheeks blushing.

The next afternoon was our betrothal. The betrothal is a simple ceremony, just the signing of the agreement promising to marry with my dowry and John's bride gift specified, but as binding as marriage vows. Surrounded by our families, John signed the agreement first, glancing up at me with a smile as he finished. I took the pen from him, dipped it in the ink carefully so as not to smudge the parchment, before signing my name. Grandfather and Isaac followed with their signatures and we were officially joined.

A small celebration followed with Alethea's honey and walnut cakes, as well as bread and cheese, almonds, apples, and wine from our farm. Braziers were strategically placed around the room for warmth on that chilly November afternoon. The windy day had blown the early clouds and rain away, but the sun gave scant warmth.

Isaac had brought Catherine and their two children, as did Donya and, for the first time, I met her husband, Michael. He looked more like a bureaucrat who shuffled papers than a soldier—not so much taller than Donya, well padded in the middle, with fleshy jowls and a friendly, if anxious, attitude.

The men surrounded John, congratulating him and, it seemed from a distance, sharing a few ribald jokes at his expense, as he was laughing while turning quite red. Isaac's humor especially had the men guffawing and looking our way, to make sure none of the women heard it. John laughed as hard as anyone at his brother's joking, even though some of it seemed to be at his expense.

At the same time, I was on the other side of the room, surrounded by the women and girls of our families, who chattered of the wedding preparations – what they would wear to it, and who they might expect to meet at the wedding. Grandmother sat next to me on the cushioned bench, too tired to contribute much to the conversation beyond a happy smile. I was never so glad to have cousin Eugenia there, bubbling over with enthusiasm and answers to every inquiry I was not quick enough to respond to.

Donya and Catherine sat nearby with their daughters, all wearing happy faces. The two women were John's closest female relatives, but I felt decidedly cooler toward them after their part in delaying our marriage. I knew it was petty to still resent the long wait their fears had caused. They'd good reasons for their apprehension, and perhaps expected it to last only a few weeks rather than over a year. Even so, it felt awkward trying to be gracious to them.

"John took Michael and me to see the house he's built," Donya said with a timid smile. "It was lovely, and with such a wonderful view on the hill."

"Thank you. We are pleased with it," I said, happy to say "we" and mean John and me.

Catherine's daughter, Marie, a subdued child of about ten years, with her mother's black hair and her father's blue eyes, stood whispering with her cousins, Donya's daughters Helena and Anastasia. They turned to me after a hurried discussion.

"Anna," Marie said, "we, I mean Helena and Anastasia and me, we would like to come to your new house and help you unpack before the wedding." Helena and Anastasia nodded agreement, and all three girls had pleading looks on their faces, eager to participate in the wedding planning and events. Their "help" might end up being more work than help, but having been their age and hoping to join in adult activities, my heart melted.

"I'd love your help," I said. "Thank you for your offer. We haven't hired any servants yet, so I will need it."

The girls' faces lit up.

Catherine had smiled wanly at the girls' unexpected offer. She was the daughter of a Bulgarian tsar, and perhaps preferred that her daughter not do chores normally assigned to a servant, but she could not gracefully back out now. I realized if the girls came, their mothers would feel obligated to join them.

"That sounds delightful," Eugenia said enthusiastically. "I think we should ask Alethea to join us, so she can get the kitchen set up for you."

Suddenly, a desultory unpacking with three soon-to-be nieces had become a party.

Two days later, Uncle Costas received the tonsure and joined Uncle Simeon at the ancient monastery of St. John Stoudion. He left behind his chessmen, his weapons and armor, his books, and his fine clothes, wearing only a plain tunic, breeches, boots, and a mantle for warmth. Eugenia, Grandfather and I accompanied him, after he embraced my grandmother, too weak to accompany us, and wished her well.

Inside the church, he bid Grandfather and Eugenia farewell before turning to me.

Embracing me, he whispered, "Anna, remember, always keep control of the center."

I could say nothing, only nodded.

My Uncle Simeon, the Hegoumenos Michael Mermentoulos, and several priests awaited him at the royal gates that led to the altar. Uncle Costas removed the mantle and stepped with them behind the iconostasis. My eyes filled with tears.

The hegoumenos and priests began chanting the service, and my uncle made the required responses, rejecting the world and dedicating his remaining days to God. The late November sun illuminated his pale skin where his hair had been shorn. He looked older, frailer than his more than seventy years. Perhaps he had been correct when he refused to consider the crown. How many tonsured years would he give to God?

The service over, he smiled briefly at us and strode to the door leading to the monastery proper, escorted by Uncle Simeon and the other monks. At their departure, Grandfather wiped a few tears with his sleeve.

I reached for Uncle Costas' abandoned mantle, still holding a faint warmth from his body. Hugging it close, I took Grandfather's arm as we left the church and returned home.

CHAPTER TWELVE

Anna and John

January 1044

I missed Uncle Costas, but John and the wedding preparations kept me busy. What little time remained I spent helping my grandmother. John moved into the house and hired a steward for us, a man named David who had been George Maniakes' steward in past times, before the rebellion. No one else would hire the poor man with his prior association, and he had been without work for months when John recognized him in a tavern. John cared little for what others thought, and offered David the position. A shy, amiable man, our new steward moved into the house and arranged the household on my instructions.

Alethea helped me with finding a cook—a plump woman named Antonina with dark frizzy hair and dark eyes, and the same no nonsense look Alethea had. Then, aside from David and Antonina, John hired an old soldier, Thomas, as gatekeeper, and two young men just with their first beards, Narses and Paulus as grooms. A maid, Martina, and a boy called Maurice to help the cook completed our household.

The wind swirled the clouds on the blustery day in early December when John's nieces, and their mothers, as well as my cousin Eugenia, and Alethea came to help me put the house in order. Leo and Patricios had already made one trip to the house with some of my boxes and furniture, and now were loading the cart for a second one.

Too weak to join us, Grandmother sat bundled in blankets downstairs, two braziers warming her. I noticed her thoughtful look as she regarded the commotion outside. I wondered if she felt as untethered as I did with the change it meant.

"Grandmother, I'm sorry you won't be coming today."

She smiled up at me. "I am, as well, child. But I feel stronger every-day. I'll go over another time before the wedding, when it won't be so busy, and I can see all you have done."

"I'd like that. I want to make sure everything is up to your standards. I don't want to disappoint you," I said.

"I don't think my grandchild could disappoint me." she said, squeez-ing my hand. "Now, go on. You don't want to be late for your guests."

Eugenia, Alethea and I arrived at the house not long before everyone else entered our freshly painted gate. Catherine, Donya and their girls tucked into sedan chairs. The men and boys, on horseback and boister-ously bantering amongst themselves, had dressed warmly in leather tunics and fur hats, and carried arrows and spears for a hunting party. Their hunting dogs dodged the horses' hooves, eager for a run. John greeted Isaac, Donya's husband Michael, and the three nephews.

John held the reins of his gray gelding as the women and girls emerged from their sedan chairs.

"We thought we would take the boys out hunting today while you women did. . ." He looked around, gesturing vaguely towards the house, before asking quizzically, "What exactly are you doing today?"

I laughed, "We will be unpacking dishes and arranging furniture and putting up curtains. You don't want our house to look like a soldier's tent, do you?"

"No, I don't suppose I do," he drawled and bent down to kiss me.

"None of that now, young man," Isaac's booming voice reverberated in the courtyard, along with the hooting and laughter of the other men, and the giggling of the girls. "I don't want to have something embarrass-ing to report to Anna's grandparents."

Grinning, John whispered in my ear, "So don't tell them." I giggled as I waved goodbye to him and the other men.

Inside, David had placed a few braziers in strategic locations. Alethea and Antonina had unpacked the silver cups that had been my parents', and started a fire to heat water to mix with the wine we had brought to chase the cold away. She also set out figs, almonds, and some of her walnut cake in what would be our dining room, although it held only a small table and a few chairs at that moment.

The house smelled young and fresh with paint, with none of the odors, good and bad, lurking in a house long lived in. My grandparents' house had always held the scent of the herb and flower gardens behind the house. Damien's house smelled of the fecund earth outside his door, and the many children within. Xene's house had smelled of what? Perhaps I had smelled marble and frost in its cold, spotless rooms, where silent servants drifted.

I had not visited the house since John moved in. Now, the rooms began to come to life with more furniture in place. My cheeks reddened when the party opened the upstairs door to what would be our bedroom, containing the bed and John's soldier's chest, but little else. The door, with its expensive metal hinges, had been an extravagance John insisted on for this room, with the other rooms having only curtains at their doorways for privacy. The bed's solitary state drew everyone's attention, eliciting giggles from the girls, while being politely ignored by my future sisters-in-law. Its windows overlooked the courtyard and had the best view of the sparkling ice blue waters of the Golden Horn, a few ships and fishing boats passing between the city and Galata. Even Catherine looked impressed.

Retreating downstairs, the young girls and I began a flurry of arranging all the household furnishings and implements. At one point, Marie and I together moved a heavy chest into the dining room, only to discover Catherine and Donya quietly sipping the warm drink I had planned to serve later, one small empty box between them.

"Anna, I hope you don't mind," Catherine said, "we were so exhausted with the unpacking, we decided to rest for a minute and enjoy this delicious wine."

The two of them did not appear to have unpacked more than that one box. Glancing at Marie, I saw her pale cheeks had blushed at her mother's excuse.

"No, of course I don't mind," I responded, hiding some slight irritation. "Please, have as much as you would like." Donya sat there placidly, saying nothing, before hiccoughing once. I wondered how much they had drunk.

Marie and I returned to our labors in the rest of the house, but she apologized later.

"Mama has always had servants to handle these sorts of chores. Aunt Donya might have helped more, but if Mama wanted company, then . . ." her voice tapered off as she shrugged.

"It is of no matter," I said. Conciliation seemed the most politic way to deal with this situation. "It was, after all, you and your cousins who made the offer of assistance. Your mother and Donya were kind to help with what they did."

The girls and I accomplished much during the rest of the day, turning the house into a comfortable home. Later, the rest of us joined Catherine and Donya for the repast, sipping the warm wine, pleased with our progress. The men returned just as we finished, exuberant in a clatter of hooves although their only kill had been a few rabbits. Flushed and famished from the exercise, they finished off every morsel of food we had brought.

Afterwards John showed the men around, commenting on our furnishings and the view from the bedroom, with the usual jokes bantered between Michael and Isaac. John returned downstairs laughing and with his cheeks ruddy.

Looking over, I saw Catherine standing by the door to the courtyard, wrapped in her thick wool cloak, Marie dutifully beside her.

"Isaac, it is getting late, I think we must return now," said Catherine with a hint of impatience.

Isaac's face was bland, but irritation flash briefly in his eyes before he clasped an arm around his son, Manuel, and the two turned to me.

"Young lady, thank you for the refreshments," he said. "The house looks perfect for you and John." He bent to give me a brotherly kiss before continuing. "The next time we'll be here will be for your wedding."

Manuel looked up at me, his young face much like Isaac's but with his mother's dark hair. He had the energy and awkwardness of a young deer, his clothes dusty from a tumble he had taken when hunting. His father nudged him into remembering his manners.

"Yes, thank you," he said, words all out in a rush. "Shall I call you Auntie, or should I call you Lady Anna? It is less than a month before you and Uncle John wed, so I think I could call you Auntie."

Taken aback, I said, "Of course you may call me Auntie. That would please me."

I thanked all of John's nieces for their help with the unpacking, as well as Donya and Catherine. In a few minutes, all were gone, giving John and me a few precious minutes alone. Leo and Patricios readied the empty cart for the return home, while Alethea tidied the dining room.

John grinned at me, and took my hand.

"Let's go upstairs," he spoke in a soft voice, looking over my shoulder to where Alethea was busy.

He led me to our bedroom where, smelling of wine and male sweat, he wrapped me in his strong arms and kissed me. His desire for me left me weak and breathless, flushed with my own yearning for him. After what seemed a long kiss, he pulled back, looking down smugly at me.

"I thought you might be willing to give me a kiss or two," and bent to kiss me again.

Too dizzy to speak, whether from the wine or from John's kisses, my arms circling him, our bodies bending together, warmer than they should have been that chilly December day. His hands around my waist felt more intense than any other touch I could recall.

Alethea called tactfully from the bottom of the stairs.

"We'll be down in a moment," I answered, reluctantly pulling back from John.

Before leaving the room, though, John pulled me to join him at the window. The evening shadows turned the waters of the Golden Horn purple. John stood behind me, hands gripping my shoulders. At that hour, the fishermen were gone, leaving only a few ferrymen lifting their oars between the city and Galata on the opposite shore. Lanterns glimmered like stars dancing in the gathering dark.

"It's magical at sunset," he whispered. "We won't have this view year round, when the trees are in full leaf, but we will in winter. It's so captivating, I don't mind leaving the shutters open to the cold."

"Well, perhaps a little, but not too long," I said with a laugh. "I don't want us dying of fever or ague before we have been wed a year."

He turned me towards him, my chin resting on his hand, his thumb lightly brushing my lower lip.

"My little Anna. I sometimes wonder how I can wait another month to be wed."

"It is only a little time compared to how long we have already waited. But I'm eager for that day, too."

The rest of that last month before the wedding flew by. There was one mild day when Grandmother visited the house. Alethea accompanied us to confer with Antonina and David about the preparations for the wedding feast, to be held at the new house.

Grandmother moved slowly through the rooms, commenting on furniture that had been my parents, and the pieces new to her. Peeking into a large empty room upstairs, she commented, eyes twinkling, "So this will be the nursery someday?"

Later we wandered out to the garden, where we had worked so diligently before Grandmother had taken ill. Most of it looked barren, although the rose bushes had taken root, even if cut back for the winter. The apple and peach trees had lost their leaves, and would not produce fruit for a few more years, but looked well settled into the earth.

"I'll give you seeds for the spring planting if you like," she said. "I've always preferred to grow as much of our own food as possible. You know the food is fresh that way."

"I think I will, too," I responded, surveying the substantial tract, already divided into areas for herbs, vegetables, fruits, and flowers.

Grandmother looked at me then, grasping my arm tightly as we stood surveying the dormant land.

"Anna, I think it is time for you to take over the warehouse. It will be yours someday and I cannot manage it by myself any longer. Samuel is experienced and trustworthy; you can learn much from him. If you have a question, you can always come to your grandfather, or me but now is the best time to take it on. I'll go over the account books with you tomorrow."

Life's responsibilities seemed to be showering down on me—marriage, filling the nursery, cultivating the garden, managing the warehouse, and my new household. It felt as though a harness had been strapped over my shoulders. Searching my grandmother's brown eyes, tired from even this short excursion, it was impossible not to accept it.

"Thank you, Grandmother. I'm pleased you think I'm ready for this."

The morning of the wedding dawned bright and cold. As was traditional, grandmother, my cousin Eugenia, and I wrapped ourselves in heavy mantles and retreated to our small brick bathhouse that morning. Earlier, Leo had stoked the fires heating the water. The steamy air and warm water scented with rose oil felt sinfully pleasant that winter's day as we disrobed and slid into the bath.

Tradition says a bride bathes before her wedding in the company of her female relatives. Those relatives had the responsibility, during the bath, to acquaint the bride with what to expect on her wedding night. I had thought, since I had lived on Damien's farm for those years, I might be exempt from that particular lesson. I soon realized, with some embarrassment, that my grandmother and cousin were strong believers in this tradition.

"I remember my bath before I married Constantine," Eugenia began. "My mother and older sisters told me the first time it would hurt terribly, but they were just teasing me. It really wasn't so bad."

"I had no other women in my family when Adrian and I wed, so your Grandmother," Grandmother said to Eugenia, "and Costas' wife Sophia went with me. The stories they told about the men in the family almost made me get out of the water and enter a convent. Stories about how big their cocks were and . . ."

That seemed an appropriate time to sink completely into the warm water and out of earshot. By the time I surfaced again, vigorously scrubbing my hair, the two of them were laughing wildly and making gestures I had only seen sailors make. This tradition had unleashed primitive traits that had never been evident before in either of them.

The laughter slowly subsided as they proceeded to wash each other's backs and helped with their hair. Eugenia glanced over at me as I sponged myself while trying to be unobtrusive on the other side of the bath.

"Auntie," she said to Grandmother, a mischievous look on her face. "I think we have been remiss in explaining things to Anna."

"No need to explain," I said, trying to end this conversation. "I know what to expect."

"Hmmm, what else does she need to know?" Eugenia asked, a humorous smile on her face.

Grandmother lounged back against the side of the pool, looking mischievous.

"Anna, you should know that the church says there should be no intimate relations on Saturdays or Sundays, or during Lent," she began. I expected a lecture on obedience to the church's strictures. "I am not sure why they say that, but you should also know that the church is wrong about that. There are plenty of babies born nine months after Lent, and not all of them are early or late. Your mother was."

I gaped at her. Grandmother had never disagreed with anything the church said.

"I don't know if John would do it, but there are many men who if their wife turns them down, would visit the nearest brothel. Or worse, take a mistress. And expecting a soldier to return home from a months' long campaign on a Saturday and have to wait until Monday to be with you is unrealistic." If possible, my jaw dropped further at these candid comments.

Eugenia nodded in agreement. "And you may not want to wait until Monday, either," she added with a thoughtful look.

"Really?" I asked, curiosity overcoming virginal reticence.

My cousin looked at me dreamily, thinking of another time and place. "Yes, with a good man, one who cares about you, it can be quite pleasant. That's what I had with my Constantine."

"You were fortunate," Grandmother said. "As was I. Not every woman is."

Xene's name hung unspoken in the air.

The water had become only tepid, so we withdrew from the pool and wrapped ourselves in towels before combing out our hair, drying it before the charcoal braziers Leo had left in the room. We were donning our mantles when Eugenia put out a hand to stop me.

"And Anna, it can be a bit awkward at first, but it really doesn't hurt so much. Just don't let John go at it too fast."

"I, I will try and remember that tonight," I stuttered out.

We returned to the house after the bath and I dressed in my mother's soft ivory silk dress adorned with elaborate gold and silver embroidery. It had been carefully packed away in a cedar chest these past twenty years, and carried the scent of lavender packed with it to deter moths. Mama's gold peacock hoop earrings hung in my ears; around my neck a gold chain held an enameled pendant cross, with the Theotokos and Christ pictured, a gift from John. My hair, combed and brushed to a glossy dark brown sheen with its reddish hints, hung loose down my back as a bride's should, was covered by an embroidered ivory silk maphorion. I kept warm in the thick red woolen mantle embroidered with gold and lined with fox fur Grandmother had once worn to the Great Palace.

John arrived pale and eyes glowing to escort us to the ceremony early in the afternoon. Grandmother, Eugenia and I tucked into the hired litters while Grandfather rode his gelding to Stoudion. The litter's curtains parted briefly when the men lifted the chair, to reveal the house that held my childhood memories. The curtains fell straight again when the men began the walk to the church, as though closing the book on childish thoughts.

My grandparents and Eugenia entered first, alerting everyone. I took a deep breath and emerged from my chair. John stood ready at the church door and grasped my hand.

"Ready?" he asked.

I nodded. Inside the church, the weak January sun gave some illumination through the windows, but it was the oil lamps on the dais that shone brightest as we passed through the assemblage. John's family was there, as were Xene and Constantine Ducas, my friend Eudokia and her mother, and other friends of our families. My cousin Romanus had been given leave from his taghmata to attend, only just arrived when we did, flashing me a shy smile as he hurried inside in the dress uniform he had received from Uncle Costas.

We stood before the iconostasis with its lavishly depicted angels and saints gazing solemnly down at us. Uncle Simeon beamed at me from behind the hegoumenos while Uncle Costas gave a surreptitious wink. The old hegoumenos greeted us, his full grey beard contrasting with a shiny pate. They wore beautiful vestments of green with gold embroidery rather than their usual simple monk's robes. Hegoumenos Michael's expression appeared phlegmatic; after seeing so many marriages over so many years, with such varied outcomes, his interest in the ceremony seemed almost academic. My two uncles showed more interest while assisting their hegoumenos with holy water, blessings, and the rings we would exchange. The priest murmured the prayers blessing the marriage while my attention drifted, glancing at John who soberly attended to the service. The sun brightened through the window, shining on a panel of the iconostasis, illuminating St. Michael, archangel and patron saint of warriors and princes, with feathery white wings, golden haloed and bearing his flashing sword. The saint's face seemed turned towards the gathering, composed of so many soldiers and their families, as though urging us on. For a moment that most military of angels crowded out all else from my mind, before the light on him dimmed and my attention returned to the priest's words.

Eugenia moved forward to hold the traditional crown over my head, while Isaac held John's crown aloft – symbols of our reigning in our family. I extended my hand to John. His hands, warm and solid, held mine as he slipped the ring on my finger. I pressed my token of fidelity on his finger where it rested firmly. The service over, I became conscious of the others in the church besides John. Isaac stood close to John, offering his good wishes. Soon the rest of our family and friends surrounded us, giving congratulations.

After the initial excitement died down, John and I thanked the hegoumenos for his blessings, bid farewell to my uncles, and departed for our house and the wedding feast. John and I rode in the litter, our hands clasped as though we would never let go, the wedding guests merrily escorting us. Behind the litter's curtains, John leaned over and we kissed, his hand firmly on my waist. I felt happy, breathless, and disoriented when Isaac pulled back the curtains.

"John, stop that. The carriers can't handle that sort of bouncing," he said to boisterous laughter.

My husband looked down at me, winked, and said, "I guess we'll have to wait a little longer."

Alethea and Antonina had roasted lambs stuffed with figs; scallops and many small bonito, fried and covered with copious amounts of a wine and fish sauce; small loaves of bread; olives of all sorts, along with pickles and almonds for luck, and other foods; and wine, of course.

The men swarmed about downstairs as the wedding feast began, taking advantage of the abundant wine and good cheer in the dining room. The musicians played, growing louder by the minute, sound emanating through the floorboards to the spacious upstairs room where the women, along with their children, congregated. For the celebration we had filled it with comfortable chairs and couches, and tables laden with as much food and drink as the men enjoyed in the dining room below. Charcoal-filled braziers warmed the house.

Xene, handsome in a dark blue wool gown, embraced me.

"Anna, you're a beautiful bride. I wish your mother could have seen how lovely you were in her dress."

"Thank you, Xene," I said, embracing her in return. "I was so happy you could attend." My hands held hers, still chilly on that cold January day. I stopped myself before mentioning my childhood recollections of her wedding over ten years earlier. She, too, had had a great feast, promising so much; that promise now long gone.

"I wasn't sure Constantine would permit it, but you married Isaac Comnenus' brother," she said with a little shrug. "Isaac's importance is growing, so he could not miss this. That, and he knew my father could not leave the monastery to come here, so we came."

"I don't care why or how, I'm just glad you're here," I said, my head bent close to her, to be heard above the rising merriment.

She gave me a sad, brittle smile. At that moment, my young friend Eudokia approached to wish me her congratulations and Xene slipped away to find my grandmother and Eugenia.

Eudokia looked after my cousin, a curious expression on her face.

"Who was that lady, Anna? She did not look very happy."

"That's my cousin, Xene," I said, before changing the subject. "I am so happy that you and your mother could attend today. Where is your mother? I have not had a chance to speak with her yet."

For the next few hours the guests celebrated with abandon, singing and dancing, eating and drinking. Early in the evening, Eugenia had handed me a small plate of food and a warm cup of wine, but I had had little opportunity to eat much else. The men downstairs became more exuberant as the evening wore on, intermittent bursts of raucous laughter streaming upstairs. It took little imagination to guess what the subject of the jokes was. It was a wedding, after all.

After several hours had passed, my grandparents had to wish me farewell. Grandmother's frail health kept them from lingering. Eudokia and her mother decided to leave with them and have an escort home through the dark streets.

Downstairs in the hallway several men stood, cups of wine in their hands, heatedly discussing the stags on a recent hunting expedition. I glanced around, looking for John when I noticed Isaac, a little apart from the other men in the hall, watching me. Our eyes met for an odd moment. It was just a moment, but his gaze was warm and appraising. Our attention then shifted to John, who noisily emerged from the dining room with my cousin Romanus, both holding full plates of food and splashing wine glasses, and I let him know of the departures.

John and I bade our farewells to my grandparents, expressing our gratitude for all they had done for me and for the wedding and receiving a final blessing from them. I helped Grandmother into her litter, tucking a warm blanket around her, while John held Grandfather's horse as he mounted, spirited in the frosty air. I turned then to Eudokia and her mother Marina as they readied to enter their litter.

"Anna, who was the young man with John when we came downstairs?" Eudokia whispered in my ear.

"With John?" my thoughts distracted, it took a moment before the memory returned. "Oh, yes, that was my cousin Romanus." Army life seemed to suit Romanus, who had a confident walk and a natural air of command.

"Really? He's very good looking." She stopped, and then laughed before asking in a teasing voice, "Is he a poet, or a soldier?"

"In my family? Oh, definitely a soldier. Before he was tonsured, Uncle Costas found him a spot in the Exkoubitores taghmata," I said.

"He could almost be a poet." she said wistfully, looking through the entrance into the hallway where we could see Romanus standing and talking to Constantine Ducas.

John and I bid Eudokia and her mother farewell before turning back to the house and our remaining guests. He grasped my hand as we stood in the lamplight and pulled me into a recess beside the door where we kissed, heedless of the guests. It was a cold January evening, but we could not feel it.

John tasted of the evening's wine and lamb, his lips warm on mine.

"I'm not sure I can wait much longer," he whispered in my ear.

"Mmm," not thinking of what else to say. I had longed for this day, too, but my upbringing had not included instructions on romantic conversations. At the same time, my body seemed to know what to do, drawn to John as though to a magnet, pressing itself against his.

After a few moments, John pulled back a few inches, holding my face between his hands.

"My little Anna, I will be very gentle. You don't need to worry about that," he said peering at me in the dim light.

I felt torn between embarrassment and gratitude. He was telling me I could trust him to care for me.

"I won't," I whispered, turning to kiss the hand on my cheek.

Isaac emerged from the entrance then, calling "John? John, are you out here?"

John rolled his eyes at Isaac's timing, and we re-entered the house.

Back upstairs the room was warm with the heat from the bodies of so many women and children, the braziers, and the hot food being served. Eugenia and Xene brought me a cup of wine and a few more bites of food. Catherine and Donya joined our little group and soon the four women were teasing me about what to expect on my wedding night. Or rather, three of them were—Xene was quiet.

"So Anna, do you think you are ready for John? He is a big man," Donya said, clearly more relaxed than usual given the plentiful supply of wine. The ladies laughed uproariously at this.

"Of course she is," Eugenia said. "Theodora and I explained everything to her this morning when we bathed." She belched gently at that.

That brought another burst of laughter, all of them telling the stories of their baths with their mothers or aunts or older sisters who had regaled the brides with stories of their wedding nights. Even Xene looked amused. At this point, all the joking about my bedding was becoming tiresome, but it did serve to take the edge off any anxiety. Perhaps that is why people did it, I thought.

David was suddenly at my elbow, trying to get my attention.

"Lady Anna, there is a senator downstairs who would like his wife to make ready to depart," he said discreetly. David did not know all of the guests, but senators wore tunicas with a red stripe, and Constantine Ducas was the only guest with that honor. I whispered to Xene, "Our steward says that Constantine is ready to leave."

The look in her eyes quivered between fear, disgust, disappointment, or some combination of those.

"Of course. I must find my mantle," she said in an emotionless voice.

Constantine Ducas waited in the hall, standing with Isaac and making plans for a hunting expedition in coming days. His smooth charm, affable and hearty, had put him on friendly terms with Isaac, who accepted the invitation. Ducas' ambitious fawning had deceived better men than Isaac.

Ducas glanced in our direction and made a curt dismissive gesture to Xene.

"I must leave now," she murmured. "I wish you great happiness in your marriage. You must come and visit me once you have settled in. I do not think Constantine will object." She glanced over her shoulder at Isaac, before turning to leave.

At that moment, the musicians started playing a lively song popular with the men, catching the attention of John and Isaac and other men. Ducas took that moment to depart, ignoring me and walking towards the door where he gave a rude shove to Xene who stumbled before catching herself. With the men's attention centered on the music and dancing, I thought I was the only one to witness Xene's degradation, until I looked up to see David's shocked expression.

Ducas' voice stabbed through the night air, "Get outside, you stupid cow."

I could not speak with shock. David flushed red with embarrassment at witnessing such degrading behavior, even as he followed them out to assist them.

I could not go outside, could not let Xene know I had witnessed her humiliation, could not comfort her in whatever distress she felt. I let her leave that night, without support rather than acknowledge her indignity. I do not know if it was the right thing to do, but it was the best I could do. Our Savior, all the saints, and the Theotokos forgive me.

After the scene with Xene, I rejoined the women, trying not to let it ruin my wedding. Inevitably the time came for the bedding. The festivities had reached their peak and some of the partygoers had begun to drift off, sated and stumbling to their horses or litters. Catherine, Donya and Eugenia hurried me into the bedroom where they removed my clothes, anointing me with rosewater, before tucking me into bed under crisp linen sheets and thick woolen blankets.

The shutters were closed tight against the winter's cold, while oil lamps gave light along with the two glowing braziers David had thoughtfully placed in the room. On a table David had left a pitcher of warmed wine, my parent's silver cups, and a covered plate of food from our feast. The thick oak door muffled the sounds from downstairs. Suddenly, thinking of the privacy it afforded, the expensive metal fittings for the door seemed a worthwhile expenditure.

I lay there only a few minutes before the sounds of the men ascending the stairs grew closer and I shrank under the blankets. The women giggled outside the door while the approaching men sang bawdy songs. Finally, the door opened and John staggered in, flushed from too much wine and embarrassment. Behind him, Isaac, Donya's husband Michael, and my cousin Romanus offered him encouragement and advice of a sort.

"If she tries to run away, tell her it's too late. You're married now," Michael chortled.

"Don't take too long the first time. You don't want to wear her out," was Isaac's recommendation, somewhat different from Eugenia's advice earlier in the day.

Young Romanus, inexperienced at this ribald humor, just winked at John with a sly grin before backing into the hall.

Finally, John wished the men a good night and shut the door, barring any further incursions. He stood there looking at me, one hand resting on his waist while running the other through his hair.

"I never realized what a great fuss weddings were before," his relief at the separation the door gave us from our guests palpable. "It's fine to be a guest at one, but quite another to be the center of all that attention."

I began to emerge from the covers I had slunk into.

I giggled nervously as I sat up, modestly pulling up the sheet. "Maybe that's why some enjoy other people's weddings so much. They don't have to worry about getting all that fuss made over them. After today, I can see why."

John sat down on a chair and removed his boots, placing them on the floor beneath the wall pegs that held our clothing. As he sat back he noticed the food and wine and glanced at me.

"Would you like some wine?"

"Yes, please, I would, and something to eat, too. I barely ate a morsel all day."

John smiled and poured the wine, then bringing my cup and the plate over to the bed, before returning with his own. He sat on the bed cross-legged and facing me while we nibbled at the almonds, apple slices and bread left for us. My hair fell over my shoulders while I tried to sit up so as to eat and drink.

"So here we are, finally in our own house and married," he said looking around our room. "There were days in Antioch when I worried you would not have the patience to wait for me."

My eyes widened, "You thought I would not wait for you? And I worried there might be some woman in Antioch you preferred over me."

"I suppose we did not really have anything to worry about, then" John said with a smile, his hand reaching to hold mine. The braziers could not overcome the wintry night air seeping in, but John's hand was warm and strong. Our eyes met, neither of us able to look away. He leaned over and kissed me lingeringly, his hand sliding up my arm with a hungry touch, before pulling back.

"Are you finished eating? Do you want anything else to drink?" he asked in a low, rough voice.

"I am finished," I croaked, handing him my cup.

He brought the dishes back to the table before hastily undressing, hanging his clothes on the pegs.

"It seemed like half the women tonight were intent on telling me how terrible it will be, while the other half said it was not so bad," I babbled while getting the first sight of my naked husband, solid and muscular, with freckles and a chest of manly red hair.

John chuckled. "Some of the men said I may have to beat you into submission. The rest just laughed as though they knew some secret."

"I wonder what that secret is," I said as he slipped into bed beside me, his body radiating a young man's heat, his hand cupping my breast as he bent to kiss me again, as hungry for me as I was for him.

"I think the secret is that I must tell you how beautiful you are."

Every inch of skin he touched seemed on fire in a way I had never felt before. My body arched toward his, almost of its own volition. His mouth moved to nibble on my ear.

"And I must tell you how much I want you," I said, my voice husky.

Grandmother and Eugenia were right—it was most enjoyable.

CHAPTER THIRTEEN

Storms

1044 to 1045

Somehow I did not become pregnant right away despite vigorous efforts, but embarrassingly enough, did during Lent. Grandmother and Eugenia chuckled at the news.

It pained me to tell Xene. John Ducas and his wife Irene had had a son, Andronikos, the year before. My pregnancy could only be another bitter drink to swallow. Still, she offered congratulations and promised a beautifully embroidered gown for the child's baptism. I would have done anything to avoid seeing the look of despondency in her eyes at the news, but there was no help for it.

John and Isaac stayed close to home with no foreign assignment that year. The empire's borders were calm after the Maniakes rebellion, the Rus attack, and the Saracens who had harried Antioch. But not all was peaceful.

Early in the year, John and I paid a visit to the warehouse my grandparents owned that I now managed with Samuel. I had been there many times, but John had never seen it before. Samuel planned to show us the entire building and review the business' affairs. A young boy greeted us on our arrival, running to summon Samuel from his office.

"Welcome, welcome, Lady Anna, Sir," Samuel said with a wide smile, his hands in constant motion as he spoke. "I see you have met my son, Joshua." He beamed down at his son, who looked about twelve years old.

"Thank you, Samuel. You've a handsome boy there. Very attentive," John said. "Does he work here with you?"

"Yes, he can read and learned his numbers, so now he helps me." The curly-headed lad had a shy smile for his father at this approbation.

Samuel escorted us into the cavernous building heaped with goods, some from craftsmen in the city, some coming on ships from the east. In a few weeks, once the sailing season began, they would be packed on merchant ships going west. After a brief tour, we returned to Samuel's office to review his account books.

Samuel led us to a large table in the center of the room on which there sat a pot similar to those used to serve wine that has been warmed, with three cups. He lifted the pot with a flourish and poured the heated beverage into the cups.

"A month or two ago, I was able to do a great favor for a merchant I know who was in some difficulty. He was so grateful that he gave me these leaves that can be brewed into a delightful beverage." He handed us the cups with a look of excited anticipation. "Please, drink, I think you will enjoy it."

Hesitating only a little, John and I took the proffered cups and sipped. A light floral scent wafted up from the liquid, which had a mild, pleasant taste to it. The heat from the drink spread through me, welcome on that chilly day.

"It's delicious," I said. "What is it?"

Samuel beamed at our enjoyment.

"The merchant called it chai. It comes from far to the east, beyond the mountains on the other side of the Black Sea. I rarely see it carried here by the caravans. I'm glad you like it." He rose from the table, striding to a cabinet along one wall, where he removed a small cloth bag filled almost to bursting.

"Lady Anna, Sir, I would be pleased if you would accept this gift. The bag holds more of the dried chai leaves. Brew the leaves in hot water at your house to make the drink," Samuel said handing me the bag.

"Thank you Samuel," I said, the floral scent emanating from the soft pouch.

Our conversation turned to business matters then, as Samuel reviewed the records. Towards the end of our discussion he stopped speaking, a worried frown on his countenance.

"I should mention there is a concern I have for the profits the warehouse can earn this coming year," he said. "I must warn you that they could diminish."

"Why is that?" asked John with a look of mild concern.

"I don't know if you've heard the news, but the emperor is starting a new building project and I've been told the plans are extensive."

"I've heard something, but my attention has not been on the emperor's activities of late," John said, with a fond look in my direction.

"Understandable," Samuel replied. "The emperor is tearing down the old arsenal at the Mangana near the Great Palace. It sounds like his plans are for almost another Great Palace, with a new palace there, a church to rival Hagia Sophia, and others buildings. The talk is it's to be named for St. George."

I was confused. "I don't understand. How will this impact the warehouse's income?"

"The word on the street is that the emperor will pay workers top wages to speed construction. So the dockworkers may take the opportunity to find employment there, unless we raise their pay," he answered.

That was unwelcome news.

John glanced over at me. "I guess we're fortunate our house is finished. The higher cost would have really drained me if this had happened last year."

Grandmother had barely turned the warehouse over to me, and already I had problems with it.

A few days after the meeting with Samuel, I spoke with Grandmother about the emperor's plans.

"I'd heard a little of these plans. Your grandfather said the emperor plans to build a palace first for La Skleraina to live in. It may be more ornate than any building in the Great Palace."

Eugenia, sitting nearby with her sewing, looked up from it and sniffed. "So much money bestowed on a house for his mistress. I wonder what his wife thinks of this?"

I rose and walked over to the brazier near Grandmother, stirring the coals to generate more heat for her. The emperor's plans to spend so much gold on a palace for his mistress, especially after the loss of the Italian taxes, was both extravagant and insulting to Zoe and her sister, the true heirs. Surely he would not try to eliminate them the way the last boy emperor had tried. I shivered recalling the blinding of two years earlier.

But that question was on the lips of many in the city.

Some days later John proposed that we rise early to attend one of the Holy Week imperial processions at the great church of Hagia Sophia. We did not often attend services there because of the family's close ties to St. John Stoudion, which lay nearer our home, but we thought to offer thanks there for the child I carried. The patriarch would be officiating beneath the high golden domes floating above us that seemed to capture heaven within them—the glittering mosaics of Christ, the Theotokos, and angels, the exquisite chanting of the day's hymns by the eunuchs' choir.

We arrived in the predawn shadows, accompanied by our groom, Narses, who carried a lantern to light our way. Even though many people stood outside in attendance, it was a quiet gathering, proper for the solemnity of the observance. As the first streaks of dawn became visible the emperor appeared from the palace gate attended by Varangian guards, his handsome face appropriately sober as he greeted the dynatoi lining the path to the church. For some reason, though, neither the Empress Zoe nor her sister, the rarely seen Empress Theodora, joined him in the procession.

It felt like a lightning bolt shot through the crowd as people peered over shoulders at the procession, searching for the missing empresses and muttering.

"I wonder what that scoundrel has done with our empress? He builds a palace for his whore, but scorns his wife?" said a thin middle-aged woman standing nearby, disgust evident in her voice.

A bulky gray haired man, still upright and with the large hands of a carpenter, next to her said, "What kind of man would humiliate our empress that way? He deserves no better than what that last emperor got." Others around those two grunted or nodded in agreement.

John and I glanced at each other as the subdued grumbling continued. The emperor's procession made its way into the church. John joined the men in the nave, while I climbed the ramp to the women's gallery.

Squeezing through the jostling crowds of women I found a spot near the railing with an excellent view of the proceedings. The center gallery where the empress usually stood was unoccupied.

The eunuchs' choir, their elegant voices rising in a hymn lamenting and glorifying the crucifixion, began the service. Acolytes swung censors, the sweet smoke rising to the heavens with our prayers. The patriarch, Eudokia's uncle Michael Keroularios, began intoning the prayers and it appeared that the angry words spoken earlier had been left outside. Then the patriarch called the emperor forward to participate in the blessings of the day, and it became clear that the crowd's indignation rose like the incense.

A black clad elderly woman near me screeched, "What have you done with our empress? She should be here with you, not your whore." I do not believe La Skleraina was there that day, so perhaps the woman was mistaken, or presumed her presence. It hardly mattered. Other women in the gallery yelled down, but the voices of the men in the nave throbbed with anger.

"No murdering our empress so you can marry your whore."

"Unworthy."

"Get back to your island, or we'll poke your eyes out too."

"Dig up his bones."

The cries incited hisses of agreement and catcalls throughout the church. The armed Varangians attending the emperor could deter a physical attack, at least for a while. The emperor stood on the dais below but, after a anxious glance around, whispered something to an attendant who disappeared through a side door.

The patriarch stumbled in his litany, unable to focus as the men continued calling out "Unworthy" and "Dig up his bones." I could not see the men's faces since the women's gallery looms so high above them, but their rough voices made it clear that the pulse of the crowd was rising into a riot.

The patriarch's disorientation worsened as he processed behind the iconostasis earlier than he should have. The emperor, however, assumed an attitude of humble prayer. The choirmaster, sensing the need for peace, started the eunuchs on a long hymn, perhaps not fitted to the day, but which reminded the worshippers of the holy place they were in, subduing their outrage for the moment.

Just as the hymn finished, a commotion came from the imperial gallery as Empress Zoe and her sister, Empress Theodora, and their ladies appeared in courtly regalia of purple robes and pearl encrusted gold crowns. The two empresses stood close, on their designated green marble circle, their raiment shining in the dawn's light streaming in from the high arched windows behind them, seen by all in the church.

The crowd sighed as the two women dropped to their knees in prayer. A woman near me proclaimed, "God bless our Empress Zoe. God bless our Empress Theodora." Other voices echoed this call and the service reached its conclusion without other interruptions.

After the service, I met John and Narses as we had agreed, in the Augustaion. A crowd milled about the large forum outside the great church, with its pillar topped by a statue of Emperor Justinian. The relief on John's pale face at my appearance was as evident as mine was at the sight of him.

"Are you all right?" he asked, grasping my arm while people swarmed around.

"Yes, fine. What of you? The men sounded as though they would attack the emperor.," I looked up into his face as he glanced around.

"I wasn't sure what I could have done. I'm not armed and with that crowd I would've been torn apart if I had tried to defend him. The Varangians would have held the mob back for a while. I don't want to think what would have happened if the empresses hadn't appeared when they did." We began the brisk walk home before he added, "Fighting in battle, in war, is ugly, but as a soldier, I know what to expect. With riots, there's no predicting."

The incident made an impression on the emperor who soon changed the plans for his project. Instead of building the new palace for his mistress, he would start with the Church of St. George Mangana.

A spring morning a few weeks after Easter, I slipped from sleep into drowsy wakefulness as the morning sun seeped through the curtains. Rolling over in bed towards John I indulged myself in viewing my husband's naked body – muscular, with luminous pale skin covered with scatterings of freckles. The red hair on his head was almost the color of oranges, while it was a darker, almost vermilion in color elsewhere on his body. I languidly ran my hand over his torso, smiling in recollection of the previous night that had begun with a game of chess, but had not ended that way.

John shuddered awake, opening one eye to peer at me. He turned towards me, wrapping an arm around me and kissing me with less intensity than the night before.

"Who won that game last night?" he asked with a quizzical smile, his hair ruffled up.

"I think we both did," I said, giggling.

"Hmmph. Well, better than you always winning. I'm not sure what I was doing when I married a woman who does not have the sense to let her husband win at chess."

"Oh, but a woman like that would be so boring. No challenge to her. You weren't bored last night were you? You wouldn't want to be bored?"

"Probably not." He then grasped one of my buttocks and pulled me closer still, sighing heavily as we lay in each other's arms. "Anna, I love you. I never thought to be so happy."

I looked into his eyes. We had been married for months, after years of waiting, and he had never said that to me before. I knew he loved me, knew it that day in the garden when he and Isaac had come to say the betrothal must be delayed. He would not have followed me out there if he had not loved me then, or thought he did. Now, after the wedding and the starting of a child, he said those words.

"I love you, too, John. I never thought to be so happy either."

We lay there together for some time as the sun rose higher before John said, "What were you going to do today? I've nothing on my schedule. Isaac and Catherine are visiting her brother Alousian, so he won't need me."

"I had a visit to Xene planned; I'd thought to ask Narses to accompany me, but I would enjoy your company more," I answered. "Eugenia was going to join me, as well." Grandmother would have wanted to go, but climbing the many stairs to the Ducas gynecaeum was beyond her capacity now.

"That sounds like a fine idea. I can speak with Ducas while you visit with her," he said.

I paused, trying to think how to explain the Ducas household. "John, he's not usually at their house when I visit Xene. I believe he's busy about the city on Senate business most of the time."

I'm not sure why I never told John then all there was to know about Constantine Ducas. I had been raised to be loyal to family, and he was, by law, family, so perhaps that was it. Or maybe I thought that someday John would come to see how vile the man was. It seemed obvious to me.

"Well, no matter. I will join you and if Ducas is there, we can speak of arranging another hunting trip," John said. John, Isaac and their brother-in-law, Michael Dokeianos, often gathered a few other men, usually soldiers they knew but sometimes Ducas, for hunting expeditions. The lack of a military campaign that year had left the men hungry for vigorous physical activity.

Later that morning John mounted his horse while I was in the sedan chair that had been hired for the day. We went first to my grandparents and, after a brief visit with them, Eugenia joined us.

Oddly enough, Ducas was home that day and welcomed John into his office while his steward escorted Eugenia and me upstairs. As we climbed the stairs I could hear the men's jovial talk below, so different from the sepulchral silence that had enveloped the house on our earlier visits. On the top floor we entered the room but saw only the sullen servant girl who was Xene's companion.

"Where is Lady Xene?" I asked her.

She made a careless gesture towards the open door to the small balcony. I relaxed, then. Of course, she would want to be outside to enjoy the fresh air on this lovely day. Looking out to the small area, though, there was no evidence of her. I looked around the small area, thinking the girl must have been mistaken. Only when I was outside on the balcony did I see her, and my heart skipped a beat. Xene was sitting on the tiled roof of the house, eyes closed and her face tilted to the sun, oblivious of me.

I could not speak for a moment, nor could Eugenia who had followed me and stood nearby in as much shock. The roof was not at a sharp pitch, but it was not flat and there were three stories between her and the hard slate in the courtyard below.

"Xene," I said, trying to appear calm, "my goodness, what are you doing on the roof? You must come down. Let me help you, please give me your hand, cousin."

She opened her eyes and looked down at our horrified faces.

"Oh, Anna, Eugenia, I am so sorry, I'd forgotten that you would be here today," she said. She scrambled toward the balcony. Our hands reached to grasp her into safety, but she shooed us back.

"Don't be worried. I'm often up here, I can manage," which she did using a chair I had not noticed earlier as a step to hop back to the floor.

Xene seemed embarrassed by our discovery.

"Oh, please don't worry about me. I'm careful. It's just that sometimes I need to feel free and out in the open. On the roof I'm above most of the other buildings, the air is fresh. I can see the seagulls circling, and hear the crowds at the hippodrome. I never climb up there when it is raining and the tiles might be slippery—only on days such as today." She spoke as though an accident was impossible.

She looked into the room where her days were spent, before turning back to us to whisper, "You must not say anything about this to Constantine. He wouldn't approve, and I would be so unhappy if he forbade it. Promise you won't."

I felt torn. Ducas had complete authority over her and could stop her, but I would never tell that vile man anything Xene asked me not to. Still, I had to stop her from putting herself in such a dangerous spot.

"Of course, Xene, we won't say anything to him."

"Xene," cousin Eugenia said, her eyes full of a sharp awareness I had not seen before, "Of course, we won't say anything to Constantine. My, that is something of an adventure, climbing up to the roof that way. Have you been doing it for long?"

Xene glanced up to the roof, her hand caressing the warm red clay tiles. "Not for so long, or so often. It was less than a year ago I first tried it."

"It's so dangerous. You could hurt yourself. Please, please do not do this again," I said in consternation. "I won't tell Constantine, but you must agree not to go up there again."

She looked contrite, squinting into the sun and grasping my hand before shrugging, "All right, Anna. If it worries you so much, I won't do it."

Eugenia said, "Why don't we go inside and have something to eat? I believe Sebastian has brought some wine and food for us. I brought along a dress that I have been sewing that I wanted your advice on. There is a stitch that I cannot get right and I thought you could help me with it."

Eugenia's light conversation during the rest of the visit masked the profound concern I knew we both felt. Later, on returning to my grandparent's house, I got out of my chair for a short visit with them.

Eugenia stopped me, "You must not say anything about Xene being on the roof to your grandmother. She's not well enough to deal with that, and she can do nothing about it anyway."

I looked into Eugenia's deep-set grey eyes, and nodded. "You're right; it would upset her." I twisted my hands together in consternation.

"Do you think Xene will stop climbing up there?"

Eugenia gave me a long look before speaking, "I don't know. She's unhappy, which can make a person take chances they might not otherwise take. We'll have to pray for her, and visit as often as we can."

John called from the door to the house, "Anna, your grandparents are waiting for you."

"Just remember, say nothing," Eugenia said.

Xene seemed to have taken our counsels to heart, for we saw no repeat of her rooftop foray. With that worry eased, I was lulled into a complacent mood with my pregnancy over the summer. Working in the garden consumed much of my time, trying to coax it into the abundant production Grandmother managed with hers. At night, I fell exhausted into bed, encircled by John's arms.

The summer heat was amplified by the heavy turgid air hanging over the city. John and I often spent our evenings in the cool waters of our small bathhouse.

Late in September, I awoke to an insistent wind rustling the bedroom curtains. The cool rush of air on my sweaty skin felt miraculous after the long sultry days, but a glance outside revealed heavy gray clouds seething across the sky.

The morning never brightened much and a light drizzle fell. By midday, the rain had grown to drenching sheets and strong gusts bent the trees low. I peered out through a crack in the shutters to see the rain pelting down in the courtyard now scattered with leaves and branches. An ominous feeling blew in as the hot air was blown away by howling winds and the unrelenting downpour.

In the afternoon, my grandparents' stable boy, Patricios, arrived soaked to the skin, rain dripping from his clothes.

"Lady Anna, General Dalassenus sent me to tell you that your grandmother has taken ill again. He wants you to please come as quickly as possible," his anxious expression told me more than his words did.

"Yes, of course," I said, looking at John.

"We'll have to walk; the horses would be too skittish," he said.

Resounding thunderclaps followed the occasional lightning bolts, jangling my nerves as we hurried through the near empty streets. My hand gripped John's so tightly my fingers grew stiff, but I hardly noticed as prayers of intercession fell from my lips.

Finally we reached the house and I rushed inside to find Alethea, looking pale, at the door.

"Alethea, what happened?" I asked. John and I hung our dripping cloaks on hooks, the pungent smell of wet wool permeating the air.

"She fell again. She had been in her workroom talking with your cousin when she said she felt tired and wanted to go to bed. We went with her upstairs but when we reached her chamber the shutters on the window there suddenly blew open and we went to close them. When we turned back, she had fallen to the floor," she said, chin quivering, her eyes filling with tears. "I am so sorry Anna."

Grandmother's fall sounded like what had happened the last time, in the garden, and she had recovered from that. Perhaps this would not be so bad.

"Don't cry Alethea, I'm sure you did nothing wrong. Who else is here? Has anyone sent for the physician?"

"Yes," she said, sniffling. "Maria Kourtikios arrived not long ago."

Upstairs we found Grandfather and Eugenia standing in the shadowy hall, awaiting the physician's report.

"Anna, I'm worried. I've only seen her eyelids flutter a few times, she's not spoken, she hardly moves," Eugenia said. This was worse than before, when she had at least been able to groan and say a few words.

Grandfather stood nearby, almost unable to speak and rubbing his hands over his face repeatedly.

It seemed we had stood this way together not so long ago when she first took ill. So much had changed since that day the year before, and here we were as though nothing had changed.

Maria emerged from grandmother's chamber, a grim expression on her face as she went to my grandfather.

"General Dalassenus," she said in a soft voice, "your wife is gravely ill. I fear I must tell you that at this point, my medical skills will not be as efficacious as your prayers. My advice is to send for the priest."

Her bluntness jolted me. "Is there nothing you can do?"

"Lady Anna," she said gently, "there is only so much medicine can do. Then it is in God's hands. Your grandmother's illness is worse than last year's—she hardly moves, she's spoken not at all, and I am only assured she still lives because of the breath I can feel from her nostrils. I think it will not be many hours. I am sorry to tell you this, but this way you can prepare her."

Grandfather appeared numb at this news.

John said, "I'll ask Nicholas to send for Simeon and a priest," and moved downstairs.

Eugenia grasped my hand, tears falling down her face to match my own. My grandmother had been the anchor for so many in the family, and she was being swept away.

Sometime later a Uncle Simeon and a priest arrived from Stoudion. Father Joseph shooed us out of the room to give her the last rites. After he finished, he emerged from the room. "Lady Theodora has received the church's blessings. She's a good woman who will be missed, but it is in God's hands."

His words did not lessen my grief, but I came to a kind of wretched acceptance. I returned to her bedside for the last hours. We took turns holding her hands during that night as the winds howled. Large limbs cracked from trees and fell noisily to the ground, sometimes with a glancing blow to a roof or building. The flames in our lanterns flickered from gusts swirling into the house.

A few times during that long night, holding Grandmother's warm hand for the last time, I felt a squeeze from her, but that was all. The agony of waiting for the end felt worse than knowing that the end was near. The noise from the storm only increased my agitation.

Finally, towards dawn the storm abated and Grandmother neither breathed nor moved again. Her hand fell slack and felt cool to the touch. Eugenia moved to the window and opened the shutters to the dawn, the clouds and rain gone, leaving behind a ravaged landscape visible now in the morning sun. Grandmother's garden was a morass of dislocated plants and mud, while the trellis over the table had blown over and smashed into sticks.

I was exhausted and my face felt swollen from crying. John stood with a hand on Grandfather's shoulder.

"It's over, Adrian. She's with the angels now," he said.

"Small consolation, that," Grandfather said, his spirit not yet resigned to his loss.

"We must see to the preparations for her funeral," said John. Gently, he and Uncle Simeon took Grandfather's arm and they walked heavily down the stairs, leaving Eugenia and me with Grandmother's body.

She had become thinner in the past year. Her body barely made an impression on the mattress, unlike the impression she had had on her family. Now, she was so still, the stillness of death, her face peaceful. The struggles of this world behind her.

"Anna," Eugenia said in a soft voice, "Will you help me wash her body?"

I nodded and wiped my eyes on my sleeve, unable to speak.

The next few days felt hazy, with an occasional light shining on the events. Alethea and Eugenia made preparations for the visitors who came to say a last farewell, sweeping the house clean and laying out food for them. They used the abundance of olive, myrtle and cypress tree branches left from the storm to scatter around her body, as was our tradition.

Isaac came with his family in the company of Constantine Ducas and my cousin Xene. Ducas used any opportunity to push himself forward, even my grandmother's funeral. Still, he would not likely behave badly toward Xene in Isaac's presence so I was grateful. Donya came also, with Michael and their children. In amongst the many offering condolences were more than a few of the traveling monks to whom Grandmother had offered food and shelter over the years. Grandfather welcomed their words of appreciation for her kindnesses.

"There are many who profess the love of the Theotokos and the Christos, but few who demonstrated it as generously as Lady Theodora did," said one.

Their kind words only magnified our loss. Even Uncle Simeon, tonsured and apart from her for so many years at Stoudion, seemed bereft at his mother's death.

She was buried beside my mother and the other children she had borne who had not survived long. She rarely had spoken of those losses, but now, as I carried a child myself, I realized how deeply she must have felt their deaths.

Grandfather, Eugenia and I made the customary visits to her grave on the third, ninth and fortieth days after her burial. By the last visit I began to feel the pall of her loss begin to lift, a final acceptance.

Back at the house after the last graveside visit, Eugenia spoke with me.

"Anna, Uncle Adrian and I have spoken about my situation here. He's asked me to remain here, tending the house for him. He's said Romanus would be welcome here at all times, but I wanted to be sure you had no objection to me staying."

I embraced her. "Eugenia, I had hoped that you would stay with him. I cannot think of him living here alone, or of him leaving the house where he spent so many happy years with Grandmother."

Over the fall and winter I came to terms with Grandmother's death. Eugenia and I sorted through Grandmother's clothes, among which I found a scarf she often wore when gardening. It carried the scent of her and the herbs she grew. I kept it in a chest in our room, holding it to my face and breathing in the smell when I missed her too much. The fragrance kept her close for a long time before I had breathed it all in.

That bitterly cold winter meant braziers burning throughout the house most days.

My pains began one night in early February, at a moment when I felt sure I was on the verge of bursting. I rose from bed, wrapping a heavy shawl around me, and began pacing about the dark room.

"What are you doing?" John asked groggily.

"I just feel as though I need to be walking," I said. On further consideration, as a pain stabbed through me, I added, "I think the baby is coming."

He startled me when he shot out of bed faster than I had ever seen him move. "Do you want me to get the physician? Your cousin?"

"No, not yet. But a candle or lamp would help. I don't want to trip over anything," I answered as a contraction tightened around my belly. He stumbled downstairs in the dark to catch a flame from the kitchen hearth before returning with a lamp and a pitcher of watered wine. I drank a few sips of it, before John consumed the rest, too nervous to realize what he had done.

The pains grew worse as night became day. Maria Kourtikios and Eugenia arrived, ready to help, but there was little to do for some hours. Grandfather kept John company downstairs. Finally, sometime after midday, I began pushing. It was not long before our noisy son slipped into the world and made his presence known in the house.

John came to our chamber to see us. "He's beautiful, Anna," he said in wonder at the small child nuzzling my breast. "We'll name him Manuel, after my father."

I looked at him quizzically. "If you wish, but he does have a cousin with the same name," I said, thinking of Isaac's young son.

"No matter. Better to remember my father that way," he said, smiling fondly at our tiny son.

Little Manuel's fingers curled around one of mine as he suckled. I gazed on his small wrinkled face and his dark red hair and thought I had never seen such a lovely creature in all my life.

CHAPTER FOURTEEN

Xene

1045

The next few years saw the city of Byzas blossom into a magnificence people said had not been seen in the world since the storied days of the first Justinian five hundred years ago. The emperor's building projects meant sparkling new palaces, churches, public gardens and theaters impressed travelers, and gave employment and prosperity for even the meanest laborer. Every visitor, whether riding his horse through the Golden Gate up the Mese or sailing into its ports with his wares for sale gazed upon the city in awe. The emperor spent gold nomisma from the imperial treasury like a spring bubbling up from inexhaustible streams, most especially on the majestic Church of St. George Mangana and its environs. Even so, one year into its construction, he decided the church lacked sufficient grandeur to be the site of his tomb and that of Skleraina. He had all that had been built torn down, beginning again on a grander scale. Few in the city questioned the waste of what he had already spent since they benefited from the work the building and rebuilding provided.

The emperor collected a menagerie of animals from distant lands, new to most in the city—elephants, tigers, giraffes, camels and zebras—putting them on display for all to see. He sponsored performances of mimes and acrobats, as well as presentations in theaters of well-known orators he invited to speak. I only heard of most of these performances from Catherine and Donya, being wrapped up in the responsibilities of new motherhood.

My little son delighted me every day with his smiling face, although that first year of his life had its low times. Uncle Costas was in attendance at the child's baptism at Stoudion, but in the months since I had last seen him he had aged perceptibly, his skin turning dry and brittle, his beard thinner. A bout with an ague left him coughing and gaunt, walking at a slower, careful pace. Still, he blessed the child enthusiastically, congratulating Grandfather on his first great-grandson.

"Adrian," he said, peering at the small sleeping bundle that was Manuel, "I think he bears some resemblance to you as a babe. He has the same large eyes you had, and cap of dark hair. Well, perhaps not hair of this lad's reddish hue, but you had as much as he does." Uncle Costas had been seventeen when Grandfather was born, the baby of the family.

Grandfather chuckled at the comparison as the baby wrapped a tiny fist around one of his fingers, a rare moment of happiness for him since Grandmother's death.

Eugenia looked down at Manuel, resplendent in his white silk baptismal gown, a gift from Xene. She had stitched a masterwork of embroidery filled with angels and flowers, doves and vines. It had arrived a few days earlier with a message apologizing that she could not join us.

"I don't know that he resembles anyone just yet, uncle," Eugenia said, giving the child a doubtful look.

Isaac stood nearby with Catherine but gave the baby the briefest of glances before saying confidently, "I think he'll look like John with that red hair." He clapped John on the back, grinning at the new father.

At the ceremony's end, I went to embrace my uncle in farewell.

"Be sure to take good care of that beautiful son of yours," he said. "And know you and your family will always be in my prayers."

"Thank you, Uncle, I will. And you, too, will be in my prayers," I said.

That was the last time I saw Uncle Costas. A few weeks later during an unexpected spell of icy weather just before spring he slipped on an icy spot, hitting his head as he fell. The accident left him insensible, although he still breathed for several days before his soul passed beyond the cares of this earth. Grandfather and my Uncle Simeon were at his side in the monastery's infirmary in his final moments.

Grandfather, Eugenia, John, and I joined Xene for the funeral service, and on the incense-filled walk to the monks' graveyard. Ducas should have been there for a final farewell to his father-in-law, but he was not. Uncle Costas would not have wanted him there; I doubted that his brief time in the monastery had graced him with the saintly ability he would have needed to forgive his son-in-law.

Grandfather looked resigned at this burial of his last surviving sibling, patting little Manuel's head absentmindedly. The bright early spring day saw pale green shoots rising from the earth despite the chill wind still blowing from the north.

Xene looked heartbroken. Tears flowed down her cheeks the entire time as though from a mountain stream. If anything, the prayers left her more desolate.

Lord, oh Lord, you are the relief of the troubled and the consolation of the mournful and redeemer of all the afflicted. Comfort those who are seized with pain for the deceased; being merciful, heal all suffering of sadness gripping their hearts, and give rest to your devoted servant resting in the bosom of Abraham in the hope of the resurrection; because you give resurrection to your servants, and we give glory to you.

She managed to muffle her sobs until the hymns ended and with the funeral service concluded, and the gravediggers began shoveling the dirt over him. The monks had left us when cries burst from her lips in grief's agony.

"Anna, I don't know how I can go on without Papa," she sobbed in my arms. "How can I go back to Constantine knowing Papa is gone?"

Eugenia and I held Xene close. Eugenia had her son, Romanus to anchor her in life, and I had John and our son. We offered Xene solace, but her weeping would not stop that late afternoon as the wind whipped around our skirts in the graveyard.

Spring warmed into summer and Manuel grew into a charming toddler who delighted almost everyone. Isaac's wife, Catherine, usually seemed uninterested, but our visits to their home were few, so she did not over trouble me.

One day John returned home and announced that we were invited to dinner the next evening at Isaac and Catherine's. Their grand estate encompassed less land than ours, but overlooked the Sea of Marmara. Its elegant gardens were tended by some of the dozen or so slaves they owned. Its opulent rooms with polished marble floors, expensive carved furniture, and large windows framed with flowing silk curtains looked out beyond the gardens to the shimmering sea.

"Really?" I asked. We did not often receive invitations from them, and they usually arrived well prior to the engagement. Isaac's and Catherine's ambition meant he had an abundance of engagements. "Why such short notice?"

John shrugged. "Isaac was asked to entertain the former king of Armenia and wants our assistance at it."

"The former king?"

"Yes, well, he thought he was king, until the emperor reminded him of a treaty his father had signed with us, giving the kingdom to the empire on the old king's death. The emperor invited him here to discuss the treaty, but then convinced him to formally abdicate," he said as he peered down at little Manuel resting in my arms. "Not that it mattered by that time. After the king left to journey here, our army arrived and convinced their capital city to surrender."

I gave John a confused look. I did not understand why the dinner was needed, and it seemed doubtful that this putative king would be happy to join us.

He continued his explanation while peering down at Manuel, trying to coax a smile from him with a funny face. "The emperor wants Isaac and Catherine to explain the benefits of becoming a dutiful citizen of the empire, as Catherine's father and Isaac's grandfather did. He's offered this king a villa on the Bosphorous, and a generous income, but the king is recalcitrant." John's efforts with Manuel were finally rewarded when a beatific smile lit up our son's face.

"He must be unhappy at fate's turn," I said casually. "But some emperors might have just executed him before he ever arrived here. Perhaps he should be grateful, even with the loss of his kingdom."

"If anyone can convince him of that, it's Isaac. He could persuade a dog to give up its bone," John said, grinning.

The next evening we arrived at Isaac's before the guest of honor. Trying to look my best, my gown was of embroidered red silk with an embroidered belt, and I wore the gold chain with enameled gold cross that had been one of John's bridal gifts to me. My efforts would never outshine my sister-in-law's, whose income and interest in fashion far outstripped my own. My estimation was confirmed when Catherine appeared a short while later, statuesque in an exquisite sapphire blue gown, and wearing a sapphire and pearl necklace. She appeared like a goddess, with her dark hair swirling about her face. I sometimes envied her having a slave devoted solely to her hair and clothing.

We were engaged in casual conversation while awaiting the guest of honor when I realized I had never learned the man's name.

"Isaac," I asked, "John never mentioned the name of this king you are hosting tonight. What is it?"

"My name is Gagik," said a voice from the hall.

We turned to see a robust young man no older than myself striding into the room, an embarrassed servant trailing behind, too slow to properly announce the impatient guest. He was dark haired and with deep-set black eyes, solidly built and of the same height as John.

"Sir, welcome. I am pleased you could join us this evening," said Isaac as he hastened to greet this king, a little flustered by the man's unannounced appearance.

"I suppose I am pleased, or should be, although I do not believe I had a choice," King Gagik answered caustically, glancing around at the lavish surroundings. His eyes took the measure of the beautifully wrought furniture, the silk pillows and cushions, the shining silver goblets, the gently billowing curtains.

After hurried introductions, and ignoring Gagik's inconvenient comment, Catherine invited their guest to have a seat on one of the cushioned benches on the terrace overlooking the Marmara. The gardens, lush with the scents of summer flowers in the setting sun, radiated tranquility after the noise and rush of the city's streets. A servant slid a cup of wine into the king's fist before retreating.

After a few uncomfortably silent moments, I said, "Catherine, you have a lovely view from here, especially this time of year. The way the last of the sun's rays light the sea at nightfall is marvelous." The sea shimmered in darkening hues of blue and gold as a few seagulls circled over the white-capped waves.

"It really is, Anna," she replied, pleased at the compliment. "I was fortunate to inherit this property on my mother's death."

"Wasn't your father the king of Bulgaria?" Gagik finished off the wine in his cup and gestured to the servant for more. He looked around at the elegant surroundings and added, "This is a fine estate, but not much of a kingdom."

"Yes, he ruled it before Emperor Basil conquered it," answered Catherine. She looked at him with the smug smile of the dynatoi she had lived among for most her life. "But the emperor was generous to us after my father's death. We had an easier life here than in Bulgaria, with so many men always on the verge of betrayal or rebellion."

"Hmmm," said Gagik with a sour look. "There's more to one's existence than just living like a well-fed cat. I'd rather watch my back for traitors than be caged." He stood and paced the terrace as though looking for an escape. "Life should be more than that of a sponge soaking up wine, accomplishing nothing."

Gagik stood in the fading light gripping the railing that circled the garden, silently looking out to the sea below. I had thought life in this most beautiful of cities would be more appealing than living in the dusty, windswept mountains of Armenia. But this was not his home, and he had ruled a kingdom. He meant what he said.

I recalled Uncle Costas and his years of exile in Egypt as a hostage. He told me in time he realized these obstacles were part of his life's journey. He had been angry at the start, but realized anger gained him nothing. The patience he learned in exile served him well when the emperor imprisoned him. Gagik would need to learn his own journey's lessons.

"So what sort of existence do you desire?" I asked.

He gave a short laugh, "Lady Anna, not one that any Roman woman would understand."

"Sir, I think you must imagine my question to be fickle. But like my husband I came from a family of soldiers and, truly, I do wonder what it is you desire." Catherine was giving me dagger eyes, while Isaac looked interested in Gagik's response.

Gagik looked into the fine silver cup that held his wine, swirling it before responding.

"I don't know now. I wanted to be the king my people need; I wanted a legacy for my sons," he said. "I do not want my existence to be wine and parties and foolishness."

Isaac looked at Gagik intently before responding.

"I agree. A man's life should not be given just to pleasure and ease. There needs to be purpose. Things done a man can be remembered for."

At that, Catherine had had her fill of serious conversation and invited Gagik to walk down to the water's edge with her.

At supper Catherine's superb chef served a feast including succulent roasted goat, fish, and the abundance of the harvest of beans and olives, and fruits. I looked across the table at Gagik, noticing his expressive dark eyebrows, and beard, black and full for someone of his young years. I tried to imagine what it must be to rule a kingdom as he had for a few years, and then have it swept away. To be told you cannot do what you were brought up to do.

Isaac was picking out succulent bits of the bronzino, cooked in olive oil with lemon and garlic, when he commented, "I understand you are unhappy with the loss of your kingdom. Still, there is no denying that Imperial troops occupy your capital, and you've signed the abdication, leaving you a guest of our emperor," he paused, I think wondering if the term 'guest' was politic, "so you don't have many choices."

Gagik looked around like a caged bear, restlessly running his hands back and forth on the arms of his chair.

"You and your family, you're accustomed to the ways of this city, of this empire," he began, looking at all of us. "I was raised to be a king, to rule a people far from here, and now I am told to forget all that, to slouch around by pools surrounded by gardens and forget all I was born to do. I am not an old man, and I do not want to be the lackey of that man wearing the purple." He sounded both fierce and desperate.

Gagik stopped. I did not often see men with tears in their eyes, but Gagik's dark eyes appeared to be deep pools.

"My people," he said in a dispirited voice, "they must think I have abandoned them, when I have had no choice."

The rest of us, even Catherine, sat in embarrassed silence before Isaac spoke again.

"Gagik, the Roman Empire holds people from many lands within its borders, including Catherine and myself; that is and has always been the Roman way. I fight for the empire now, as does my wife's brother, Aron, who is governor in Vaspurakan. Armenians are part of it now. You may find serving the empire, as I have done, can lead to a position of greater power and influence than you might ever have had as a king."

Gagik sat with his elbows on the table, head bent with his fingers massaging his temples in frustration at these circumstances. He looked up and eyed Isaac warily.

"So you say I should accustom myself to soft Roman ways, and even fight for this emperor who has taken my throne?" he asked.

"I say you should accustom yourself to Roman ways, that are not always soft, and fight for the empire, which now includes the people of Armenia," said Isaac. "Not exactly the same thing."

Gagik sat back in the chair then, giving Isaac a deep look as he pondered that observation. A spark of interest crossed the young man's face, which lost some of its bleak despondency.

He sighed heavily, "I will give your words thought. But I could never take up arms against my people."

"I would not expect you to, nor would the emperor. If you would like, I would be pleased if you joined the troops I lead. An energetic young man such as yourself, with experience leading soldiers, would be a welcome addition, wouldn't he, John?"

"I agree, Isaac," John replied. He gave an encouraging smile across the table at Gagik, who appeared heartened by the invitation. At that moment, I realized John had been correct – Isaac could talk a dog out of its bone.

Fall arrived and with it memories of the previous year's terrible storm and Grandmother's death. I still wept for her sometimes, pulling out her scarf from the bottom of the chest where I kept it, breathing in the garden scents that always clung to her. Her voice echoed in my mind, repeating my name.

Xene seemed to have recovered from her father's death. At least, she did not appear as distraught as she had in the early days when Eugenia and I found her weeping on every visit. She held to her promise not to perch on the roof, or so we thought, since we never saw her there. Eugenia, without the responsibility of an infant as I had, visited more often, but neither of us ever observed her there.

I breathed an inward sigh of relief as I saw her becoming calmer over that summer. She kept busy embroidering many small shirts for my little Manuel, and a few larger ones for Eugenia's Romanus. Even so, Eugenia said she still felt some trepidation at Xene's behavior, a sense of grief hidden, like a sea monster ready to rise from the ocean's depths.

At one visit, the three of us were together in the Ducas gynecaeum sewing and taking turns holding baby Manuel when Xene reached into a wooden chest in the room and removed a small parcel wrapped in soft kid leather, handing it to me, while taking the baby into her arms.

"Here, Anna, I would like you to have this," she said. "Your mother gave it to me when I was a girl, but I do not have the time to read much these days and I thought you would enjoy it."

Opening the wrappings, I saw a book with a deep brown leather cover and the words "Holy Psalms" embossed on it. Inside it was beautifully illustrated with a drawing of a golden harp on the first page next to the words of the first psalm, carefully inscribed on the ivory parchment in black ink. I read the first few lines, "Happy are those who do not follow the advice of the wicked, or take the path that sinners tread." Leafing through the pages interspersed among the holy words I saw drawings of snowy lambs and shining swords, of jugs pouring red wine and delicate pink roses surrounded by lush green leaves.

"Xene, you cannot wish to part from this. It is too generous of you," I protested.

She smiled, pleased at my surprise. "It would be no more generous of me than your mother was when she gifted it so long ago. You know I prefer to spend my time in sewing, not so much reading. And you are just the opposite. I think your mother would be pleased to know you now had it."

Eugenia was giving Xene a quizzical look, one eyebrow raised. Xene turned to her then, pulling another wrapped parcel from her chest.

"I have not forgotten you," she said, and handed the new package to our cousin.

Inside was an Egyptian sandalwood box, the lid inlaid with an intricate design in mother of pearl.

"Papa brought it back from Egypt when he was there, for my mother. It has been mine since she died, but Constantine wants me to get rid of things he does not think I need anymore, so I thought you might like it."

The small casket held a few dried red roses within it, curled and brittle.

"The roses are from the bush Papa planted at the house in Amaseia for my mother," she said.

"I remember it," I said, thinking back to the garden where John and I had sat one evening with Grandmother, first getting to know each other.

"Xene, you are too generous," Eugenia exclaimed as she reached over to hug Xene. "I'll treasure it always. Your parents were so dear to me."

Xene beamed at our pleasure in her gifts, looking the happiest I could remember seeing her as she bounced Manuel on her lap.

Later, when we were outside getting ready to depart, I remarked to Eugenia at Xene's gifts.

"Yes," she said as she gave a worried look up at the balcony jutting from the gynecaeum, "she was kind." She looked at me then, and shrugged before adding, "She did seem happier today, so maybe she is finally getting over Uncle Costas' death."

I smiled at that thought, and wished Eugenia farewell.

A few days later Manuel came down with an ague, feverish and with a dripping nose for days, so it was almost two weeks before I could again visit Xene. The weather had turned cooler with gloomy overcast days and rain, while the leaves changed color and began floating to earth.

John had the time to escort me to Xene's that day. It had rained earlier, but the sky was clearing when we left, I in my sedan chair and John on horseback. I regretted not returning sooner to Xene's house, wondering if she might think me ungrateful for her gift, despite the notes I had sent her about Manuel's illness.

Our party approached the Ducas house, plodding carefully in the still damp streets. Curious to see how close we had come to their residence, I peeked out through the curtains and saw the house was within sight. Glancing ahead, I gasped in shock. Xene was, again, sitting on the roof.

"Anna," John said, a peevish tone to his voice as he heard my cry, "what is wrong?" He had been riding along side of my chair and was annoyed by traffic. He heard the noise I made but had not seen what I had seen.

I pointed to the house. Words would not come and John looked exasperated at my inability to explain. But he peered ahead and after a few seconds, saw what I saw.

As I watched, Ducas emerged onto the balcony, searching for Xene before noticing where she was perched. I heard his angry shouts, but could not make out his words, lost in the wind and the sounds of the street. He tried to reach for her. Xene looked at him and seemed to be answering him while trying to slip further away from him. She wiped her cheeks with her sleeve.

Xene's husband climbed onto the chair she used to reach the roof's peak and began pulling her—or was it pushing?—off. They appeared to be arguing, shouting accusations at each other, anger and frustration in every push and pull. Xene slid closer to the roof's edge, shoved there, or slipping away from her husband. I could not be sure what exactly happened, but then she plunged down to the hard slate tiles of their courtyard. Her scream vibrated in the air.

In moments John and I had reached the house, as servants emerged and surrounded the limp body of their mistress, my beloved Xene. Her face was a hideous shade of purple I will never forget, sprinkled with red flecks of blood, her eyes rolled back in her head. I knelt next to her, holding her hand with the final beats of her heart pulsing, hoping somehow for a miracle that would keep the heart and body alive. But there was no miracle that day, only, perhaps, a blessing as she found a peace she had not known on this earth for many years.

It was sometime before Ducas had descended the many steps to the dead body of his wife. He was not there to give comfort in her last seconds, nor ask her forgiveness. He did not reach out to her or touch her. He stood staring from the mansion's white marble doorway under gray skies amid the dripping leaves, dispassionately surveying the remains of his wife, before giving an instruction to the shocked servants.

"Send for the priests. They will need to take care of this."

John was kneeling next to me when he heard Ducas's voice. He composed his face and glanced at the man. He squeezed my arm, quietly asking, "Will you be all right? I can take him inside."

Through tears, I nodded and the two disappeared somewhere into the house. Ducas' steward, his face pale and voice stuttering, ordered servants to bring Xene's crumpled body into the house. I stood weeping in a corner of the room where servants placed her so they could wash her before wrapping the body in a plain burial shroud the steward hastily procured.

Eugenia eventually arrived, looking stunned. We clung together. I reached out to touch Xene's hair, still a rich chestnut shade, so like my own, with no hint of silver before the shroud finally covered her face.

The rest of that day is blurred in my memory. The priest looked in briefly to say a few prayers over her, before going to speak with Ducas about the funeral.

I saw little of Constantine Ducas the rest of that day. As the sun began to set, John pulled me away to remind me of the living, of our son waiting at home, and we departed. I wept in the privacy of the curtained sedan chair.

Early the next morning John and I first went to Grandfather's house to meet with him and Eugenia before making our way to Ducas' house to greet the mourners. John and Grandfather sat talking quietly in the dining room, sipping watered wine and eating bread while Eugenia and I walked in the garden. Eugenia's interest in gardening was not like Grandmother's was, so it held a more disheveled look than before. But a few late roses still bloomed.

"Eugenia, what was she doing up there? I thought she had stopped that, I thought she realized how dangerous it was."

Eugenia gave me a thoughtful look, before putting her arm around my shoulders.

"Don't blame yourself. Xene knew it was dangerous. You could not have prevented this."

"What are you saying?" My mind tried to twist around Eugenia's implications.

She said nothing, unnaturally quiet for her, and then spoke carefully. "Xene was sad and had little left to live for after her father died. I don't think she did this deliberately to end her life, but she became reckless when her life had so little left in it."

"How can you say something like that? You're almost saying she wanted to fall to her death."

"I can say that because I have lived with losses like hers and came close to something as careless as what she did." Her eyes were dark and grim as she spoke, swirling with pain. "When they told me that my husband had hanged himself, that he was a traitor and his estate confiscated, I didn't want to keep living. I'm not saying I would have ended my life or that Xene did, but there can be times when you do not care what happens anymore. It was only my son that pulled me from that edge."

Eugenia never spoke of the shameful death of her husband, Constantine Diogenes, who the Orphanotrophus had imprisoned and tortured. One night, rather than succumb to the torture, and name others as conspirators with him, he hanged himself. Either that, or the Orphanotrophus had him hanged to appear a suicide when he could not extract what he wanted. Uncle Costas had never thought him a suicide. Even so, Eugenia's husband was buried in the windswept area of unmarked graves for suicides. Her son was a small child, not much older than my little Manuel, when his father was buried.

A short while later, the four of us left to greet the mourners alongside of her despicable husband. I would never know whether Xene had wanted to die, or wanted to live. All I did know was that Constantine Ducas was, in some way, the cause of her death.

Most of the mourners were friends of her father who had known Xene as a bright, beautiful child. After the last of them left, I sat watch over the body during the night before she was buried. Eugenia was with me some of the time, but in most of the dark hours I prayed alone while she slept elsewhere. Ducas had played the bereaved husband when visitors had paid their respects, but disappeared when they were gone.

Xene's cold body lay unmoving in the candlelight. If Christ could raise Lazarus from the dead, then why not my dear cousin, who was surely as sweet a person as Lazarus had been. My prayers were unanswered and my mind wandered in a hopeless maze of wishes.

At one point, I sensed another presence in the room. Turning, I saw Ducas watching me from the doorway, a wineglass in his hand. I had nothing to say to him, and turned back.

"D'you really think your prayers will help her?" he asked, his words slurred.

"I do," I responded curtly. "Your prayers might also be of assistance."

He snorted. "I doubt it." Tradition said a man should spend the night before his wife's burial praying at her side. "Barren woman that she was, she's better off where she is."

I swallowed my bitterness and turned away from him, hoping he would just leave. He would be of no benefit to Xene now, either in body or in spirit.

I had no intention of confronting this monster my cousin had married. Pointless. But then something gripped me – a spirit or ghost demanding justice that would not let go. I turned back to face him.

"Did you push her off the roof?" I asked, the words tumbling out.

"What?" he appeared shocked at my question. "I wouldn't push her. I was trying to get her down from there when she slipped off and fell. She was crazy, going up there."

"Then why were you up there? Xene said you never visited the gynecaeum. Why were you there?"

Ducas looked irritated. "You tell me," he sneered. "She sent her slave down to me, asking me to come see her. I thought she'd finally agreed to a divorce. I didn't see her when I got to the room, so I went to the balcony and realized where she was."

"You had asked her for a divorce?" I was incredulous at this.

He appeared nonchalant at my question. "Didn't you know? I'd told her I wanted it a month ago, but she would not agree, even though Myrelion had agreed to accept her. What use is a barren wife?"

A month ago was not long before my last visit, when she had given me the book of psalms and the Egyptian box to Eugenia. What had Xene planned? Had she decided on the tonsure or a darker solution?

"Don't you think she wanted children, even more than you did?"

"Maybe she did, but she never produced any. The church says I have a right to have children, and put her aside. I just needed her to agree. I thought she'd finally seen sense."

I bowed my head again, too appalled to look at him.

"She didn't want to leave you; she still loved you," I said, my voice just above a whisper.

He shrugged, as though that was of little importance. "Well, now I'm rid of her and her blasted father, that stinking, farting, old buzzard got me caged with him for seven years. Always yammering on about making the best of a bad situation, wanting me to play chess. I'll be glad to never see another chessboard again. I'll never have those years back, wasted in four walls with a man I loathed. Who could blame me?"

I could, was the thought that came to me. It was long after midnight and long before dawn. I was suddenly too tired to continue the argument, too tired to defend Uncle Costas who deserved no such incarceration. I turned back to my prayers for Xene's soul.

Ducas, deep in his cups, was not finished with me.

"Don't you dare blame me for her death. She was a useless, stupid woman who did nothing for me," anger pulsing in his voice.

I looked up sharply at him, "Is that all that matters? What someone can do for you?"

He looked confused at that, as though all the rest of the world was there to do the bidding of Constantine Ducas, and why did I not realize it?

"None of what happened was Xene's fault. She wanted children. And yet you treated her as though that was all her fault. Why couldn't you just accept it?"

Ducas looked at me with a raised eyebrow for a long moment before confiding something I never expected. "Because I want a dynasty."

"A dynasty?" Where did his ambition end? But perhaps I should have guessed. He had married Xene because her father was the preeminent general of the Empire at that time, almost Empress Zoe's first husband.

"Why not? The empress has no children. The Ducas family has had generals in the Empire since the days of the first Constantine. It's time one of us should rule," he said as he straightened.

The light in the room dimmed as one of the candles sputtered out. Ducas' face was in shadows, set like a stone against any criticism. He saw nothing but his own thwarted desires. Xene counted for nothing.

"I see you have no understanding of my position," he said looking down his thin nose at me. He glanced at the shrouded body before turning away. "I'll leave you to your prayers then, Lady Anna." He left the room and made his way to the stairs.

Arrogant bastard, I thought. What a desolate life Xene must have had with that man. Anger flashed through me like lightening.

I spent the rest of that night alone with Xene for the last time, keeping watch over her as she had with me when I was a child who longed in the night for a mother who had departed with the angels.

The morning dawned windy and overcast, but there was no rain. I stood fatigued from the lack of sleep among the mourners at her graveside. The new widower had donned a suitably mournful expression, along with his mourning attire. Of course, John came as well as Isaac and Catherine, and Donya and her husband.

Eugenia and Grandfather stood with me at the graveside, tears streaming down their faces, for they had loved Xene as I had. I thought it was only us three there who truly knew her, loved her, and mourned her that day. Her brother, my cousin Damien would have, but he was far away in Amaseia and would not learn of her death for weeks.

A glance at Ducas revealed no tears, just impatience to get the matter done.

The priest's words offered some slight comfort.

God of spirits and all flesh, who has vanquished death and trampled on the devil and given life to the world, give rest to the soul of your servant, Xene, in a place of light, a place of refreshment, a place of repose, from which pain, sorrow, and sighing have fled. Because You are so good and love mankind, forgive her every offense, whether in word, or in deed, or in thought, for there is no man living and never will be who does not sin. But You alone are without any sin, your righteousness is an everlasting righteousness, and your word is truth. For You are the life and the resurrection of the dead, and we give glory to you.

At the funeral's end, the other mourners moved away from her grave, returning to their lives, leaving behind this woman who had been nothing but sweetness and kindness my whole life. John waited with Isaac some distance away from the grave as I made my last farewell to Xene.

Ducas and his brother strolled toward their mounts, giving a brief farewell to the priests. It felt as though an arrow pierced me as I watched their perfunctory actions. I wanted to scream at him to return, to fall on his knees to beg her spirit's forgiveness, to say he had some small love for her, to offer prayers for her. Instead, I saw the brothers laughing at a shared joke as they turned their horses toward home.

The gravediggers shoveled the dull clods of dirt mercilessly onto her shrouded body.

I wiped my eyes with a damp sleeve and peered into the dark hole. I gripped my maphorion as the autumn wind whipped up my skirts. A seagull called as it made a slow circle above us.

"Xene, I don't know what happened on that roof, when you fell," I whispered to her spirit. "But whatever happened, I know Constantine Ducas bears its responsibility. I promise you this—I don't know how or when I will make it happen, but he'll pay for what he did to you. I promise you, he will pay."

And in that moment, though I had a husband I loved, and a beautiful son, it was hatred of Constantine Ducas driving me forward.

CHAPTER FIFTEEN

Emperor Constantine Monomachos

1045 to 1047

The next year John left with Isaac and his army not long after Easter for Armenia, planning to meet with the Turks at their border. John and Isaac spent many hours closeted with Gagik at our house before leaving, learning about the terrain and the growing numbers of the barbarian Turks and Persians who tried to pierce the border, no matter whether that border was called Armenian or Roman.

"Roman armor is stronger than anything the Turks have," Gagik said. "But their horses are faster than you have seen before, and their men shoot easily even while they are racing away. If you must fight them, it would be better in the mountains where their horses' speed will not give them that advantage, but plan ahead to avoid ambushes."

"We've no plans to fight them. The emperor just wants to know more about them," said Isaac.

Gagik shot him a cynical look. "Go well armed. Look impressive. Don't let them think you're easy to take down. They will seize any opportunity."

Isaac shrugged, and nodded. "Good advice," was all he said.

John told me there had been few reports of Turks attacking the new border with the empire. Even so, I worried, and not just because of the memory of the two Turks who had attacked me years earlier. Every few months reports of attacks on our borders buzzed through the city. I was far from the fighting, but my husband would not be.

John sent us only one letter that long summer:

My dearest Anna:

Isaac and I have had good fortune in our visit to Armenia, meeting no aggressors on this trip. The land here has few inhabitants, mostly sheep and goat herders. The city of Ani, which was Gagik's capital, is a fortress with high walls that could have long withstood a siege. The empire was fortunate that its rulers had no taste for combat after Gagik departed.

The Turks are fierce warriors—strong, fast, and relentless in their pursuits. Isaac made sure our considerable forces wore all their weapons when we met them, thoroughly impressing them, so at present they have no interest in attacking. If you see Gagik, you must tell him we are grateful for his advice.

Isaac keeps us moving constantly, to avoid showing these Turks any sign of weakness. We always have the sense of being watched, although we rarely see signs of the barbarians apart from our official meetings.

I find myself often thinking on you and our son, looking forward to the day that I can sleep in our bed again and bounce our son on my knee. You must make sure he does not forget his father, off on the emperor's errand in distant lands.

Your loving husband, John.

I was grateful for even this one missive that long summer. I saw Gagik every few weeks and gave him John's words of appreciation. His wife, Hija, had been scooped up from her castle in Armenia and brought to Byzantium with their son. She had recently had a second son, and was recovering her health. I visited her with gifts after the child's birth, but she was shy and spoke little Greek, which kept our conversation brief.

Gagik would sometimes visit us at Grandfather's house, and the two of them would play a game of chess or with my cousin Romanus when he was on leave. The two of them had much in common, both being soldiers not far apart in age, and having had responsibility thrust on them early. Gagik was a garrulous man, either asking Romanus about military matters, or recounting his experiences from when he had been King Gagik of Armenia.

One afternoon the two of them had been contending over the chessboard for hours when Romanus moved his king to a square protected by one of Gagik's elephants. Gagik raised a dark eyebrow, looking distinctly cynical.

"This game teaches many lessons," he said, his Armenian accent heavy. "The king has little power without his knights and castles, his vizier and elephants, and, of course, his little pawns. Even the pawns can do more than the king can. I wish I had known that a few years ago."

Romanus looked up at that, curious at the observation.

"I don't think that's the case with our emperor."

"You don't? What would your emperor be without his soldiers, the palace, the bureaucrats who do his bidding, and, of course, the empress? And if any of them became disloyal, betrayed him, he would be lost, just as a captured chess piece is, and lose the crown." A keen observation but Romanus still looked perplexed.

"Gagik is right, Romanus," I said. "The loss of a knight or a castle, or even a single pawn may not lose the game, or in life, the throne. But the more pieces, the more supporters the king has, the stronger he will be, the better able to defeat opponents, whether foreign armies or usurpers."

"Gagik, I think you have discovered the heart of chess," I added.

He gave a short, rueful laugh. "Maybe, but not soon enough. If I had learned as a child, I might not be here today."

"So, what did you do that put you here?" Romanus asked, pushing back his hair.

"Well, first of all, I left my side of the board, venturing to the other side without sufficient men accompanying me for protection. A king should never do that, but the advice I received from this piece," and he picked up the vizier, "and from this piece" and he picked up an elephant, "was to do it. I did not realize I had already lost those pieces since they had plans of their own and no loyalty to me."

"Well, you could not have known they would betray you," Romanus said.

Gagik looked at my cousin for a long moment before answering, his expression sour.

"When I look back, I remember small things, whispers and false smiles hiding their treachery. I thought they accepted me as their king, but they lied. Their ambition blinded them. They thought the emperor would make one of them king. Instead, POOF and there is no more king in Armenia. They are chess pieces with no king to defend and fight for. My game is over, but so is theirs. Checkmate."

Thinking out loud I said, "A king needs loyalty more than anything to keep his throne. The question is how does he get it and hold it?"

Gagik glanced over at me and shook his head. "That will depend on what each man wants – it could be money, or a title, or honors. Some are generous with their loyalty asking little, some miserly demanding much. And if a man wants what you have, your gifts to him may be great, but they will never suffice."

"Gagik, you sound so cynical," Romanus said, uncomfortable with the serious turn the conversation had taken.

"Perhaps. But I think only experienced," he said ruefully.

Gagik then made his next move and indeed, he had checkmated Romanus who appeared abashed at his loss.

At that moment, Grandfather and Eugenia returned from a walk in the garden with Manuel, who toddled along between them. My son grasped the stem of a red poppy in his fist, a big smile on his face as he came running to me.

"Here Mama, a fritty plower for you," his confused words breaking the tension that had grown in the room.

"Thank you Manuel. It is a pretty flower, isn't it?" I kissed him on his round baby cheeks then, and lifted him onto an embrace on my lap.

John and Isaac returned home in September, with Isaac reporting to the Domestic of the Scholai on their meetings with the barbarian Turks. Manuel had almost forgotten his father in the months of John's absence, but they quickly reacquainted themselves. Unlike many men, John enjoyed his time with Manuel.

I knew before we wed that marriage with a soldier would mean lengthy periods alone. The reality of so much time alone was different from the contemplation of it. While John trooped through Armenia I learned that his absence meant many long solitary nights in my bed, worrying about him and missing him. Some women did not seem to miss their husbands so much; Catherine never appeared to. In fact, she looked as though she enjoyed her freedom during those months. Still, she greeted Isaac enthusiastically on his return, so I may have misread her.

Our reunion, after many months apart, sparked memories of the hunger for each other we had felt on our wedding night, but better now with the knowledge we had of each other. It may not have been that evening, but within those first few passionate nights of his return I was with child again.

I welcomed his warm body close to mine, as the autumn nights grew colder.

"John," I said, half asleep one evening after making love.

"Hmm," he barely responded, exhausted from a day of chasing Manuel around, and a night of chasing me around.

"What is it like when you are on campaign? I mean, do you miss me?" I did not want to ask, were there other women he turned to in my absence. But I did want to know if there might be.

"Of course I miss you. You are my wife. I have no desire for any others." His armed curled about me, warm and secure in the chill night air. "There are no others for me."

Comforted by that thought, I drifted off to sleep.

That long winter passed uneventfully as my belly grew with the next child we would have.

Although our lives were placid then, other forces grew beneath the surface. Late in that spring, just after Easter, the emperor recalled his cousin, Leon Tornikios, from Armenia where he had been strategos amid reports that Tornikios was planning a rebellion. The emperor soon had his cousin tonsured and packed away to a monastery, thinking the matter resolved.

This news seemed so distant and unimportant to me. My mind was preoccupied with our child who was due in June. Mid-month, I went into labor and quickly delivered our daughter, a sweet child with my coloring we named Maria after John's mother. Soldiers' concerns held little interest for me then, although John and Isaac often spoke of Tornikios' attempted rebellion.

We were in the garden behind the house with the children, John and Manuel running about with a ball and stick, Maria sleeping in a basket next to me. Isaac arrived unexpectedly and sat in the dappled sunlight on a bench across from me under the arbor, watching his brother and nephew playing.

"Reminds me of when my Manuel was little. He was just as busy, running everywhere." He tapped his foot impatiently, waiting for John to join us. His eyes darted back and forth, looking anxious.

"What's wrong, Isaac?"

He glanced over at me, seeming to consider whether I could be trusted not to become hysterical at the news he brought. Men thought that of women, and perhaps Catherine or Donya might, so he hesitated. His intent gaze reminded me of the way he looked at me the night John and I had married. I felt suddenly warm, not just from the bright sun that day.

After a moment, he bent forward, resting his elbows on his knees, hands clasped, before speaking.

"Tornikios has bolted from that monastery the emperor tucked him into. We think he's gone to Adrianople."

"What?" I asked. My fingers curled tighter around little Maria's hand.

"Must've bribed someone. His family is from there, and he's got friends stationed nearby. We found the horses kept at the Imperial rest stops going in that direction were killed to prevent pursuit."

My jaw tightened.

John and Manuel finished their playing and joined us under the arbor, John hoisting our son onto his lap as they both caught their breath.

"I was just telling Anna the news. Tornikios has escaped. Gone to Adrianople," Isaac blurted without preamble.

"What? Really?" John asked sharply, as he handed Manuel a cup of water to cool off that warm morning. He pushed back the hair fallen in his face while roughhousing, looking straight at Isaac.

"Yes. Monasteries are not as secure as prisons, which would have been a better place for Tornikios. But he is the emperor's cousin," said Isaac, unsmiling.

"What's the emperor doing now?" asked John.

"Sent scouts out to learn what Tornikios is up to. But he'll be here soon with his army. Maniakes had to make his way all the way across

Greece in winter; Adrianople is closer, and it's warm," he finished as he rose and began pacing on the terrace.

John looked out into the garden, and then at his brother. My husband never assumed the worst. John loved and admired Isaac, but I had come to realize he lacked his brother's clear vision and surefooted decisions. "So we'll wait to see what the scouts learn. No point in worrying yet."

Isaac stood up, his eyes hooded. "Perhaps not, but it will not hurt to round up what soldiers we can find, should they be needed. Can you meet me at the office of the Domestic at daybreak tomorrow?"

"Of course," John replied, although his tone implied he thought it was decidedly premature. Even if Tornikios was planning a rebellion, how fast could it occur?

After Isaac departed, John voiced his confidence that his brother was premature in his concerns.

"I think Isaac is letting Tornikios distress him without reason. The man is miles away; it will be months before he approaches the city, if ever." John, I was realizing, rarely chose to worry about what the fates might have in store.

Even so, Isaac's deep concern weighed on my mind. In the morning I sat with David and Antonina to assess what foodstuffs, firewood and oil for lamps we had on hand, and what we might need should the city come under siege. For several nights in lamplight I cursed my foolishness for not learning how to sew better. I repeatedly stabbed myself while embedding gold coins in our garments.

John was wrong. Tornikios moved faster than anyone expected, even Isaac. Even before Isaac's visit, the usurper announced to the people of Adrianople that Empress Theodora, who theoretically shared the throne with her sister Zoe and Zoe's husband, had named him emperor. A lie, but the people there believed it and acclaimed him. News arrived in Byzantium a few days after Isaac's visit that Tornikios had gathered all of the empire's soldiers from north and east of Adrianople, to the border where the Danube emptied into the Black Sea. These thousands of soldiers stood guard at the empire's margins against the barbarian Pechenegs, whose fierce nomadic clans had long been a thorn in our side.

That these soldiers so quickly and willingly deserted their posts to fight for a usurper was more worrisome. What had happened to their loyalty?

Less than two weeks after his escape from the monastery, Tornikios and his army began marching to the city, ravaging the countryside as they went. The panicked emperor called in as many troops as he could, sending for the thousand or so Exkoubitores from Bithynia where they were stationed across the Bosporus. He sent other messengers to Armenia where an army was stationed, but it would be weeks before they would arrive. In consequence, there were precious few other soldiers available since most had gone home to tend their fields and bring in the harvest, as was the custom that time of year. The city had local conscripts assigned to the walls, the numeroi and teichistai, but they numbered only about four thousand and few had battle experience. They knew better how to interrupt drunken brawls and haul broken carts out of the roads than how to fight the battle-hardened themata troops Tornikios led.

I was hardly less panicked than the emperor. We had enough stores of food set aside to last through a lengthy siege, and when word of Tornikios's approach reached us, I convinced Grandfather and Eugenia to stay with us along with Alethea and Maria, leaving Nicholas and the men servants to guard their gates. John and Isaac manned the walls with the other soldiers.

On the afternoon of the day the rebel troops appeared outside the city's walls, I paced about the house, wondering if I should pack our belongings. John had left hours earlier with Isaac and there had been no word from him since. The numeroi and teichistai had manned the city's walls, dragging ballistae into position for assaulting the enemy.

"Anna," Eugenia said, "there's nothing more you can do now. You should relax. You won't have enough milk for the baby if you keep this up."

I paused at her comment, as Maria had been fussy that day. It may have been due to my worries leading to insufficient milk for her, or she may have picked up on my anxiety. I forced myself to calm down, sit down, and think. Our high stonewalls and the gate constructed of thick oak planks could deter many attackers. If a determined assault occurred, the swords and knives wielded by Grandfather and the other men of the household should suffice for a while. My imagination ran wild worrying about what might happen. I rose and went to the hall, calling for David, who was not far.

"David, I want you to send someone out to find out what is happening," I told him.

David, his faced pinched with anxiety, replied, "Narses can be trusted. I'll send him."

An anxious hour later Narses returned, sweating in his brown linen tunic, shaking his dark haired head while his eyes darted around the room.

"Lady Anna," he said, "I've been up to the battlements. Many men from the city are up there, not just the numeroi and teichistai, but ordinary citizens. Many looked to be there only to watch the fighting, not to actually fight." He paused, to recall what else to tell, bouncing from one foot to another. "I never saw your husband, but I was not permitted to approach the taghmatas – they surrounded the emperor."

Grandfather stood nearby, shaking his head.

"Civilians on the walls – hope they aren't there when arrows fly," he grumbled.

"What of Tornikios' troops? Does he have many? How do they look?" my questions galloped out.

A frown flashed across Narses' swarthy face. "The rebels' numbers exceed what I saw on our side of the wall. Many of our men on the wall carry neither sword nor shield. The rebel camps went from one end of the walls to the other, from the Golden Gate all the way here to Blachernae. Many thousands of soldiers," he said.

I could feel my face drain of color at this news. How could the emperor's motley assortment of defenders, most of whom appeared to have no training, best these tough rebels? Conquering armies typically had free rein to rape, steal, or kill whatever and whomever they chose.

Narses began again. "And Lady Anna," he said before hesitating.

"Yes? What else is there?"

"The emperor, the emp. . ." he stammered, "he is on the walls at the Blachernae Gate."

"Blachernae? He's at Blachernae? Not at the Romanus Gate, or the Golden Gate? What of the rebels – where are they?" I asked, appalled at the thought of the fighting likely to go on so close to our house.

"As I said, their great numbers are spread all along the city walls, but their general has pitched his tents near Blachernae."

Blachernae. Close to home. I felt faint then, sitting down heavily.

"Thank you Narses," I muttered, dismissing him. I turned to Grandfather, unable to think. He was a soldier; I had to depend on him.

"Anna," he said, "the news is bad, but the emperor is not defeated yet. You know the city walls have never been breached. The emperor may not have the troops he needs to defeat these rebels, but the walls will defend the city better than twenty thousand men could without them."

Eugenia stood nearby, listening and turning paler each moment before speaking.

"I'm sure you are correct, Uncle. But when the fighting does start, the emperor will send in the best trained soldiers he has, won't he?"

Grandfather did not need to answer. Eugenia and I looked at each other, cold at the thought that John and Romanus would be among the first to fight.

During that long night, we heard shouts echoing from the city walls, although we could not discern the words. Grandfather said the soldiers were calling each to the other side, first to abandon their emperor; and failing that, they would yell insults to each other. The distant noise haunted my night, while the children slept like the innocents they were.

David and the two grooms, Narses and Paulus, kept watch at our bolted gate in the darkness. The house did not lie on a main road, but we heard the nearby clopping sound of horses' hooves, and light glimmered from torches and lanterns as the city's inhabitants prepared for the battle. The night held eerie reminders of the one so many years earlier, before we had been sent into exile. The same fears flooded me, but worse now, with a husband and children to worry over.

I slept fitfully, sinking into a deep sleep for a few hours before dawn. Rising with the sun, I combed and plaited my hair and washed my face before going to the baby who needed feeding by then. Sitting with her small warm body snuggled next to mine in those quiet early hours gave a brief respite from worry.

As the world became lighter, sounds from the direction of Blachernae's walls grew louder. Soldiers would have noisily roused, performed their morning ablutions, ate, donned armor, and strapped on their swords. A routine the more experienced of them had performed many times in the past, but for some, it would be their last. I wondered what John was doing at that moment.

Grandfather and Eugenia emerged from their rooms looking as unrested as I felt. Samuel had sent over another bag of chai leaves a few weeks earlier, so Antonina brewed a pot of it for us to share with the bit of bread we managed to choke down. Afterwards, Grandfather took Manuel outside to play in the garden while I paced with Maria until she fell asleep.

At mid-morning the sounds from the city walls grew louder with the crash of rocks thrown by the ballistae, and the screams of men crushed by them. The battle had begun.

Eugenia looked anguished, consumed with worry for her son, her only child. I must have looked just as worried. When Maria was awake and fussing, we took turns walking her—her baby cries a welcome distraction from sitting with our sewing while the cries of wounded and dying men echoed in the distance.

The fighting did not seem to have been going on for long, for it was no later than midday when the rumble of many people running, screaming in fright began at the walls and grew, passing through the streets in frenzied flight away from the enemy.

Grandfather looked out onto the street from an upstairs window.

"We'll need to ready ourselves, but whether to hide, escape, or to fight off Tornikios' soldiers, I'm not sure yet." His calm, professional demeanor kept Eugenia and me from joining the hordes racing away. "Tornikios won't want his soldiers destroying the city. He needs the people's support, so they won't have free rein to pillage," he reasoned.

His dispassionate analysis of the situation calmed us. In the end, Grandfather was proved correct.

The first wave of escaping combatants passed through our neighborhood, and the ranks of the fleeing had thinned. Through it all, David and the grooms kept the gate firmly bolted, refusing entry to any, whether looter or soldier, passing by. Grandfather stood by with his sword at the ready. Suddenly, a fierce hammering on the gates demanded entry.

"Let us in. I have your master, John Comnenus," Isaac's deep voice boomed out.

Relieved but terrified wondering why John himself had not called out, I ran to the gate as David pulled back the bolts to let them in. Outside, Isaac stood alongside a donkey with John astride it, but hunched over and blood on his clothes.

I gasped at the sight of him, raising a hand to my mouth. His dull eyes did not register any recognition of me. He was moaning in pain and smelled of shit and the coppery tang of blood.

"David, open it wider. It's the master," I said, my voice shrill.

In seconds they were within our walls, the gate slamming behind them. I almost cried to see John covered with ugly bruises and painful cuts—slash marks on his forearms and calf, whatever flesh armor had not covered. He was barely conscious, with the side of his face scraped red and mud splattered. I gritted my teeth, determined not to give way to womanly tears.

We struggled to get John up to our bedroom. I cleaned his wounds; it took many buckets of warm water before I could bind them in clean bandages. John was too dazed to say much, just whispering my name.

Grandfather said to Isaac. "Tell us what happened."

Isaac's eyes looked wildly around, as though searching for a way out. "You want to know what happened? It was a slaughter that happened this morning; that's what it was," his voice rising hoarsely. "The emperor sent out his cavalry, what cavalry he had, to fight the rebels. We had maybe a thousand mounted soldiers. John was one of them. Tornikios had four or five times that number. They slaughtered our men."

Isaac took the cup of wine Eugenia handed him, running a hand through his hair.

"The only reason John survived was Gagik dragged him out of the melee when it became clear our men were doomed. If there were even a hundred men who survived, I'd be surprised."

I said a silent prayer of thanksgiving for Gagik's fortuitous presence as I washed the blood and filth from John's leg.

"General," Eugenia spoke, "did you see my son, Romanus Diogenes?"

Isaac looked over at her with a crooked smile. "Did I see him? That I did. I suppose you haven't heard, have you?"

Eugenia, looking anxiously puzzled, answered, "No, we've heard nothing since yesterday."

"Your son's a hero. He got assigned to guard the emperor. Yesterday afternoon, the emperor stood atop the battlements, surveying Tornikios' army, when he suddenly moved to one side to get a better view. Just at that moment, an arrow flew by and would have killed him if he hadn't. Instead, it flew a little distance further, banged against your son's helmet, clattered to the ground, and hurt no one. So even though he did nothing, the emperor claims your son saved his life. And he decided it was time he started wearing armor," Isaac finished drily.

Eugenia's face beamed with pride at this, but still sought confirmation of his safety. "So Romanus is fine, then?"

"Last I saw him, he survived and was well." Isaac gave a long appraising look at Eugenia. Although they had met briefly in the past, he had not spoken often with her. "The lad has a promising look to him. Do you mind if I ask if he's been betrothed?"

Eugenia looked startled, but answered, "Betrothed? No, he is still only eighteen. With his father gone, I thought to wait longer." Her voice trailed off in embarrassment.

Isaac nodded thoughtfully at her comments, with a slight smile on his face and a raised eyebrow. As busy as I was with John's wounds, I wondered what he was thinking.

John lay dully on the bed as I finished tying the bandages, appearing shocked by the battle and his wounds. I asked David to fetch some blankets to warm him, and send for Maria Kourtikios. I held John's head so he could sip a little watered wine.

"So where are Tornikios' men now?" I asked.

"That is the strangest part of what happened. After the survivors of the battle made it back through the Blachernae gate, we shut it behind us. I don't know what has happened since we pulled John through and I left to bring him here, but the rebels made no move to push through the gate then." He sounded puzzled by this odd climax. "They should have. It was a great chance."

Grandfather gave a disgusted snort. "That was foolish of him. He'll lose momentum."

Isaac nodded. "Only a fool hesitates when the battle is going your way. Might as well surrender. But that's his mistake, not mine." He quaffed the last of the wine in his cup.

Isaac looked sweaty and dirt smeared, his beard matted in spots and with some of the lamellae on his corselet missing, so he must have been in the fighting, too. He had not mentioned his own part.

"I can tell you the emperor won't be reopening that gate to welcome his cousin's men in." He laughed ironically. "I wonder if Tornikios thinks he would?"

It took a moment to understand the implication of what he was saying, but I slowly realized that while some were fleeing the battle and city walls, at this moment no reason for those departures presented itself.

"You mean the rebels have not breached the walls yet?" I asked, seeking verification.

"No," he answered. "Not last I saw."

"Then why were all these people fleeing? I thought Tornikios' men had killed the emperor and started pillaging and slaughtering."

Isaac glanced over his shoulder towards the street, giving a scornful shrug. "Those weren't soldiers fleeing, just numeroi and teichistai, a bunch of shopkeepers and fishermen buckling on their grandfathers' rusted swords, pretending at being soldiers. Worse than useless. The frightened rabbits did not wait to see what really occurred, and deserted at the first sign of fighting."

"So what will happen now?" I asked, amazed at foolishness of it all.

"Anna, I wish I knew. Maybe Tornikios wanted the citizens to welcome him in and avoid the inevitable pillaging. That would be a credit to him. But no one in this city will welcome him after seeing the slaughter today." Isaac glanced over at John, his gaze concerned over his younger brother's wounds. "Too much blood."

"Where is Gagik now?" I asked. "I need to thank him for saving John."

"He's safe, back standing guard on the walls." Isaac looked amused at that, "Not exactly the type of assignment a former king expects but after the gawkers and all the numeroi and teichistai scampered away, we needed every soldier we could find. You'll have a chance to thank him after this is over."

John's eyes had slid closed, oblivious to my conversation with Isaac. He looked so pale with the loss of blood, even his freckles had almost disappeared.

I called Antonina, instructing her to assemble a basket of provisions for Isaac and his soldiers manning the walls. Eugenia put together cloths for bandages for the soldiers, and asked Isaac to send word to Romanus that she and my grandfather were safe.

Eugenia, Grandfather and I saw Isaac outside, so that he could return to the city's walls.

"Anna," Isaac began almost as an afterthought, "can you send word to Catherine that I am safe, that she and the children are not to worry?"

"Of course. I'll send a groom to let them know. Thank you for bringing John home. And for word on Romanus."

Isaac strapped on the parcels and climbed onto the donkey he had used to bring John home, and started for the gate before turning back to us.

"This was an awful day. I thought I had almost lost John." His face turned red and contorted at the recollection. "Seeing soldiers fall like sheep in a slaughterhouse—the men and horses struggling to escape, trapped in mud slick with blood, surrounded by enemy swords, and one of them my brother. They should never have been sent out."

Grandfather nodded somberly. "But you're both safe."

Isaac shook his head. "I'm just grateful it was not my brother's day to die." With that, he swung the reins around and galloped back to the walls.

That night after the slaughter of the imperial infantry saw great celebrations in the rebels' camp with much drinking and feasting, still expecting a quick victory. Meanwhile, the emperor's men regrouped and fortified the walls. The two armies fought no battles during the next few days, although Tornikios' men called to our soldiers on the battlements, urging them to abandon one cousin emperor for the other. None did.

At home, Maria Kourtikios had stitched up John's deeper wounds. He slept for most of the next couple of days, waking only to the pain of the doctor's needle stitching his wounds, and for the small bowls of broth I spooned into him. At night I slept on John's camp bed, afraid to disturb him. On the third night he insisted I join him in bed, so I knew he was recovering.

"You know I sleep better with you next to me," his voice barely above a whisper. "You will keep me warm."

"All right, but you must tell me if I disturb you at all." I lay next to him, gathering him gently into my arms, careful not to tug on the bandaged skin. We lay folded together like that, hardly moving, all that night.

The following morning John began looking like himself again, if scraped and a little thin. I helped him downstairs, so he could enjoy the warm day and Manuel's playful company. The medicinal smells of the healing ointments Maria had left dissipated in the breeze blowing from the Golden Horn.

"I think I am feeling like something other than broth for dinner today," he said in the afternoon, exhausted just from watching Manuel scrambling around the garden chasing a toad that had dared to venture there.

At that moment, I heard visitors arrive at the gate and went to see who had arrived.

"John," boomed Isaac's voice. His eyes lit up at the sight of his brother sitting in a chair. "Last I saw you, you looked little better than a dog who's had the worst of it at a bear baiting. How are you feeling?"

John's eyes lit up at the sight of Isaac, as well as Gagik, who followed close behind. John tried to rise, but the wounds still ached and he had to make do with a manly grasp of arms.

"Isaac, it's good to see you, and you too, Gagik. I'm much improved from a few days ago. Anna's physician has been in. A woman physician who's exceptionally fond of stitching. Her stitching hurt more than the bite of the sword did. The sword had a sharpen edge at least," he said with a grimace.

Isaac and Gagik laughed at that.

"You've always been stubborn when it came to getting patched up. The only reason you survived all your childhood cuts and falls is because the monks frightened you into submission." Isaac looked up and winked at me, then. "Anna must have done the same thing."

"So you must ridicule me, and in front of Gagik, when I am too weak to defend myself?" John joked.

Isaac cocked an eyebrow at that. "Well, he already thinks Romans don't have the sense to not engage in a battle they have no chance of winning. But he was kind enough to notice you were not dead and drag your sorry carcass back behind the walls."

"Little enough good it would have done me, if Isaac had not pushed aside a couple of Varangians who'd been told to bar the gate. You were not in a fit state to notice, but your brother let us in before those two blond bears regained consciousness. Isaac better hope they didn't get a good look at who hit them." Gagik grinned.

John looked down, embarrassed at the trouble the two of them had gone to. "Thank you both, I owe you."

"Yes, thank you, both of you," I reiterated. I stood behind John's chair, holding the hand of the less injured arm.

Isaac reached over to grip John's shoulder, as much to steady his own emotions, as John's. "You'd have done the same for me. Just tell me you won't make a habit of getting slashed into pieces?"

John shifted in his seat, in a vain effort to get the sore parts of his body comfortable, and glanced up at me. "I'll try, if not for your sake, then to keep Anna's physician and her blunt needles from poking me again."

"John, they were not blunt. And you are healing better for them." I gave him an affectionate wifely look before turning to Isaac and Gagik. "Please, I know you want to see your families, but stay for a few minutes and tell us the news. I've been too busy with John and the children to learn anything. Let me get some wine and food while we talk."

In a few minutes Antonina had assembled a small feast of fish, bread, and apples, along with wine to entice our visitors to remain a while longer.

We ate on the terrace, basking in the early autumn sun as Isaac and Gagik took turns recounting events of the last few days.

"It's difficult to believe," Isaac said, "but Tornikios' delay in pressing his advantage proved fatal. He lost the momentum and never regained it."

"So after a few days of minor skirmishes," Gagik interrupted, enthused about sharing the story, "Tornikios was out with his soldiers yelling taunts at our soldiers, daring them to do battle, when I moved the ballista I was manning to a slightly different spot and let the rocks fly. They just barely missed him, but it must have scared the fool, because he went riding off in total panic before returning to their camp." Gagik appeared smug recounting his efforts. "You should have heard the men on the ramparts howling at him."

"I couldn't tell with certainty immediately, but it looked like the camp had fewer tents not long after Gagik's near miss. A general goes running off like a scared rabbit at something that didn't hit him? Men won't follow a coward." Isaac took a sip of the wine before continuing. "Even more deserted, slinking off last night. His siege will be over soon."

Isaac and Gagik soon made their farewells, and I walked them out to the courtyard and their horses. As Gagik mounted, Isaac bent down in an embrace and spoke softly to me. "John is fortunate to have you as wife. It's a relief to know you're caring for him."

I pulled back from the embrace before responding. "Isaac, I'm fortunate, too, in my husband."

Isaac turned and mounted his horse, a dark look in his eyes, before the two men gave quick salutes and rode to their homes and wives.

The Tornikios' rebellion did not last much longer. A day or so after Isaac and Gagik's visit, what was left of the rebel camp scattered. By December Tornikios had been dragged from a church where he'd sought sanctuary and returned to Byzantium.

The emperor was magnanimous in his clemency to the rebels, seeking no punishment or penance from any except Tornikios who he had blinded on the night of the Christ's nativity. Isaac said Tornikios howled and pleaded in vain for clemency. I felt nauseated when the image of the blindings I had seen came back to me.

Despite the emperor's clemency, many soldiers stationed along the Danube never returned to their posts. They had already gone too many months without pay or supplies from the capital. This left the northern borders of the empire ragged and frayed, relying only on the local troops, poorly trained and armed. The Pechenegs seized the opportunity to cross the unprotected river and begin raiding. And the emperor's jeweled church of St. George kept rising on the promontory above the Bosphorus.

CHAPTER SIXTEEN

The Matchmaker

1048

John's wounds healed by the Nativity, leaving him with a slight limp in his right leg and a stiff right arm, but nothing worse. He was lucky. Most of the other soldiers who survived that day with him beneath the walls at the Blachernae Gate still suffered. Isaac visited often during his brother's convalescence and made a habit of collecting John at least twice a week, insisting they go riding or hunting to recover his strength and agility. His encouragement and good humor made all the difference in John's recovery.

One day, as I fed Maria in the library near a brazier while Manuel and John played outside in the garden, I complimented Isaac on his fraternal devotion.

"Did you know we had another brother?" he asked with a quizzical look.

"John's mentioned it. Didn't he die before John was born? Named Nicephoros?" I stretched a little, moving Maria to get more comfortable.

"That's right. Died of plague, killed him and our mother. I had it, too, but somehow recovered. Nicephoros was a few years older, but always made time for me, even if his friends were with him. After he was gone, I was desperately lonely." He bent forward resting his elbows on his knees, hands clasped before him. His brow was furrowed, a look of raw desolation about him as he recalled those days. For a moment, the ghost of that forlorn child sat between us.

I looked out the window into the garden as John chased Manuel among the sleeping plants that winter's day, sad for Isaac's loss.

"What was John's mother like?" I asked. John recalled little of her.

Isaac leaned back against the cushion in his chair. His soldier's face softened at the recollection. "She was Greek and named Maria, brown hair and eyes like Donya. No blood ties between us made no difference to her. My own mother, well she had a temper. But not Maria; she was such a sweet lady."

"She sounds much as John is," I said, wishing I could have known her.

"Yes, I guess she was. Sad she didn't live long enough to see her children grown. John was just four and Donya six when Maria died. That last year she just wasted away. The physicians could do nothing to help. And then our father died the year after that. But he'd put us under the emperor's protection, at a time when the emperor's protection still meant something." A frown crossed his face.

"One day, near the end, I found Maria weeping at the thought of losing them. Her tears anguished me so much I promised I'd always look after her children. Thought I was old enough at thirteen, young pup that I was. But I've done my best for them; I've tried to keep my promise."

"Oh, Isaac you have," I said. "I had no sister or brother to compare with, but when I see you and John together, and with Donya, I see how it should be between brothers and sisters, not fighting and bickering as we sometimes see."

"Thank you. Some days I think I do better than others." He gave me a half smile before finishing the cup of hot chai sweetened with honey Antonina had brewed for us.

Putting the cup down, he turned to me with an altogether different look on his face.

"Anna, were you aware that Catherine has been after me to find a husband for her niece? Alousian has not had any luck finding a husband for his daughter. Not surprising given his antics a few years back. He must have thought people would forget, but they haven't."

"John's mentioned it," I spoke cautiously. John had told me of Isaac's complaints about Catherine's nagging him on this matter. Alousian was still a man of wealth, but few dynatoi parents wanted their son wed to the daughter of a rebel, even an ostensibly forgiven one. Alousian, son of a Bulgarian ruler, would not look beneath the dynatoi.

"The girl is not much to look at, but a pleasant disposition, and an even better dowry when she does wed," he said. "I thought of your cousin Romanus as a possibility," he finished.

I pursed my lips in pretended concentration at this suggestion. Isaac was right – the girl was not much to look at, with a round face and mousey brown hair, but a friendly enough smile. Eugenia and I had been discussing this question after Isaac's blunt inquiry the day he brought John back from the walls. I had suspected this girl, who was at least twenty years old, and so two years older than Romanus, was the one in need of a husband. Romanus was a Diogenes, and related to both the Dalassenus and Argyros families, all prominent members of the dynatoi.

Eugenia had done nothing about finding a wife for her son yet. The Orphanotrophus had confiscated her husband's wealth, leaving only her small dowry. Romanus would not bring much beyond a distinguished family name, a military appointment and salary to his marriage, but that might suffice for Alousian.

"Would you like me to speak with Eugenia about it?" I asked.

My cousin Romanus and Alousian's daughter, also named Anna, were betrothed within a few months of that conversation. I served as the intermediary to resolve occasional points of disagreement in the arrangements.

The day of their betrothal, Grandfather signed for Romanus, as the most senior man in that household, while Alousian signed for his daughter. Eugenia had given her son the lovely gold and lapis necklace her husband had given her on their betrothal for him to give his Anna.

The betrothal celebration Alousian hosted that early spring day far exceeded the modest one John and I had had. With the benefit of an open purse and her Aunt Catherine's stylish suggestions, the future bride wore a flattering dress in a rich red with gold embroidery, with a sheer veil dyed the same red covering her head, and the gold and lapis necklace complementing her attire. Her face radiated happiness as she shyly looked up at Romanus' handsome face. Romanus did not radiate the way his betrothed did, but appeared pleased enough.

"I must thank you for your help in arranging my niece's betrothal," came a voice from behind me. Catherine had been speaking with other guests and just then approached me, putting a smooth hand on my arm as she spoke in a confidential voice.

The compliment pleased me. I so often felt inferior to her, with her royal father, her sense of style, her wealth, and Isaac's prominence.

"Catherine, I was happy to do it. Your niece is a sweet girl, she'll make Romanus a good wife," I enthused. "She'll be happy with Romanus, too. He's done well in the Exkoubitores, and Eugenia could not ask for a more a devoted son." Everyone knew a son who was good to his mother would be a good husband.

Catherine glanced at Romanus, standing tall and straight next to his Anna, wearing the shining dress uniform that had once been Uncle Costas', the one he had worn on our visit with Empress Zoe. My cousin's neatly combed light brown hair fell to just below his ears, a darker beard full now on his face. His muscles had developed during his time in the Exkoubitores, giving him more bulk than he'd had just a year or two earlier. He looked like a great bright eagle standing beside a delicate, red bird.

"My niece looks quite satisfied with the betrothal. They've not spent much time together, but I think she already fancies herself in love with him," Catherine said.

"Always best to start out that way," I said, trying to be humorous.

Catherine gave me a sharp look, but did not add to my comment. Not much of a sense of humor.

After an awkward silence, I said, "I understand the wedding itself will be in just a few more months."

"Yes, we expect it will be in late September. My brother Aron may be back for it," she said. "He's been governor of Vaspurakan for over two years and it will be his first chance to return."

Catherine came from a large family of at least ten children. I sometimes wondered if her mother had surrendered to Emperor Basil after the death of Catherine's father because of the promise of munificent gifts to her many offspring, saving her the trouble of providing for them. I looked around Alousian's elegant mansion perched on the side of the Marmara.

It may have cost a great deal, but less than the cost of a war. Emperor Basil knew well the value of what he gave, and what he bought.

I made my way over to Eugenia, who was in full bloom as she basked in the lavish celebration for her only son's betrothal. After years of living on family charity, her marital expectations for Romanus, the penurious son of a traitor thought to have killed himself, had been low. Now it looked as though the Fates had something better in store for them both.

"Here," I said, handing her a cup of wine. "You've not had a moment's peace since we got here."

"Thank you Anna," Eugenia replied, sipping thirstily. She was glancing about the room at the guests, smiling at some of them. "Alousian invited a few people I knew when Romanus was a baby, but not seen since. Irene Phocas is now married to Alousian's brother, Troian. Her mother and I had been friends so we had much to talk about. Everyone has commented on how handsome my son is," her pride obvious. It was superstitious of me, but I thought she came close to hubris with her joy in this moment.

Just then Donya joined us.

"Anna, Catherine tells me you deserve much credit for this matchmaking," she said, her eyes glowing with interest.

"I did so little," I protested, but pleased Catherine had seen fit to flatter me to others.

"It may not have been much, but one does not need much yeast to leaven bread," Eugenia answered. "We would not be here today without Anna's help."

I blushed at the compliment. In truth, my efforts stemmed partly from my recollection of my own unhappiness at a delayed betrothal. I did not want to see another girl experience that frustration. At the same time, this experience taught me how betrothal contracts were arranged, a valuable skill to have.

"Well, I hope when the time comes for my children to be wed, you will sprinkle some of your yeast on them," Donya said. "Helena and my boys are not so many years younger than Romanus."

And so here began my reputation as matchmaker for the family.

That summer I had time to devote to the family's warehouse. John had long since disclaimed any knowledge of business affairs and and left it to me.

Samuel and his son, Joshua, worked tirelessly, supervising the loading and unloading of merchandise, and maintaining their records. In prior years, most of the trade goods coming into the city were rare spices, perfumes, furs, and other rarities such as the chai Samuel sometimes found for me. Now, as the emperor's building of the church of St. George Mangana continued, the goods more often included fine metal tools for the builders, glittering tesserae and smalti for the mosaicists, and elegantly veined marble blocks for carving and polishing. The goods flew in and out of the warehouse, in response to the emperor's unrelenting demands.

By this time, the church, along with its monastery, palace, gardens, hospital, and home for old soldiers, had been under construction for five years. The emperor scheduled the consecration of the church, the first building on the grounds to be completed, for that summer. He invited as many of the dynatoi as could fit in it, John and Isaac among them, with Catherine and myself accompanying them.

Curiosity about this great church was rampant. Few had seen its interior aside from the workmen, the emperor and empress, and a few courtiers. The magnificent rectangular building had five domes covered in gold leaf, four at each corner, with the great central dome dwarfing the rest. Three sets of massive bronze doors, as tall as three men, faced the road on one of the long sides, while the opposite side looked over the promontory to the Bosphorus. Arched windows rose gracefully above the doors, bringing light to the interior.

The bronze doors had been wrought with images of saints and angels on the panels. Floral mosaics surrounded each entranceway, and the icons on the doors gave the impression that one entered the garden of heaven on entering the church. Gasps of amazement came from those ahead of us as Catherine and I crossed the threshold into the church on the consecration day. I thought it strange that people accustomed to the splendor of the Hagia Sophia could be awed at any other church, until I saw the interior of this new church myself.

Within the great dome itself was a mosaic of Christ Pantocrator, with his mother the Theotokos on one side and St. George on the other, opposite them was a mosaic of the emperor and empress holding a model of the church, as though handing it to our Savior. The tesserae and smalti were covered with lavish amounts of gold glittering in the sunlight streaming through the arched windows. Each of the smaller domes contained scenes from the life of St. George—his holy parents, his defeat of the dragon, the inquisition before Diocletian, his torture, and being thrown into the quicklime pit. I had to wait to glimpse the rest as I followed the other women upstairs to the women's gallery. I ran my hand along the exquisite mosaics lining the stairway as I climbed the marble steps.

Once in the gallery, I looked down from the tableaux in the domes to the walls whose mosaics told the story of the life of the Christ, from His birth on the wall above our women's gallery, to the crucifixion on the wall above the altar. We could view the nativity scene, close above the women's gallery most clearly. The eyes of the Theotokos, St. Joseph and the Infant shone brightly, while the garments of the magi appeared to have been dazzlingly embroidered. I had never seen mosaics shimmer as these did. As I gazed on them, a ray of sunlight shone through the window onto the scene, and my mouth gaped open. The mosaics held gemstones – sapphires for their eyes, rubies and pearls decorated the garments of the three kings. The Theotokos' blue gown was depicted with sparkling lapis flecked with gold.

I looked around the church, wondering if other mosaics glinted the way the one above us did. It was difficult to say with certainty from the distance, but the larger ones did have the added brilliance that gemstones would provide. Catherine stood nearby me, and I looked at her for confirmation.

"Do you think those truly are . . ." I whispered.

"Hush," she said with some urgency. Her eyes were on the lapis gown of Mary, and the bright robes of the magi. "Say nothing. Not now."

Catherine's critical sense of the appropriate was greater than mine, so I decided to hold my tongue for the moment.

A few minutes later Empress Zoe arrived with the emperor. For all the paint she wore, she appeared much older than when Uncle Costas and I had our audience with her six years earlier and moved creakily towards her throne. Her imperial purple gown, richly embroidered in gold and scarlet, covered her bent shoulders as she processed among the women in the gallery to the imperial box at the railing's edge. Her maphorion hid her hair, which surely had faded to white.

The patriarch, Michael Keroularios, led the service with numerous priests and bishops assisting, swinging their censors and intoning prayers blessing this holy shrine to St. George. Even from where I stood, I could see the floor of the altar had been laid in a checkered pattern with bright green malachite tiles, alternating with white marble and bordered with black marble. The emperor sat ensconced on a golden throne near the altar's iconostasis, flanked by Varangians in dress uniforms but carrying their rhomphaia. John stood among the crowd in the nave, undoubtedly near Isaac, but even with their bright red hair, I could not find them.

I kept glancing around at the mosaics as the patriarch intoned his words of blessing and the voices from the eunuchs' choir rose in harmonies along with the pungent incense filling the air. The abundant gold showered on this place and the unmistakable gems twinkling in the sunlight astounded me. The empire was wealthy, but enough for this extravagance?

Catherine's tight lipped face said to keep silent as we filed out. John and Isaac rode horses back to Isaac's house, while she and I were carried in sedan chairs.

Once we emerged from the chairs into the privacy of her courtyard, I could not restrain myself any longer.

"Did you see those mosaics, all the gems embedded in them?" I asked Catherine incredulously.

"Yes, but we need to get inside before we speak of it any further," she whispered, guiding me into the house.

John and Isaac followed from the stables where they had left their horses. Both were uncharacteristically silent.

Finally, the four of us were in their dining area, where a light repast had been spread for us. I kept silent as the servants moved about the room, pouring wine, setting out cakes and fruit; unsettled at the thought of this magnificent, but horribly expensive, church. Finally the servants had departed.

Despite my earlier attempts to say something to Catherine, I was now silent, shocked into wordlessness by John and Isaac's quietude. Finally, Isaac spoke.

"The Church of St. George is magnificent," he said after a sip of the wine.

"Did it require the use of gems?" I asked.

"We cannot know that they are gems; they could be colored glass," Isaac said, eyebrows raised and waving a hand in denial.

Catherine rolled her eyes and sighed with exasperation. "Maybe you do not know, but would Monomachos make do with just glass? And I have never seen any glass that looked like lapis. Or malachite." She sipped at the excellent Thracian wine brought up from their cellar.

Isaac scowled but nodded in unwilling agreement.

"So much gold," John said, shaking his head. He bit into a juicy plum before continuing. "I swear there is as much gold in that church as would pay all of the empire's soldiers for at least two years."

It was no wonder that so many soldiers had revolted with Tornikios a year earlier. If that church required so much gold, and had been under construction for five years, there would have been nothing left to pay them.

"Not much we can do about this. The money is spent and he is emperor. No one will stop him from building, certainly not Zoe. Nor all the hangers-on at the palace with their hands outstretched for golden gifts. I saw Constantine Ducas this morning; he and the other senators look as prosperous as Croesus these days."

I stiffened at Isaac's mention of my cousin's widower. Anger blew through me like a fast-moving summer storm. My vow at Xene's graveside almost three years earlier still lay deep in my heart, but opportunities were nonexistent. The philosophers say forgiveness is better than revenge but I could not agree. Ducas may have thought his brazen cruelty to his dead wife would be forgotten, buried deep in the ground with her, but I remembered it everyday.

"Hmmm. And yet the emperor sees no benefit to rewarding his generals with something other than the tokens he gave you after Tornikios rebelled." Catherine's observations cut as sharply as her tongue. The 'tokens' included a dinner with the emperor for the generals and officers, a purse with a few gold coins; hardly seemed worth my husband's injuries or the loss of so many lives.

"No," Isaac dragged out that word. "No, he didn't."

Catherine sipped her wine. Wine often had the effect of relaxing an imbiber. With Catherine, it seemed to sharpen her edge. I glanced at John, and in the unspoken language passing between husband and wife, I told him we should soon be leaving. He gave a slight nod back at me.

"Maybe you should do something about that then." She gave Isaac a scornful look. "I thought soldiers took what they wanted."

"Perhaps Bulgarian soldiers do, but we are Romans," came Isaac's short retort.

With that, John and I made our excuses and our way home. As I sat in the sedan chair while the bearers threaded their way through the city streets, my thoughts returned to the emperor's grand new church, its gold domes shining like beacons over the Bosphorus. It was a beautiful church, truly exquisite. But the city was full of many beautiful churches. Did it need another?

And there was Catherine's tart but correct observation on the miserly rewards the emperor made to the soldiers who defeated the rebels, while he was so generous to others like Ducas who had done little.

That summer John and I took the children for a month long visit to my grandparents' farm near Tzouroulon, which lay on the way to Adrianople. I had hoped to bring Grandfather with us, but he had passed his seventieth year and grown too frail for the journey. Eugenia, in the midst of her plans for Romanus' wedding, would stay with him.

Instead, we asked John's sister and her family to join us. Donya and Michael's faces lit up at the invitation to take their children and escape the city's hot confines. A few days later, our cavalcade left the noises and smells of Byzantium behind. Our nephews, Theodore and George who were then twelve and ten years old, proudly rode their own horses rather than being relegated to the donkey drawn litter Donya and I and the other children rode in. Paulus, our groom, drove the cart full of luggage behind the litter. Donya's girls, Helena almost grown at fourteen and Anastasia a sweet seven year old, kept Manuel occupied with games and stories whenever he tired from riding with John.

We left early one morning, making our way to the Golden Gate, the Porta Aurea, happy to wave farewell to the four great gilded elephants shining atop it, and cross the bridge over the moat on the road to the farm. Even in the summer's heat, crowds already bustled about, heavily laden carts coming and going about their business. The dry summer weather meant muddy roads would not slow us, but it also meant there had been no rain to wash away the city's stench, leaving us more appreciative of the clean air of the country.

Donya and I had rarely spent time alone together, most often being in Catherine's dominant company. Her quiet, subdued personality differed from Isaac's expansive nature and John's sunny disposition. Perhaps it came from the years she had spent in the company of nuns at the Myrelion monastery, after her parents had died. Curious about this place that might have been Xene's home if her husband had had his way, I asked her about it in the sultry afternoon as the children sharing the litter dozed around us.

"I spent over eight years at Myrelion," she said softly with a smile, not wanting to wake the sleeping children. "I feel certain the nuns thought it was seven and a half years too long."

I gave her a sidelong glance with raised eyebrows. "Donya, I cannot believe you were a problem for them," I said.

She smiled ruefully. "I was. At first, I think they thought to make me into one of them. Later, they were glad they had not. John may have mentioned the energetic boys sent to St. John Stoudion. Well, their sisters had no less energy."

"And probably not many chances to visit outside their walls, as the boys would have had, I would wager."

"No, not many. I only met Michael when he visited with Isaac. Isaac served with him under General Kekaumenos when they were young, and brought him along. After a few visits, Isaac said the hegoumena had complained and he would either have to stop bringing Michael, or we would have to be betrothed. So we were betrothed and married not long afterwards."

"So you had no family besides Isaac to arrange a marriage?" I asked in a subdued voice.

"No, only Isaac, and John were left. Isaac, of course, had been betrothed to Catherine since they were young, long before our father died. Father had promised Isaac's mother to marry him to a Bulgarian, since she was Bulgarian. Isaac received a rich inheritance from his mother, leaving John and me to split the remainder. It was much smaller than what Isaac received, but my portion satisfied Michael."

I yawned. Donya's story held my interest, but the stifling summer heat left me drowsy.

"Had Catherine and Isaac married before you and Michael married?"

"No. Even though they had been betrothed for eight or nine years at the time we wed, Isaac had been on campaign in Bulgaria and on other assignments. Isaac's ambitious and wanted some standing before marriage. But it was just a few months after our wedding when they finally married."

Manuel dozed next to me, a little pink with sunburn and his sweaty hair matted to his head. Maria slept peacefully in my lap. I felt torn between continuing the conversation and joining my children in their naps.

"I don't think Catherine was happy to wait so long. You know she was twenty-five at the time. Isaac is a couple of years younger than she is but I think he was reluctant to settle down." Donya glanced over at her own sleeping daughters.

"Perhaps we should rest a while ourselves, before the children awaken," I said.

"Yes. They'll be awake soon." Donya curled into some pillows, closing her eyes.

I leaned back against cushions padding the back of the litter, resting easily with Maria held in my arms, as I contemplated the Comnenus family history. Despite Donya's circumspect comments, it did not sound as though Isaac had been enthusiastic about his marriage to Catherine. Still, he had honorably kept his betrothal commitment when some would have sought an impediment. Isaac's loyalty shone through as his most defining attribute—faithful to a marriage promise his father had made, to a brother and sister with a different mother, and to his empire and emperor.

We had sent word ahead of our visit, so the house had been cleaned and the shutters opened, but it still held a musty, unlived in smell. It did not take long for that smell to dissipate as the six tired children tumbled into their beds after a light supper.

The steward, Simon, and his wife, Priska, lived nearby. They had brought us cheese and bread, plums and melons with pitchers of milk for the children, as well as wine, for our first meal at the house. Michael, Donya, John and myself sat outside on the small terrace eating, drinking and talking convivially long past sunset.

Looking at him, Michael's innate good temper was evident from the affection he showed Donya and their children. It was more difficult to see the soldier in him. His soft face and rounded belly belied the title of general he had earned and the many assignments he had been on. He never spoke of his time as catepan of Italy in Bari, and the Frankish pirates who overwhelmed his defenses. Still, any Roman general, even one as lacking in martial appearance as Michael, hungered for the chance to redeem his reputation.

Finally fatigue overwhelmed us and we retired to our rooms to sleep in the blessed quiet of the country.

"I think Michael and Donya are happy they came with us," I said to John, curling up next to him in the bed.

"Of course they are. They don't have a place outside of the city of their own. I'm glad you suggested it."

"I can't imagine inviting Isaac and Catherine here, though. A bit too rustic for their tastes."

"Well, I think Isaac would enjoy it, but not Catherine. Not enough servants around," John whispered into my ear, as he gave it a little nibble. His hands began roaming over my body, rousing it with sensations I had almost forgotten in the exhaustion of travel, and I put off sleep for a little while longer.

We settled into a routine with the children, sending the boys out to gather firewood for cooking each morning. Even little Manuel had a small sack that he dropped twigs into. Helena and Anastasia would fetch in buckets of water, and do their best to keep an eye out for Maria, an unsteady year-old toddler. Afterward, John and Michael might take the older children fishing, or have them harvest whatever had ripened in the fields. The oldest children helped with milking Simon's old cow and his goats, returning with pitchers of milk.

Donya and I spent our time chattering together, cooking, cleaning, and with the sewing that never seemed to end. I learned how merry she could be when free of the stultifying formal rules of behavior.

She and Michael, while not poor, lacked the family wealth Isaac and Catherine had, or that my grandparents had provided me and John with, so she knew well how to cook much more than I had ever had to learn. That summer she and, I am embarrassed to say, her daughters taught me how to prepare delicious meals.

Donya kept her children busy with tasks to make them feel useful, and helpful to her. I had not been raised around many other children, aside from the time we had spent in Amaseia, so I learned much about raising them that summer.

For my part, I had brought with us a book with several plays of Euripides, and had Donya's children learn the parts to *Medea*. By the end of our time there, they had learned the lines well enough to perform the play for the adults, with even little Manuel and Maria playing the parts of Medea's small children.

The children made their presentation a couple of days before our departure home. Theodore had the role of the handsome, faithless Jason; his sister Helena performed as the vengeful Medea. A few shards of golden light still glowed in the darkening sky as Donya's four children carefully spoke the chorus' closing words that sultry evening. The children's sweet young voices sang out the chorus:

Manifold are thy shapings, Providence!
Many a hopeless matter the gods arrange.
What we expected never came to pass,
What we did not expect the gods brought to bear;
So have things gone, this entire experience through.

The next evening, our last of that summer's visit to the farm, was a night of feasting. Simon slaughtered a lamb for us, roasting it most of the day on a spit in the fire pit. The boys climbed the apple trees to pluck the early-ripened fruit, so we had an abundance to eat that day and to bring back to the city. Donya's girls had made bread for the night's meal and for our journey home the next day. It was not so fine a feast in a palace in the city, but no one seemed to notice. The happy sunburned faces of the children and the relaxed countenances of John, Donya and Michael said much about this holiday.

After the children had gone to their beds, the parents had a few minutes to relax. Moths circled the lanterns, and we enjoyed the last pitcher of the summer's sweet wine.

"We really have to thank you for inviting us to join you," said Michael. "I don't believe we have ever had such an enjoyable holiday."

"Michael, Donya, we were so pleased you and the children could join us. I think the time here would have been much duller without all of you. John and I have spoken about making this an annual holiday, and I hope you could all join us again next year."

Michael and Donya exchanged a half-smiling glance.

"Some of us may be able to join you, but perhaps not all of us," said Donya, and then sipped at her wine.

"Not all of you?" asked John.

"There is no formal announcement we can make as yet, but Helena is almost fifteen, and by next summer will be almost sixteen. So we are thinking to betroth her soon." Michael's satisfied smile proved his pleasure at the news.

John's eyebrows rose with the corners of his mouth, happy at the news for his niece. "Do you have someone in mind for her?" he asked.

"We do. Phillip is a nephew of General Kekaumenos and serving with his uncle. The rest of his family is gone, so the general is all he has. He knew we had a daughter approaching marriageable age and approached us about her."

I smiled at this news. General Kekaumenos had been friends with Uncle Costas. My uncle had said he and Kekaumenos were in agreement on all matters military, although in another area they sharply disagreed. While my uncle saw no need for the women of his family to be relegated to a gynecaeum, Kekaumenos held firm opinions about sheltering his women and children there. The old general may have been well intentioned in his protective inclinations, but as a practical matter the custom would be difficult for any family other than the wealthiest to live with. For Helena's sake, I hoped this Philip did not agree with his uncle about the gynecaeum for Helena's sake.

John picked up the pitcher of wine, swirling it about in the weak light to determine what was left. Satisfied at the sound, he poured out all that remained into our cups.

"Let us give a toast to Helena and wish her best of luck with her betrothal," he proclaimed.

"And for a holiday as wonderful as this next year," added Michael.

We clinked our glasses together merrily, drank our wine, and forgot for that moment Euripides' words.

We returned to the city in early September, a few weeks before Romanus' wedding, the cart driven by Paulus full to overflowing with baskets of apples and nuts, cheeses and olives, and amphorae brimming with wine and olive oil. We embraced at our parting after reaching our house near Blachernae, as Donya and Michael left with a cart full of a generous selection of the summer's produce.

A few days later, I sent a note to Samuel, asking him to visit me at home. He arrived the next morning with his son, Joshua, his records, and another small sack of the precious chai he sometimes found for me.

I sat down to go over the accounts with him, but was amazed to see records not as tidy and clear as Samuel customarily prepared. I gave him a quizzical look.

"Lady Anna, I do apologize for the sloppiness. These days we have almost more business than we can accommodate. With the emperor's requirements, rope, and tools, marble and precious stones come in and are sent out sometimes within a few hours, and often in just a day. The workmen sent to retrieve them are sometimes unsure about what they have been sent for." His wrinkled forehead and frown, on a face usually so cheerful, testified to his earnestness.

"Is it this common?" I said, curious.

"For all those taking in building materials. As well as the furs and spices the palace requires."

I shook my head in wonderment. Almost under my breath, I mused "After that opulent church, and he's still building. Where can he be getting the money for all this?"

I happened to glance up at Samuel, whose dark eyes looked steadily across the table at me as I perused the accounts. He did not look away. Quietly, he said, "The Venetians."

"The Venetians?"

"Yes. And the Genoese, but mostly the Venetians. They have been generous with loans to him." Standing beside his father, I saw Joshua nod his head in agreement.

"But what of the Treasury?" I asked incredulously.

He shook his head. "The gold leaves the Treasury faster than it comes in."

I looked down the page filled with entries for marble blocks, exotic wood, and spices, with amounts written over and changed, and X's where illiterate workmen signed for them when they were picked up. Such a confused mess.

I shrugged my shoulders; I had no control over what the emperor spent. "I guess he expects to repay the loans from taxes once his new palace and gardens are completed. Assuming he has no new plans," I added wryly.

So I should not have been surprised when a few days later John came to me with the news of the annual tax our household was assessed for.

"One hundred solidi? Are you sure of that? We've never had to pay more than eighty before." A poor family could live for a month on just one of the shiny gold solidi, so we were fortunate. Still, I had not expected such a burden.

"That is what the eparch said. He mumbled something about taxes being increased. I was not inclined to question him whilst the dozen or so soldiers in the room surrounded him. If it helps, everyone's taxes are rising."

I rolled my eyes at that. "Well, at least we won't be the only ones who have to make economies." Arguing with the eparch would be pointless, so I pulled out the key to unlock the chest I kept our coins in, opened it, and counted out the hundred he needed.

"Be sure to take Narses with you. I wouldn't want to lose you or the money to thugs."

"I will," he said and kissed me, leaving me in glum contemplation of the depleted chest. It gave little satisfaction to realize who, in fact, was paying for the elegant new church and palace the emperor had built.

The end of the month saw the wedding of my cousin Romanus and Anna Alousiana. The service took place at the church attached to the Myrelion convent, where Donya had been raised. This small church with its arched windows, mosaics, and many side altars felt intimate when compared to the great Hagia Sophia, or the extravagant St. George Mangana.

During the ceremony John and I stood opposite the wall whose mosaic told the story of Mary's birth to St. Anna and St. Joachim, childless for many years before having their beloved daughter. Glancing back at my cousin, standing tall and handsome in gilt-edged armor, his golden brown hair brushed glossy and with a full beard—not at all the scraggly affair some young men have—I hoped his marriage would not suffer the pains of childlessness. I shivered recalling Xene.

Afterwards, the feast at Alousian's grand estate far exceeded any celebration I had attended before. The summer's heat had dissipated and a breeze fluttered through the gardens while servants quietly padded about with trays heavy with delicacies and pitchers of wine. The women congregated in a shaded portico with cushioned benches while musicians played for our entertainment.

I looked around for my sisters-in-law, but found only Donya and asked her where Catherine was.

"Catherine is with her brothers," she said looking casually over her shoulder in the direction of the room where the men had gathered. "One of them, Aron, just returned from Armenia yesterday. He had been in a battle with the Seljuks and was regaling them with the story. He seemed to have the attention of many of the men. Isaac, John, and Michael were in the crowd."

I recalled Gagik's descriptions of the Turks, the speed of their horses and their unrelenting aggression. A sliver of worry cut through me for Damien and his family. Amaseia was not that far from Armenia.

Just then Eugenia entered the portico, her face glowing with pleasure at the success of the day. She had never dared hope for such a prosperous marriage for Romanus, or to celebrate it with such a grand feast.

Grandfather had generously paid for Eugenia's scarlet silk gown, embroidered with gold thread and small pearls adorning the collar, so she would appear as elegant as her new relations.

"I hope you both have had something to eat. Alousian has practically emptied the markets of all the best food for the festivities," she said, waving a hand at the tables weighed down with platters of assorted seafood, meats, cakes, olives and fruits.

"I've never seen so many delicacies in one place," I said, reaching an arm around her for a hug. "I won't need to eat for a week."

Looking around, I spotted the bride greeting the guests with her mother, across the room from us. The young woman's embroidered pale blue silk gown with a braided gold belt and veil of the same blue flattered her coloring and her stolid figure. As I watched her I smiled, wondering if I had blushed as much as she was blushing when John and I wed. I realized many people believed most of the fun at a wedding came from embarrassing the bridal couple, as this Anna was being embarrassed with bawdy comments.

"Eugenia," I said turning to her and recalling Donya's news. "Donya said one of Catherine's and Alousian's brothers had returned from Armenia."

"You mean Aron? He just barely returned in time for the wedding. Alousian had almost despaired of him arriving, but he rode in yesterday afternoon. Delayed because of fighting, I think."

Clearly, in the midst of her only child's wedding she would have little interest in Armenia. I would have to learn more from John or Isaac later.

The celebration went late into the night, with dancing and singing long past the time when the young couple was bedded in a room in Alousian's house. John enjoyed himself so much that I considered putting him in the sedan chair and riding his horse myself. But he insisted he would manage and he made it home through the dark city streets without tumbling off, for which I was grateful.

The next day I questioned John about Aron.

John looked up at the ceiling, scratching his neck through his beard thoughtfully as he recalled the conversation. "Yes, it sounded like a confused muddle. He's not sure whether we won or we lost."

"What? How can he not know? He fought in it." I felt frustrated at John's reticence.

"So Aron sends scouts out regularly to check for any foreign incursions into Roman territory, and about a month ago, several returned with news of Turkish soldiers approaching. He sent for Kekaumenos who's living in Gagik's old capital city of Ani, and to Iberia where Manuel Liparites is governor, for assistance. The two of them arrived with their men a week or so later, and the battle occurred a few days after that."

I was becoming irritated with my husband for dragging out this story for so long.

"So what happened then?"

"Aron said the three Roman armies each stood opposite separate Turkish armies on the battlefield, with Liparites in the center and Aron and Kekaumenos on the two sides. Trees covering the hills meant each army had no clear view of the other. Aron and Kekaumenos each easily defeated the armies they faced. Afterwards, they were flabbergasted to discover that Liparites had not only lost his fight, his nephew had been killed and he was captured. By the next morning, the Turks had disappeared, along with their captive. Aron had only returned to the city to report this to the emperor, not attend his niece's wedding."

In this first battle between Romans and the Seljuk Turks what should have been a Roman victory looked more like a defeat.

CHAPTER SEVENTEEN

The Patriarch

1049

At the Nativity, Eugenia happily shared the news of the child Romanus and his bride were expecting by the summer. In anticipation of the joyous arrival Eugenia busied herself sewing and embroidering innumerable small shirts and dresses for her first grandchild. This sweet news kept that year from total disaster.

Before the end of January came the news of a disastrous defeat by the Pechenegs near the Danube. General Kekaumenos, the uncle of the young man betrothed to Donya's daughter, had been sent there from Armenia with his troops by the emperor and had almost been killed in the battle. He was found, still alive, among the thousands of dead bodies left on the field, and slowly nursed back to health, although missing part of one hand. His nephew, betrothed to Helena, had barely escaped with minor injuries.

As winter's deep chill settled on the city in February with snow and ice, Grandfather took ill with an ague, coughing as though he could not catch his breath. I stayed at his house trying to nurse him through this illness. Uncle Simeon visited when he could from Stoudion, often accompanied by the monastery's physician who offered ointments and herbs to ease Grandfather's suffering. Alethea prepared her most appetizing broths to tempt his fading appetite. Despite our efforts, his condition only worsened.

Grandfather demonstrated the least concern of us all about his health. He was over seventy years old and survived many battles. All his brothers and sisters had died, as well as Grandmother, whose loss he had felt each day of the last four years.

One night I sat sniffling beside him as I listened to the rattling in his chest that came with each breath. He had been a part of every day of my life. I could not imagine life without him. Suddenly I felt his thin hand reaching out to me.

"Anna, my child, you must not be so sad," he whispered in his hoarse voice.

Unable to speak, I rested my head on the side of his bed, my wet cheek against the rough wool of his blanket. He laid his hand in blessing on my head, as he had so often when I was a child. But then it had been a hand of strength; now it felt as light as the snow falling in the dark outside.

"I've lived a good life. Better, I'd wager, than most; certainly longer than most. And I've missed your grandmother, your mother, and my brothers; it is time for me to be with them again."

I looked up at him then, his face gone so thin and his cheeks ruddy with a fever. When had his steel gray hair turned so white and crumpled? Surely, though, he must recover.

Even as I tried to catch that thought, it was gone. The light flickering in his eyes was almost extinguished. His time was short. I clasped my hands around the cold hand that had rested on my head.

"What would you have me do?" I asked as I dried my tears.

"Once I am gone, remember to give a generous gift to Studion for prayers on my behalf. And I know you would not force her to leave, but you must let Eugenia stay in this house as long as she wants. She's been good to help me these past years." He stopped then, out of breath and hacking with cough.

I nodded and brought a cup of warm honeyed wine to his lips to sooth his raw throat.

He rested against the pillows finally, and closed his eyes. After a moment, he spoke again.

"Now, I think it is time for the priest."

Grandfather's time on this earth ended the next grey afternoon as snow fell heavily over the city. Uncle Simeon, Eugenia, John and our children surrounded him with our presence and prayers in his last moments.

Then, his face relaxed into a peaceful visage as this world's cares fell from his shoulders.

The following day visitors arrived to express condolences and bid a final farewell to Grandfather. Grizzled soldiers he had served with, friends, and family all came in a steady stream, trudging through the snow-covered roads. It was consoling to hear them praise Adrian Dalassenus for himself, not just for his famous brothers or father, and more than a few of these tough greybeards wiped away a tear as they said their farewells.

Early in the afternoon, my friend Eudokia Makrembolitissa and her mother, Marina, arrived in sedan chairs. Even modestly covered in her maphorion and heavy wool mantle, Eudokia's pale oval face with serious blue eyes and blond curls slipping out caught the attention of the men gathered in small groups.

Her mother Marina greeted me first, expressing her sympathy on my loss, before walking to the bier where she knelt in prayer.

I had not seen Eudokia in several months, and she appeared thinner than I recalled.

"Thank you for coming today," I said. "It's been so long since we've spoken, you and your mother must come and spend the day with me."

She smiled wanly at me, a smile that did not reach her eyes.

"Anna, I must tell you my news. I am to be betrothed. My uncle has found a husband for me," she said as she nervously twisted her hands.

I looked at her with curiosity. As patriarch, her uncle would have great influence over whom she wed. I wondered who could she be betrothed to that would cause her such disquiet.

"Eudokia, what is amiss? You do not look pleased with your uncle's choice. Who is this man?"

For a long moment she gave me a doleful look before saying, "It's Constantine Ducas."

My mouth gaped open in shock. Eudokia knew how he had treated my cousin. No one should be forced to put up with him, least of all a friend I cared for almost as much as I had my poor Xene.

"How did this happen?" I asked stupidly.

"My uncle. He says Ducas has become quite wealthy of late, and influential with the emperor. The connection to the patriarch with marrying me means Ducas will not require so much dowry. And with me married to Ducas, my uncle will have influence in the Senate. Mother is grateful I can make such a prestigious match. She had thought I might only find some poor soldier." The only person not pleased was Eudokia.

"Eudokia, I'm so sorry," I stammered, anguished for her fate. She had few choices other than those her uncle found for her. I had thought her fortunate in his position.

"Anna, he is so much older than I am, almost as old as my father. And after all you told me of your cousin. . . I've met the man and he has been cordial, but . . ." her voice trailed off, as her eyes filled with tears.

"You and your mother must come visit me next week. We can talk more then. Perhaps we can think of something," I said quietly to her.

She gave a quick nod and wiped her eyes but said, "We'll come, but I think nothing less than a miracle will stop it."

Instead, Marina said preparations for Eudokia's impending betrothal would not permit the time away from their home and would I please visit them? A few days later I visited them at the Patriarchal residence near the Hagia Sophia, where they lived under Keroularios' protection.

Eudokia greeted me on my arrival, insisting on bringing me to meet her uncle awaiting us in his office with Marina. The two of them sat with lap blankets in chairs near a brazier. I had seen him at a number of religious celebrations over the six years since he had been patriarch, but always from a great distance. Even from that distance, though, he appeared unlike the devout men who had previously held this honor.

This patriarch was not the pious greybeard one would expect, but a man in his late forties, still with a soldier's vigor in appearance, and only a touch of silver in his thick brown hair and beard, just around his temples. His face held the lean look of the soldier he had spent so much of his life as before being forced to accept the tonsure. He wore informal black monk's robes that day, with a gold and enamel cross hanging from a chain around his neck. Deep-set dark eyes regarded me sternly as I knelt for his blessing.

"Lady Anna, Eudokia has told me of your late cousin, who was wife to Senator Ducas," he said in a commanding voice.

"I, I. . ." I fumbled for words to respond to this powerful man. "Yes, Holiness, Xene Dalassena was my cousin."

"I'm sure you were loyal to your cousin, but you need have no concerns on Eudokia's behalf. I have spoken with Ducas about his first wife, and he has assured me of his devotion to her despite her shortcomings, and his terrible disappointment that there were no children."

I blinked at him, stunned at his ridiculous statement. Did Xene's childlessness justify Ducas' rough treatment?

"Even if he were inclined to unkindness, I'm sure he'll treat my niece well," he finished smugly. He stood and laid the blanket to one side before walking to his desk.

I spoke without thinking, then. "As having General Constantine Dalassenus as her father helped my cousin."

"Eh?" he glanced at me. "Really, Lady Anna, I think you're being too emotional. We have no concerns for Eudokia, do we sister?"

Marina timidly looked up at her older brother, a lifetime of deference to men apparent on her face. Even if she had been inclined, Michael Keroularios' commanding attitude and voice brooked no opposition.

"No, we have no concerns, brother. Eudokia's betrothal to the senator exceeds my most fervent prayers."

"As you can see, your worries are baseless," he said to me dismissively. "Now, I have work to do." A young deacon sat to one side in the room, scratching his quill on parchment sheets. He glanced up with a look of gentle concern for another's welfare that was lacking in his master's.

The three of us women made deep curtseys to the patriarch before turning to leave the room. Returning to the entrance hall, Marina made some embarrassed excuse and left us. Eudokia then led me to the sunny upstairs room where she did her sewing.

I was seething. He thought I was too emotional? I had witnessed Ducas hitting his wife, had held her hand as she breathed her last, and knelt through the night where Ducas should have been praying beside her bier. I felt as disgusted with Michael Keroularios as I was with Ducas.

"He will not change," she said gloomily.

I felt as helpless as I had when visiting Xene in her attic room, and angry too. I asked her about how Ducas came to ask for her.

"He visited my uncle one day on a senate matter and saw me with my mother. He spoke with her for a few minutes before addressing me. It had been so long, I did not recall him from your wedding. Only when my uncle told me the name of the man seeking to betroth me did I realize who it was."

"So he was willing to marry you with only a small dowry?" I asked.

"Not at first, he wasn't," she said. "Uncle Michael insisted. Eventually, he relented."

I looked at my friend, her blond hair curling around her face, soft eyes and full lips, with flawless skin and graceful figure. I thought if the patriarch had held out a little longer, Eudokia Makrembolitissa's great physical attractions might have induced Ducas to pay the dowry himself.

"So Ducas wants to bed you," I said, with one eyebrow raised. "You have that advantage."

"Anna," Eudokia said, blushing, "you are so blunt."

I laughed. "You will be, too, after you've been married."

Thinking a little more, I said, "He wants children. He told me he wants a dynasty, so he needs children. That was his worst complaint about Xene."

"He wants what?" she asked with some incredulity.

"A dynasty. He wants the throne, and with the empresses childless, someone will have to succeed them. He thinks he could be emperor someday and wants children for the Ducas dynasty." I shrugged.

Eudokia started laughing at this ridiculous notion. "So all I need do is bear him children for his dynasty, and sit next to him on the throne as empress." She sounded almost hysterical.

I nodded agreement. The thought that she might be empress some-day was ludicrous.

Early in the spring that year, my cousin Romanus approached me about buying my grandparents' house.

"My wife and I have been trying to decide where we want to live. We've been staying in her parents' house, but now with the baby coming she wants her own house. Your grandparents' house wouldn't be far from them, but just far enough." Romanus gave me a knowing grin.

"What of your mother?" I asked cautiously.

"Oh, my Anna will be pleased to have her as a companion. They get along marvelously, and my mother will be a wonderful help when the baby arrives."

We soon arrived at a price for the property and I cleared out the last of the possessions I would keep from my grandparents—silver wine cups and forks, the worn wooden plates they always ate from, a chess set, books, and icons from their icon corner. Aside from the books and the silver cups and forks, most of the items held little value, except in my heart's memory. It gladdened me to know the house would remain in our family.

At about the same time, Donya arrived one day with the news of the emperor's appointment of Michael to the post of Vestarches with the army, and his imminent departure for the area south of the Danube, where the Pechenegs had been attacking our forces.

"Of course I'm concerned about him leaving, but this is the best opportunity he's had to regain his reputation after the terrible mess in Bari all those years ago," she said, eyes bright. The Bari episode was still a sensitive issue.

The news of this prestigious appointment was gratifying, but on remembering the news of the Pechenegs' bloody defeat of Kekaumenos, one of the empire's best generals, I felt some trepidation. Michael could not have been a better husband or father, or friend to John and me, but he reminded me more of the bureaucrats scurrying about the city than the bold warriors of my family. Still, he had been a soldier his whole life, and good enough to win the post in Bari. I shook off the wisp of anxiety I felt and offered my congratulations.

Eudokia's betrothal to Constantine Ducas occurred soon after Easter, speaking their marriage vows in the early summer. John and I were not invited to the festivities, which I was glad of. However, Ducas, ever the social climber, did invite Isaac and Catherine to attend.

Catherine told me the groom had spared no expense for this celebration, with the emperor in attendance accompanied by his latest mistress, the daughter of the king of the Alans. Catherine spoke at length on the emperor and his woman, their sumptuous attire and exquisite jewels, with hardly a mention of the bride.

"She was lovely," Catherine finally commented after I had asked the third time about Eudokia, her head bent to one side as she recalled the scene. "She seemed stiff, though."

"Stiff?"

"She walked as though she were a piece of glass, trying not to break, slow and stiff. Her dress was magnificent, pale blue with embroidered flowers and birds, pearls and gold trim. The silk looked like it was of the highest quality – must have been a gift from the emperor. It was better than anything I've ever found in the marketplace."

My poor friend. Her sparkling good looks only an ornament on Ducas' arm; his marriage to the niece of the patriarch bringing him priceless prestige. I almost wished I had never said anything to Eudokia about Xene. I regretted the worry it gave her, but not the warning she received.

A few weeks later, I returned to the house I still thought of as my grandparents'. I had promised Romanus' wife to help her become familiar with the gardens Grandmother had planted. Anna understood little of gardening, and knew I had spent many years working at Grandmother's side there, so invited me over for my advice.

The house was now Romanus', and he and his wife would arrange things in it as they saw fit. It felt strange to walk in and see new, more expensive curtains on the windows and in the doorways; walls bright with fresh paint; the finely carved furniture that was part of Anna's dowry; her silver cups shining on the table instead of the ones now moved to my house. The shadows of Adrian Dalassenus and his wife Theodora lingered, but the world had moved on and new life filled their spaces.

The sleeves of my dress stuck uncomfortably to my skin in the June heat after travelling in a stuffy sedan chair. I had brought my big straw hat along, to keep the sun off my skin while we worked, but little could be done for the warmth. Eugenia and Anna came out to greet me when I arrived. Or rather, Eugenia came out; Anna waddled out, billowy and large. Her baby was due in another week or two and I wondered how she thought she might do any gardening when she probably could not see whether she had pulled out a weed or an onion from the earth.

After a refreshing drink of water flavored with lemon juice, and small cakes Alethea had baked, we ventured outside under our broad brimmed hats. The sun shone down from a cloudless sky as we walked among the beds, and I pointed out where Grandmother had planted certain vegetables; why they were in one spot rather than another; where the flowers were planted, how to trim the rose bushes. Before long, though, Anna tired under the sun's sharp rays, excusing herself to rest on a bench under the grape arbor, Eugenia solicitously joined her.

I worked in the garden. I almost felt Grandmother spirit working beside me with the particular mix of the odors of fecund earth and herbs. It had been almost five years since she died, and yet I could still hear her voice and felt her presence close by. The heat did eventually drive me to join Eugenia and Anna where we all sat chattering in the arbor's shade.

Anna had been laughing at Eugenia's description of a peddler who had tried to sell them day old fish as though it had been fresh, when her face became red and pinched.

"Anna," I said, "Are you all right?"

"No, no, it is nothing," she said, gasping a bit. "I've had a few pains like these before, but they meant nothing. I still have time before the baby comes."

She seemed confident until a moment later when a look of surprise came across her face and she stood up, a puddle of water accumulating at her feet.

Eugenia gave her an ironic smile. "You may have time, child, but not much. We must get you inside and send for the midwife. I'll send a message to Romanus."

A few hours later I went home for the night, before returning the next morning not long before Romanus' daughter Theophano was born. I had brought Manuel with me, and bent down to show him this delicate pink infant not long after she had been swaddled.

He studied her with mild curiosity before deciding it would be more interesting to take his ball outside to play than to continue looking at her.

I congratulated Romanus and his wife on their new daughter, and Eugenia who could not stop smiling at her granddaughter, and left with Manuel for home.

As quickly as a summer squall can ruin what had promised to be a joyous day, grim news arrived spoiling the day's delight in this new child. When I arrived home, John's face held a stark look.

"News from the northeast. About Michael, Donya's husband," he said tersely. "A battle with the Pechenegs. Our troops were defeated and Michael. . ."

John was having difficulty speaking, could not seem to even finish his sentence. He looked pale and in shock.

"What's happened, John?"

"Michael was captured. And killed." John spoke slowly, reluctant to divulge the words. "They may have tortured him first, but we don't know. They mutilated his body, cut off his hands and feet."

He rubbed his forehead before continuing. "They cut him open and stuffed his hands and feet inside."

"Oh, dear Christ," I said, sitting down and trying to comprehend this news. "Does Donya know?" I asked, stunned.

"Isaac's gone to tell her and their children. Young Phillip Kekaumenos arrived today with the news; he went to Isaac first. I was there when he told Isaac." John ran a hand through his hair, his face bleak.

Donya's husband had seemed ill fitted to military life, but he still strove for a distinguished career. He had been so intent on regaining his reputation, no matter the cost, but the cost to his wife and children was high.

Within an hour John and I arrived at Donya's house to express our condolences and offer whatever assistance we could. The poor woman was prostrate with grief, and had been taken to her room by Catherine who sat with her. The children, adrift without either mother or father, cried mournfully in quiet corners. Peter Kekaumenos held his betrothed's hand, stroking it in consolation. John joined Isaac who stood greeting mourners who arrived as word spread.

The atmosphere in the house was one of loose ends—nothing quite the way it should be. Donya had fewer servants that even John and I did and a thin gray dust covered much of the furniture, with toys scattered about the main room. The house needed order. I found the cook and instructed her to bring out the available food and drink for the mourners, sending another servant out to local shopkeepers with my own coins to augment what was in the house. I found a rag to dust with, and John sent our groom to the Myrelion Monastery where Donya had been raised, to ask for a priest. The children were sent to change into suitable attire, and I picked up forgotten stray toys. In a few minutes, the house was arranged in a sober fashion appropriate for the family's loss.

My own desolation at Michael's death would be nothing to what his family was experiencing. I climbed the stairs to Donya's room, dreading this visit yet knowing Donya needed the company at this time.

Donya lay on the bed, speaking tearfully to Catherine who sat in a chair next to her. They looked over at me as I pushed aside the curtain to enter the room. Donya reached out crying in fresh paroxysms of grief, "Anna, he's gone. My Michael is gone."

Catherine slipped out, and for the next hour we spoke and cried, recalling the month we had spent on the farm the previous summer. Donya had almost twenty years of memories of her now dead husband. We hardly know all the strands that bind us to our spouse until they are sheared away and we are left untethered, on our own.

Eventually the priest arrived to offer consolation and prayers for the dead and I left them to speak in private. I found Catherine greeting visitors with John and Isaac. She soon expressed a desire for Isaac to take her home.

"I cannot leave now, Catherine. Donya is my sister and I fought beside Michael. It would be unseemly." Isaac spoke impatiently, barely hiding his anger at her request.

John, ever the conciliator, looked back and forth between the two of them, before speaking up. "Catherine, I can escort you home."

Catherine quickly gathered up her mantle and walked out to a waiting sedan chair while John whispered to me that he would be back as soon as he had seen her home. I squeezed his hand in gratitude for smoothing over Catherine's peevish demands.

"Hurry back," I whispered.

The stream of visitors went on for at least another hour with Isaac and me greeting each of them, trying to be sure to recall names and faces so we could tell Donya of all the friends who had visited. Finally, as the day drew to a close, the callers dwindled and I sent the children to the nursery where they could eat supper.

At last Isaac and I could sit down and sip the last of the wine put out for the visitors and await John's return.

"I was surprised to see old Issiates," said Isaac. "I did not realize he was still alive, or that he had known Michael. It was good of him to stop by."

"And Bryennios stopped by with his son, Stephanos. The boy seemed a promising lad," I added.

The conversation lapsed then, and I took the opportunity to eat a few berries that had been left behind by the mourners. Isaac sat across the table from me, looking down into his swirling wine cup.

Finally, he spoke. "I'm sorry Catherine did not stay."

I shrugged. "I am sure she did what she could for Donya. It was good of her to be here when you broke the news." It would be impolite to criticize Catherine's abrupt departure, but I had wondered about it. I tried to give her the benefit of the doubt.

He looked up at me with a blank stare, before he gave an ironic snort.

"She only came because I insisted. She wouldn't have otherwise." He grimaced at this statement.

"Oh." I said.

Isaac looked away, not meeting my eyes.

I felt embarrassed for him. Idly, I picked up a solitary wilted blackberry left on a platter and ate it.

"John is fortunate to have you," Isaac said. His face was flushed and his eyes bright in the diminishing light.

"You're kind to say that, but I'm also fortunate in him," I replied honestly.

He shook his head. "No really, he is. I had no idea how to handle this situation today, and Catherine did little to help, but once you arrived you arranged everything. You made all the difference today. Thank you for all you did." He reached out his hand across the table then and grasped mine.

His hand larger and stronger than John's engulfed mine. I looked at him and felt transfixed as his eyes searched my face. We sat like statues for what seemed an eternity when around us noises arose signifying arrivals. The kindly priest from Myrelion descended the stairs from Donya's room; while from the small courtyard came John's hearty voice instruct-ing the stable boy on the care of his horse.

Slowly, I slipped my hand from his warm grasp, barely managing to croak out a "You're welcome. I was happy to help Donya. Michael meant a great deal to us." I turned then, self-consciously, to greet John.

John and Isaac spent most of the next few days with their sister, helping her to arrange the Trisagion prayer service for Michael, his body having been buried near Adrianople several days earlier. The third day following his death had already passed but there was just enough time to arrange the ninth day service. The fortieth day service, a month later, would be the last commemoration. The church's services help us take the steps to part from our loved ones – recalling them as they slip away to heaven.

The emperor provided a death benefit for the family, but John and Isaac would have to help their sister's family. Donya, like many women, had little understanding of matters pertaining to money, and needed their assistance.

We all needed a respite. The day following the fortieth day prayer service for Michael, John and I and our children, along with Donya and her children, all made the trek again to our Thracian farm.

Donya spent most of the journey weeping, hugging her daughters close. I comforted her as best I could, but there was little consolation in the face of such a loss. Sadness overwhelmed her, like the hot sun wilted a plucked flower lying on the ground.

"I was so happy when Michael was named Vestarches. He should have won great honors on this campaign; he shouldn't have been killed," she kept saying through her tears.

Grandfather and my uncle had told me battles were confused affairs—communications misunderstood, lucky or unlucky attacks, and hidden enemies. Michael's battle would have been no different, but this time he had been the unlucky one. Those words would have been no comfort to Donya.

"I know," I said, trying for some vain comfort. "Michael fought bravely that day; people will remember his courage. He would be proud to know that."

Donya nodded as she wiped her tears. "He would be so glad. He wanted our children to be proud of him." She glanced then to the corner of the litter where the girls had curled up to sleep. "But I still miss him," she whispered. She rested her head on my shoulder then, weeping softly, and slept.

Outwardly, our time on the farm that summer was much like it had been the previous year. John took the boys fishing and hunting, while the girls helped with cooking and harvesting the apples and apricots from the orchard. Manuel and Maria loved the attention Helena and Anastasia lavished on them, although they did not understand the tears their cousins sometimes shed.

Donya spent most of her days resting on a bench outside the house, in the shade of the elm tree towering over the house. The children would show her the baskets of fruit they had picked, or the fish they had caught, with little response.

"That is lovely, dear. You must take it into your aunt. We shall have it at supper," was her undeviating response.

She ate little, but always seemed to have a cup of wine nearby. At dinner in the evening she drank more than John and I did, perhaps to help bring on sleep, but her muffled sobs troubled the darkest hours of the night.

After a couple of weeks, Helena broached a concern she had with me.

"Aunt Anna, can I ask you something?" She was a pretty, dark haired young lady, almost sixteen now, but her face held an anxious look.

"Yes, of course, Helena." We were walking down to the stream where the boys were fishing. Anastasia had run ahead with Manuel, while Helena and I held little Maria's hands, swinging her up and down in delight as we walked.

"I'm supposed to be married soon, in October. Do you think I should still go through with it? I am worried Mama will need me at home now that Papa's gone," she said, her voice trailing off.

With Michael's death crowding out all other thoughts, I had almost forgotten about Helena's wedding. My niece's eyes held a confused look as she spoke. Donya had not mentioned her daughter's upcoming marriage since we received the news.

"Helena, you're a good daughter to be concerned about your mother. I cannot think what her feelings might be about your marriage, but I'll speak with her."

At least, I thought, forcing Donya to think about the future might shake her from her lethargy. Either she would want to hold onto Helena longer, or she would want to see the marriage take place as scheduled. As we approached the stream where John and the boys were fishing, John's bright red hair flamed amongst the summer's green leaves, tugging at my heartstrings. It must be terrible to lose a husband, particularly in the gruesome way Michael had been killed. Donya's torpor might be understandable, but she had children depending on her.

That evening, after the youngsters had gone to bed, John and I asked Donya about her plans for Helena. Finally, a spark lit in her eyes.

"I do want Helena to marry as Michael and I had planned, in October. I guess I've been too upset to think about it." She sat straighter as she spoke, as though reminded of a forgotten task.

John sat beside his sister and put an arm about her, while I reached across the table to grasp her thin hand.

"Perhaps John and I can help with the arrangements," I offered.

Donya nodded with a faint smile, and a look of renewed purpose coming to light on her face.

In the morning, she greeted her daughter with energy we had not seen since before Michael's death. Helena had packed in the baggage the rose colored silk fabric purchased months earlier for her wedding dress, hoping to spend time on its preparation on our holiday. But without her mother's interest, it had stayed packed away.

The delicate blush of the fabric flattered Helena, contrasting beautifully with her dark hair and eyes. My sewing skills had improved to the point where I could do simple mending, or a straight hem, but the more complex work required Donya's accomplished hand. Now, she set to the task with vigor. Her elegant embroidery, a legacy of her years living as an orphan in Myrelion, embellished the soft fabric with scrolls, doves, and flowering plants. I doubted the empress' seamstresses could have done better.

The embroidery took most of the remaining time we had planned to spend on the farm, with another day needed to assemble the dress' pieces into one garment, for which I provided some modest assistance. During those weeks, Donya avoided the wine jug in daylight hours when needlework could be easily accomplished, although she still partook of it generously at the evening meal. She continued to mourn Michael's death, but regained enough equanimity to care for her children's needs.

We again roasted a lamb for our last night's feast, its rich aromas mingling with those of baking bread and sweet apples. The celebration had the sheen of a happy ending to our holiday, but covered a somber undertone. As the setting sun streaked the sky with ever-deeper shades of pink and gold, and white moths fluttered around us, we danced to music played by Simon and his wife, and John. Simon strummed the lyre, with his wife, Priska, on the flute, while John pounded a beat on the drum.

Donya shied away from the dancing at first, content to sip her wine and watch the rest of us. Then, towards the end, not long before the only light came from the lanterns, her older son Theodore pulled her to her feet for a dance. Theo resembled his father in height and face and coloring, although his demeanor held an alert edge his father had never demonstrated.

Donya and her son danced as the shadows deepened, and it almost seemed as though it was Michael she was with. I twirled nearby with my little Maria while Anastasia spun Manuel until he was dizzy and laughing.

That evening was one of shapes and shadows; of ghosts and the living; of Donya's flushed cheeks and faint smile as she danced, and the joy I felt with the still secret knowing that John and I would have another child. After the grief we had endured, it seemed a glowing future was dawning.

CHAPTER EIGHTEEN

Donya

1050

"Anna, you have another boy," Donya announced happily as she helped the midwife swaddle the squalling newborn. I lay in bed panting, sweat soaked after hours of labor and at that moment not caring about anything other than the worst of labor being finished and grateful for a healthy son.

"He's beautiful," said Helena as she looked over her mother's shoulder at the babe. She had the dewy-eyed look of a young woman who had no idea how much work that child would be, dreaming of the child in her own belly, her first, due in a few months.

"He may be beautiful, but he has a job to do now," said Maria Kourtikios, the physician I had come to rely on so often. She took the baby and brought him to my breast for feeding with a practiced hand. He was a hungry little man and latched on without much urging, sucking energetically while my milk sluiced down in a rush. The afterbirth was expelled within a few minutes, and soon my new son fell asleep, exhausted by his recent exertions.

"So his name is to be Isaac," Donya said sometime later. I had washed and sent the physician home with her coins, so we were alone.

John was on campaign in Bulgaria with Isaac and Gagik, sent to quell the Pecheneg uprising that had killed Michael. Before he left he had said that if the child was a boy, he wanted it named after his brother, with the promise that the next one would have a name from my side of the family. I could not object, knowing how close the two brothers were.

"Yes, Isaac," I said. I gazed down at the babe in my arms, whose hair at least resembled mine, nut brown with copper highlights. He opened an eye partway, before succumbing back into fatigued sleep.

Helena knocked on the door, before opening it a crack.

"May I bring the children in? They want to see little Isaac," she said.

"Of course," I said, giving her a weary smile. "Bring them in."

In an instant my little Manuel came barreling through, with plump little Maria following closely, and Theodore, George and Anastasia not far behind. John had thought it would be helpful to have Donya and her three remaining children with me while he was gone, so I would not be alone when I gave birth. Helena, married the previous fall, had arrived to help with the birth that day.

Manuel had a perplexed look on his face as he looked down at this tiny new brother in his swaddling, while Maria's held the same awestruck expression she had had when we had given her a kitten a few months earlier.

"Manuel, here is your new brother, Isaac." Helena pulled back a fold of the swaddling to show the sleepy baby better.

My oldest, a sturdy five-year-old full of boundless energy, looked down disgustedly at Isaac.

"Manuel, why are you looking at him that way?" I asked. He had often said he wanted a brother, but now appeared unhappy.

"He's so small. I wanted a brother I could play with," he answered, disappointed in this diminutive bundle.

Theodore, standing behind him, rolled his eyes. "I explained babies start out like this. He didn't believe me."

Donya and I looked at each other, suppressing a laugh.

"He will get bigger every day, Manuel, and soon he'll be able to play with you," I told him. "You were once a little baby like him."

"How soon can he play with me? Before Theodore and George have to go back to their house?"

"Not that soon," I told him. "But then you will have your father home again, and he will play with you until Isaac is big enough."

Mollified somewhat, Manuel and the rest of the children left the room as Antonina brought in some broth, lamb stew, bread and wine for Donya and me. My cook knew I felt ravenous after labor.

The sky outside my window turned a deep purple as the day drew to a close, the shutters still open to let in the sweet spring breezes. The world felt fresh that day, renewed with new life, especially following the death a week earlier of the aged Empress Zoe. The emperor's histrionic grief over his wife's death had seemed excessive given the many mistresses he'd had over the years of their marriage. Her silver encrusted mausoleum seemed just another excuse for more gaudy excess. I was grateful that my advanced pregnancy had excused my attendance at her memorials.

"Any word from Catherine?" I asked as I lay down my bowl after finishing the broth. Her brother's wife had been feverish following her recent delivery of a daughter.

She looked uneasy at my question, which told me all I needed to know.

"She's died, hasn't she" I said, referring to Irene Phocas, the wife of Catherine's brother, Troian. She had given birth ten days earlier, her first child. I had heard it had been a difficult labor. Catherine sent messages saying she could not visit since her sister-in-law had childbed fever. Some women survived it, but many did not. I did not know the woman well, but of course Catherine had been concerned since it was her brother's first child.

Donya nodded. "I didn't want to upset you."

A few tears slipped down my cheeks as I grieved for the poor motherless girl, and the woman who would not see her daughter grown up. I reached out a hand for the baby sleeping beside me, seeking solace.

"I'm sorry. I barely knew the woman, but it's so sad to hear the news. Troian cannot even know yet," I said, weeping afresh at the thought of the news the girl's father would receive. Like John and Isaac, he had been sent to fortify the empire's borders. Troian had been sent to the Armenian city of Vaspurakan where his brother Aron was governor, taking my cousin Romanus with him.

Donya reached over to pat my arm.

"Catherine will find a good wet nurse for the baby, and take care of it as if it were her own."

I nodded, sniffling noisily. The pain of knowing a woman who has died in childbed sent my emotions onto storm-tossed waves, and tears still fell. After a few minutes, I regained control.

"So the baby is named Maria?" I sniffled, trying to recall what I had heard earlier.

Donya nodded.

"I thought if you were feeling better, I would visit Catherine tomorrow and see if she needs any help," Donya said.

I nodded and tried a nibble of Antonina's succulent lamb stew, spearing a piece of meat on the fork before setting it aside. Perhaps my appetite would return later.

"I'll be fine, so please give her my condolences on her loss. Will you take any of the children?"

"I don't think the boys would be much help, but perhaps I'll take Anastasia," Donya responded reluctantly. Catherine's tendency to treat those not born with high titles as though they were her inferiors grated on both of us. Still, Catherine was family and an unavoidable obligation, especially now.

I sipped the wine, wondering when the men would return.

"Has there been any word from Vaspurakan?"

"None that I have heard," Donya said.

The Turks had been snapping at our borders, sending raiding parties to attack the towns and villages in Armenia, which is why Romanus as well as Catherine's brothers Aron and Troian were there. These barbarians should be no match for the empire's taghmata troops, but Uncle Costas and Grandfather had taught me one should never assume victory. Even more, they had taught me that those who assume victory are more likely to be defeated. So I did not share the complacency so many in the city felt.

September

I cooed at the little boy in my arms, a sweet blond child, small for his age.

"Eudokia, he is precious," I said as I held her child. "Your husband must be ecstatic at finally having a son." My friend had finally found an opportunity that early September day to visit me and show me her new son, Michael. The emperor had sent Constantine Ducas to review the troops assigned to the Black Sea, giving her a small measure of freedom.

"He is," she responded without enthusiasm. She was looking down at four-month-old Isaac trying to roll over in his basket, grabbing the side of it in his efforts, while her own Michael, now seven months, lay placidly in my arms. We sat on benches in the garden, in the mottled shade of the grapevine trellis, sipping watered wine and eating small cakes Antonina had baked.

I took a deep breath before asking.

"So how are things with you and Constantine?"

She gave me a level look. We had known each other for many years now, confiding in each other. I did not know what to expect.

"He isn't cruel to me," she said with a sigh. "But I don't think he cares much for me." She gave a shrug. "I don't think he cares much for anyone. Well, aside from his brother John. And it isn't that he's not glad of a son, he is. But I could be a chair, or a table, or a building he owns. I feel like I'm just an ornament; nothing more."

Eudokia had succeeded where Xene had failed, giving her husband a son. Yet Ducas treated her little better than he had Xene. Both women had come from the dynatoi, and both quite lovely. Eudokia had the look of an angel in an icon, even with her blond hair in a maternal plait, stray ends curling about her face. At least he had not forced her to wear the rough clothes he had forced Xene to don, and she had the freedom to occasionally depart from the gynecaeum.

"You are no mere ornament," I said, laying a hand on hers. "And now you have this handsome son who will surely love and respect you."

I laid Michael back in her arms. At the sight of his mother's face, he broke into a toothless grin of happiness and rubbed his face on her bosom. Eudokia held the baby close, fierce in her love of him.

I pushed a strand of damp hair behind my ear, and picked up little Isaac who had begun to fuss. I could hear male voices coming from the house and rose to learn who was within before putting Isaac to the breast.

A voice—not John's as I had been hoping for—said, "I'll just go out and surprise her." A moment later my cousin Romanus strode out of the house, his hair still damp from a bath, and embraced Isaac and me. It was obvious the months he had spent in Vaspurakan had chiseled away the softness of youth. He stood tall and lean, his blue eyes bright against his tanned skin.

"Romanus, when did you return? I had no idea you were back."

"Just returned today; I came to see your new son, and see if John has returned yet," he answered, a weary smile on his face.

Isaac, unhappy at the delay in his feeding and the uncomfortable feeling of being squeezed between us, began crying in earnest. I bent over trying to sooth him while urging Romanus to sit down. David had followed Romanus out, and I asked him to bring another cup.

"I didn't mean to interrupt anything," I heard Romanus say as I was settling Isaac to nurse.

I glanced up to see him staring at Eudokia, who was rising with her son in her arms.

"Romanus, please excuse my manners, I don't think you have met my friend Eudokia Makrembolitissa, visiting with her son Michael. Eudokia, do you remember my cousin Romanus? He was at our wedding."

Eudokia blushed, but gathered her things together and said, "Yes, I recall that. I'm glad to meet you, Romanus, but I must be going. I promised my mother I would bring Michael for a visit today."

She bent to kiss me goodbye before leaving. Romanus gave Eudokia a lingering glance as she made her way gracefully on the garden path around to the courtyard where her litter waited.

"Your friend is an attractive woman," he said.

I looked after Eudokia as I heard her bidding David farewell. "She is, and married to Constantine Ducas," I said.

A sharp twist of his mouth said more than words about his feelings on that unfortunate pairing. He had not known Xene well, but he knew how Ducas had treated her and Uncle Costas.

"That man is too fortunate," he said with a shake of his head.

David emerged from the house with fresh wine, filling a cup for Romanus. My cousin drained the cup, before pouring another. Little Isaac had settled into a contented suck, finally allowing conversation.

"What brings you here so soon after getting back? I would have thought you would be spending time with Anna and little Theophano after being gone for so long."

Romanus bent forward, elbows on his knees, swirling his wine in the cup as he thought what to say. He glanced up, his forehead creased with concern. His time in Armenia had aged him beyond his twenty-one years.

"I need to see John," he said, appearing as tense as a new strung bow.

"He hasn't returned from Thrace yet, but he should return within the month. Why do you need to see him?"

"The situation in Armenia reeks like raw meat left in the sun. I thought if I told John he could tell Isaac, who may have influence with the emperor."

"What do you mean? We've heard no ill tidings here." Most expected the soldiers sent to the empire's borders would make quick work of the barbarians. I was more realistic than most, but his stark words still stunned me.

He ran a hand through his hair as he regarded the bees buzzing around the last of the season's flowers. He gave me a thoughtful look before standing and speaking again.

"I guess I can tell you. My Anna would not understand, but you would."

"Tell me what?"

"The Armenian border is a ragged mess. The Turks harry our troops to exhaustion, and the emperor sends almost no supplies and arms to the men. The soldiers are holding their own, barely, but I don't know for how much longer." He sat down again, pouring another cup. "Nothing devastating has happened yet, but if he doesn't send money and reinforcements soon, it will."

"But what about Aron?" I asked, speaking of Romanus' wife's uncle. "He's the governor, shouldn't he say something?"

"He's tried. His letters have done nothing. The Armenians care nothing for the emperor and won't fight for him the way they might have for your friend Gagik when he was their king. Aron's troops are always short of men. And trying to collect taxes to pay the themata troops is a joke. The land is poor and mountainous, and the farmers well practiced at hiding from tax collectors. What troops there are often have to buy their own equipment."

"So there's no gold going to pay these soldiers?"

"Oh, some solidi reach them. The emperor learned something from his cousin's revolt. The men are still being paid, but oftentimes late and receive little else promised to them."

I sat speechless.

He shrugged. "Look around Byzantium, cousin. I saw the emperor's fine new buildings with stonemasons and carpenters hammering and sawing as I made my way through the city. The money is paying for all the sparkling new buildings, not for weapons and grain for its soldiers."

This had been in front of our eyes. It would have been costly enough if the emperor had confined himself to just building the jewel bedecked church and monastery of St. George Mangana. Instead, the city boasted of new theaters, a new palace next to the new church, exquisite gardens for his enjoyment. The extravagance continued with lavish furnishings inside to match their glittering exteriors.

Emperor Constantine Monomachus was known for his luxurious attire, and for his generosity to his mistresses, as well as with the hangers on at court. The feasts at his palaces were legendary, which may have led to the increasingly debilitating gout he suffered from. I had certainly realized he was spending the empire's treasury on these opulent indulgences sprinkled throughout the city. But even I had not realized what that meant for the rest of the empire.

Emperor Constantine was managing to empty the treasury in plain sight.

"You'll have to speak with John and Isaac when they return," I said. "Perhaps Isaac can help."

I spoke without thinking, but it was natural to expect Isaac to be the one who might offer a solution. John did not aspire to great leadership, and men did not look to him for it as they did Isaac, but he was a conduit to his brother.

"I hope so," he said gloomily.

Voices drifted from the house. Soon Donya emerged into the garden, with Anastasia and my daughter Maria in tow, returned from a visit to her daughter Helena and her new baby boy. Her sons Theodore and George along with Manuel were ensconced in the nursery with their slates being tutored by a scholar I had hired for them.

"Romanus, I would have expected you to be with your wife and baby, not visiting us so soon," said Donya after greeting my cousin.

"Well, I wanted to see cousin Anna's new son, too. You are correct, though, I do need to get back home to my Anna and the baby. I hoped to see John, but Anna's promised to let me know as soon as he returns," Romanus said.

With that, we bid him farewell.

Romanus' report on the precarious situation in Armenia still preoccupied me the next day when I welcomed Samuel to the house for our weekly meeting to go over the warehouse's activities and the account books.

"Lady Anna, I do apologize for the state of the account books. As I've said before, the emperor's stewards have so many deliveries and shipments that it can be difficult to keep it all straight," he said. Samuel sat on the edge of his chair, squinting at the book and clearing his throat. "They're so impatient that I have little chance to be sure to log in their shipments correctly before they are sent out again."

Aside from baby Isaac asleep in the basket beside me, we were alone in the room. Samuel's son Joshua was of an age to manage the warehouse in his father's absence. Donya was catching up with the mending with our seamstress Sophia.

"Samuel," I asked hesitantly as I set the account book to one side, "do you have any idea how much the emperor has been spending on his new buildings?"

Samuel looked at me through narrowed eyes; he then glanced around to be sure there was no one close enough to hear, leaned in, and spoke softly.

"Lady Anna, I don't know what exactly he has spent, but it's a great deal."

That was a teasing kind of response, inviting further questions.

"What do you mean 'a great deal'? As much as the treasury takes in during a year?" I asked.

"No, I do not think so," he said. I felt relieved until he continued. "No, he has spent much more than the empire pays in taxes to the treasury every year for at least the last five years, perhaps since he married the empress. Some years I have heard it was twice as much."

My eyes widened in shock, a nasty suspicion crawling up my spine. "Is he still borrowing from the Venetians?"

Samuel lowered his voice further. "In the past he borrowed from the Venetians, but the total has grown so great they have become unwilling to advance him more. Lately it has been more from the Genoese. I have no idea exactly how much. The Italians have plenty of gold and the emperor is happy to sign their notes, even at exorbitant rates of interest."

I sat back shocked at this state of affairs. What would happen when the notes came due? I knew too well how taxes had risen in recent years. His great church of St. George was built, and yet the emperor was still borrowing more to build his marble halls and clothe his mistresses in expensive silk robes. And yet the empire's soldiers fighting on distant borderlands lacked armor and weapons. If Romanus was correct, then the soldiers had been suffering from inadequate rations and arms for some time.

I thanked Samuel for the information and we finished our meeting. Afterward I sat shaking my head at the foolishness of it. There was nothing I could do about Emperor Constantine's flagrant waste of money, and with three small children to care for I had little time to even think on what it meant for my family.

Mid-October

Manuel squealed with delight as John swung him high in the air upon arriving home. Little Maria jumped about excitedly while I held her hand, determined to keep her from getting underfoot as John unloaded his kit, no easy task when also holding a squirming five-month-old baby. John's seven months on campaign had been the longest we had been apart since our marriage, and his absence left a hole in the fabric of our lives.

John swung Maria up as he had Manuel, and then produced toys for them both from a pocket. Maria squealed at the small doll, while a carved lion dropped into Manuel's hands. The noisiest ones thus distracted, he pulled me into a tight embrace.

"Anna, I have so missed you, sweetheart," he whispered in my ear. His hands held me close, roaming over my body as though to verify I was not a ghost or a dream. I know I felt as though my body had come back to life, with the feel, the smell and the taste of him reminding me of how it was between us. His mouth found mine in a lingering kiss, interrupted only by the cries of baby Isaac squeezed between us.

I found myself crying happy tears. Always in the back of my mind lay the worry he might not return, or might return with a grievous injury. But he was back, and whole, and after laughing at the baby's irritated protests, I introduced John to his newest offspring.

"John, this is your son Isaac," I said, handing the child to him. Five-month old Isaac gave this unknown father a look of deep suspicion until John jollied him into a smile by making silly faces at him.

Dinner that evening was a celebration, with Antonina outdoing herself, serving smoked sausage drenched in her special fish sauce, with cheeses, fresh greens, dried figs and spiced wine, warming for the cool, early nights of autumn. Donya and her brood were still with us, but would return to their own home soon now that John was back.

The boys listened to John's stories of the campaign without interruption, but he told only the stories that would not frighten the children. John was a fine soldier, strong and brave, but gentler than most I had known. Grandfather and Uncle Costas had not softened their stories for me, thinking it was better to know the truth than romantic nonsense. It left me impatient sometimes at John's softness, although on that night I was happy for it.

Later that night, alone and behind our closed door, our coupling was as passionate as when we first wed almost seven years earlier. I recalled Grandmother's oblique mention of the pleasure to be had when a husband returns from a long campaign, and knew its truth.

We lay nestled together afterwards, quietly talking of the past months' events.

"I wish I'd been here for the babe's birth," he said while cupping a breast still heavy with milk and nuzzling an ear, "but you've recovered well from it. Did it help to have Donya here with you?"

"She was wonderful. I'm not sure what I would have done without her and Helena when Isaac was born. Manuel loved having her boys here everyday. I'm glad her children will stay with the tutor I hired." Donya had gratefully accepted my offer to have them continue. Manuel needed a tutor since he was old enough for schooling and he enjoyed his cousins' company, while Donya had few extra solidi to pay for their own tutor.

"I had not asked before, but how did the fighting go?"

John shrugged. "Better than before, when Michael was killed. Leontios Bryennios was assigned ethnarch over Isaac and all the other generals, and he had some good ideas. We avoided any big battles. The Pechenegs had spread out and were raiding towns all through the area so we laid traps for them and managed to wipe out a lot. We never learned who the bastards were who killed Michael, but we did what we could to avenge him."

I rolled over so John could curl around me.

"John, could you tell if the soldiers on the border have been receiving their usual allotments of weapons and supplies?" I asked.

"Why would you ask such a question? Now? In bed?"

"I know but I just remembered about something Romanus told me a few weeks ago, after he returned from Armenia. He said the soldiers in the east have not been getting the supplies they'd been promised. He was worried about it and I wondered if that was true elsewhere."

John snorted. "I've never known a soldier to say they had all the weapons and supplies they needed. But there was more grumbling than I usually hear up near the Danube," he conceded.

"Romanus wanted to talk to you about it when you got back," I said, before yawning as sleep settled on us.

John and Isaac did speak with Romanus about the supply shortages, but another tragedy befell us before Isaac could decide how to address these concerns.

The autumn weather had been full of chilly rains and gloomy days, and the whole city seemed to be coughing and wheezing. Donya and her three younger children had been back in their home only a short time before she became ill with the morbid sore throat. I went to her house to help nurse her, hoping she might recover.

She was flushed a deep scarlet from the heat of her fever, her skin dry to the touch. I sat in a chair beside her bed and tried to help her drink the heated sweet mead the doctor had recommended. She shivered as she raised her head enough to swallow a gulp.

DONYA

"Thank you, Anna," she said, her voice hoarse.

"Is there anything else I can bring you? Antonina sent over some broth she thought would help."

Donya shook her head, her throat was too sore to speak and she ignored a few drops of the honey sweet wine lingering on her chin. I dabbed them away with the corner of a linen towel since her normal fastidiousness had burned away with the fever. She lay there with her eyes closed so long I thought she had fallen asleep until I saw the tears slipping down the side of her face. I pulled another blanket over her and gripped her hand to comfort her while autumn rains fell outside.

She turned to me then, her eyes fever bright in the room's dim light.

"Anna, a favor?" she asked in a low voice.

"Anything, Donya? What can I get you?"

"If," she said halting to cough roughly, "if I die, will you and John take my children?"

"Donya, you know John and I would do that for you, but there is no need to ask. You'll recover," I said, trying to sound encouraging.

"Hope so. Thank you." Calmer then, her eyes closed, and she drifted into sleep.

Donya's illness took her the next day. She left this world surrounded by her children, and brothers, and me, and after anointing by a priest. She had overcome the grief of losing her husband, and welcomed her first grandchild two months earlier, only to be gone from us.

Isaac made a perfunctory offer to take Donya's children, but John and I knew they would not be happy with Catherine who was focused on her own children and on her motherless niece. We kept them.

Even so, Isaac often took her two boys out hunting with his own son and John, and promised to find them a place in the army when they were older. Isaac's visits during this time filled the house with boisterous male banter and camaraderie. He often invited one or another of the empire's generals—Botaneiates, Bryennios, Melissenos, Kekaumenos, and others—to accompany them and meet the boys. I overheard disturbing scraps of the men's conversations. Like Romanus, many were unhappy with the emperor's spending, and knew or suspected of the Italian loans. The comments never rose to the level of treason, but would not have been spoken if they had not trusted Isaac.

Isaac and I were never alone. John, our children, servants, and the soldiers he brought with him constantly present. I would sometimes recall the night we learned of Michael's death when he had held my hand so intently, grateful for my kindness to Donya. And like the generals who visited, I found my respect and trust in Isaac growing. He led men, and John was happy to follow him. I loved John, but he lacked the strength and boldness I had admired in Grandfather and Uncle Costas.

CHAPTER NINETEEN

The Eparch

1051 - 1053

"That will have to satisfy the boys until we return," John said as he sank exhausted into a chair. Despite the early spring chill, his exertions when he, Isaac and the older boys had been out hunting for hours had left his hair plastered to his head.

"Hmmm" I said, barely paying attention. I had used the past few hours of relative quiet, with the boys out of the house, to go over my account books. No matter how I worked the numbers, though, they did not look good.

Aside from the cost of raising our own and Donya's children, our recent tax bill had again been much larger than expected. A few weeks earlier Samuel had told me of rumors that the emperor's ability to mortgage the empire to the Italians had finally run its course; they had begun to demand repayment. The eparch and his tax collectors strove daily to fill the treasury to pay the Italians. We weren't paupers, and what I had inherited from my grandparents was mostly untouched, but I had never had to be so careful with money before.

John's hand reached across the table to grasp mine.

"Is something troubling you? You look preoccupied."

I did not want to worry him just two days before his departure and forced a smile. "No, it's just been a busy day. So many things to get ready."

He stood up and pulled me up into his arms, kissing me energetically. "I'll miss you when I'm gone, Anna. The softest feather bed without you cannot compare to whatever bed I'm in with you, even if we were just in a blanket on the ground."

I reached my arms around his neck, breathing in his musky scent, the smell of his horse, and the smoke from the campfire when they had prepared a meal. His warmth and solidity never failed to hearten me, even on the worst days.

"Well, don't let Isaac keep you away any longer than necessary. It isn't just me who will miss you; the children will too."

After he left me for a bath and clean clothes, I looked again at the account books and sighed. I could not recall my grandmother worrying about money, but she had only two children to raise, while I now had six, including Donya's three. And there were always the taxes, always going up.

Romanus had already left for the eastern border with the Turks, when John, Isaac and Gagik departed for Cappadocia. Life in their absence fell into a sedate routine of lessons for the children and a few visits from women I knew. The older boys—Donya's Theodore and George, and my Manuel and Isaac's Manuel—burned off their energy learning the basics of swordplay with a retired soldier I hired to come in three days a week.

Isaac and Catherine's daughter Maria came over with her brother one day for his lesson, along with the motherless child of Catherine's brother, born at the same time as Isaac and also named Maria. John's niece had grown into a lovely and intelligent young woman, with dark brown hair, warm brown eyes, and a quick, friendly smile.

The boys were in the courtyard, practicing with their wooden swords. My niece and I worked in the garden while little Isaac and Maria toddled along with Anastasia and my own little Maria. We thus had three Marias and an Isaac, and that did not include the two Manuels practicing with wood swords in the courtyard. I had to shake my head over the lack of originality in the family's name choices. The next child would have to be different.

Our steward, David, announced an unexpected visitor. The ambitious cabin boy we had met nine years earlier on our return from exile, Michael Maurex, was calling. He visited us and Isaac a few times a year, always grateful for the opportunity that chance encounter had given him. He had since risen far in the navy, distinguishing himself during the attack by the Rus. After many promotions, he had received command of a squadron of ships. He was in the city that bright summer day to receive the honorary title of Ostiarios from the emperor – a minor honor, to be sure, but a steep climb from his modest origins. He brought the medallion the emperor had awarded him for this honor.

I introduced him to Maria, who stood blushing, giving him a shy smile.

"Congratulations Michael," I said, looking over the enameled gold disk hanging from a silk sash tied around his neck. The medallion was imprinted with the image of the Emperor in the center with his title 'Basileus Constantinos' above and Michael's new title curving around the bottom edge. "I'm so proud you've received this honor at such a young age. John and Isaac will be pleased you've done so well."

Michael had no family left, and while his shipmates and fellow officers provided comradeship, he looked up to John and Isaac almost as older cousins. A tall, lean young man with a full head of black hair, dark eyes, and a trim beard, he walked with a sailor's rolling gait. That day he was attired in his best, a long red and gold tunic belted with black leather and boots of the same black leather. The tunic and leggings were not of higher quality silk, but for one of his modest beginnings, it was a more than acceptable costume for his first court appearance.

"Thank you," he said. "I had hoped to see General Comnenus and his brother at the ceremony, but I was told they are in Cappadocia."

"Yes, my father and Uncle John have been there since before Easter." Maria's smile, always cordial, seemed warmer than usual as she appraised the handsome sailor. "This is the second year they've been sent on campaign there."

I did not think Michael and Maria had met before, but I could see my niece's interest in Michael was reciprocated. The young man was smiling at her as though she was the first girl he had ever seen.

"I've received instructions to sail that way myself in a week or so. If there is anything you would like me to bring them, I'd be happy take it with me."

"Michael that would be wonderful. John's sent me a list of items he's in need of. Maria, has your father asked for anything? How soon should we have it ready to go?" I tried to divert the young people's attention from each other. Catherine would never condone a romance between her daughter and a man of such low birth.

Michael's gaze wavered and moved to me. He appeared confused for a moment, but then answered.

"I leave a week from Thursday. So if I stopped by next Wednesday, would that give you both enough time to assemble your packages?" he asked.

"Yes, plenty of time," I answered as the little ones piled on me in a rush after a muddy chase through the flowerbeds.

"So who are all these little people?" Michael asked, smiling and bending down to their happy faces.

I laughed and raised an eyebrow at his question. "So this little man is my son, Isaac. And the little girls are Maria and Maria. Maria my daughter," I said as I put an arm around my wide-eyed four-year old. "And, this is Maria who is the cousin on her mother's side of the oldest Maria," and I nodded to my niece as I smoothed back the baby Maria's flyaway golden brown hair.

Michael threw back his head and laughed at this surfeit of Marias.

"Lady Anna, I think your family needs to find some novel names for its children. Perhaps Michael?" he suggested playfully.

My niece and I laughed. Michael was almost as common for boys, as Maria was for girls.

The little Marias and Isaac kept the adults' attention focused on them for most of the rest of Michael's visit, so that he and my niece had little chance to continue flirting. Michael was an attractive and accomplished man, despite his lack of dynatoi ancestry. Even so, I knew without asking that Catherine expected her daughter to wed a man of high standing and wealth. Higher than to the station the Ostiarios' medallion had lifted Michael Maurex.

"So I will be here at the sixth hour next Wednesday to pick up anything you want to send to Lord John," Michael said as he readied to leave, but nodding in Maria's direction "or your father, General Comnenus." His eyes were on Maria, who returned his gaze with her cheeks blushing.

"I will have a box ready for you then," I answered.

THE EPARCH

Maria gave me a brief glance before responding, "I'll be sure to have a box here for my father, as well."

After Michael had left, Maria turned to me with a dreamy look on her face. "Auntie, he must be the handsomest sailor in the navy," she said.

I clucked my tongue at her, trying to bring her back to what her mother undoubtedly expected of her. She was seventeen, an age when a girl dreams of young men. "Maria, yes, he is an attractive man. But, no, he is not the man for you. He has no family to speak of, he is not dynatoi, and he has no money. Your parents, especially your mother, expect better for you than that." I tried to dispel any illusions she might have about what Catherine would think of him.

Maria looked down, abashed at my admonition. She sighed as she traced the outline of the design on the rim of the plate on which Antonina's small cakes had been served. The curling waves continued around the rim; was it the tide coming in that they depicted, or going out?

"I know," she said dejectedly. "You're right. But I see so few young men, and you must admit he is handsome. I was just daydreaming a little."

"I know many girls who are already married at your age. But I did not marry until I was almost nineteen, and your mother was even older." I laid a hand on hers, remembering those long years in Amaseia when I wondered if I would ever wed. Even scrawny Irene Pegonitissa had married before me. "Your parents will find you a fine husband, I am sure of it."

She sighed. "I suppose I shouldn't worry about it. I'm not; he was just so handsome I let my imagination get the better of me."

After that afternoon, I did not see Maria again until the day Michael Maurex returned to pick up the parcel I had prepared for John. Maria and her niece Maria appeared at my door at mid-morning with a sturdy wooden chest filled with sandals, belts, whetstones, extra tunics and wide brimmed hats to keep the sun off during the summer heat.

As midday approached, my niece Anastasia alerted me to a nosebleed that little Isaac had come down with. I went to care for my son, fussy and upset with blood gushing from his nose, oblivious to Michael Maurex' impending visit. By the time I had stopped the blood and cleaned Isaac and myself, Michael had arrived and was in the cool, shaded library with Maria.

I came downstairs after leaving instructions for the nursemaid and entered the room to welcome Michael. He and Maria sat some distance from each other, but both had flushed a deep red despite being out of the sun.

"Auntie, I hope you don't mind but I asked David for refreshments," said Maria, looking redfaced.

I glanced down at the carved wooden tray where a half-filled cup lay on its side, its contents puddled on the tray.

"Not at all. Michael, I really do appreciate your offering to take these boxes to John and Isaac." I stood in the center of the room, befuddled with lingering worry for my little Isaac, wondering if I had assembled all that John might need, and an amorphous concern about what mischief Michael and Maria might have indulged in when alone. I needed to seize the bull by the horns.

"Maria, I think your little cousin is getting fussy and wants to see you," I said, thinking up the only reason why Maria might need to leave the room.

Maria excused herself, leaving Michael and me alone.

I looked at Michael as his gaze followed Maria into the hallway and up the stairs. This would be uncomfortable.

"Michael," I said, "come sit down here." I patted the cushioned seat in the chair across from me.

He looked at me with a guarded expression but followed my direction.

"Michael, you know John and I think well of you," I began, "and Isaac, too. But Isaac's wife, Catherine, has high hopes for a great marriage for her daughter."

Michael looked down at the floor for a few seconds, contemplating my words. He rubbed his hands up and down his thighs as he gave my comments thought. His gaze flickered toward the door Maria had left by before he looked up at me.

"So you don't think I'm good enough for her."

"No, I did not say that. I said her mother aspires for her daughter to have a husband of the dynatoi. I wish it were different."

Michael gave me a long look, before nodding in reluctant agreement. He sighed, rose, and gestured towards the box I had packed for John.

"This one is for your husband? Is there one also for General Comnenus?"

"It's in the hallway, you'll see it as you leave."

I walked Michael outside to the cart he had hired to bring the boxes to the ship. He mounted his chestnut gelding after stowing the boxes and was preparing to leave when Maria appeared, little Maria in her arms.

"You're leaving so soon?" she asked, flushed at her hurried descent down the stairs.

"Yes, Lady Maria, I have much to do before we set sail. I promise to give your warmest good wishes to your father when I see him. And yours to Lord John, as well, Lady Anna," he said, with a quick nod in my direction.

"Thank you, Michael," I said as I eyed my niece. Maria's face had a hurt look on it, as though he had disappointed her somehow.

"Lady Anna, Lady Maria" he said with a quick salute, as he turned his horse towards the gate and the piers on the Golden Horn where the navy's ships were docked.

I noticed Maria knuckling away a tear as we returned to the house. I felt terrible at separating the two of them, but little good would come if they were left in each other's company since Maria was of an age to be married. Catherine did not confide in me but I hoped she had marital plans for her daughter.

The lean times worsened in the following year as the emperor's taxes bit ever more deeply into everyone's purses. I was grateful for the produce from our garden and what came from the farm in Thrace, carted in by Simon since we did not visit it those summers when John was gone. Less fortunate were the beggars who found their way to our gates despite our location far from the city's main thoroughfares. I could never send them away without some food, especially the children.

Income from the warehouse dwindled then, since the Italians would no longer lend their gold to the emperor for his palaces and pavilions, instead requiring repayment. For long weeks the building stood empty, and when it did hold merchants' wares, the fees paid were a sliver of what they had been.

One day that spring, Samuel arrived for our regular review of the warehouse's affairs. This man, whom Grandmother had first hired for the position almost thirty years earlier, had a buoyant personality, always eager to see the best in life. On that day, however, his brow was furrowed, his face drained of color, his hands shaking.

"Lady Anna," he said in a rush, "there's been some trouble in the warehouse district. The eparch's men have been arresting some of the managers, accusing them of cheating the emperor in their business dealings in the past. They're being imprisoned in the dungeons of the Great Palace."

I was confused. "Really? What could they have done?"

"Nothing, which frightens me. You remember Yonas, the Ethiopian who runs the warehouse owned by the Taronites family? The most honest man I know; I would trust him with my life and honor. He was dragged away yesterday. And Azat, the Tatar who worked in the Melissenos' warehouse, was taken away the day before. Not so honest as Yonas, perhaps, but not so foolish as to cheat the emperor. There've been others, too."

"Was there proof of cheating?"

"I was nearby when the soldiers came for Yonas. They had no proof, just swords and spears. Yonas tried to explain but got knocked to the ground for his trouble. He was only half conscious when they threw him into a cart with two others. His wife and children are frantic with worry. They've no idea what's become of him."

"It must be some sort of misunderstanding," I said without conviction. "Why else would the eparch do that?"

"I've no idea. But the rest of us warehousemen, we're wondering if they'll be coming for us next. A few of them, the newer ones, have just disappeared."

I frowned. I had always thought it a good idea to stay out of the eparch's way - unnoticed and inconspicuous. Ostentation had a way of getting his attention, leading only to more taxes. But it left me without a connection to discover what was happening. Still, other paths might lead to answers.

"I'll pay a visit to the Taronites house. They must know something about what's happened to Yonas." I looked at Samuel's worried face, which did nothing to relieve the knot growing in my stomach.

An hour later I presented myself at the Taronites gate with David. Gregory Taronites was off with John and Isaac, leaving his wife, Thekla, behind at home with their children. A few moments after I knocked on the gate, the small window in it opened, and the pale face of a nervous youth about fifteen looked out at me.

"Good day," I said to the boy. "I would like to speak to Lady Thekla, if she is at home. I'm Lady Anna Dalassena, and my husband John Comnenus is in Cappadocia with General Taronites," I noted, by way of introduction. I did not know Thekla well, but we had met on a few social occasions.

The boy's glance moved to a spot inside the gate, where he must have received permission, because the gate creaked open to allow us in. Many people with houses large enough for a wall kept their gates closed unless they needed to be open, but this felt different. I wondered if it was just my nerves on edge after Samuel's report, but when I got inside the gate and saw Thekla's frightened face I knew my instincts were correct.

"Thekla, are you all right? I heard about Yonas."

Her hand gripped the arm of the boy who had opened the gate, every muscle in her face tense.

"I just don't know what to do," she burst into tears then, her maphorion slipping to the side of her head. "Yonas has been arrested."

"Let's go inside and talk there," I said.

She nodded her head, but seemed unable to speak further.

"My mother's been upset since we heard yesterday," the boy said as we walked towards the house. "She's never had to deal with this kind of problem before."

"You are the general's son? What is your name?" I asked.

"Michael. I sent our steward, George, out about two hours ago to see the eparch about what has happened to Yonas; to see if he could clear things up. He hasn't returned yet though," he said, nervously glancing at his mother. The boy, a slender child with a mop of brown hair tumbling into his face, seemed to be handling this better than his mother who continued to cry.

I settled Thekla in a chair inside while asking a servant to bring wine and water in hopes of calming her down.

"So tell me what happened," I asked.

Thekla seemed incapable of answering, so young Michael filled me in with much the same information as Samuel had related earlier. After hearing nothing more, Michael had the idea of sending their reluctant steward to the eparch's offices to learn what was the problem. As he finished speaking, a commotion outside announced the return of the steward.

A slightly pudgy man with wispy nondescript hair, George hurried into the room, his face flushed with the effort and panting heavily.

"Lady Thekla, I apologize for my lengthy absence, but the crowd at the eparch's offices made it difficult to speak with him. It appears Yonas was not the only one accused of theft from the emperor. At least a dozen other warehousemen have been imprisoned, along with a number of the merchants."

"So what did the eparch say when you spoke to him? Did you tell him Yonas would never have stolen from the emperor?" Thekla asked, trying to regain some composure while continuing to sniffle.

"Yes, Lady, I did. It made no difference. He had a list of names with numbers listed next to them, the amounts they were accused of stealing. Yonas had the number four hundred next to his name," George said.

"Four hundred? Four hundred what? For what?" she asked, her voice pitched high and a perplexed look on her face.

"Solidi, for compensation to the emperor," George answered bleakly.

Four hundred gold solidi was an enormous amount, more than most people saw in a lifetime. I could see from the fine furnishings of their house and Thekla's expensive silks that the Taronites were a wealthy family but that amount would be substantial even for them.

Michael spoke defiantly then, "What if we refuse to pay?"

"The eparch made me to understand besides keeping Yonas imprisoned, the emperor would next investigate whether the instructions for the thefts came from General Taronites," George said.

"My father would never do anything like that," Michael responded vehemently.

George held up his hand to stop Michael. "Of course he wouldn't, but if Yonas were tortured, he might make such an accusation. Clearing the family name could cost even more than the four hundred solidi." George looked resigned as he finished his report. "I could see the eparch had a subordinate in an office near where I met him. There was a line of men already there with bags heavy with gold coins."

"Ransom," I said softly.

George's eyes lit on me, noticing me for the first time.

"I'm Lady Anna Dalassena. My husband is John Comnenus who is with General Taronites in Cappadocia."

"I think you are correct, Lady Anna. It is a kind of ransom, or a tax. Whatever you call it, it is filling the emperor's coffers as we speak."

And then going to repay the Italian loans, or perhaps the emperor has some new building he wants to construct, or new favorite mistress to indulge.

It came as no surprise then, when I arrived home to find Samuel's son, Joshua, waiting for me, deep lines of worry on his young face. He did not need to speak to know what had happened.

I sent David with Joshua to the eparch's offices to learn what amount our household had been assessed. The sooner I came up with the money, the sooner Samuel would be freed.

The two men returned an hour later with the news that Samuel had been accused of stealing two hundred solidi. I retrieved the shiny gold coins from the locked chest I kept them in. John and I had thought to spend that much outfitting Theodore when it was his turn to join the Exkoubitores, but now would have to find some other source with the chest so depleted. I then went back to the eparch's with David and Joshua, the bag of coins tucked in my robes.

The eparch's large brick dwelling stood at a bustling crossroads on the Mese near the Forum Tauri. The first level held his offices, while living quarters were upstairs, presumably with a family, though they kept out of sight. The crowds had thinned by that time of the day, but it happened that Michael Taronites and George had arrived to pay his household's assigned penalty a few minutes before us. I stood waiting our turn behind Michael as the tax collector spilled the bag onto his table and began counting. A few minutes after he began, the taxman carelessly knocked a few coins to the floor, which Michael and George rushed to pick up. While they were thus distracted, I saw the taxman drop a few solidi into a pocket in his greasy sleeve before continuing to count. Naturally, he came up short.

"Boy, I can't let your man go. You are three solidi short," the plump tax collector said, a look of feigned sympathy on his swarthy face.

Michael looked frantically down at the stacks of coins. "But I am sure we had the right amount. We counted it twice to be certain."

I spoke up then, calmly observing, "Michael, I'm sure you counted them correctly. Sir, perhaps when the coins fell to the floor, some fell into your lap, or your sleeve. I'm sure I saw some roll there."

The man scowled at me, displaying one of the uglier sets of teeth I had ever seen, stained, black and broken by turns. "You're mistaken, woman. The coins only fell to the floor," he growled irritably.

The eparch entered the room then. He had the morose grayish look of an efficient bureaucrat doing what he had been told to do, but not particularly liking it.

"What's amiss, Paulus?" the eparch asked the tax collector.

"Nothing sir," Paulus answered. "This boy lacks three solidi to cover the thefts at his family's warehouse."

"I don't believe that is correct. I am sure I saw three coins fall into the taxman's sleeve," I said pleasantly. "Paulus may have overlooked them as he was so busy counting."

The eparch glared at his underling. "Paulus, I want no accusations of thefts from this office. Search your clothes."

Glaring at me, Paulus shook his sleeve out of which, to no one's surprise, appeared three bright solidi.

A short while later, after I had handed my coins handed over to the surly tax collector, I stood outside under the eparch's portico with Michael awaiting the release of Yonas and Samuel. We stood concealed behind David, Joshua and George who had struck up a lively conversation about horseracing.

"Lady Anna, thank you for your help. It would have upset my mother if I'd had to go back for more gold," said Michael, looking relieved.

"I was glad. . ." my voice drifted off as I caught sight of several men sleek in their elegant red banded Senator's robes approach the eparch's building. The four men spoke jovially, without the anxiety and defeated looks those of us paying ransoms wore. Constantine Ducas was one of the group entering the building, the door shut behind them.

Michael and I continued a desultory conversation as we waited. The soldiers retrieving Yonas and Samuel and a few others were not rushing. Some while later, as the cart arrived with the men being released, the eparch's door opened and the four senators emerged, slapping the functionary's back, and commenting, "Well done, Eugene," and "The emperor will be pleased at how much you've collected," and "Be sure to get the chests over to the palace tonight. And double the guards," Ducas instructed the eparch. I stood in the shadows during the commotion of the prisoners' release and the senators' departure, overlooked but hearing all.

A man in his fifties, heavy with steel gray hair thinning on top I recognized as the Senator George Probatos, clapped Ducas on the shoulder and applauded him saying, "Ducas, the emperor really owes you a debt for all we've collected."

The exorbitant taxing schemes ran rampant throughout that year and the next. Every coin they could squeeze out of pockets, they did. Somehow, though, it never appeared to affect the senators, whose households sparkled with beautiful silks and elegant jewels, and whose tables groaned under the weight of the finest foods.

John returned home at the end of October, shocked at the change in our circumstances. Our household had barely managed. Clothes were patched and mended until they fell apart, while we relied more than ever on the garden's produce to put food on the table. But compared to many others, we were fortunate. It often appeared the only meal the children's tutor ate on the days he taught them was the one he shared with us.

There were some happy times, though. My cousin Romanus and his wife had a son, named Constantine after Romanus' father. And that winter I found myself pregnant again. I summoned Maria Kourtikios about the end of my fourth month, concerned about how quickly the baby seemed to be growing, as I felt swollen to the size I had been when five months or more pregnant with the other children. That wise woman asked a few questions, wondering if I had somehow miscalculated. That was not possible since I appeared to have gotten pregnant within a day of John's return. Then she felt my swelling belly, looked at me with a narrowed eye, and said, "You may be having twins, Lady Anna."

I blinked at her in shock and sat down heavily. Outside Donya's two boys and Manuel played a raucous game with wooden swords, their noise reaching fever pitch; Anastasia and Maria squabbled in a nearby room about their dolls; and almost three year old Isaac clung to my skirts while glaring suspiciously at the physician. I was trying to raise six children on a dwindling income with my husband gone much of the year and she was telling me I would soon have two more. I didn't know whether to laugh or cry.

A few weeks later, news arrived that my friend Eudokia had given birth to her second son, named Andronikos after Ducas' father. As a senator's wife, she had no concerns about money, but I did not envy her her situation. Samuel's discreet inquiries had confirmed Constantine Ducas' involvement in the emperor's extortionate plan for ever-weightier taxes, fines and fees. Ducas received generous gifts from the emperor in compensation. I hardly needed the confirmation of his involvement after what I had heard outside the eparch's office.

I was just over eight months into my pregnancy in early June and barely able to waddle about. The physician had instructed me to stay off my feet as much as possible, and I tried to obey. But with John still in Cappadocia, the children appreciated my presence at meals. Helena often visited us bringing her son, called Michael after his grandfather. Just a few months younger than my little Isaac, the two of them had become great friends.

After the midday meal, Helena and I sat outside on the veranda in the shade of the grape arbor, trying to cool off. Like most women, my everyday dress could be loosened to accommodate pregnancy; but this pregnancy had stretched it to its limits and it chaffed roughly against my belly. It was one of those early summer days when the earth seemed to sizzle and the plants wilted in the heat. The children were becoming irritable, whining over the smallest disagreement. I found it difficult to muster the interest in moderating their childish arguments, and left their resolution to Helena. A bee buzzed around me and I raised a hand to brush it away when I realized a trickle of moisture was dripping down between my legs.

"Helena," I said, the trickle quickly becoming a stream, "would you please ask David to send for Maria Kourtikios? I think it's time."

"Auntie, already? Don't you have a few more weeks?" she said, looking concerned.

"Babies come when they are ready. I think if there are two of them in there, they may be feeling a little crowded." I had come to reluctantly accept the physician's judgment that I would be having twins. There were simply too many feet and elbows and knees jutting out to be just one child, not to mention the tandem hiccupping.

Labor lasted the rest of that hot day and into the night. It was in the darkest hour of the night when the air had finally cooled that I gave birth to two small girls, one a red head like her father, and the other a blond surprise. Even with their different coloring, though, their faces were so alike it was a blessing their hair color so different.

Helena had stayed with me through the long pain filled hours, and held the fussing blond babe as the red haired one nursed at my breast.

"What will you name them?" she asked.

I could see the first shards of light in the eastern sky outside the window, heralding the new day. Smiling down at the peaceful child in my arms, her small fingers clutching one of mine, I said "We thought to name one of them after my grandmother, Theodora, and the other one Eudokia after your mother. And, of course, we would call her Donya as we called your mother."

Helena wiped a tear away at that.

"Thank you, Auntie. I know my mother would have liked that." Helena gazed down at the small blond girl and said, "Welcome, little Donya."

With that, the red haired one received Grandmother's name of Theodora.

CHAPTER TWENTY

Schism and Plague

1054 to 1055

I am a woman, and an only child, but I have raised boys so I know a pissing contest when I see one. For the first half of the year the Patriarch Michael Keroularios, Eudokia's stubborn and cantankerous uncle, and the equally stubborn and cantankerous envoy from the pope in Rome exchanged angry words and insults arguing about how we say the Divine Liturgy as opposed to how the Latins say theirs. Every pronouncement elevated the harsh rhetoric to new levels, with threats of eternal damnation over trivial matters shot back and forth between them like barbed arrows. Of course, the Roman cardinal was wrong in his demands about the Divine Liturgy but I knew from my one dreadful meeting with the patriarch how irritating and dismissive he could be of any opinion other than his own.

The city buzzed with talk of what first one said and then the other. The emperor tried to conciliate the two of them since he hoped for papal assistance in regaining our lost Italian territories. The patriarch did soften his rhetoric, but their relations did not improve. Finally, in mid-July, in a fit of pique the pope's envoy stormed into the Hagia Sophia ostentatiously attired in his red cardinal's robes. As the patriarch celebrated the Divine Liturgy he strode through the church and flung a rolled up piece of parchment onto the altar, bellowing something in his barbarous tongue. He then turned and walked out, the congregation watching in horrified fascination. The parchment excommunicated the patriarch while falsely

accusing him of simony, the closing of Latin churches, encouraging cas-
tration, and many other ridiculous theological errors.

The citizens of the city were outraged at this insult to their patriarch,
rushing to demonstrate their support of him and their own Church's cus-
toms. The Italian merchants in the city hid themselves away until calm
returned. The patriarch himself responded to the excommunication in
kind, anathematizing the cardinal. Meanwhile, the blustering cardinal
soon sailed back to Rome in tact and with generous gifts from the emperor.
A ridiculous piece of nonsense; I'm sure it will be soon forgotten.

Theodore's brother, George, gave a skeptical look at the helmet, wincing
as it pressed on his nose when he tried it on, "Why do you need a nose
guard? It pushes down on your nose and hurts."

His older sister, Helena, sat nearby with her baby son and laughed.

"Better a little push on your nose than to get it chopped off," she said.

After three years of serving in Cappadocia with Isaac and Gagik,
John and the other men had no assignment that year. Instead, they spent
their days helping Theodore purchase items for his kit, while at the same
time regaling the young man with stories that alternated between terri-
fying and uproarious. Theodore's face held a strong resemblance to his
fair haired father, but his sturdy build was not so inclined to plumpness
as Michael's had been. In that way he seemed to resemble his Comnenus
forebears more.

Theodore would soon join the Exkoubitores to begin his military
training. John and I, with help from Isaac, had scraped together the
money to see him outfitted with the equipment a young soldier required.
The sword he carried had been his father's, as was the lorikion – his chain
mail. These were two of the more expensive items, but he still needed a
pair of horses with saddles and all their fittings; shield; mace; his uniform, including heavy wool cloak and heavy boots for the cold winter
months; assorted other clothing; and the helmet with nose guard. And
of course the sturdy chest a soldier needs to keep it secure.

His departure in the spring following Easter felt as though I was
sending my own son off, after being with us almost four years. I would
miss him, but the tears did not last long with seven children remaining
under my roof.

We decided to visit the farm in Thrace again that summer, not having gone for the four years when John had been gone on campaign. At the end of July, we packed up the cart, hired a litter, and eagerly left the hot and smelly city behind for the quiet, fresh air of Thrace.

Manuel, now nine, rode his own horse, along side his father and his cousin George. From time to time I would peek out from the litter to watch him, sitting with confidence on the even-tempered filly we had procured for him. I am not sure which of us was prouder—John, me, or Manuel himself. I felt a pang when I realized how few years it had been since Theodore had ridden with us at the same age, and how few years it would be before Manuel would be putting together his own kit.

From time to time John would grab young Isaac and set the excited boy on his saddle, much as he had done with Manuel on earlier trips. Anastasia and I were then left with Maria and the fussy twins in the litter.

This journey brought back memories of trips to the farm from the past and of those who no longer joined us on them—Donya and Michael, and my grandparents. There were even faint memories of my own parents eating sweet summer peaches, and holding their hands as we walked to the creek to fish. More than anything, I wanted my children to have memories of this place they could recall with happiness in later years. Happy memories can sometimes be the only things that temper life's heartbreaks.

We had been settled at the farm for only a few days when Simon hurried back from the market with frightening news. I had been working in the garden with Anastasia while trying to keep an eye on the babies, who giggled and rolled about on an old blanket we had put out in the shade of a tree for them to play on. John had taken the boys and Maria to fish. I stood up, shading my eyes when I saw him turn in our gate at a quick march for a man his age. He looked at the house, before I waved and got his attention.

"Lady Anna," he croaked out, winded and barely able to speak.

"Simon, just catch your breath. No need to rush. Can I get you some water?" I asked. But he shook his head at my offer, pulling up the water skin he carried at his waist. He took a drink of water, and after a minute his breathing returned to normal.

"Lady Anna, terrible news from the city. Plague."

"Plague? Are you sure? There was no sign of it when we left." We had been gone from the city only a week.

"Don't know. All I know is people are streaming out of the city to escape it. Crowds coming through, talking about it, trying to get as far away as they can. Been a long time since I last seen plague. Would've been happy not to see it again. Things go crazy, people go crazy when it comes." He ran a hand through his sparse white hair.

Plague sometimes haunted the clogged and smelly streets of Byzantium, thick with the press of men. It did not always spread into the countryside, or at least not until after the pestilence had had its fill in the city. It would be safest if we stayed where we were on the farm for the present, but take precautions.

John and the children returned late in the afternoon with a string of plump fish for our supper. He paled at the news, but his first concern was for his brother who had planned to remain in the city with his family that summer.

"It won't do them any good if you return to the city," I said, "and it certainly won't do me and the children any good if you leave us behind. Why don't you write to Isaac, just to reassure yourself that they have not taken ill? And invite them to come stay with us, if they want."

He considered my suggestion, glancing at the children and running a restless hand over his face.

"You're right. That would be best." He leaned over and kissed me. "I'm not a doctor; there's nothing I could do and I can't leave you here alone."

He found a messenger willing to carry the letter back to the city, but we had no assurances he would make it there or whether there would be someone to receive it on arrival.

Scruffy travelers passing on the road outside our gates looked wretched and desperate. John hired a couple of young men from the neighborhood to guard the farm at night, to prevent thievery, so he and Simon could sleep. We also left a basket of food and amphora of water outside the gate each day for the indigents, which were empty by sunset.

The gate and wall beside the road were not high and little impediment to any determined thief, but they kept most away. A bold few did still venture in, hiding in shadows to look for more fruit, or the odd egg or chicken that might not be missed. While I did not welcome these,

I was sympathetic to their plight knowing their terrible circumstances. John kept close to the house most days after encountering some of them. He also hoped for a letter from Isaac.

After being confined like that for almost two weeks, John became bored. The older children also needed to find something more interesting to do, away from the house.

"Why don't you take the boys and Maria and Anastasia down to the creek to fish? Simon and Priska should be back from the village soon. It's been weeks since you've done that and the children would enjoy it," I said. In fact, I would enjoy it too. With the twins napping and the older children out of the house, I would have those few blessed moments of peace that are the golden coins of any mother's life.

I waved goodbye to the merry group, them as eager to leave as I was to have quiet before the babies awoke. I relaxed on a bench in the sun behind the house, the endless mending any mother has beside me. The peace and warmth of the day lulled me into sleep, and I lay down for a few minutes to nap before the twins awoke. I could not have slept for long before a voice disturbed me.

"Lady Anna," it said in a sly, nasty tone.

My eyes cracked open, my mind confused. The voice sounded familiar in a long ago way. I bolted upright, realizing it was not the voice of a friend, wiping the drool that had slipped from my mouth with the back of my hand.

A man, tall and in a filthy, disheveled juppe and breeches, stood nearby. Two other men hovered behind him, equally shabby and grubby, grinning unpleasantly at me. All three had a hungry, emaciated look to them. The first man became familiar as I focused on him. It was Nicholas, my grandparents' old steward, thinner and grayer than when I had last seen him. Romanus and his wife had not had the patience with him my grandparents had, and dismissed him not long after they acquired the house.

"Nicholas," I said, still groggy, "what are you doing here?"

He sniggered. "Just passing through the neighborhood and thought to pay a visit to the farm of my old employers." His two companions laughed at that.

"Oh." That comment felt inane, but it was taking me some time to gather my wits about me. They made no overt, threatening move, but their rough appearance made my skin crawl. I remembered the twins, asleep inside, and forced a smile. "Would you like some water? It's hot today."

The men glanced at the pitcher of water I gestured to without appreciation. It seemed they wanted stronger drink.

"Or, if you would like, I can get some wine for you and your companions," I offered. "And can I offer you some bread and cheese?"

The men's eyes glittered at my suggestions. As thin as they were, they may not have eaten for some time. I invited them to sit down and left to bring the food and drink to them.

Inside the house, I briefly contemplated running to the road and calling for help, but realized I couldn't leave with the two babies sleeping upstairs. I broke the bread into pieces, sliced the cheese for the men, and added a bowl of red cherries. As a precaution, I found a sharp knife, hiding it in a fold of my gown so the men could not see it.

Outside I set the tray with food and drink on the table where we ate most of our meals, and tried to appear calm and oblivious to any threat. I sat down nearby, pretending attention to the sewing in my lap, before starting a conversation with these undesirable visitors.

"How did you men come to be here in Thrace? When did you leave the city?" I asked. "We've heard terrible stories."

Nicholas finished a bite, washed it down with a long drink of wine, before answering.

"If you've heard of plague in the city, it's true. Leo, Matthias and I left over a week ago, after over five hundred died in one day. Or so we heard." He laughed unpleasantly. "Not like we seen all the bodies; just enough of them."

Leo and Matthias grinned like a couple of mimes in the emperor's theater.

"Plague must've come in on a ship; first thing, lots of sailors and dockworkers got it," Nicholas continued between bites. "Then women in the brothels started dying."

Leo gave a howl of laughter at that. "Sailors go right to the girls when they reach port, even when they's sick."

"After it got to the brothels, it spread like the fire the emperor's ships fling on their enemies. Nothing stopped it," Nicholas said.

"It was wise you left when you did. How is it you happened this way?" I asked in an effort to maintain the conversation. I strained to hear the sound of John or Simon approaching.

Nicholas shrugged while looking out of the corner of his eye at me. "Just happened. When we got close I recognized the area from when your granddad brought me here. Decided to pay a visit."

I nodded and pretended to work at a knot in my threads, my arm held close to my side where I had tucked the knife, while trying to think what to do until John returned. I glanced towards the wooded area where they would come from the creek, but saw nothing. The men were not slow to pour themselves more wine, and I was glad I had filled the pitcher close to the brim. Perhaps the wine's soporific qualities would soon take effect.

"Where's your husband?" Nicholas asked. He had stopped eating, appetite satiated, and glared across the table at me in bold curiosity.

"John?" My mind tried to come up with some reason for his absence that would also indicate his imminent return, but it turned blank and I told a version of the truth.

"John has taken the children fishing. I expect him back any time now." In fact, I did not expect their return until mid-afternoon. Judging from the sun, I could not expect them for some time. Nor did I mention the children asleep in the house. I said silent prayers that the babies would not wake and start to fuss, but my breasts felt full, which meant their stomachs would be empty.

"'E shouldn't leave a pretty wife alone these days. All sorts of ruffians on the road, trying to escape the plague," said one of Nicholas's companions with a smirk.

Nicholas laughed at that, a nasty twist to his mouth. I went to clear the table, and was about to offer to get another pitcher of wine when he grabbed my wrist. He pulled me down close to his face, his hot breath foul smelling.

"You were always a pretty one. Filled out well, I see," he said as his other hand clutched at my breast. The memory of the attack by the Turks so many years earlier rushed through me like a lightning bolt. Forgotten anger at what those men had done turned me fierce in fighting these men.

I tried to jerk free, but his grip held firm. Leo and Matthias watched in lascivious fascination as Nicholas pawed me.

"Let go of me now, Nicholas," I said, my voice rising as his fingers probed.

"I'll let go when I'm done. But Leo and Matthias will want their turn." He grinned and leaned into my face. I turned away, sickened. It was then I heard one of the twins begin to cry, and the other one soon joined in.

Nicholas turned at the sounds, unsure of them, before he realized the noise came from the house.

"Whatzatt?"

"My babies," I said. I twisted my arm in an effort to get loose with his attention distracted by the infants. Terrified but desperate, I broke free and made a run for the house, before he caught me and pinned me against a wall, his back to the others.

"Looks like she's no interested in you," cackled Leo, or maybe it was Matthias. "Wants me instead. Let me have a go."

"You two wait your turn. I got her first," said Nicholas, his voice rough and eager.

Nicholas held me against the wall with his right arm, while attempting to unlace his breeches with his left. His filthy body was so close I could feel his hardness press against my belly. A surge of revulsion for this disgusting man cut through me like a white-hot knife. At that moment, it felt as though a foreign spirit had taken over my body and my hand found the knife hidden in the folds of my gown.

Later I could not recall every detail of what occurred, shocked at what I had done. I know I pulled the knife from my skirts. I know I stabbed Nicholas, I recall his body vibrating as the blood gushed out onto me. I remember hearing Matthias, or was it Leo, say, "Quick one, is she?" confusing my assailant's death shakes with shivering pleasure. I remember Nicholas's eyes as they looked at me in surprise, before the light faded in them, and he crumpled to the earth in a bloody heap.

What I do not recall, though, is actually thrusting the knife into him. I must have been lucky to cut into a vein big enough that his life's blood would gush out. Odd, I thought. I had slaughtered animals before for a meal and never seen so much blood.

I stood trembling against the house, knife in my hand, the blood that had splattered onto my dress causing it to adhere to me like the skin on a piece of fruit. The expectant grins on the faces of Nicholas's two scrawny companions transformed to panic as they realized what had happened.

The babies' cries grew more insistent. I had to protect them and get rid of these two vermin. I started toward them and pointed my bloody knife at them.

"You're right. I am quick. Who wants to be next?" I yelled. Later I thought I must have looked like the nightmare of an avenging angel, blood everywhere as I swung the knife. The two of them scrambled in a rush to their feet and ran up the path to the gate, as I followed after them, screaming like a feral cat with threats to unman them before I killed them.

I watched them race north up the road away from the farm and look back in terror at the sight of me, covered in blood, knife in hand and pointed at them. I stayed there until I was sure they were gone, and returned to behind the house where Nicholas's body lay, dark blood pooled around him. The thick, metallic stench of blood permeated the air and flies had begun feeding. I would have stood there longer, exultant at his death, but for the babies crying.

I stripped off my gown and left it in the grass. The pitcher of water washed over me to get rid of some of the gore. I wheeled more water up from the well, eager to clean myself. I began to shake while I washed, as the realization of what had occurred became as sharp as the knife I had stabbed Nicholas with.

Naked but clean, I stepped around the body and went inside to dress and put the babies to the breast. Their small bodies felt sweet in their innocence, grateful for me. I sat with them in my lap, my thoughts about the attack alternating between horror of what I had done, and awe of what I had done. I may have been the daughter and granddaughter of brave soldiers, but a woman does not expect to ever kill a man. Yet I had done so.

A short time later I heard the sounds of John and the children returning – first merry and excited at their catch, then shocked silence as they came upon the dead body and my bloody dress. John called my name many times, becoming more desperate.

"I'm here, here with the babies," I tried to call down to him, but my voice would not go above a whisper. I wiped the tears that started falling down my cheeks in frustration.

John searched downstairs, before he came upstairs and found us.

"Dear God, Anna, what has happened? Are you hurt? Or the girls?" he asked.

I looked at him, my face wet, and shook my head.

Nicholas was buried in a far corner of the cemetery in the nearest town, far enough away I had no fear his ghost would haunt me. His two mangy companions were never seen again. John blamed himself for that frightening moment's laxity. Afterwards, he hired men from the village to stay with us if he needed to be gone.

Worse news came from Byzantium not long afterwards in a letter from Isaac.

John and Anna –

Many have fallen to the plague, with hundreds dying everyday in recent weeks. One of those fallen is my beloved son, Manuel. We had planned to leave the city for safer climes on the day he took sick, but he had the swellings on his body and was gone in two days. Catherine and I are heartbroken. I have prevailed on her that we should take Maria and go to Bulgaria until the illness has passed. We leave in a few hours on a ship commanded by our old friend, the Ostiarios Michael Maurex. Remember us, and our son, in your prayers. I hope you are all well. I received word from our nephew Theodore and he has been spared thus far.

Your grieving brother,
Isaac.

The death of Isaac's son was a sharp pain in our hearts. Our own Manuel had looked up to his older cousin with whom he shared the name that had been their grandfather's. He cried for weeks in the night after learning the news. Our nephew George had been of an age with his poor dead cousin; they had often gone hunting together. Weeks passed before even the slightest smile passed over his young face.

The shock of killing Nicholas and the grief at this news meant I gave little thought to my niece Maria's sailing on Michael Maurex's ship. Isaac and Catherine knew nothing of their earlier flirtation. So it was many months before I wondered at what might have occurred on that journey.

Leaves began to turn gold and red, loosening their grip on the trees and falling into heaps on the ground. Reports from the city of the terrible death tolls grew fewer as the weather cooled, but John was not eager to return to the site of contagion, until we had not heard word of plague deaths for over a week. We stayed in the country that year for over three months, waiting for the cloud of illness to dissipate and did not return to the city until the middle of November.

All the sunny days, and hunting and fishing with John had left the children as brown and tough as one of the nuts they cracked on the stone wall by the road. Even the babies had lost their city pallor and crawled everywhere so they could not be left alone.

We shut up the house for the winter when the cold winds had started to blow from the north. I left the farm that year changed in profound ways from when I had arrived. Nicholas's attempt to rape me had disturbed my sense of safety, security. He had been a trusted servant of my grandparents for many years, and even if I had not been fond of him, I would never have expected such an attack. Nor had I expected my fierce response.

The rhythms of the horses' hooves clopping on the road lulled the girls to sleep in our litter. I brushed a few blond curls from little Donya's face, nestled against me. Her sweet face stood in sharp contrast to the persistent memory of Nicholas. Yes, he had frightened me, but I had fought back and killed the monster. I was not helpless, and that was the greatest change from that day. I knew I could fight back.

The streets of the city of Byzas wore somber hues when we passed through the Porta Aurea on a gray November day. The few people still on the streets did their business with dazed expressions, as though unable to fathom the tragedy that had befallen them. Faces looked sallow and emaciated, some with scars still healing. Many shops along the Mese, the city's busiest street, were shuttered and deserted.

John raised his fist and knocked on our gate while calling for the gatekeeper, "Hello, Thomas?" The servants had barred the gate against unwelcome visitors, as they should have in our absence.

I exited the litter and stood next to John, bouncing little Donya on my hip while we waited. Little Isaac and the girls had been cooped up in the litter for too long. Manuel and George looked ready to drop off their horses with fatigue. We had sent word of our delayed return months earlier, but never received a response. The servants treated our absences in the country as their holiday; visiting family if they chose to, while a few remained at the house.

John and I exchanged a look of concern at the lack of response, and he pounded louder on the gate, before he raised his voice more.

"Thomas, are you there? David?"

We finally heard a shuffling sound from the other side of the wall, and a plaintive, "Coming sir."

The gate creaked open and a man I just recognized as our steward, David, stood alone in the courtyard. David had always had a robust physique, aided by a hearty interest in the pleasures of the table. The gaunt man standing before us bore only a passing resemblance to the David we had left behind in late July.

"Good God, man, what's happened to you?" asked John.

The question was needless, but I forbore to criticize my husband. Instead I hurried our party inside the gate and supervised the unpacking of the baskets of fruit, jars of olives, and other foodstuffs and wine we had brought back with us. Anastasia and George took the younger ones to the nursery and fed them while I joined John in the dining room where he sat talking with David and learning of the past months' sad events.

Thomas, our gatekeeper, had died over a month earlier, as had the little seamstress, Sophia. Antonina had taken ill not long after, but recovered with David's nursing of her. David himself had fallen ill after Antonina had begun to recover, and she, in turn, had nursed him. Neither had returned to full health yet, in part because, lacking the energy to shop for food, they had often gone hungry.

"Can you tell us what you know has happened?" John asked.

"Well, sir, it was maybe a day or two after you left when we first heard of the plague. Word is that it came in on a ship the harbormaster had not checked as thoroughly as he should have." All ships entering the city's harbors were supposed to be checked by the harbormaster's staff for any signs of illness in the men on board. If any are sick, the ship is turned away.

"At first it seemed like it might not be so bad; a few deaths down at the dock, like other times, and in the bawdy houses as happens. Then, one day I had gone to the market and saw three people collapse with the swellings right on the street. Right in front of me." He paused to wipe his perspiring brow. "Those were the killing days, when the gong of the semantrons in the churches never stopped."

"Didn't people try to leave?" John asked.

David nodded. "The emperor and his household left first on the imperial dromon, and most of the dynatoi left soon after, but not soon enough for some." He gave me a sad look before saying, "You will recall the Lady Taronites? She should have left sooner. And I expect you will have learned of your nephew?" The effort to speak left him out of breath.

"Yes, my brother wrote of Manuel's loss," said John, his head bowed. We still mourned for the young man.

"Did you receive word of your warehouse man's death?" David asked.

"Oh, no. Not Samuel," I said in shock. That cheerful, honest man was now in his grave. "What of his family?"

"His son's been around. Joshua. Been running the warehouse for you since his father died. Don't know about the rest," he said.

"I cannot tell you of all who are gone, the number is so great. " David stopped for a moment and bit into one of the figs we had brought back. He swallowed with visible enjoyment. "Oh, I must tell you of one other loss. Your grandparents' old cook, Alethea, and her son the baker, died in September. I passed by his shop before Antonina took sick and it was shuttered. Someone on the street said he and his mother had died."

Of all the deaths, the news of fat, bossy Alethea's death cut me the worst. She had always been a part of my life, even after Grandfather's death when she went to live with her son and his family. She worked in his shop and we often bought bread from them. Another childhood tie broken. Tears streamed down my face, for Manuel, Thekla Taronites, Thomas,

Samuel, and Sophia, and now, most of all, for Alethea. I mourned them all, but Alethea opened the floodgates.

CHAPTER TWENTY-ONE

Isaac and Alexios

January 1056 to August 1057

Theodora, the despised younger sister Empress Zoe had tucked away in a monastery only to need her assistance years later to regain the throne, outlasted Zoe and all of her husbands. Constantine Monomachus took a chill bathing at his Mangana palace one January day and soon died of it, mourned only by those minions he had supported. Over seventy and the last survivor of her dynasty, Empress Theodora displayed unexpected prescience by fostering relations with courtiers who alerted her to Monomachus' impending death. She made it into the palace, grasped the throne and was acclaimed by the Varangians before any competitor could shove her once again into a forgotten corner. Theodora now ruled alone.

I had no complaints about Empress Theodora. She had no grandiose building projects; married no one who thought the throne only worthy of looting; excited no rebellions. The most grumbling about her taking the throne came from the patriarch, who believed it unseemly to have a woman ruling without the aid of a man.

Theodora also relieved Isaac of his military appointments. Not only was Isaac known to be loyal to Monomachus, who had promoted him to Stratopedarch, but years earlier there had been an incident involving one of Catherine's many brothers and Theodora. Catherine's oldest brother, Preslan, had plotted to overthrow Zoe and supposedly planned to marry Theodora and sit as emperor. No one knew for certain whether the prospective bride had agreed to the plan. This plot had been the ostensible reason for Zoe depositing Theodora in her monastery for most of the past thirty years. Isaac's relationship by marriage to Preslan meant he got a share of the blame for it.

"Not much a man can do in this situation," said Isaac, making the best of it. He was not naïve and would bide his time. Theodora could not last many years on the throne at more than seventy years and with the full responsibility for ruling.

Even so, the demotion only added to Isaac's gloom. He often appeared lost in thought with a veil of grief across his face since Manuel's death. These were stormy days for Isaac and Catherine. The winds of their sorrow and disappointment alternately pushed them close and then apart in angry swells.

Catherine often took their daughter with her on visits to churches to pray for Manuel's soul, the Hagia Sophia, St. John Stoudion, the Church of Saints Sergios and Bacchos and others, wandering in search of some comfort.

Men seek solace in other ways. Isaac and John spent many days hunting in the forests just outside the Blachernae gates, often with other soldiers. Our house, with its proximity to the gates, was often the meeting place for the men before the hunts, and where they would stop afterwards to drink wine and chew over recent events. The only unpleasant side of the gatherings was when Constantine Ducas joined them. He had always been friendly to my brother-in-law, who knew little about what Xene had endured at his hands. Ducas ingratiated himself with Isaac whenever possible. I suppose I could have insisted on excluding him, but I felt loathe to add to Isaac's troubles.

I had my Manuel and my nephew, George, help serve the men after John and Isaac had been hunting so the boys could get to know the generals they might someday report to. The young boys had a few careless mishaps early on, but in time learned.

Manuel asked a question one evening at dinner.

"Why do we have an empress, but there is no emperor? We used to have an emperor."

"When Empress Theodora inherited the throne, she was too old to get married," replied John as he forked cheese onto his plate beside the fish.

"Wouldn't it be better if we had an emperor instead of an empress?" Manuel asked.

"Yes, of course it would," said John while he picked out tender bits of fish.

I raised a skeptical eyebrow. The last emperor had been a pathetic failure, but his empress had been no better.

"Perhaps most of the time, but there have been some bad men who were emperors, as well as good ones," I said.

John looked at me, a quizzical expression on his face at this unexpected contradiction.

"Yes, but only a man can lead an army," he said, stating the obvious.

"Not every emperor leads an army," I said. Manuel's eyes flickered back and forth between John and me. "The great Justinian never lead an army. And I don't think Monomachus ever wielded a sword, even if he did buckle on shiny armor on occasion."

"Anna, you know any ruler may have to lead an army; he could be called on to fight battles to defend the empire and his throne," John answered back, as though the conversation was just between us. "Only a man could do that."

I snorted at that. "I've killed a man, to defend myself and my children. Does that mean I could become emperor?"

He flushed, "No, of course not. I'm just saying that it is better to have a man as emperor, than to have a woman ruling alone. Even Empress Zoe realized that."

"And look at the fine men she married," I answered drily. None of Zoe's three different husbands had a great aptitude for ruling, much less her putative nephew.

"Anna, you have to admit an emperor must be able to go into battle. How else can he lead an empire?" John asked as he put down his fork and leaned back in his chair to glare at me, impatient at my disagreement.

I looked at him with a steady gaze. "John, I can't imagine a more incompetent or frivolous emperor than Monomachus. Zoe was no better. So far as I have seen in my lifetime, it matters little whether it's a woman on the throne or a man. The mettle of the person who wears the crown matters more."

John gave me a long look before he commented, "Perhaps, but it is better to have a man on the throne who can lead an army into battle. You have to agree to that."

I flushed. In truth, he was right on that point. The empire could only be strong so long as it fielded men to fight its enemies, and best to have an emperor leading them. Perhaps a woman could lead the empire if there was a loyal and talented general commanding its armies, but then that general might depose her.

"Yes, we can agree on that," I said reluctantly, as I picked a fish bone from the food on my plate.

John reached across the table to pat my hand once he though I had acquiesced to his argument. At least, I did cease arguing with him. I loved my husband although he shared the common view that most women were ignorant and helpless, me being the exception. Men like Ducas and the patriarch relished the power to bend women, as well as men, to their will. Not for the first time did I whisper a prayer of thanksgiving that my grandparents had not forced me to marry someone like Ducas.

John and I had been married ten years. Perhaps he took for granted the smoothly running household, the food on the table, the care I gave to our children and his sister's children, and did not realize how much I did. Perhaps he had forgotten what I had done when threatened with rape, what I had done to protect my children.

"Maybe the empress will get married and we will have an emperor again," Manuel said in his high, piping nine-year-old voice.

"Perhaps, so," said John as he scrutinized our son's plate. "But that doesn't mean you won't have to finish your dinner."

Manuel looked back down at his dinner, all but forgotten during our verbal repartee. He took his fork and stabbed manfully at the piece of fish on his plate, fragrant with garlic and lemons.

"I wish the empress hadn't relieved Uncle Isaac of his command," said George, a robust sixteen year-old. His hair fell across his face, obscuring his eyes, while his first beard shaded his chin. It would not be long before he left us. "I would have liked to serve with him."

John shook his head at that. "You could still get the chance, George. I think he may lead another army someday."

The plague returned that summer, but less virulent than in the year before. Isaac agreed to accompany us to the farm that summer for a few days. He said he wanted to visit it after hearing so many of our stories reminiscing of the summers spent there, but I think he and Catherine needed time apart. Catherine and their daughter, Maria, and niece, Maria, had sailed for Bithynia to her brother Alousian's estate, where Isaac would join them after his stay with us.

We arrived near sunset, with the sun slipping behind the distant mountains darkening to purple. Simon and Priska greeted us, bringing out baskets with bread, eggs, and cheese, and the early peaches for our supper. The children called out, excited to see the old farmer and his wife again.

"Simon, Simon, look at me. Look how big I've grown," crowed little Isaac, puffing out his chest.

"Priska, we've brought you ribbons from the city," cried Maria.

John, Isaac, and the boys, their clothes heavy with dust from the long ride, dismounted and stretched before leading their horses to the stable to brush down and feed.

Anastasia and I and the little girls emerged from our litter and began unpacking our belongings from the cart our stable boy, Narses, had driven. Anastasia and I soon had the chests with our clothes hauled to the proper rooms while Maria kept her mischievous twin sisters from getting under foot. By the time the men returned from the stables and it had reached full dark, we had lanterns lit outside and a light supper on the terrace tables.

"Lady Anna, I've brought you a pitcher of fresh milk," said Priska, appearing out of the dark. "I remembered how much the little ones love the milk."

"Thank you Priska," I said gratefully, taking it from her. "Children, show me your cups so I can fill them with this delicious milk."

Maria ran over to Priska and threw her little arms around the old woman's waist in an ardent embrace, "I love you Priska. Thank you for the milk."

Priska beamed at this spontaneous show of affection, hugging Maria back. "We'll have more tomorrow. Perhaps you can help me milk the cow?"

"Oh, yes. Mama, may I please?"

"Of course. But you'll need to be up early for that."

The happy chattering of the children continued as they made plans for the next day's activities. In their excitement, they spoke of all their favorites, as though they must all be done in that one day, forgetting they would have many days to enjoy them. I looked over their young heads to the table where John and Isaac sat with their wine cups. Isaac cut a piece of cheese and ate it while they spoke and laughed at the youthful enthusiasm on display. It was the first time I had heard Isaac laugh in the year since his son had died.

Later, after settling the children in bed, I sat outside with John and Isaac as we finished the last wine in the jug. Moths flitted about the lanterns, their pale wings like midnight flowers in the light. Isaac looked relaxed in a way I had not seen in a long time, perhaps ever.

"I don't think I've seen those children as excited for anything as they are to be here," said Isaac before raising his cup to his lips.

"Of course they are," said John, exuding the look of a contented paterfamilias. "No tutors, not confined to just our house in the city, plenty of fresh air and outdoor time. How could anyone not enjoy this?"

Isaac sat with a half smile and a raised eyebrow at that question, and I wondered if he was thinking of Catherine.

"Still, it's a tribute to you both that all of them, from George, who's almost of an age to join the army, all the way down to the little twins couldn't be happier. Even after what happened last year."

John reached across the table to clasp my hand, and winked at me.

"We were fortunate none of the children witnessed what happened. By the time I'd returned with them, the worst of it was over," said John.

I could feel the muscles in his hand tense as he spoke. The palms of my hands grew sweaty, and I glanced to the wall Nicholas had pinned me against before I stabbed him. The blood had long since washed away, but the memory of the crumpled body and swarming flies never would.

"We were here almost another two months after the attack. Plenty of time for them, and me, to recover from the shock," I said, shrugging in an attempt to be casual.

Isaac looked into his cup, his eyebrows drawn down as he swirled its contents.

"I think I'll go to bed now. The children will be up early, so best be ready for them," I said.

I took one of the lanterns inside to light my way, but at the doorway looked back at my husband and his brother as they sat in the remaining lantern's glow, like a halo around saints in an icon.

I rose early the next day, but not so early as Maria. I checked in the girls' room and saw she had already left, eager to help Priska with the milking. In the early morning half-light I set about preparing the morning's porridge. The boys would need to gather wood today if we were to have supper.

As the porridge bubbled away, grumbling came from outside. Isaac stood at the door wiping his face and peering over his shoulder to the cowshed.

"Isaac, are you all right?"

He turned towards me, a half-abashed, half-amused look on his face.

"Do you know what your daughter just did, the little minx?" he asked.

I tried not to smile. The sun had barely risen, the dew still damp and sparkling on the grass.

"Can I guess? She squirted you with milk from the cow's teat? Looks like her aim has improved from last year. I'm sorry, I should have warned you of her trick. I had no idea you would be up so early." I handed him a towel to dry off with.

"Yes, well, I'm often up early, if I even get to bed. I saw her leaving the house and she invited me to come with her."

"Ah, caught like the spider with a fly. Why don't you sit down at the table and I'll bring you a bowl of porridge."

As he handed me the towel back, I caught sight of Maria walking towards the house in a deliberate fashion, a pail of milk in her arms. She caught sight of her uncle and burst into giggles.

"I don't see why you are laughing so hard at your old uncle. Was that respectful of your elders to squirt milk at me?" Isaac said, tongue in cheek.

Maria had the grace to look faintly abashed by this reproof.

"I'm sorry, Uncle Isaac," she said, worried now she gone too far.

"Aww, you know I'm just joking with you," he said, breaking into a grin as he took the heavy pail from her and handed it to me.

I left them on the terrace, joking with each other and returned to the house to finish preparing breakfast, pouring the fresh milk into the bowls with porridge. Placing three of them on a tray with spoons and the honey jar, I made my way outside to the terrace and the early risers. We enjoyed a companionable meal beneath the rising sun before the other children and John rose, hungry and eager to start the day.

Isaac stretched out his visit by a few more days than planned and did not depart for the city until more than a week after our arrival. Each day the grayness in his face faded as he rediscovered his old energy. He raced horses with Manuel and George, and joined the crowd that went to the stream most days to catch fish. Little Donya and Theodora insisted on sitting in his lap each evening as we told stories around the fire before bed, giving John a pang of jealousy at the twins' rejection.

The night before he finally had to depart we roasted a goat for supper with greens, chickpeas, and more peaches. The boisterous children urged Isaac to stay another day, and sad when he had to refuse. They wished him farewell then, since he would be leaving before first light. Maria was the last to hug him.

"Next time you come, Uncle Isaac, will you help me milk the cow again?"

"Milk the cow again? Will you promise not to squirt me then?" Isaac asked, a sparkle in his eye.

"Ummm, maybe," she teased him.

"Then, maybe I will," said Isaac, teasing her back.

The children settled in their beds, John, Isaac and I again enjoyed a few cups of wine as the sky darkened and the stars came out. John and I would be up to see Isaac off in the morning, but this would be our last night with adult companionship before returning to home.

"I can see why you look forward to this trip," said Isaac. "I've had more fun than I've had in a long time, if ever."

John's face lit up at this compliment. Isaac was his older brother, wealthier and a more successful soldier than he was. He rarely received a tribute of this sort. But John deserved it; while the farm may have been my patrimony, it was he who made sure everyone had fun.

"We're glad you could be here this year. Perhaps you could induce Catherine to come next year," I said.

He smiled, but shook his head.

"No use planning too far in advance. Best just to enjoy today, and let tomorrow take care of itself. Next summer is a long way off."

"Well, you know you and Catherine and Maria will always be welcome here, anytime," said John, still glowing from Isaac's compliment.

Isaac reached over to squeeze John's shoulder in acknowledgement, and drank down the last of his wine before heading to bed.

I crept barefoot down the stairs in the early hours to pack provisions in Isaac's saddlebags for his trip home. Bread, dried fish, and cheese wrapped in a towel, along with a skin of watered wine. John was still stumbling around upstairs when Isaac appeared in the doorway, startling me. He had been up and saddled his horse already, knickering faintly outside.

"Isaac, you surprised me," I said, jumping at sight of him. I was dressed in a loose linen gown, comfortable in the summer's heat, with my hair in a night plait down my back.

"I'm sorry. Didn't mean to startle you. Where's John?"

I shrugged.

"Oh, you know John, never the earliest riser. He'll be down soon."

Isaac nodded agreement, but there seemed nothing more to say. A few birds chirped outside, while we heard John as he stumbled about upstairs putting on some clothes. Isaac caught my eye and we stood gazing at each other in the light of a single lamp, unspeaking for a long time. His face had a questioning look, while I felt flushed.

"Anna, you. . ." and he stopped as we heard the sound of John's sandaled feet on the stairs.

"So, are you all set? Is there anything else you need?" John asked when he came in the room. I had turned back to the saddlebags, checking its contents.

Isaac smiled at him, reached out and gripped him in a manly hug.

"No, John, I have all I need. Thank you. I had a wonderful holiday with you and Anna and the children. Thank you both."

I handed Isaac his saddlebags, giving him a sisterly embrace.

"We enjoyed having you, Isaac. I hope you can come next year as well," I said and offered him my cheek for a farewell kiss.

In a moment he was off, a barely visible figure in the gray dawn.

We stayed more than our usual month on the farm that year so as to avoid the return of the plague, but not as long as in the previous year, returning home by the end of September. Isaac and his family had returned a week earlier from Bithynia. As the cooler fall months settled in, Isaac and John embarked on more hunting trips than before, as well as arranging and attending dinner parties for the many soldiers and senators they knew.

Isaac's visits were as frequent as before, but the tenor of the men's conversations changed. They discussed less about the game in the forest and more about the politics in the Great Palace. John accompanied Isaac to other men's dinner parties around the city energetic debates went on about who would succeed Theodora.

John only hosted one of these dinner parties that year, since I was again expecting a child, as well as having to care for the other seven. At this dinner, deep in the winter months after Epiphany, I lurked outside the room, listening.

"I don't know what it's like elsewhere, but the Armenian border could be pierced through by the Turks whenever they want to. There've already been raiding. If we don't stop them, someday we'll wake up and find we've lost a lot of territory," said a voice I recognized as Romanus'.

"It's too late in Bulgaria with the Pechenegs. They know how weak we are," said a deep voice. "We pushed 'em back; just don't know how long they'll stay back."

"The soldiers on the border's aren't getting the supplies they need." This voice, unusually high pitched for a soldier and speaking fast, had the distinctive sound of Katakalon Kekaumenos. "The tax collectors are doing their job, but where's the money going?" he said, his voice rising in anger.

Their general consensus was that the problem stemmed not from insufficient revenues for the empire, but what the Palace chose to do with the taxes. I wanted to speak up from my spot in the shadows outside the dining room, let them know where the gold went, but this gathering of men would not welcome a woman's opinion.

The smooth, sinuous voice of another man rose among the cacophony of talk from the group. "I know what happens to the empire's revenues," he said.

Constantine Ducas must have gotten the men's attention because the room quieted. Finally, Isaac spoke.

"All right Ducas, you have our attention. What happens to it?"

"It's paying for all the fine buildings Monomachus built. He borrowed millions from the Italians to pay for them; they expect repayment."

"But Monomachus is dead. Are we still obligated to pay?" asked the high-pitched voice of Kekaumenos.

"Oh, yes. The Italians required the Senate to confirm the debts, so it doesn't matter who sits on the throne. The empire pays."

I had told John of this before, and never one to take too keen an interest in financial affairs, he had been skeptical.

"So how much of this debt is left? Monomachus spent the last few years of his life squeezing money out of us. That should have paid down a lot," said Isaac, intrigued by this disclosure.

There was a pause before Ducas replied with carefully chosen words.

"I'm not certain of the amount, but I believe a great amount still needs payment."

The men all began speaking again, outraged at how our future had been mortgaged. I slipped away then, back upstairs to the children. Ducas' duplicity at pretending ignorance of the debt, or of the schemes he helped devise to extort money from the people was breathtaking. Still, I wondered how monstrous the debt was if he dared not say the amount.

One advantage of the growing relationship between Constantine Ducas and Isaac was the freedom it gave Eudokia to visit me. I could not bring myself to return to the house where Xene's life had ended, but Eudokia could bring her children to our house, where they played in the garden with mine.

By this time, Eudokia had given her husband three children. Michael, the eldest was of an age with Isaac. My son's lively temperament differed from Michael's timid one, but Isaac's friendly disposition left him happy with any playmate. Eudokia's second son, Andronikos, was a few months older than the twins, while her baby Anna was just a few months old.

We sat under the trellis one spring day, my expanding belly limiting the room on my lap for baby Anna, a quiet child with serious eyes.

"Constantine must be pleased to have so many children now," I said as I rocked the little girl.

Eudokia's mouth twisted into a frown as she shrugged.

"He says he is. But he's so old, fifty years now, and has no patience for them. He expects them to be as obedient as a dog, but gives them less time and affection than he gives our dogs. They're ornaments to him. He tells me to keep them in the nursery. I think children need to be outside playing, too. But I'm just their mother, so of course I know nothing."

"I'm sorry to hear that." Sorry, yes, but not surprised.

"He's hired his old friend from the palace, Michael Psellus, to tutor Michael. The man is pleasant enough, if a bit of a social climber, but he's never tutored a small child before. And Michael is so young still." She looked out into the garden where the children played.

"I thought Psellus had been tonsured, was in a monastery?" I asked.

"Oh, he was, but Constantine must have persuaded the hegoumenos to allow the visits, probably because of my uncle."

Eudokia reached over and took baby Anna who had begun to fuss, putting her to the breast. Isaac and Michael ran over, sweaty from whatever game they had been playing and begging for a drink of water. I poured them each a cup from the pitcher David had brought out. Like any six-year-old boys, they drank messily, dribbling and spilling all over themselves. Still, there was something odd about Michael, who made no effort to swipe away the water he had splashed on his face, as Isaac had done. He just stood there, watery blue eyes staring vacantly at his mother, mouth agape and face dripping.

"Come here, sweetheart, let me wipe your face," she said, her own face such a picture of gentle maternal love. With the infant in her lap, she could have been painted into an icon of the Theotokos.

Little Michael moved to her, turning obediently to her waiting towel, smiling up at his mother.

As he ran off again to join Isaac playing with toy swords, I wondered what life would hold for this awkward child and his ambitious father.

We delayed our visit to the farm by a month that year due to the impending birth of our next child, expected at the end of July. George's departure for the army in the spring had decreased the household by one child, but this birth would return it to seven. Isaac had given George most of his dead son's armor, weapons, and horses, saying he knew Manuel would have wanted George to have it.

When the pains began, I sent for Helena and Maria Kourtikios while fifteen-year-old Anastasia took care of the younger children. Helena, her belly swollen with a second baby due in another three months, arrived as John was walking me back and forth in the garden while the pains came and I flung curses at him for getting me pregnant.

"You're the son of a toad, a devil, for doing this to me," I screeched at him, along with other deprecations. Sweat poured off me, worse when we happened into the sun. John's face held a worried look, unaccustomed to such invective from me. Labor is never easy but the pains seemed worse with this child and the unrelenting heat made them more unbearable.

"Anna my sweet, look, Helena has come," said John, glancing gratefully at her.

"I saw that look. Do you think Helena will stop you from being the worthless grub you are?" I said as the muscles in my belly contracted into the hardness of a rock. A wave of nausea surged over me and I vomited into a flower bed before we got inside. Wiping my mouth, I stumbled away from him and allowed Helena to take my arm to escort me to the bedroom where I would give birth.

"I'll be waiting down here for news, my dear," John said as I disappeared upstairs. He may have thought waiting would be a useful thing for him to do, but at that moment I thought he should instead be catapulted over the city walls. Mumbling to myself, Helena walked with me until the arrival of Maria Kourtikios a short time later.

The heat in the room felt as hot and oppressive as a blacksmith's furnace. My hair came lose from its plait and clung damply to my face and shoulders as I labored. At one point Helena and the physician stripped me naked since my gown had become soaked through with sweat. About two hours after sunset a squirming wet body emerged, squalling almost before his body and mine had separated.

I lay on the bed, weak with exhaustion and waiting to expel the after-birth while Helena cleaned the child, swaddling him in fresh linens in the lamplight.

"Looks like you have another redheaded boy," she said as she handed the snug bundle to me.

I put him to my breast where he immediately began to feed. This new son looked irritated by all he had been through, but as the milk let down into his mouth, his eyes opened wide at the pleasure of it.

"What will you call him?" Helena asked.

John and I had discussed this. It was my turn to name a son after someone in my family.

"This one will be called Alexios, after my father," I answered, smiling down into the wide eyes of my new son, almost forgetting the hours of labor.

As it turned out, we were fortunate to be home that August. Three weeks after Alexios' birth, Empress Theodora died after ruling for less than two years. Her last illness was not long, but rumor said it was painful. Few aside from the priests and eunuchs she had brought from the monastery mourned her loss. On the whole, she had been a good ruler, or at least not a bad ruler. The people had never learned to love her as they had her sister, the ever-frivolous Zoe.

In the empress's last hours, when she knew her time to leave the earth approached, her advisers proposed a successor, one Michael Bringas with the nickname of Stratiotikos, whom she accepted without hesitation, by then beyond caring. He had served as the empress' finance secretary for the military, but was old, never married, and childless. Isaac said he and other generals had chaffed at his tight-fisted ways when he controlled the military's purse strings. At the same time, this new emperor had not appreciated their belligerence when they petitioned for funds. It was a mixture as certain to combust as the ceramic balls full of Greek fire were when launched at an enemy.

CHAPTER TWENTY-TWO

The Bureaucrats

August 1056 to August 1057

Empress Theodora's forty days of funeral services—prayers, processions, and the public lying-in-state—required the presence of many personages into the middle of October. Catherine and I carried flowers with other high born women in the final winding procession to her tomb at the Church of the Holy Apostles, already crowded with sarcophagi of emperors back to the first Constantine, praying for her departed soul. The censors swung, emitting sweet smelling smoke, while the eunuchs' choir sang hymns for the dead. I peered through the crowd and smoky haze at the purple marble tomb she was laid in, squeezed in a corner not far from her sister's and wondered how the bickering sisters would feel about spending eternity in the same church. Theodora may not have been a likable woman, but she tried to rule well, which was more than I could say for foolish Zoe.

Isaac spent his time working to ingratiate himself with the new emperor, hopeful for an assignment. Isaac thought they had gotten on tolerably well before Emperor Michael reached the throne. Even so, I worried that Isaac's forceful personality may have angered the former bureaucrat.

The emperor, short and gone to fat in a bureaucrat's easy life, looked more inclined to keeping accounts than wielding a sword. He had toiled away in an imperial office for decades, following orders from whoever sat on the throne. He had taken abuse from soldiers who believed there was more money available, with only a desk and a quill pen to defend himself.

"I saw some soldiers browbeat him for their coins back then, pushing for more than their allotment. Truth be told, I may have been pushier about it than I should have been. Now I guess we're paying for that," Isaac said one day after waiting fruitlessly for an interview. Isaac and some friends had been trying for an imperial audience for weeks. Even John grew frustrated.

"Isaac, no long-suffering functionary could imagine a more complete triumph than to make us wait on his pleasure," said John as he sipped wine one chilly November afternoon. "He still needs us, though. It isn't as though the Turks and the Pechenegs and the Bulgarians decided to pack up and return home."

Isaac grunted and threw back the rest of his wine.

As the months of Michael's reign passed, he reveled in raising fellow bureaucrats to titles such as Proedros, Strator, Vestarches, and Ostiarios, while ignoring the military. This revenge may have seemed a sweet wine, but it might turn to vinegar if so many humiliated soldiers lost their loyalty to the emperor.

Michael Bringas had been on the throne for seven months when Isaac and Katakalon Kekaumenos, and several others including even the Ducas brothers decided the time had arrived to press their case.

"I cannot believe that eunuch Theodorus was named Proedros. What has he done to deserve such a title besides stick his nose up the arses of Michael and Theodora?" said Kekaumenos testily of a particularly useless bureaucrat. He and the others had been hunting with John and Isaac, and stopped for refreshments at our house afterwards, just bread, olives and watered wine, it being Lent.

Isaac shook his head in disbelief. "Yes, and then there's that toady, Leo Strabospondylos. How he could receive a title and all the income that goes with it when all he has done is . . . what? What has he done?" Isaac raised his arms to the heavens, as if asking angels to explain it to him. "Nothing that I can see."

"We've been on the front lines of battle for the empire. I was almost killed, and lost half of my hand fighting the Pechenegs," said Kekaumenos, raising his maimed hand to demonstrate his loss. "Don't I deserve something? I put up with waiting for old Monomachus. And Theodora, what could you expect from a woman? But this one? He should know."

"Utterly bizarre, what he's done," said John.

Isaac's mouth twisted into a grimace as he took a swallow of wine from the cup I placed before him.

"He knows, but he doesn't care. He must think pushing a quill is equal to winning battles. We need to speak to him; tell him we expect fair compensation." Isaac was willing to give the emperor one more chance to remedy his oversights.

General Kekaumenos, one of the empire's most respected generals, gave Isaac a long considered look, arms crossed on his chest. He'd already made his decision.

"And if he refuses?"

Isaac poured himself more wine and slowly sipped. He leaned back in his chair before he spoke.

"Then we'll have to make our own decisions."

Kekaumenos' face brightened and he reached over to grip Isaac's shoulder.

"Good man."

John, Isaac, Kekaumenos and a few other overlooked generals decided to petition the emperor on Easter when he should be in an expansive mood. The long tradition of imperial generosity with Easter petitions made them optimistic.

Isaac and the other soldiers who approached the throne had served the empire faithfully, putting themselves in situations where they could have lost their lives as Donya's husband had and left their wives and children bereft. To be passed over when ink-stained clerks who spent their days sharpening quills earned great titles and looked down their noses at the fighting men seemed little more than criminal.

The sun shone brightly that Easter, the tenth day of April, when the men, armor shining and in their best court attire, walked through the Gallery of the Forty Holy Martyrs to the Chrysotriklinos where the petitions were heard. They took the same path past the mosaics depicting freezing martyrs that I had a dozen years earlier, a lifetime ago it seemed, when I had gone with Uncle Costas to see Empress Zoe when she had wanted to marry him. Was the name of the old doorkeeper Paris, or perhaps Hector? He must have long since been in his grave. Michael Psellus still lived and was somehow again the imperial secretary as he had been on that day.

They entered through the polished silver doors, into the antechamber with its mosaics of Christ Pantocrator gazing down on them over the doorway to the throne room, before being admitted. A crowd of petitioners and imperial servants thronged the room. Isaac and Kekaumenos, the leaders among the soldiers, waited patiently for their turn to speak, hopeful as the emperor answered many requests generously. Finally, their time arrived and Kekaumenos, the most senior of the men, stepped forward.

"Your majesty, I have come respectfully with my comrades to bring you Paschal greetings of the day, and to ask your indulgence for our petitions."

The emperor, short, graying, and nearsighted, with a scraggly beard and greasy lips, looked pained as he tried to put on a beneficent smile. About twenty burly Varangians surrounded him, the only ones in the room permitted to carry weapons.

"Thank you for your greetings. You may approach with your petitions."

Isaac's group approached the foot of the dais where the old man sat on a golden throne, and made their obeisances. On bended knees and with head inclined, General Kekaumenos spoke in a firm but courteous voice.

"In the past, emperors have bestowed titles and benefices on the empire's soldiers after services such as we have performed, winning victories, serving in distant lands for long years, receiving grievous injuries in battle. For myself and for General Comnenus, accomplishments such as ours have often been rewarded with the office of Proedros. These others with us have served the empire and in the past would have been awarded the titles of Spatharios, or Strator, or Vestarches. We petition you now that we might receive the rewards we have so hard earned."

The dozen or so soldiers who accompanied John, Isaac, and Kekaumenos clustered behind their leaders. But this time their imposing sight did not intimidate the emperor. Now he had the Varangians protecting him, not just his sharpened quills or accounting books.. Emperor Michael sat motionless for a time, until his mouth curled down at these soldiers of the empire and he spoke.

"I am under no obligation to award anything to any of you. I've listened to you soldiers whine about what you think you deserve for years and I'm sick of it. You'll get no more than what the paymaster gives you. Be gone and be glad you aren't in prison," the old man said.

Kekaumenos stood in shocked silence at this indignity, unable to find a response. He had not expected a warm reception from the emperor, but this humiliated them all. Isaac flared up in anger and raised his voice as he addressed the Emperor, defending their requests.

"Your majesty, we come before you as loyal subjects who have fought for the empire for most of our lives. General Kekaumenos almost lost his life to the Pechenegs just a few years back, and did lose part of his hand in that battle. In that same war my own sister's husband died." Isaac waved a hand to the men with them. "All of us have risked our lives for the empire. Past emperors rewarded our service; we ask for nothing more than what the empire has given its soldiers in past times."

The emperor looked down his pinched nose to the brawny men gathered before him. Time seemed to stand still as the soldiers waited, the emperor raising an eyebrow while the corner of his mouth turned down before words erupted from him. He darted a look at the Varangian guards who stood on either side of the throne, to be sure of their protection before speaking.

"I've told you, you get nothing. You deserve nothing. Don't think I haven't heard the stories about you, Comnenus, and your embezzlement when you were dux in Antioch. I've told you to leave, but if you need assistance, the Varangians can assist you. Now, get out." He waved a hand in sharp dismissal as a couple of guards moved forward.

Isaac flushed red at the unfounded allegation. The crowd in the throne room had stopped their chattering to watch this performance, eyes glittering at the opportunities for gossip the scene playing out before them provided. Kekaumenos, his face purplish with fury, jerked his head towards the door and the soldiers followed him out, armor clattering, while the hushed audience looked on.

Some people explode when angered, flinging dishes about, yelling obscenities and frightening children and small animals. Others hold their anger in, quietly using it to drive them on, exacting whatever retribution or retaliation they believe they are owed. It is more like a bolt of lightning striking hot, burning, and silent, with the clap of thunder coming after the damage is done. Explosive anger is bad enough, but the quiet sort you can't see coming deserves more fear. Isaac's and General Kekaumenos' anger was of the quiet sort.

In the weeks following Easter, Isaac and the rest of the spurned men often huddled together at our house ruminating about the emperor's treatment. Loyal soldiers their whole lives, none had ever opposed an emperor or empress before, no matter what their own opinion might have been. Now, faced with such manifest contempt from this former bureaucrat and following years of casual indifference from the previous few, coupled with what they knew of the parlous state of imperial defenses, they began to think the unthinkable.

"I don't believe that old man will ever find a soldier worthy of acclaim. He's hardly ever been out of the city, much less fought a battle. I doubt he even came to the seawalls to witness the Rus attack, or to Blachernae when Tornikios rebelled. He has no idea what wretched condition our borders are in now. So he finds what we do for him, for the empire, to be trivial," said Kekaumenos in an angry growl.

I put a plate of bread, cheese, and olives on the table on the terrace for the men to share, while pouring wine in their cups. I wanted no servants nearby who might overhear conversation that verged on treason. It was also easier to learn what was going on by hearing their talk, rather than wait for John to tell me in his abbreviated fashion.

"So if we can expect no reward, what do we do?" asked John.

"As I see it, we have a few options. We continue as we have, but without our just compensation. That would make us fools. We can stay home; refuse to fight and let the barbarians overrun the empire. That would make us both cowards and even more stupid, since we could lose everything to invaders," said Isaac, his mouth set in a grim line.

"And what else?" asked John.

Kekaumenos' eyes had a spark in them, seeing better than John did where Isaac was leading them.

"The final option would be to take matters into our own hands. Rebellion. There's no telling where we might end up. We could be dead like Maniakes, or we could . . ." He shrugged his shoulders.

It was the first time any of them had spoken aloud of overthrowing the emperor. Isaac never said that he should be the one on the throne, but it must have occurred to him then that he could be a candidate.

The thought of rebellion left me anxious, recalling the failed attempts when Monomachus ruled. At the same time, I knew from what John and the other soldiers in the family told me that our borders were often left unguarded. The gold in the imperial treasury went more to Italian moneylenders and sycophantic courtiers than to pay soldiers. The empire was in a terrible downward spiral. If someone did not take the chance to stop it, barbarians would be at our walls before my children were grown. I dreaded this course, but saw no other for us.

I caught John's eye. He looked uncertain. I gave him a slight nod before speaking.

"You'll need allies if you are to accomplish this. None of you is commanding an army at present, and you'll need men to support your claim. And not just soldiers in the field, you'll need someone of standing in the city who will come forward at the right time, and bring the church and the people to our side."

The wily old fox, Kekaumenos, sat back in his chair while he stroked his beard with the few fingers left on his maimed hand and contemplated the problem. The scars shone white against his soldier's tan, the skin stretched taut over the remaining bones of his hand. The emperor, or rather, the 'old man' as Isaac's friends now referred to him, knew little of what made up a soldier's life if he could count such a wound as nothing.

"You're right, Anna. I think I could get Constantine Ducas to speak with the patriarch; Keroularios is really angry at how the old man pays him no attention," said Isaac. "And Ducas brings the senate with him. He's been unhappy with the emperor's lack of gifts for senators. All the senators probably are."

My dead cousin's greedy husband would be, I thought, but said nothing. His avarice might benefit us now. Kekaumenos nodded, his excitement growing.

"Then we'll need to find someone who has command of an army and is as angry at the old man as we are."

That problem turned out to have an easy solution, since Emperor Michael managed to antagonize just about any soldier he came across.

Nicephoros Bryennios had been more prominent and successful than Kekaumenos during the reign of Constantine Monomachus. But for some reason, empress Theodora took an even greater dislike to him than she had to Isaac, stripping him of his titles, confiscating his property, and sending him into exile. On his accession, Emperor Michael had generously allowed Bryennios to return from exile and restored his titles to him. However, he refused to restore to Bryennios his property.

"You'll get your property back when you've earned it," the emperor told him as he sent Bryennios with an army to Anatolia to attack a swarm of Turks raiding towns and farms there. Consequently, he had not joined the others at the palace on Easter because of that assignment.

Bryennios, now back in the city and still waiting for the return of his lands, soon became an eager partner in the plans for rebellion.

This new conspirator was well known, respected, and liked by Isaac, John, and Kekaumenos, and the other conspirators. All the men were of an age, and had served together on several campaigns over the years, in Bulgaria, Anatolia, and Sicily.

The men first had to decide who among the three leading generals—Isaac, Kekaumenos and Bryennios—would be put forward as candidate for the new emperor. The decision was not difficult. Kekaumenos, with his maimed hand, could not be emperor since a physical deformity of that sort was an automatic disqualification. That left Isaac and Bryennios; but Isaac did not have quite the stature of Bryennios, and neither did he have an army. That left Nicephoros Bryennios to be the next emperor, if they succeeded.

The conspirators met in early May at our house to finalize their plans.

"I'll sail on Wednesday for my estate in Paphlagonia, and start calling up the thematic troops. It will take some time to do that without alerting the emperor, maybe two, three weeks," Kekaumenos said, addressing the entire group. "Isaac will be at his brother-in-law's estate nearby, marshaling what men he can there. Bryennios, you'll move with your army to the town of Amorion as though planning an attack against the Turks. But, once there you'll need to begin convincing the men to support you."

"How do you plan to do that?" asked Nicephoros Botaneiates skeptically, glancing at the prospective emperor. Botaneiates was a stubby little man with a bullish personality; not likable, but one with a grudge against the emperor, like the rest of them.

Bryennios, a handsome man with even features, tall and slim, gave a slow conspiratorial smile. He smiled easily, but kept his own counsel most of the time. He stood aloof in a corner of the room, arms crossed on his chest, although every eye was on him, curious about how he would manage these conversions.

"In the usual way. I will ply them with gold, and if that doesn't work, I will encourage them with a blade."

Botaneiates asked, "So where's the gold coming from?"

"From the old man. Who else would have enough?"

Botaneiates scratched his chin through an abundant beard before speaking.

"How do you plan to do that? I doubt he would be willing to pay for you to unthrone him."

"Let me worry about that," said Bryennios, looking sure of his plan.

"What about the rest of us?" asked Romanus Skleros.

"You'll be arming what men you can. You'll need to be ready at a moment's notice to join with Bryennios' army, no later than mid-July, perhaps sooner. How many men can each of you bring?" Kekaumenos asked as he looked slowly around the room at the men.

The men glanced at each other, assessing each's ability to contribute to this rebellion. Too few men, and they would never stand high in a victorious new emperor's court; too many and the risk of word getting back to the old emperor increased.

Skleros spoke first.

"At least five hundred, maybe six hundred," he said.

"Nine hundred, maybe thousand for me," Botaneiates averred.

"Wonderful," said Bryennios, clapping him on the shoulder.

The two sons of Basil Argyros looked at each and decided to up the bidding.

"I think we can bring at least three thousand from Opsikion," the elder one stated emphatically. These nephews of Zoe's first husband had endured many years of ill treatment by the palace, and were more than ready to see a friendly face on the throne.

After all the men had stated how many they could bring, it turned out Bryennios would have at least seven thousand men, plus his own five thousand troops.

Isaac and Bryennios looked at each other and then at Kekaumenos, considering what this number could accomplish.

"Will it do?" asked John.

"I think so," said Bryennios, with a steely look in his eye. "It will have to."

John and I made a great show of telling the servants we and the children would be accompanying Isaac and Catherine to her brother's estate in Paphlagonia, allowing them to visit their own families during this holiday, leaving only David and Antonina behind. These two faithful servants had wed not long after recovering from the plague, and had no other family left. I trusted them, but feared to leave them open to arrest should matters go awry.

"David, in our absence, if news arrives that gives you concern about us, or my husband's brother, I think it would be best if you and Antonina left the city for a time. Do not be concerned about the house; just lock it up as best you can and leave."

My hands had been shaking almost all the time the past couple of weeks, and I'd lost my appetite with worry about this plot. Either the emperor had spies who would soon have us arrested for treason, or he was too stupid to suspect a plot by soldiers he had treated badly.

David looked at me quizzically, but ever discreet, said only, "As you wish, Lady Anna."

In the cart bearing our chests to the ship was one with a false bottom packed snugly with what gold we had—several thousand gold solidi. I knew not whether they would be needed for the rebellion, or for our escape from the emperor's wrath, but I knew gold would be needed.

We arrived at Alousian's estate in early May. Catherine's brother and his family remained in Byzantium, unaware of the drama about to take place. While awaiting word from Kekaumenos and Bryennios, my nieces Anastasia and Maria and I kept busy with the children. Isaac and John spent their days gathering men willing to fight for a new emperor, but not having great success.

One evening, after the children had been sent to bed, Isaac, John, Catherine and I debated how best to gain the men Isaac needed.

"The problem is the men here don't know me well. They aren't willing to risk their lives and families for me as they might for someone they knew better" said Isaac. "Bryennios needs more than the two hundred men I've found."

Catherine looked at her husband as a thought came to her and her mouth twisted into a sly smile.

"Your father would think up some trick. He always had a few brewing; I think it was his favorite part of being a soldier."

Catherine was the oldest of us, and probably recalled my late father-in-law better than anyone. I recalled Grandfather and Uncle Costas laughing about some trick Manuel Comnenus had played on a general attempting to rebel years ago against Emperor Basil.

John looked at Isaac, eyebrows raised in question.

"What do you think Papa would have done?"

Isaac glanced from his brother to his wife, a mischievous gleam lighting his eye, and said, "I think he would find a way to get the emperor's troops to fight for us. And I think I know how to do that."

Isaac strode from the room. We heard him fumbling through his army chest in his room, before he returned, dropping a carved wooden box on the table.

"I keep the seals from letters I've received from the emperor. Never know when you'll need proof you've done what the palace wants. I've received only one from the old man, but it may be all I need." After peering into the box and fingering a number of letters with lead seals, he found the one he was looking for, raising it up for the rest of us to behold.

"Michael VI" he exclaimed.

The lead seal held the blurred image of a bearded emperor garbed in his embroidered lorum and holding a long cross. The emperor's seal.

"All we need to do now is forge an imperial letter from to the strategos in the Chaldean theme instructing him to send troops to me, use this seal to authenticate it, and get it to him in a way that he believes it is from the Great Palace," declared Isaac.

"That's all? And why the Chaldean theme?" asked John drily, eyebrows raised.

Isaac threw him a withering glance that said "Oh ye of little faith", and answered.

"Yes, that's all. Chaldia because it's too far from the city to give the strategos time to verify the instruction. In fact, don't you know the strategos? It's Eustathios Maleinos now, isn't it? You'll be the messenger."

"I do. But Isaac, you know you can't melt the seal so that it adheres properly to the letter without destroying the image," John answered skeptically.

"We'll figure that out. Right now, we need to find someone who can write a hand as well as the imperial secretaries do."

John looked over at me, and I gave a quick nod. With Uncle Simeon serving as Stoudion's Master of the Scriptorium, I had learned to write with a clear, polished hand.

"Anna could do that," he said.

And so we set to work forging a letter to strategos Maleienos instructing him to send at least five hundred of his best troops to Isaac in Paphlagonia, for Isaac to use in fighting the Turks with Bryennios' troops. We had to scrape the parchment clean a few times to get the letter in a convincing enough form, but after a couple of days it was finished.

The seal presented a more difficult problem. A lead seal stays solid until heated to the point where it melts in an instant, becoming liquid. We could not chance destroying the seal. Instead, we had to find a glue that would not be obvious to the casual observer and reuse the seal in that way. With the help of a local carpenter, we found glue from cowhides that would serve our purposes, and after several practice attempts, we sealed the letter to the strategos so he would never suspect a forgery.

It was the third week in May when John set off for Trapezus, the Chaldean capital, the forged letter tucked in his saddlebags, ready to bluff his way into Maleinos' good graces.

A week later Kekaumenos arrived with news, having ridden hard to reach us. Sweat soaked and dust covered, he gulped a cup of well-watered wine, wiping his mouth with the back of his maimed hand. He then explained how Bryennios' plans had gone terribly awry.

"Started well enough. Bryennios led his army to the outskirts of Amorion as planned and got his paymaster to agree to our plan. He spoke with the men who were more than happy to go along with him when they received the extra gold. We were congratulating ourselves on our success when some obnoxious accountant the emperor had sent along objected loudly to these excess payments. He attacked Bryennios and tried to grab the chest holding the pay. Bryennios struck the man down, putting him in irons and under guard in a tent."

Kekaumenos caught his breath, and took another drink. Isaac looked on, impatient at the delay.

"Then what happened?"

"The old man had some other bureaucrat attached to the army. The old man must have had some suspicions. Anyway, the accountant somehow got word of his imprisonment to that other bureaucrat. That man had the wits to realize Bryennios was planning to rebell, and gathered his men. They attacked Bryennios, and freed the accountant and, in a surfeit of loyalty to Emperor Michael, then blinded Bryennios as a rebel. I escaped before they tried to do the same to me."

My stomach churned—the scorched flesh, the anguished cries of the blinded, the smell of human waste when the pathetic victim lost all control. Worse than that was the thought we might be betrayed, that our lives, homes, children could be forfeit. My children.

We had brought Kekaumenos into the house's main room to deliver his news. The room had windows with views of the golden grain ripening in the fields as well as of the roads approaching the estate stretching for miles in each direction. I had been watching these roads, wondering when John would return.

"If we turn back now, all will be lost and at best we will be kneeling before the emperor for the rest of our days. He would treat us like the rugs under his feet. Or worse, he'll coerce our names from Bryennios and we'll be blinded or dead. Someone must take the throne and take it now." Kekaumenos' eyes blazed. "As I see it, the choice is between you and Constantine Ducas. Ducas has the patriarch on his side, but he has no army and not much money to pay soldiers. Do you want the throne? Do you have the men and gold to take it? Keroularios will help Ducas, if you don't."

My head swung sharply around at hearing Ducas' name. I could not speak for the lightning flash of outrage that burned through me at the thought of him sitting on the throne.

"Isaac, you know the Roman empire needs a strong man like you, after the old women and fools we've had for the past thirty years. The people will rejoice at a leader such as you," said Catherine.

Isaac glanced at his wife, bent forward in her urging.

"So you think I should lead the rebels and, with luck, take the throne?"

"I do," she responded without a moment's hesitation.

"I'd prefer you to Ducas," said Kekaumenos. I had set a fresh cup of watered wine before him that he drank quickly to get the dust from his mouth.

Isaac sat looking at them, lips pressed tight and eyes half-closed as he took in their urgings. Finally he spoke.

"I'm willing, but there's still the matter of men and gold. I need more than what I've got now."

I shook my head, dizzy at how quickly the world had changed. I knew what I had to do but still hesitated. I looked back to the road I had not checked in a few minutes. Before, the horizon had appeared clear and sharp, but now a cloud of dust blew up from what must have been the hooves of hundreds of approaching horses. I stood up and walked to the window to be sure. I was sure when I saw a banner John used, a double headed eagle, raised leading the men.

"Isaac, look. John's returned. He must have hundreds of men with him." I was crying at relief to see them.

Isaac, Catherine, and Kekaumenos rushed to join me at the window. Kekaumenos had a look of elation on his face as he realized the number of troops that large a cloud of dust must mean. Catherine glowed at the thought that she, the daughter of a deposed Bulgarian king, could be the wife of the new Roman emperor.

I looked over at Isaac who was flushed with excitement at the arrival of the soldiers. Swallowing hard at the thought of what I had to do for Xene, I pulled him back from the window, to speak with him away from the others.

"Isaac, if it's gold you need, I can help," I told him. My grandparents would approve of using my inheritance to keep Ducas from the throne. Xene would be avenged.

Isaac's face paled, understanding now that he had the means to take and wear the crown. His hands gripped my shoulders and he kissed my forehead, murmuring "Thank you". Then he straightened, pushed a hand through his hair, and went out to greet his troops.

Isaac and John soon convinced the Chaldean theme troops to join the rebellion. They had no love for Emperor Michael, who was uninterested in improving their poor lot as they struggled against Turkish raiders. But the key to their support was, as Bryennios had said, gold. The gold coins I had brought with us when we left for Paphlagonia bought us their loyalty for a time. That, and Isaac's promise to them of greater rewards after he sat on the throne.

The first week in June, Isaac's troops joined with Kekaumenos' and those of the men raised by the other conspirators. It was on June 8th, once they had met with Skleros, Botaneiates, Bourtzes and the Argyros brothers on the field of Gounaria, and their men numbered over seven thousand, that Kekaumenos stood up before the men and spoke directly of what they planned to accomplish.

"Men, I come before you today as a loyal soldier of the Roman empire. You know how hard I have fought for us, what it has cost me. But despite its cost, I have remained loyal to whoever wore the crown of Constantine," he said and raised his maimed left hand high as proof. The men shouted in support.

"You know for the past ten years the palace has not seen fit to send us sufficient supplies; to send our pay on a regular schedule; or to reward those who serve it in the manner they were rewarded in years past. I am speaking not just of myself, but of us all. Who among us has not wondered how the emperors could build such fine palaces, while soldiers make do, or go without. Or when the pay is late or disappeared. Or when we have to buy our own weapons, and not depend on the country we defend to give us what we need."

The men, sitting on the ground surrounding the rise where Kekaumenos stood with Isaac, John and the other conspirators, shouted their agreement.

"When Empress Theodora lay dying last year, Michael Bringas was proposed to succeed her. You know he's jokingly called Stratiotikos, the military one? But how soldierly can you be when all you wield is a quill? Those advisers were priests and eunuchs. We know what sort they would propose, don't we?" Kekaumenos stopped his harangue as the men laughed and made crude remarks and gestures. "I doubt our empress knew much of the man, so close as she was then to crossing the bridge to heaven. She could not have known how little he cared for the empire's well being. So she made a mistake by allowing him to succeed her. But this mistake cannot continue, or the empire, our people, will suffer grievously."

The men were calling out their support for a new emperor and getting to their feet, stomping and calling out Isaac's name. The crowd's energy had reached a boil, simmering over.

"Roman soldiers, I ask you now—who is to be our emperor?" Kekaumenos called to them.

"Isaac, Isaac, Isaac," they answered and rushed to surround the chosen man with congratulations and support. Isaac stood tall among them, accepting their nomination, their praise a balm after the emperor's humiliating rejection.

Catherine and I watched this from a distance in a litter. The cheering voices gave me goose bumps and my throat almost closed at the enthusiastic applause. Catherine sat tall beside me, putting on a regal air as though already wearing a crown. Isaac glowed with the accolades and affection of his fellow soldiers. I was glad to see him where Ducas had dreamed of standing, but wondered if Isaac felt conflicted about rebelling. The gospel of loyalty had been the narrative of his life; to his parents when he married the woman they chose; to the empire, despite foolish, greedy rulers; and to his brother, John. As bold a man as he was, rebelling meant Isaac might no longer see himself as a man of honor and loyalty. But he was set on this path, with many depending on him, and there was no turning back.

The next day, Isaac spoke to John.

"I know you want to be with me in this fight, but I need you to take Catherine and Marie, as well as Anna and your brood to Pemolissa for safety. It's on the coast and far from Nicaea, where we're heading. If the fighting goes badly, I'll want you all to sail as far from the emperor's reach as possible."

John flushed, disappointment at this safe assignment writ all over his face, but he conceded its wisdom. The retaliation of vengeful emperors could be brutal - our sons killed, or at best castrated; our daughters raped or sent to a monastery.

I slipped my hand in John's, looking up at his face. For the only time, with the money we would need in exile gone, I wondered if I had been right to give the gold to Isaac. But the first pawn had been moved in this game. We could not go back, and needed to protect our children in case the emperor checkmated Isaac.

Pemolissa, with thick stone walls surrounding a central keep, was an ugly place, but remote enough and impregnable enough that few would think to search for us there. If they did, it would take some time to batter down the walls. A small ship waited not far from us on the coast if the rebellion failed.

The uncomfortable journey to this old fortress on twisting dusty roads with so many children was nightmarish. We arrived in mid-June, hot, tired and hungry. It stood in the east, near the Black Sea, perched high on a hill. Its few small, cramped rooms barely accommodated the eleven of us, plus the two servants Catherine had brought and three soldiers brought for protection.

John and our two oldest sons, Manuel and Isaac, spent their time exploring the fortress and its environs. They discovered its hidden escape tunnel one day, elated at the possibility of ghostly excitement. The passageway exited in an old Roman tomb dug into the side of the hill, but they saw no ghosts. They hunted often, too, bringing back their kill for supper. John probably spent more time that summer teaching the boys swordplay and other fighting skills than at any other time in their lives. It almost seemed like a variation on our usual excursions to the farm, except we had Catherine and Marie with us now.

Catherine paced the battlements for hours each day, watching for the messengers Isaac sent every week or so with letters while her daughter, Marie, and I cared for the little ones. We all waited, tense and impatient, for news of any battle, or skirmish that might tell of a definite victory or defeat for Isaac. The weekly letters held precious news of a bridge destroyed that restricted the emperor's men to an area Isaac favored; then word that Catherine's brother Aron was among the men fighting for the Emperor. Finally in August we heard the two armies were both near Nicaea, a battle imminent.

John was a mountain of frustration after hearing of the impending battle, pacing and short-tempered, more restless than the children. Catherine barked at everyone more than before. Marie helped me with the little ones, playing little games to distract them. One day in late August I noticed her sitting with a sleeping Alexios draped across her lap, his head on her shoulder, and her hand wiping away tears.

I put an arm around her shoulders and bent my head beside hers. "Marie, all we can do is pray. Pray, and have confidence in your father's skill at leading men. All else is in God's hands." Even though I had John close by, we all had much to lose if this battle went badly for Isaac.

She nodded and produced an anxious smile. "I know. I'm praying always."

We kept close watch on the horizon for days. Then, as the sun was setting on August 21st, dust rose above the trees from a solitary soldier riding to the fortress as though chased by a lion. Possibilities crashed through my mind as I tried to guess what the message would be. Would we enter the city as the imperial family through the shining Porta Aurea, or escape to another land as impoverished relations of a defeated rebel?

Catherine scrambled down the ladder to greet the man before he got too close and calling out to John who had been watching Manuel and Isaac practice with their wooden swords. I was on the battlements with her when we saw the rider, but I remained there a few minutes longer watching the man approach. The rider was Donya's older son, Theodore. My heart pounded faster and my palms grew sweaty.

"Isaac's sent Theodore," I called down to the others before climbing down myself. Manuel and young Isaac hooted in glee at the thought of seeing their cousin and old sparring partner again, and ran to open the gate for him.

Once inside the walls, Theodore jumped down from his horse, both of them sweat soaked, a smile broad across his face. Dirt smeared his face, and his tunic torn and bloodstained.

"Aunt Catherine, Uncle John," he said, winded from his ride, "Uncle Isaac was victorious. Yesterday he defeated the emperor's forces in battle outside Nicaea, near Petroe. You're to meet him in Nicomedia from whence he'll make his entrance into Byzantium."

Tears of relief and joy welled up in me. John, standing next to me, put his hand to cover his eyes for a moment, whispering, "Dear God, thank you."

Catherine fell on her knees, crying and euphoric with the news. "Oh, thank God. I prayed everyday for this."

She wiped a sleeve against her eyes suddenly and asked, "And my husband was unharmed?"

"It was a near thing, Aunt Catherine, but he was not wounded. Some of the Varangians came close to killing him, but Gagik and I stopped them. That's when the battle turned our way and they started fleeing." Theodore wore a satisfied grin, pleased at his decisive role in the battle.

"The old man sent a eunuch to lead his army. A eunuch who had spent his life as a bureaucrat. He'd no idea how to fight. The old man must think you don't need any practice to be a general. Anyway, the eunuch escaped to the city, but he was lucky not to be killed," said Theodore, laughing the laugh of the victorious.

John embraced his nephew, thanking him for bringing the news, then embraced me and whispered in my ear.

"We can go home now."

I blinked away happy tears at that thought and at Isaac's victory. He would be emperor, not that foolish old man, and most definitely not Constantine Ducas. The gold had been well spent. I had won the chess game for Xene.

In the morning we joyfully departed that dusty, old stone fortress to join the new Emperor Isaac and his army at its encampment at Nicomedia, less than a day's journey to Byzantium and the Great Palace. And home.

CHAPTER TWENTY-THREE

Isaac Comnenus

September 1, 1057

"Soldier, where can we find our new emperor?" John called out to the sentries at Isaac's camp outside Nicomedia's walls as our party approached. The sentries recognized John and pointed us to Isaac's tent.

We expected to see the triumphal procession ready and preparing to depart for Byzantium, but instead the men and beasts looked to be settled in and going nowhere at present.

Catherine's mouth had turned down in a frown, her eyes darting around the camp looking for signs of an imminent departure.

"What could have happened to delay the emperor's entry into the city?" she said, her face reddening. She was already referring to Isaac as emperor.

John, Catherine, all of the children and I entered the camp, ready for public acclaim as relations to the new emperor but we received scant attention. Catherine had been preening and layering herself with cosmetics and jewels all the way from our little fortress in anticipation of the honors she would receive, but she was barely noticed.

We arrived at his tent in the camp's center and Catherine hastily scrambled out of the litter, straightened her dress, and marched inside ready to spur Isaac on to the city. I followed behind, Marie with the children trailing us.

"Isaac, I don't understand what is happening. Why we aren't you preparing for our entry into the city? You won. When is your coronation?" Her clipped tone already sounded imperial.

Isaac had been reviewing a map with Kekaumenos and looked distracted, startled at our sudden appearance. He stared blankly in his wife's direction for a moment until John and Kekaumenos shrugged their shoulders and looked away in embarrassment. Finally, Isaac pulled Catherine aside. Unfortunately, it was the corner where I was standing, leaving me unable to maneuver away from the fractious couple.

"Catherine, calm down. We are negotiating with the old man. You have nothing to worry about."

I could have told him that telling her to calm down would not work.

"I certainly do if you are not demanding the crown and throne immediately," she said, her voice knife sharp. "You won the battle. When you win, you take the throne." Her chin jutted out.

Catherine's determination for Isaac to take the Roman throne exceeded anything I had imagined. She had no doubt she was meant to sit beside her husband in the golden throne room in the Great Palace. That was her only interest.

"I will. The old man's lost, but hasn't figured it out yet. If I try to enter before he leaves, I'll have to lay siege to the city and fight the Varangians. That won't help. Once he is gone, I can enter the city with the people welcoming me—not fighting me. He's lost; he just need time to realize he's lost."

Catherine scowled at her husband and fixed him with a steely gaze.

"Isaac, I don't care what the emperor says. You won, you should be crowned."

He returned her gaze acidly.

"It's not that simple. I need to talk to the men he's sent to negotiate. Otherwise I'll have to attack the city. Not a good start and too many have already died. You haven't asked, but over four hundred men were killed, with many wounded. I won't add to the bloodshed if I can help it. Ducas is working for us inside the city."

I groaned inwardly, hearing the name of Ducas. There never seemed to be a good time to tell Isaac what I knew of the man.

"What men could the old man be sending? None who matter, that is certain," Catherine responded as she arranged her maphorion carefully around her face. I did not enjoy being a witness to this marital spat but there was no way to slink away unnoticed.

"He's sent Michael Psellus, and a couple of senators." Isaac looked irritable.

Catherine rolled her eyes at the mention of Michael Psellus.

"That toady? He's as much use as a barnacle chipped off the emperor's ship. He'll just try to wear you down with mindless chatter if you meet with him."

"Catherine, I'm aware of Psellus' ways. I'll be meeting with him and the rest within the hour; they won't get the better of me," Isaac said with enough force that he heard no more objections from Catherine. He let go of her arm and moved to rejoin the men.

Catherine tried to shake me off as I pulled her away.

"Catherine, why don't we get the children settled and fed, and then we can return to see what these negotiators are suggesting," I said as we left Isaac's tent.

"Hummphh. All right, but I must be back here within the hour. Isaac won't dare give into the old man's demands if he sees me here," she said, her face set like stone with determination.

We soon returned, accompanied by Manuel who was twelve and had begged to witness this historic moment. Isaac and Catherine's daughter, Marie, also joined us. My niece looked apprehensive in the crowd of jostling soldiers and I put an arm around her to steady her nerves. John found a spot for us in the packed tent, and procured campstools for us to sit on.

The two senators made some flowery speeches of little consequence, but then Psellus stepped forward. His grand oratory that day did justice to his years as a court functionary, saying little with many words. He looked to be about fifty and with the ever-eager puppy dog look of one always trying to please those in authority. A man who loved the sound of his own voice, he wove a long discourse on why this was just not the right time for Isaac to take the throne. He chastised Isaac for being ungrateful for the favors and honors the emperor had bestowed on him. I thought perhaps it had somehow slipped Psellus' mind that that was the reason for Isaac's rebellion. Further along in the speech his tongue twisted around new implications that the emperor had adopted, or would adopt Isaac, so Isaac would naturally succeed Emperor Michael on his death. Catherine was clicking her tongue in disgust at every liberty Psellus took with the truth.

The man's words bubbled up and reminded me of the many years he had spent smiling sweetly at emperors, speaking anything to make them happy and gain their favor. I could not help but wonder how he had so lost track of the truth, and if he really believed what he said.

Other men in the tent called out these fabrications, outraged that he would attempt to imply they had no justification for their rebellion. Psellus backed down, and admitted they might have reasons, raising his hand in concession.

"All right, I will admit some of you may have been overlooked when Emperor Michael awarded honors. Those were unfortunate omissions, but just an oversight. An oversight and still, nothing justifies revolution. Suppose you were emperor and some of your generals were to conspire against you, finding fault with you somehow. Would that justify rebellion? Of course it does not."

"Maybe not for an arse-kisser like you, it doesn't. But it does for me," yelled out one soldier from the back. That got the rest of the soldiers laughing.

"And you have not even suffered so much, except that you did not get what you had expected to receive," the unctuous man finished. That remark earned him some some angry shouts.

Isaac sat in his chair, almost a throne of sorts, listening and politely nodding his head at this speech although his eyebrows rose at the remark about "unfortunate omissions" and "oversights", but not speaking. Psellus pressed on, thinking the polite nods meant he had convinced Isaac.

"In truth, you should turn back from this shameful path and take the path of justice. As we have been taught from old, you must honor your father, Emperor Michael, and in doing so you will receive the blessing of a legal inheritance of the throne."

Catherine almost glowed she was so livid at the implications of the little bureaucrat's sermon, but she was not alone in that feeling. Catcalls and ridicule erupted from the soldiers in the tent, Kekaumenos loudest among them. The men pushed forward towards Psellus, armor clinking and swords rattling, and he almost shriveled in fright. Isaac rose, gesturing for the men to back off.

"Now, now," he said, raising his hands in a conciliatory gesture to his men. "There's no need to become angry. He's only the messenger."

He glanced at Psellus and the two frightened senators and turned back to his soldiers.

"Men, I'm grateful for your support, but if you don't mind, I think I need some time alone with my family to consider what these envoys have said and what my response will be."

The tent emptied over the next few minutes amid calls to Isaac to stand firm. Isaac held Psellus back as the rest departed. Catherine and I joined Isaac, Kekaumenos, and John on the dais. Psellus spoke again, his voice just above a whisper, now with a private message for Isaac.

"Sir, Emperor Michael has empowered me to offer you the title of Caesar, and to say he is willing to designate you as his successor if you will end this rebellion. He has no desire to continue this conflict, as I am sure you are as well."

That little bureaucrat spoke out of both sides of his mouth. Hadn't he just said the emperor would have Isaac succeed him? Now he was whispering about it as if it were something more than he had promised before. Did he think Isaac was stupid?

Isaac sat in his chair, stroking his beard and contemplating the man's words. He glanced over at Catherine who was rolling her eyes at the foolishness of agreeing to anything Emperor Michael, whose men had already blinded another conspirator, might offer. He gave a small smile before speaking.

"Ah, you are most correct in that. I've seen too many good men die in battle to want to see any more unnecessary deaths. If the emperor agrees to these terms you have mentioned, then I can agree also. However, I will need to have his agreement in writing, in a Golden Bull, before I can announce anything."

The bureaucrat was beside himself with elation at his easy success with Isaac. He expressed his gratitude in the ornate language of a courtier before rushing out to gather up the two senators and return to the city.

Catherine, on the other hand, had flushed a deep red. Her eyes were almost popping out of her head but she held her tongue until Psellus was gone. Before she could start berating Isaac for trading the throne for a promise, he raised his hand to her to stop her from speaking.

"Don't say a word. I know what you're thinking. But Psellus does not know what I have learned today."

Catherine looked at him warily, hands on her hips.

"So what have you learned today, might I ask?"

"I just received word from Ducas. The patriarch is with us, and most of the Senate as well. They've given the emperor the final push. He'll abdicate and be tonsured today, or at the latest tomorrow. When Psellus gets back, he will find the old man is no longer emperor. Once Ducas sends word it is accomplished, we can enter Byzantium without a fight. I'll have the people's love for that alone," Isaac said in a satisfied voice.

I looked over at John, who winked at me, a grin barely restrained on his face. I could not help smiling back at him, both of us ecstatic at Isaac's success. The only dark cloud was Constantine Ducas' role in Isaac's elevation, which would mean high honors and a prominent position for him once Isaac was crowned.

Messengers flew between our camp and the city with word of the uproar the senators made until Emperor Michael abdicated. On August 29th our army marched to Chrysopolis, just across the Bosphorus from the city of Constantine, made camp and waited for the final word on Emperor Michael.

The morning of August 30th, a messenger, his horse spinning up the dust on the road, raced to the camp with his news. The man almost fell off his horse, panting and coughing, before approaching Isaac and kneeling before him.

"Your grace, the people and the Senate have declared they will not have Emperor Michael on the throne any longer; they have acclaimed you. He has accepted the tonsure and left for the monastery of St. Demetrius in Thrace. In the city, all I heard on the streets were the people saying they are ready to welcome you as their new emperor."

Isaac appeared calm at the news as he thanked the messenger and handed him a gold coin. Michael Psellus stood nearby and his face rearranged itself. Ever ready to work his way into the affections of who-ever sat on the throne, he knelt before his new ruler.

"Sire, let me be the first to offer you my loyalty and devotion. I will do all in my power to serve you as I have served your predecessors on this august throne." It was startling how fast the man could change his alle-giance. Then again, I suppose his true allegiance was only to himself, with whoever sat on the throne merely being the path to that true allegiance.

The last day of August was a euphoric day, the waves sparkling with sun-light as our ships sailed far to the west, for Isaac's triumphal entry by the Porta Aurea, the Golden Gate. The elated populace waved banners and shouted welcome from the mole walls and ships floating in the harbor near the Hippodrome as we passed. Isaac waved to them, resplendent in his dress armor etched in gold with an eagle at its center, its claws clutch-ing arrows. After landing, he, John, and Kekaumenos mounted their great warhorses. Catherine, Marie and I were provided a gold curtained litter, drawn by four white horses. We processed through the center gate, the angels and elephants atop its walls gazing down in benediction, and onto the Mese's broad thoroughfare leading to the palace. People appeared in the streets and leaned out of upper floor windows. They rained flowers down on the parade, joyous at the thought of a man of Isaac's energy taking the throne after years of dissolute, decrepit, or incompetent rulers.

"Isaac, Isaac," came the voices as they caught sight of us.

Despite the summer's heat, a scarlet cloak embroidered in gold covered the new emperor's shoulders so its bright colors would catch the onlookers' attention. John rode on one side of his brother, with Kekaumenos on the other, the three of them waving and smiling to the well-wishers.

It felt exhilarating being in such a procession, with huzzahs surround-ing us, so many happy people before us. Catherine's face was upturned in the sunlight to the people and the flowers, and radiated a happiness I had never seen before. That day was one of the brightest of my life—the sun shining on us, flowers everywhere, welcomed with the affection of the whole city. I think that day we were all as happy as we could ever be.

It took over an hour to make our way through the crowds to the Milion, the Golden Milestone at the heart of Constantinople that marked the beginning of the Mese. The patriarch and a group of senators led by Constantine Ducas greeted us there as Isaac shouted his thanks and good wishes to the cheering throngs. We then retired to the Great Palace where the eunuchs greeted us, eager to flatter and curry favor with the new emperor, his family and retainers.

"Lady Catherine, may I show you to your rooms?" asked a tall, thin eunuch in a professionally obsequious voice.

"Of course. Anna, you'll be coming with Marie and me?" It was not as much a question as it was a statement.

John stood beside me, and nodded for me to join her.

"I'll be with Isaac. We have to arrange his coronation," he whispered in my ear.

"I would be pleased to, Catherine, uhh, Your Grace, I mean." It would be difficult getting used to speaking to Isaac and Catherine with such formality.

The eunuchs escorted us to the opulent rooms set aside for an empress. Since the old man had been unmarried at the time he was elevated to the throne, these rooms had been unoccupied for at least a year, perhaps longer if Empress Theodora, as sole ruler, had chosen the rooms designated for an emperor. No matter, they had been thoroughly aired by the time we arrived, with exquisite emerald green silk curtains swathing the windows and masses of flowers in bowls throughout the room, sweetening the summer air.

Maidservants brought silver trays laden with pitchers of wine and delicate glass goblets as well as bread and fruit for us to enjoy, setting them on purple marble topped tables. Eunuchs from the empress' wardrobe appeared bearing cedar chests filled with bejeweled robes from which Catherine would choose her attire for Isaac's coronation the next day. Other chests soon arrived, with clothing beautiful but less fine than Catherine's, for Marie and me to choose from.

The silk from which these garments had been sewn was of a finer quality than I had ever seen, or better yet, felt. As soft as a down feather, light as a whisper, the colors deeper and the embroidery more luxurious than any but an emperor or empress could afford. The garments were of such great value that they were stored in cedar chests in their own wardrobe building whenever they were not being worn, and sprinkled with fennel leaves and lavender.

As we tried on various gowns, I recalled Grandmother's comments about the clothing provided for imperial processions, how they would often smell of those who had worn them on prior occasions. Sniffing the blue silk tunica banded in gold that I thought to wear, it seemed as though there was a hint of roses. It reminded me of the heavy perfume Empress Zoe had worn the day I had been on the palace grounds so many years earlier with Uncle Costas. She had been dead over seven years now, so perhaps I imagined it.

"What do you think of this?" Catherine asked us as she tried on a magnificent purple and gold silk gown with wide, hanging sleeves sewn with pearls along the cuffs. She looked every inch the empress, with her dark hair, just starting to be threaded through with silver, piled high on her head.

"Mama, you're beautiful." Marie, draped in a green silk confection, gazed in awe.

"Yes, you are. There may be other gowns to look at, but I cannot think any would complement you more," I added.

Catherine appeared pleased at our comments as she gazed at herself in the polished mirror set on one of the tables.

In mid-afternoon servants brought us to the baths where they helped us wash before combing out our hair. The warm scented water eased the muscles strained to excess by the weeks hidden in the fortress and then with Isaac on his road to the crown. One of the servant girls insisted on massaging my scalp while washing my hair, relaxing me so I almost fell asleep in the pool. My life to that day had been a fortunate one, never experiencing great hunger or backbreaking labor, but neither had I experienced such self-indulgence. It almost felt sinful.

That night Isaac threw a celebratory dinner for the men who had supported him in his bid for the throne, hosting it in the new palace Monomachus had built near the sumptuous Mangana church. Constantine Ducas and patriarch Michael Keroularios attended, as well as the Argyros brothers, Botaneiates, and Romanus Skleros and a few others. John and their Dokeianos nephews and my cousin, Romanus Diogenes sat with them.

Catherine held a dinner in her rooms for the female relations of the men at Isaac's dinner. Katakalon Kekaumenos' wife arrived during the ninth hour, accompanied by our niece Helena whose husband was the general's nephew. Kekaumenos' wife was a dun little bird of a lady; she looked so timid I wondered how she managed with her great blustering husband. My cousin Romanus' wife, Anna, who was also Catherine's niece, arrived a little later with Eugenia who was agog at the palace's splendor.

Eudokia arrived in the tenth hour, in an elegant fawn colored gown with an ivory under tunic, which set off her pale gold hair. She dipped down into a deep bow before Catherine, congratulating her on her husband's success.

"I'm sure my husband could not have succeeded in this endeavor without the assistance of both your husband and your uncle. It is we who should be thanking you," Catherine answered graciously, and seated her between the two of us.

The imperial kitchens prepared a grand feast for us—shrimp, clams, delicious fish grilled with lemon juice and garlic, beef pastirma, greens, bread as good as any Alethea had baked, fine wines chilled in the ice kept in the Palace's cellars. A group of musicians played for us near the doors leading to a lush rose garden. Eunuchs lit lamps for us as the sun dipped below the horizon.

Eudokia and I walked outside in search of a cool breeze after we had had our fill of the delicacies. The other women clustered into their own knots of friends, or surrounded the new empress with flattering attention. In the garden we could hear both the music drifting from the dining hall, and the faint sound of waves lapping at the nearby shore.

"You know, before yesterday I never would have thought I would spend even one night in the palace. I'm loathe to admit it, but we wouldn't be here if it weren't for your husband and uncle's help. What made them do it?"

Eudokia gave an ironic smile and shrugged.

"The usual problems. Constantine had grown used to Monomachus' favors, which were fewer when Theodora was empress, and disappeared entirely when the old man sat on the throne. As for my uncle, after he crowned the old man, the emperor just ignored him and refused to see him. Neither of them were used to such imperial indifference."

"So they will expect a lot from Isaac," I said as I reached to pull one of the blooms to my nose.

"You can be assured of that. I think they already have lists drawn up."

"Isaac will be crowned in the morning; I hope they give him a little time before they start pestering him."

Eudokia snorted with a new cynicism. "Maybe a day or two, but no longer."

We sat quietly for a few moments, enjoying the silence and peace of the place.

"How are things with you and Constantine?" I asked quietly.

"Oh, the same. He ignores me unless he needs something. He ignores the children, unless they irritate him. But there are worse husbands," she said in flat tones as her foot tapped rhythmically on the path's slate tiles. "And I'm pregnant again. Due in the spring."

Looking inside the dining hall, it appeared that the party was breaking up, with some of the women starting to gather their belongings together. We stood and I took Eudokia's arm as we returned inside.

"I am sorry about Constantine," I said.

"You shouldn't be; it isn't your fault. It's just fate," Eudokia said as we passed the musicians on our way to say farewell to our dinner companions.

I gave her hand a squeeze as we parted at the door. We both knew women had little say in their destiny, told by their parents to marry a man who might be kind or brutal. Then told by their husband what to do. Even though John loved me dearly, would never beat me, and allowed me do as I preferred, I knew he had the final say if he wanted it, and the law would always permit it. My voice would be ignored if we disagreed. Among women, only widows had voices that could be heard, and rights before the law. So I was luckier than many with my sweet husband.

At the fifth hour of the following day, September first and the start of the new year, the coronation procession started from the Great Palace to the Hagia Sophia. Soldiers from the Exkoubitores, including our nephews Theodore and George Dokeianos, bright in their dress uniforms and polished armor led the parade. Monks from the Monastery of St. George Mangana followed, chanting hymns of praise as they walked; trailing the monks came the Senators in their gold-banded robes, Constantine Ducas leading them, glittering collars around their necks and rings on their fingers. More monks came next singing more hymns.

The people pushed as close as they could get, despite the soldiers who kept them a little distance off. The crowd gazed jubilantly at the dazzling spectacle, throwing flowers at our feet.

The Varangians escorted Catherine, Marie, me and the other ladies of the dynatoi chosen as escorts for the new empress—Romanus' wife, Anna, and my friend Eudokia among them. As we walked, an uncomfortable recollection of the first time Varangians had escorted me, the night my family was sent into exile echoed in my mind. It reminded me that great power was a blunt weapon, whether used for good or ill.

Finally, the other generals who had fought with Isaac processed toward the church, and then John and Kekaumenos on either side of Isaac who was clad in the purple robes of a Roman emperor—an under tunica embroidered in gold topped with a purple silk tunica with an eagle embroidered on it and a gold belt circling his sturdy waist. He walked bareheaded, still uncrowned, waving at the people who greeted him with glee.

I looked back at Isaac and John as the procession made its way the short distance to the church. John looked handsome in a forest green tunica, his red hair bright as a flame, while Isaac walked boldly looking every bit the emperor in his purple. I tried to catch John's eye, but the crowds distracted him. Isaac saw me, though, and winked at me as he waved to the crowds. I relaxed at that moment, realizing he would be the kind of emperor we needed after so many years of the old, the tired, or the bad.

In the church most of the women processed up the ramp to the upstairs gallery while the men stood in the nave. Isaac had the seat of honor, the throne at the front of the church, John, Kekaumenos and Constantine Ducas standing behind him. Catherine was given a smaller throne near her husband, with Marie, Eudokia, Anna and I standing as her attendants.

The patriarch, a gold mitre atop his head and clad in ruby vestments embroidered with gold keys and scenes of the Crucifixion and Resurrection, began the Divine Liturgy. The eunuchs' choir in the gallery added their high angelic voices to that of the monks. The patriarch, for all his pomposity, sang the Liturgy in a rich tenor, as beautiful and smooth as the silk gown I wore.

"For the peace from on high and for the salvation of our souls, let us pray to the Lord," he chanted.

My attention drifted during the litany I had heard at least every week my whole life. The Great Church of Holy Wisdom, the Hagia Sophia, had to be the largest church in Christendom, but it was filled to overflowing with guests and onlookers. Dust motes danced in the shafts of light shining through the windows high above us in the dome. Catherine looked the happiest I had ever seen her, now empress of the same empire who had defeated her father's. Marie, who stood on her other side, had a more somber expression.

"Lord God, save your people and bless your inheritance; protect the fullness of your Church, sanctify those who love the beauty of your house, glorify them in return for your divine power, and do not forsake those who hope in you," the patriarch continued in his lovely voice.

The bright gold mosaics depicting the apostles in the dome glittered in the morning light. Angels and saints gazed down on us, solemn in their exhortations to the true faith. Overhead was the great mosaic of the Theotokos and the Christ Child.

The heat of summer and the packed church meant some in attendance might pass out in too lengthy a service and the patriarch moved the service along. Before long he processed through the Beautiful Gate in the iconostasis, behind which lay the altar, holding a golden chalice containing the Holy Communion for Isaac and Catherine. Fragrant smoke swirled out of the priests' censors, rising above our heads into faint clouds in the great dome. The choir's voices grew louder and the tempo more intense.

The singing continued after Holy Communion until the patriarch placed the chalice on the altar behind the iconostasis and returned to the nave. All fell silent.

"Let us pray for the new Emperor of the Romans, Isaac, and for his Empress, Catherine," the Patriarch sang.

Isaac and Catherine stood and walked a few steps to the dais, kneeling on the lowest step. The rest of the assembled bowed their heads in prayer.

"We pray that the Lord God might give all blessing to our new emperor, Isaac, and his wife, Catherine, and make His face to shine upon them; we ask that the Lord God never forsake Isaac and give him victory when he must battle our enemies; that while he reigns the empire is blessed with favorable weather and an abundance of the earth's fruits; and that his reign might see the deliverance of all affliction, wrath, and danger for the Roman Empire, the Lord's most blessed and holy people. Grant this, oh Lord."

"Amen," the crowd sang, the voices filling the vast space.

"Bow your heads to the Lord," called out the Patriarch.

"To you, O Lord."

Isaac and Catherine rose, each escorted by priests on either side bearing golden candlesticks with lit beeswax candles, and followed the patriarch into the ambo perched high above the heads of even the tallest in the crowd. Most coronations took place in the omphalion, the marble circle where his throne now sat, but Isaac had wanted to be seen by all.

The glorious ambo stood atop seven green marble pillars, with one at each corner of its hexagon and one supporting the center. The platform and its railing, carved in centuries past of the purple marble used in much of the Great Palace, was itself capped with a golden dome supported again with green marble pillars. Priests usually read the liturgy of the day's service in it, but it was spacious enough so that at least seven people could stand in it, as was needed for a coronation.

Isaac stood in the ambo with the patriarch, priests at either side holding their candles high as the words of blessing were intoned. Patriarch Michael held a small silver dish with holy oil in which he dipped his thumb before making the sign of the cross on Isaac's head. After wiping his hands on a white linen cloth, he took the jeweled crown from a nearby table.

The patriarch held the crown high for all to see. Its gold sparkled in the bright light of day with cabochon rubies, sapphires and amethysts encircling it. Enameled images of angels and saints sat above the gems, with another image of Christ on the cross in the center. Four pendants with small pearls dangled from its sides, completing the crown's magnificence. Whispered gasps of awe came from the crowd. Even in this magnificent city, the Queen of Cities, which had seen the elevation of many emperors in recent years, the people could be filled with reverence at this spectacle.

The crown was rested on Isaac's head as songs of joy burst from the choirs. I noticed his red hair, no longer the brilliant color it had been when I first met him sixteen years earlier, had faded to a russet color with age. He was fifty years old as he took the throne, still energetic and more than capable of leading an army, unlike the irascible old man he had replaced. I breathed a sigh of relief as the crown settled firmly onto his brow, elated at not just seeing Isaac ruling, but also to have thwarted Ducas. A new day had begun.

Concluding the ceremony, the patriarch, assisted by two priests, placed the mandyas, the large heavy cloak of embroidered purple silk, on Isaac's shoulders, symbolizing the great responsibility he now bore as emperor.

The patriarch spent some time getting the cloak arranged and the golden clasp closed on it. This part of the ceremony dragged on, and I glanced around at the men who accompanied Isaac. John stood solidly at attention, eyes fixed on Isaac, wearing a proud smile, as did Kekaumenos. Constantine Ducas' gaze, though just for a moment, held a look of pure envy, his bottom lip pursed out, hands balled into fists, teeth slightly bared as he stared at the crown and mandyas Isaac now wore.

I dropped my eyes before looking over at Eudokia. She, too, had seen her husband, before lowering her eyes to the floral pattern of the marble floors beneath our feet, her face like stone. Still, I thought, what could he do? Isaac was now crowned, was supported by the people of Byzantium, and well deserved this honor. Constantine Ducas had even helped him reach it but, it appeared, with some regret.

I gave a mental shrug of my shoulders at the thought of Ducas as the crowd roared when the final clasp of Emperor Isaac Comnenus' mandyas was closed and he stood before them, arms raised to the heavens.

"Isaac, Isaac, Isaac."

Emperor Isaac waved to the crowd. He looked as strong and vigorous as though he would rule for twenty years more. Ducas, a year or two older, his gray hair thinning already, appeared almost as tired as the old man had been.

The ceremony concluded a few minutes later with the much less important crowning of Catherine. Her crown lacked the size of Isaac's, but its exquisite gems still glittered in the bright light of morning.

The coronation accomplished, the Varangians led Isaac and Catherine and their attendants in procession from the Hagia Sophia into the Augustaion, the forum outside the Great Church. More crowds awaited us there.

We who had been named attendants had been given pouches of silver and copper coins to distribute to the waiting onlookers. We threw handfuls into the throngs. As one pouch emptied, I opened another one until by the time we reached the palace gate I had thrown the contents of three bags to the ecstatic crowds.

The feasting that night was beyond anything I ever experienced. The men, of course, had their own feast in the Daphne Palace, while Catherine's was in the Boukoleon Palace overlooking the Sea of Marmara. The wine flowed and the platters of delicacies never seemed to cease appearing on the tables. After several hours of this, Helena and I left the table, more than sated, for a breath of cool air.

I was still unfamiliar with the many assorted buildings that made up the Great Palace, most of which were over one hundred years old. Curious and giggling, we opened creaking doors into many of the Boukoleon's old rooms, some dusty and unused, others furnished with the finest furniture I had ever seen.

We entered one room furnished with desks and chairs, and beyond that lay a door leading outside. We passed through the door to a portico above the quay where the emperor's personal ship docked. Lit torches lined the walls to show our way, and I realized I recognized this place, but had seen it before from a different vantage.

"Helena, I've seen this place before. When I was a girl and the Orphanotrophus sent our family into exile, we sailed right past here."

I bent over the railing and peered down into the early evening shadows where the two marble lions still stood. Now, though, there was no eunuch masquerading in monk's robes to see us into exile. He had died years earlier, exiled to a remote island far from this palace after the death of his brother, the emperor.

Helena gave a quick look down, but all was peaceful as the dark waves lapped against the seawalls.

"It makes me sick thinking of all he did, Auntie."

"I felt so helpless being forced to leave my home, knowing no one in my family had done anything wrong. He used Empress Zoe's love of his brother, the loyalty of the Varangians, and money, to coerce people to do their bidding. They used their power and thought to gain everything. But in the end, they lost all."

Helena put an arm around me.

"You're right, Auntie. They lost everything, and they're all dead. Now, Uncle Isaac wears the crown. He's a good man. He won't end up as they did."

Perhaps it was too many glasses of wine that left me with a maudlin feeling as I looked out at the waters we had sailed through seventeen years before. Or perhaps the ghosts of my grandparents were still out there on that ship, doing their best to protect me from harm. Tears slipped from my eyes and it was almost as though I could see the oars of the dromon as it moved towards the Bosphorus, a man with wild hair looking like a sea serpent as its master.

The next day the celebrations continued with special performances and races at the Hippodrome. John and I joined Isaac and Catherine in the Kathisma, the emperor's private box of seats. We passed through a hidden passageway in the walls between the palace and the Hippodrome, and climbed narrow old stairs, the treads worn deep over the centuries, our way lit by lanterns hanging on the walls.

At the top of the stairs we emerged into the sunshine to the cheers of tens of thousands of men calling out "Isaac, Isaac" until he showed himself, garbed in his purple robes and golden crown, trumpets blaring to welcome him. The crowd roared when Isaac walked to the edge of the box and waved his arms at them as they stood and clapped in excitement. Their enthusiasm reverberated around the stadium, like a blanket wrapped around us.

The Kathisma sat near the top of the Hippodrome with a magnificent view of the racecourse and the city. To the far right at the north end were the starting boxes, six on each side of a high central tower on which stood the quadriga – four gilded bronze horses with a gilded bronze chariot and charioteer. The spina, the center around which the racers ran, held fountains, other statues, and monuments including two obelisks, a bronze statue of an eagle fighting a snake, and the ancient serpent column brought from Delphi.

The crowd began to settle down as jugglers and mimes appeared from the starting boxes at the sound of trumpets, tumbling onto the race-course. From our high perch, they looked like nothing so much as many bright bouncing balls flung onto the field.

My mind drifted as the performance went on. I winced recalling my conversation with Xene so many years earlier on her small balcony when we had promised to be in the Kathisma together. She was dead a dozen years that day, and instead I sat beside her husband's new wife, as dear to me as Xene had been. I glanced over at Constantine Ducas, chatting with Isaac, John, Kekaumenos, Botaneiates and a few others. The men looked to be placing bets on the chariot races to come. The memory of my promise to Xene from all those years ago, and my vow to avenge her death, echoed.

"Xene, I'm here in the Kathisma. Do you remember the promises we made? You can't be here, but I am," I whispered to her ghost. I glanced at Ducas, joking with the other men, but not wearing the crown. "I spent my gold to keep your husband from the throne he so wanted. I've done what I could to avenge the way he treated you. You can rest peacefully now." I stood alone at that moment feeling a bitter satisfaction, my eyes blurring with tears. I knuckled them away and turned back to Eudokia.

"Have you been here before?" I asked her.

She nodded noncommittally. "Monomachus invited us to join him and his mistress a few times. He really liked Constantine." I gave a rueful smile at that.

Looking at her face, I realized she knew nothing of her husband's extortionate scheme to extract money from the city's citizens to repay the Venetian loans. The money would have had to come from taxes anyway. But his plan terrorized innocent men with false accusations and imprisonment. It reminded me of the wrongs done to my family by the long dead Orphanotrophus.

I rarely thought of the Orphanotrophus, but he had been revived in my memory twice in two days. Perhaps it was the proximity to the buildings he had lived in and ruled from. I shuddered, trying to shake off his memory.

Helena joined us then, bringing a plate heaped with cheeses and olives and gripping a glass of wine. The Kathisma had a table behind the seating area where she had found this repast. She placed it on one of the low tables that stood before us.

"Help yourself," she said as she turned her attention to the performances below.

I nibbled on a piece of cheese while contemplating fate's twisted threads. There were some men who sought power over others, like the Orphanotrophus, but aroused such resentment and fear from those they coerced that the people eventually rebelled, and their power evaporated like the mists on the Marmara in the morning sun. Others, like Emperor Basil and my Uncle Costas, inspired loyalty and respect; some may have feared them, but it was affection that kept men speaking of them with devotion years after their deaths.

Isaac sat on the emperor's dais, speaking congenially with his friends standing nearby. The men's faces were all happy and smiling, as they looked at Isaac, even Ducas', the envy I had glimpsed on the previous day hidden away. I wondered how Isaac would handle the fawning and flattery that anyone in a position of authority, an emperor most of all, inevitably received. Sycophants sought titles and gold, thinking that was all there was to life. Some succumb to it and come to believe his own opinions to be unflawed. But I hoped Isaac would see through the honeyed words, look for honesty.

John would give him honesty, I knew that much, as would Kekaumenos. I would too, but I was a woman, just a sister-in-law. Ducas, or his generals—Skleros, the Argyroi, and Botaneiates—would not be so scrupulous. The other courtiers, especially that unctuous Michael Psellus, had had many years of practice telling emperors exactly what they wanted to hear, or could be convinced to believe.

Perhaps just a few honest advisers would be enough to keep Isaac from believing he was incapable of mistake or failure. I hoped so.

"Anna, how long will you be staying in the palace?" asked Eudokia, shaking me from my reverie.

"What? Oh, I'm not sure, maybe another day or so. I'm eager to return the children home. The eunuchs have been spoiling them with rich foods and sweetmeats, and I've not had the time to be sure they have stayed on a schedule of any sort, so they get whiny."

John appeared at my elbow then, giving me a look.

"Sorry, I forgot to mention it to you, but Isaac wants us to stay, too. He asked me before we even reached the city," he said, looking flushed and happy from the excitement and the wine.

It was a generous offer, and one I should have anticipated. Part of me was thrilled at this invitation, but I longed for the routines and familiarity of home. John had slipped his hand into mine and winked at me, expecting me to be as pleased at this honor as he was.

"Aunt Catherine has asked that I move in for a while, to keep her and Marie company," said Anna, my cousin Romanus' wife. "She said I could bring Eugenie and the children since Romanus is returning to Armenia."

"Constantine wrangled an invitation for us, too. I wasn't eager to leave our house, but I'm expecting another baby in the spring and I thought I might enjoy the next few months being pampered by the palace servants," said Eudokia. "Anna, it will be wonderful if you were with us, too."

I put on a grateful smile, "So it seems that I will be there too." The other women, all friends and relations, chirped happily about how delightful it would be to be so close. John squeezed my hand, gave me a peck on the cheek and returned to the men.

The palace's many buildings would easily accommodate all of us. I just wasn't sure this was what I wanted. I was reminded of the old saying about being careful what you wish for.

A eunuch approached us carrying a silver tray holding several glasses of watered wine appropriate for the time of day. The pale red wine in them sparkled in the sunlight and I sipped its contents before I decided to join Catherine, seated on her throne in a whispered conversation with Marie.

"Not another word, young woman. We'll discuss this later," said Catherine, her voice sounding irritated.

"But Mama, I'm almost twenty-one. How old do I have to be?" Marie asked sounding frustrated.

"I was years older than you are when your father and I wed; no need to rush, especially now you are a princess. Many fine men, better than some sailor, will want to be your husband; we must find the best one for you, and that will take some time," said Catherine.

Marie noticed me then before looking away, red-faced. Michael Maurex still.

"Aunt Anna, how are you enjoying the performances?" Helena asked, trying to bring up a less troublesome subject.

I gave a quick glance down onto the race track where a bear was performing at one end, while an acrobat danced on the back of a bull rumbling down the course. The actual races had not yet begun, but it looked as though the opening entertainment was closing.

"The performers are wonderfully talented; I wish I could do half as much as any one of them manages."

"Lady Anna, I am sure you could dance like a bear any time you chose," said a voice behind me, low enough that only Helena and I could hear clearly. Constantine Ducas brushed past me as he approached Catherine to make his obeisance to her. Helena's face turned red at the insult Ducas had thrown at me, while Catherine's wore a confused expression as though she was not sure what she had heard. The insult stung a little, before I remembered that much of the reason why he was not wearing the crown today was because of my gold coins. I could not help the small smile of triumph that crossed my face; I wondered if he suspected what I had done, and why.

"Your grace, the day is hot. Is there anything I can bring you or your lovely daughter?" asked Ducas, changing from catty to sweet in an instant. He was so eager to meet any needs Isaac or Catherine had, jumping about like a fish in a net, pulled fresh from the sea; it was ridiculous. The eunuchs were already falling over each other bringing the new ruler and his wife drinks and delicacies. Ducas was simply trying to ingratiate himself with Catherine.

"No, Senator, really there's nothing we need at present," Catherine said. She looked up at him but his eyes were fixed on Marie, sitting demurely next to her mother, eyes focused on the track. Catherine noticed Ducas's gaze fixed on Marie. She reacted like a mother bear protecting her cub.

"Thank you, Senator. There's nothing we need now." Catherine's voice held an edge that caught Ducas' attention, as did the sharp look she gave him. He bowed and returned to Isaac's side.

I stole a glance at Eudokia, who sat stone faced between Helena and Romanus's wife, as the other two chattered away. Her husband's fixed stare at Marie had not escaped Eudokia's attention. Still, he was a married man, with three children and one due in a few months; what interest could he have in Marie?

In a flash, I realized what it was. He had not given up on the throne. If he were married to Marie, he would be seen as the natural successor to Isaac since Isaac had no living son. Ducas would be the next emperor. He would have to coerce Eudokia into a divorce, to taking the veil and entering a monastery, but he had almost done that with Xene. Perhaps he thought she might die in childbed; she had delivered without difficulty in the past, but that did not mean it could not happen. There was also the legal problem that it would be his third marriage and frowned on by the church, whose head was his current wife's uncle. The patriarch would be unwilling to see his niece put aside, so that would be an impediment to such a plan. Of course, accidents happened, and there was poison.

I bit my lip at these sickening thoughts. I settled back in my chair next to Catherine and tried to calm down as the horses lined up for the day's first race. The handsome animals pawed the ground restlessly in their boxes, sending up plumes of dust, waiting for the starter's signal. Isaac and the other men on the Emperor's side of the Kathisma—Ducas, John, Keroularios, and Botaneiates—gathered at the railing. Isaac stood front and center, tallest of the men. The rest jostled each other for a spot beside him, eager to see if they would win their bet, or lose. Ducas and Botaneiates pushed their way next to Isaac, while John and Keroularios hung back, looking over the other men's shoulders.

The crowd fell silent waiting for the race to begin. The starter in the referee's box opposite the Kathisma stood holding the purple moppa, a weighted square of cloth used to signal the start of the race. He held it high and the spectators hushed in anticipation. All eyes were fixed on the purple, floating like an imperial banner on the breath of a hundred thousand spectators. The starter dropped the moppa, the crowd roared as it had the day Xene and I listened from her balcony, and the race began.

Author's Note

I have been fortunate that there were three excellent contemporary historians who wrote about this period in the Eastern Roman Empire. Michael Psellus' history is a breezy, gossipy book about palace politics. His friend, Michael Attaleiates, provided a lawyerly bent to his history. Then there's the relatively anonymous John Skylitzes, whose scholarly history often has its striking illustrations copied in modern histories. For anyone interested in reading primary sources, these are all excellent books. Readers with a more rudimentary knowledge of the Byzantines would do well to first find John Julius Norwich's excellent volumes on this amazing civilization.

I have tried to keep as close to the historical record as possible. Areas that I have had to improvise on include the names of some of the women in this book, since many of them never had their personal names recorded. Not long before publication, another fan of the Byzantines pointed out to me that Manuel Comnenus, the father of Isaac and John and their sister, may not have had two wives; it could have been just one. Unfortunately, it was too late to change this novel. Mea culpa!

None of the Byzantine historians I mentioned above record anything about the incident that resulted in the Great Schism between the Orthodox and Roman Catholic Churches. It was a complete non-event to them; Rome was a backwater in those days and the pope barely worth consideration. I included Anna's perception of the event only because it was colorful and involved characters already in the novel.

Harald Hardrada was a renowned member of the Varangian Guard in Miklagard (Constantinople) during the period of this novel, and later the king of Denmark. He was killed at the Battle of Stamford Bridge, fighting against Harold II of England, shortly before the Battle of

Hastings. A man so involved in power politics in so many distant worlds needed to have at least a walk-on!

While growing up I had often thought of writing historical novels, but the topics I knew best (English history, the Julio-Claudians) were well covered on library bookshelves. It was only after reading Norwich that this time and place rarely tackled by novelists drew me in. And it was only after reading about Anna Dalassena that I saw someone whose story was calling out to be told. It was almost as though some spirit tapped me on the shoulder saying, "This is it."

The histories that include Anna Dalassena invariably mention that she loathed Constantine Ducas. Most implied that her hatred of him was politically motivated, but something so visceral seemed to have a deeper source. It was only when a footnote mentioned that his first wife was a Dalassena and that they never had children, that I knew what could have motivated Anna's hatred of the man. Obviously, no one can prove something like that a thousand years later, but like any novelist, I recognized a good plot point.

I would like to thank my editor and cover designer, Jenny Quinlan, for all of her guidance, help and efforts in assembling this novel. Mike Lewis provided great help in pulling together a finished product. Also, my beta reader, Jane Rawoof, and writers' group partners, Bruce Bustard and Hal Stull, whose honesty and attentive critiques were invaluable to the finished product.

Finally, to my husband, Ken, and the rest of my family, thank you for tolerating my obsession with the Byzantines and traipsing around so many obscure locations in Ravenna, Istanbul, and Sicily to visit anything with a remote connection to them. I love you all and hope you have come to appreciate, at least a little, my obsession.

Final Note

Reviews are critical for all authors, but especially for those like myself who are just starting out. If you enjoyed this novel (and even if you didn't), please consider leaving a review at Amazon, Barnes & Noble, Goodreads, or other author websites you might frequent. Learning what readers like or don't like is the only way to get better.

Please visit my website and blog to learn more about the endlessly fascinating Byzantines:

Eileenstephenson.com

Or follow me on Twitter, *@byzyeileen*

Thank you for reading!

Glossary

Anatolia—Also known as Asia Minor, this is the geographic area currently occupied by the Asian side Turkey. The Bosphorus and the Sea of Marmara separated it from Greece and the rest of the Eastern Roman Empire. It extended east to the borders with Armenia and Mesopotamia in 1025 and appears to have been divided into about 16 Themes, or provinces, during Anna's lifetime.

Black Sea—The Black Sea has been known by several names over history, sometimes by the name Euxine Sea, the hospitable sea. For ease of understanding, I am calling it only the Black Sea.

Bracca—Trousers.

Cheese Week—This is the week before Lent starts, when devout Greek Orthodox members begin abstaining from meat but may still consume dairy products. During Lent, they are expected to abstain from meat, fish, dairy and eggs.

Chess—It is unknown exactly when chess arrived in the Byzantine Empire, possibly earlier than this book posits. In any case, chess in the 11th century had a "Minister" instead of a "Queen" and "elephants" instead of "bishops". The possible moves for rooks, kings, knights, and bishops/elephants were roughly the same as they are today. The rules of the game for Queens and pawns expanded in the 15th century to about what they are today. The additional flexibility for Queens and pawns sped up the game. In the 11th century, a single game could go on for a day or more.

Chrysotriklinos—The main throne room, audience and formal dining hall at the Great Palace. It was a large octagonal building with the main entry door of silver. Records indicate that the inside was covered with magnificent mosaics, lavish with gold, as well as gold lamps, and a throne of gold. There was a private entrance to the Boukoleon Palace for the monarch's use.

Constantinian Walls—Emperor Constantine built these walls when he established the city as the capital of the Eastern Roman Empire. They encompassed an area roughly equal to 2/3's the area later encompassed by the more substantial Theodosian Walls. In this story, Anna's grandparents' home was between what then remained of the Constantinian Walls and the Theodosian Walls.

Domestic—A military leader. The Domestic of the Scholai was the leader of the Scholai elite taghmata, a regiment, and was the most senior military leader in the Byzantine Empire. The leaders of the six taghmata generally had the title of Domestic.

Dromon—The Greek term for a warship. The word comes from the word that means "run". Rather than the Latin/Western idea of sailing the seas, the Greeks from at least the time of Homer thought of ships running on the back of the sea.

Droungarios—A military leader, usually referred to the admiral of the imperial fleet, but could also be the leader of one of the elite regiments, such as the Vigla Taghmata.

Dux—The leader of regional command cities on the frontiers of the Empire during the 10th and 11th centuries. Anna's Great Uncle, Constantine Dalassenus, had been Dux of Antioch in 1025, the year of Anna's birth and the year that Basil II died.

Dynatoi—The term used for the Byzantine aristocrats.

Eparch of Constantinople—the city governor's office. It had wide-ranging powers, from maintaining public order, to resolving business disputes, and tax collection.

Fish Sauce—Garum, or fish sauce was a common fermented condiment popular in Byzantium, roughly equivalent to catsup in America or soy sauce in Asia.

Franks—The Norman soldiers, generally the younger sons of the Norman nobility, who left in search of land and wealth in the south. Many of them settled in southern Italy and Sicily.

Genoese/Pisan/Venetian/Almafitan Quarters—These were areas in Byzantium designated for the traders from Genoa, Pisa, Venice and Amalfi. The Byzantine government tried to keep these outsiders from mixing too much with their citizens.

Greek Fire—Also known as Median fire, it was a napalm like substance whose formula was a state secret, long since lost. The Byzantines used it primarily in naval battles, sending it through long ceramic tubes onto enemy ships. The fire it ignited could not be extinguished with water. It was remarkably lethal and one of the most powerful weapons the Byzantines had against their enemies.

Gynecaeum—Many families in Byzantium kept their women, as much as possible, in separate women's quarters for protection. While not a universal practice, it was common, particularly among the upper classes.

Hagia Sophia—The Church of the Holy Wisdom of God. This basilica was built in the reign of Justinian about 575 and is considered the finest example of Byzantine architecture. It was the main church of the Eastern Church until 1453 when the Mehmet II conquered Constantinople and converted it and many other Orthodox churches to mosques. The Hagia Sophia is now a museum in Istanbul.

Hegoumenos/Hegoumena—The Greek term for the abbot/abbess of a monastery.

Hippodrome—The stadium located near the Great Palace where chariot and horse races were traditionally held, as well as some imperial ceremonies. Finished by Constantine the Great in the 4th century, it could hold about 30,000 spectators and by Anna's day it was at least 600 years old. There was a central tower at the end with starting gates upon which stood a quadriga of horses. These four horses were taken from Byzantium during the Fourth Crusade and are now at St. Mark's Cathedral in Venice where they can still be seen.

Icon—Paintings of Christ, angels, the Mother of Christ, and other saints, to be venerated by Orthodox Christians.

Iconostasis—A screen between the nave (where worshippers were located) and the altar, where the priest, bishops, and/or deacons would be located. It was typically adorned with paintings of Christ, the Theotokos, angels, and saints, as well as Biblical scenes to aid the community in its worship.

Juppa—A man's long-skirted tunic or shirt, falling to the upper thigh.

Kataphraktoi—The armored cavalry of the Byzantine army, typically fighting with either lances or bows.

Kathisma—The Emperor's box at the Hippodrome, reached by a spiral staircase from the Great Palace, which was adjacent to it. It was spacious enough to include a banqueting hall and could accommodate the imperial family and entourage.

Maphorion—a mantle, or veil, worn by Byzantine women when they went out.

Mese—The main road in Byzantium, beginning at the Milion marker near the Great Palace and the Hagia Sophia. It continued past the city walls as far as Thrace.

Michael Psellus—This man was a high-ranking imperial bureaucrat for decades, who wrote a remarkable history of the fourteen emperors and empresses who ruled during his life. His history comes to us as authored by "Michael Psellus", but he took the name Michael when he retired to a monastery. Psellus means "stutterer", but it seems likely that this was an inherited moniker since it would be unusual for a stutterer to teach rhetoric and oratory.

Milion—A marker near the Great Palace and the Hagia Sophia, where the Mese began, near the heart of Byzantium. It was a sizable structure, described in historical texts as a tetrapylon, or a vaulted open area supported by four tall piers. It was first built in the time of Constantine and was similar to those in other Roman cities. A small piece of it can still be seen in Istanbul today.

Moirarches—A Byzantine military title, roughly equivalent to captain or colonel.

Paphlogonia—The area, or Theme, in Anatolia on the Black Sea, where the family of Michael IV, Michael V, and the Orphanotrophus originated.

Prinkipo—One of the Princes' islands in the Sea of Marmara where abdicated/exiled rulers and political enemies of the rulers of the Empire were sent, typically to be tonsured as a monk or nun, to live out their days in the monastery or convent there.

Purple Room—The room in the Great Palace where Byzantine empresses traditionally gave birth. This room was built with walls of reddis/purple marble from Egypt called porphyry. Children born in this room traditionally bore the moniker of "Porphyrogenitus/ Porphyrogenita".

Rhomphaia—The weapon commonly associated with the Varangian guard. It appears to have consisted of a blade attached to a long shaft. The blade was single edged and could be either straight or slightly curved. The Varangians also were known to carry battleaxes and, of course, swords.

Sea of Marmara—The body of water to the south and west of Constantinople. Called the Propontis in ancient Roman times.

Solidi—(Solidus—singular) The traditional gold coins of the Byzantine Empire. These were highly regarded for centuries for their quality and value, and were often traded into Western Europe where they were called "bezants". These coins have been found as far north as Scandinavia and as far east as Japan. During the period of this novel, however, the coinage became gradually more debased to fund profligate imperial spending, resulting in inflation and popular dissatisfaction with the empire's rulers.

St. John Stoudion Monastery—This was the largest and best known of the monasteries in Byzantium, surviving for hundreds of years. It was commonly referred to as simply as Stoudion. Portions of the ruined church, originally built about 500 years prior to the time of this story, can still be seen in Istanbul today.

Strategos—Governor of a Byzantine Theme; often a general since they had defensive responsibilities, or possibly a large landowner in the Theme.

Street of Porticos (Makros Embolos)—I have translated the name of this street known for its many shops to English.

Taghmata—These were the Byzantine Empire's six elite regiments—Scholai, Exkoubitores, Ikanatoi, Vigla, Arithmos and Athanatoi. Any usurper would require the support and consent of the Taghmata in an attempt to take the throne.

Tesserae—The small bits of stone, colored glass or marble that make up a mosaic.

Theme—The regional "provinces" within the Byzantine Empire. Each theme's defined borders could be altered, with the number of themes changing over the centuries. There appear to have been about 16 Themes in the Anatolian part of the Byzantine Empire during Anna's lifetime. Armenia (different from the Armenian kingdom), where Anna's family lives during its years in exile, was one of them.

Themata—These were the provincial army corps. Each province had their own, composed of professional soldiers and local troops who held land in exchange for military service. Over time the dynatoi, particularly in Anatolia, began acquiring the lands held by these soldiers, eventually starving the empire of these critical defensive men.

Theodosian Land Walls—These nearly impregnable walls were built during the reign of the Emperor Theodosius in the 5th century, extending in an arc from the Golden Horn in the north, to the Sea of Marmara in the south. They consisted of a main fortress wall with numerous towers and watch posts, a lower outer wall, with a trench between the walls that could be filled with water. These walls were an amazingly effective deterrent for centuries and only fell in 1453 to the cannons of Mehmet II and the Ottoman Turks. Most of the walls can still be seen today in Istanbul.

Theodosian Harbor—One of the two large harbors on the south side of the Byzantine peninsula. By Anna's time it had partially silted up from the Lykos River that fed into it, although it was still in limited use. It no longer exists but there is a large archeological dig underway where the harbor had been.

Theotokos—The Greek term used commonly to refer to Mary, the mother of Jesus. It is literally translated as "God-bearer". Mary is a frequent subject of Byzantine icons, but always pictured with Jesus.

Varangian Guard—One of the most renowned mercenary corps in history, the Varangians were Scandinavians, Anglo-Saxons and Russians who had wandered south in search of wealth. They dedicated themselves to serving the Byzantine emperor, however needed, beginning in the early 10th century until the late 14th century. In chapter 1, Anna's Grandfather greets the leading Varangian of that time, Harald. Harald, also known as Harald Hardrada, served the Byzantine emperors from 1035 to 1044. He later became King of Norway after returning to his homeland. He perished at the Battle of Stamford Bridge a few days before the Norman Conquest in 1066. That battle is thought to have so weakened King Harold II Godwinson that it resulted in William the Conqueror's success at the Battle of Hastings.

About the Author

Eileen Stephenson was born in Fort Worth, Texas, but has spent most of her life in the Washington, D.C. area, earning a living in the finance industry before discovering the enthralling world of the Byzantines. She has degrees from Georgetown University and George Washington University, and is married with three daughters. Her first book, Tales of Byzantium, is a collection of short stories of love, war, and destiny in medieval Byzantium.

Please visit my website, *eileenstephenson.com*, and blog to learn more about the Byzantines.

www.ingramcontent.com/pod-product-compliance
Lightning Source LLC
Chambersburg PA
CBHW020323140726
47905CB00012B/163